NO
LIVING
SOUL

NO LIVING SOUL

JULIE MOFFETT

WORLDWIDE®

TORONTO • NEW YORK • LONDON
AMSTERDAM • PARIS • SYDNEY • HAMBURG
STOCKHOLM • ATHENS • TOKYO • MILAN
MADRID • WARSAW • BUDAPEST • AUCKLAND

PLEASE RECYCLE • THIS PRODUCT IS RECYCLABLE

Recycling programs
for this product may
not exist in your area.

No Living Soul

A Worldwide Mystery/September 2017

First published by Carina Press

ISBN-13: 978-0-373-28424-5

Copyright © 2017 by Julie Moffett

All rights reserved. No part of this book may be reproduced or transmitted in any form or by any means, electronic or mechanical, including photocopying, recording or by any information storage and retrieval system, without permission in writing from the publisher. For information, contact: Harlequin Enterprises Limited, 225 Duncan Mill Road, Don Mills, Ontario, Canada M3B 3K9.

This is a work of fiction. Names, characters, places and incidents are either the product of the author's imagination or are used fictitiously, and any resemblance to actual persons, living or dead, business establishments, events or locales is entirely coincidental.

® and TM are trademarks of Harlequin Enterprises Limited. Trademarks indicated with ® are registered in the United States Patent and Trademark Office, the Canadian Intellectual Property Office and in other countries.

Printed in U.S.A.

To Vanessa Visagie, from South Africa, for forming my VERY first fan club. Also to the members of the fan club (thank you SO much for joining) and to all readers who enjoy Lexi and the gang as much as I do. Thank you, thank you, thank you for spending time in my world. Lexi and I greatly appreciate it. oxox

ONE

O<small>N MY NINTH</small> birthday my father gave me a puzzle in the shape of an Egyptian pyramid. It was one of those brainteasers, the kind with movable pieces you had to assemble. Super challenging for an adult and nearly impossible for a normal nine-year-old.

I solved it in one hour and forty-nine minutes.

It wasn't the challenge that made that particular puzzle memorable—I've done a thousand since that were much more difficult. It's because the pyramid puzzle was a present from my dad. By that, I mean a present that wasn't bought by Mom and labeled "To Lexi, From Mom and Dad."

Amid the pink ballet shoes, girly dresses and shiny necklaces I'd never wear, the pyramid puzzle stood out. My dad had handed it to me unwrapped, grinning when he saw my eyes light up.

"Here you go, pumpkin," he said, ruffling my hair.

My fingers had itched to start solving it, but then he'd tipped his head meaningfully toward my mom. Even though I was only nine, at that moment, my dad and I came to an unspoken agreement. While the puzzle was his way of acknowledging I was never going to be that bubbly beauty queen my mom dreamed about, we both knew I was still going to have to deal with Mom's hopes for me.

My dad cleared his throat. "By the way, your mom

and I thought you might be willing to give ballet another try. We found a different studio. No one needs to know what happened during your last recital. You willing to give it another shot?"

I took one look at my mom's hopeful face and shrugged. "Sure. I can do that."

Unsurprisingly, it hadn't ended well. But that moment of understanding with my dad had gotten me through another year of falling off the stage, inadvertently setting fire to a tree prop, and surviving the humiliation of the other ballerinas dancing as far away from me as possible. Finally, I mustered the courage to tell my mom I was miserable. To my surprise, she dropped the entire ballet thing, suggesting I might enjoy piano lessons instead. And, oh, by the way, wouldn't it be fun to go shopping together to pick out the perfect recital outfit?

It hasn't always been an easy road to traverse for any of us, but we work on it because we're family. That's what families do.

The puzzle was on my mind as I drove the few miles to the house of one of my best friends, Elvis Zimmerman, because I'd just packed it into one of the large moving boxes currently at my apartment. In a few days I'd be moving into a house that my Italian boyfriend and hacker extraordinaire, Slash, had recently purchased and was remodeling.

For a geek girl like me this was a huge step. I was twenty-one before I got my driver's license, twenty-four before I bought something other than white cotton underwear, twenty-five before I went on my first date, and I'm still afraid to go shopping alone. Although Slash and I had been dating for several months, certain life-threatening events had brought us closer, drastically shifting our priorities. Part of that shift had been a realization we no longer wanted to live apart.

I hate packing, so I'd been grateful when Elvis called, asking me to come over. As much as I was on board with the living-together thing, it also meant change, and I'm not a big fan of shaking things up.

The early evening weather in Jessup, Maryland, was lovely for late May. Humming, I put the top down on my cherry-red Miata. My long brown hair was pulled back into a ponytail, the way I usually like to wear it, and the radio was blasting nineties music. I tapped my fingers against the steering wheel. The Miata had recently been in an accident and I'd missed it. Now that it was back, my life seemed to be getting on track again.

Things were going my way.

I pulled the Miata into the driveway behind Elvis's new car, then picked up my cell phone. I tapped a quick text to Slash, letting him know I was at Elvis's house, and then listened to two messages from my mother. "When are you coming for dinner, darling?" Then she gave me a callback reminding me *not* to forget Slash. After that I listened to one from my best friend, Basia. "Lexi, I'm having the final alterations made on my wedding dress on Thursday. Can you come?"

Ugh. It was a big no to all three, but I had to figure out ironclad excuses, and that would require some thought. I shoved my phone into my purse and got out of the car, wondering what Elvis wanted to show me.

I rang the bell and a minute later the door opened. Elvis stood there, barefoot as usual, his glasses askew, brown hair in disarray and dressed in khaki shorts and a T-shirt with the phrase Will Code for Food on it.

"Hey, Lexi," he said, giving me a smile. "Thanks for coming."

"Thanks for giving me an excuse to stop packing. I can't wait to hear what's up. You were so mysterious on the phone."

He opened the door wider and moved to the side so I could enter. As I took a step across the threshold, he suddenly looked alarmed.

"Elvis, what's wro—?" I yelped as something cold pressed into the small of my back.

"No sudden moves," a man said. "Just step into the house nice and slow and no one gets hurt."

TWO

THE STRANGER PUSHED me the rest of the way into Elvis's house. I stumbled, turning around as he slammed the door shut and locked it. I'd never seen the guy before, but I did recognize the gun. It was a 9 mm semiautomatic pistol—the same kind Slash had given me for Christmas. He stood with his back against the door, studying us. No matter how many times I'd had a gun pointed at me over the past year, it didn't get any less terrifying. I exchanged a worried glance with Elvis to see if he knew what was going on, but he seemed as surprised as me.

"In there." The stranger jerked his head toward the living room, where the twins had set up what they affectionately referred to as the Computer Command Center. It was essentially a computer lab with dozens of expensive laptops, monitors, routers and special cables. I loved going in there…except for now.

We both hesitated, which seemed to energize the intruder.

"Don't even think about trying anything. I'll hurt you."

His threat wasn't idle. He was six foot three, by my calculations, with olive-colored skin, curly black hair and overly thick biceps. His accent was British. I studied his face. I had an eidetic, or photographic, memory, which meant I remembered everything I saw.

Not that it helped at the moment. It only meant I was one hundred percent certain I'd never seen him before.

Apparently neither had Elvis.

"Dude, what are you doing in my house?" Elvis asked. "If you're MasterSlayerMan in Dorks and Dragons, I swear the annihilation of your kingdom in Quadratic Land was purely strategic."

The guy waved the gun. "This isn't chat time. Shut up and do as I say and you might live. I've got limited time, not to mention patience."

Seeing as how I didn't have much choice, I entered the living room. I wondered if this was some kind of random home invasion. I hadn't seen Xavier's car, which meant Elvis's twin was probably out with my best friend and his fiancée, Basia Kowalski. They were house hunting for a place to live after their wedding, which was exactly one week and five days from today. I was the maid of honor, assuming I survived this encounter.

"Take those two chairs and back them up together," he instructed, pointing at two swivel chairs. "Now."

Elvis grabbed his chair and I wheeled Xavier's to the spot he'd indicated.

"Now sit down and put your hands out behind you."

I looked over my shoulder at Elvis as we sat. We held our hands behind us as the intruder pulled out a roll of duct tape and bound our wrists to the chair and each other's. At least he hadn't shot us.

Yet.

"Are you going to tell us what's going on?" Elvis asked as the guy worked in silence.

The way he spoke, with more exasperation than fear, almost made it seem like facing down a guy with a gun was just another day at the office. Although, the way our lives had been going lately, maybe it was.

The intruder didn't answer as he ripped the final piece of tape off with his teeth and secured it around our wrists. He'd bound us tightly, professionally. My shoulders and arms had already started to ache.

He returned the duct tape to the bag, then stood, brushing his hands off on his black jeans. "Now, we can make this easy or we can make it hard. Which one do you prefer?"

"That's a rhetorical question, right?" I preferred a scenario that ended with Elvis and me alive and unharmed.

He strode over to me, leaning down so his nose almost touched mine. "Don't push me."

Elvis nudged me, warning me to stop talking. But I was mad. Couldn't I go *anywhere* these days without being accosted by some nutcase with a weapon?

"I wasn't being pushy. The question was genuine. I'm not very good at reading between the lines."

He gave me a long, hard stare, then circled around the swivel chairs. It sounded like he stopped in front of Elvis.

"It's pretty simple. Hand over the package from your father and I cut you both free. No one gets hurt."

Elvis's father?

That couldn't be right. Elvis and Xavier had been estranged from their father for ages. They never talked about him, not even to me.

"I don't know what you're talking about," Elvis said. But the way he said it made me wonder.

"I know he mailed you a package," the intruder said. "You already started the experiment, didn't you?"

Experiment? I tried to twist in my seat so I could see what was going on, but it only made the chair move.

The guy stuck out his foot to keep the chair from rolling. "Do that again and I'll shoot you on principle," he snapped.

When Elvis didn't respond, his voice grew rough. "So, your answer means we do it the hard way. Starting with her. On the count of three."

He walked back into view and stood in front of me. I swallowed hard.

"I'll pop her in the kneecap first," he said. "There's sufficient pain and usually a lot of screaming, but she shouldn't die or bleed out right away. That gives me plenty of time to shoot her other kneecap, followed by random other body parts, just in case you don't think I'm serious."

"Hey!" I said as indignantly as I could muster, given that my heart was galloping like a group of geeks rushing the minifridge for the last Mountain Dew.

"Leave her out of this," Elvis shouted. "She doesn't know anything."

He raised the gun, pointing it at my knee. "One."

I brushed my fingers against Elvis's, then started to recite Fermat's Theorem in my head.

Let N be the set of natural numbers such as 1, 2, 3...let Z be the set of integers 0, +1, +2...

"Stop," Elvis said to the man, desperation creeping into his voice. "You don't know what you're dealing with. You won't understand."

"Two."

I looked at my knees, which were shaking, and then back at the guy with the gun. "Don't I get a say in this?"

"You know where the package is?"

"No, but—"

"Then both of you had better understand I don't care what I have to do to get it. This is your last chance. Give me the package or she loses her knees. Your choice."

"Okay, okay!" Elvis said in a rush. "You can have it. If you'll let me loose, I'll retrieve it. But I guarantee you'll have a hard time figuring it out."

"Not my problem. Not my job."

"Package? Your father? Elvis, what's going on?" I tried unsuccessfully to twist around again and our chairs scooted a bit across the floor. The guy stuck out a foot to stop us and glared at me.

"Do you ever follow directions?" he asked.

I shrugged the best I could, considering my arms were duct-taped behind my back. "You heard from your father? Really?"

"Really. If he'll let me loose, I'll get him what he wants."

To my everlasting relief, the guy lowered the gun from my kneecap. "How about you tell me where the package is instead?"

Before Elvis could respond, the doorbell rang.

Frowning, he looked between us. "Expecting someone?"

"Not me," I offered. "Then again, I don't live here."

He approached the door, gun out, then peered through the peephole. "Pizza?" He looked at Elvis. "You ordered a pizza?"

"I was hungry," Elvis said. "Just pay him and he'll go away."

The doorbell rang again.

"Sod off," he shouted through the door. "We don't want the pizza anymore."

"Oh, man, don't do this," the pizza guy yelled. "Cut me a break. You'll be the third customer today to stiff me. My boss will fire me."

"Not my problem," the intruder said. "Get lost."

"You better open up." Pizza guy pounded on the door. "I'm going to call the cops if you don't. You're interfering with my livelihood."

The guy stiffened at the word *cops*. "Fine," he said between gritted teeth. "How much?"

"Twelve bucks, plus a tip for me. Three extra bucks should cover it."

The guy pulled out his wallet and extracted some bills. "You can forget about your bloody tip." He opened the door a crack, pushing the bills out. "Leave the pizza on the porch and I'll—"

He didn't finish his sentence as a gun slid through the crack, pressing against his forehead. At that same moment a side window in the living room shattered and someone with a hood and dressed all in black rolled in and came to a crouch, gun out.

"Drop your weapon nice and easy," the man from the living room said. "One chance only."

The intruder stepped back, dropping the gun as several guys muscled in through the front door, pressing him against the wall and cuffing him. I recognized them as the two FBI agents on Slash's protection detail. That meant the guy who had come through the window was...

Slash!

My boyfriend turned toward me, pulling off the hood as shards of glass slid off his jacket and onto the floor. He strode to my side, taking a knife from his boot and slicing the duct tape around mine and Elvis's wrists. "Are you hurt, *cara*?"

"No, thank goodness." I stood, rubbing my wrists and wincing at the tender spots rubbed raw from the tape.

"How about you, Elvis?" he asked.

"I'm good, too. Thanks, man."

Slash looked around. "Where's Xavier?"

"At Basia's place," Elvis said. "Thankfully he missed this little party."

"Yeah, lucky him." I touched Slash's arm. "How did you know what was going on?"

"Would you believe I'm mysteriously in tune with you?"

"Sometimes I wonder. But the real answer is…?"

He smiled and kissed me on the cheek. "The real answer is Elvis invited me here, too. I got your text and arrived just in time to see this guy push his way into Elvis's house behind you. I alerted my tail and we quickly parked and reconnoitered. When I saw he had a gun, Shavis here alerted the authorities." He jerked his head toward one of the FBI agents. "We weren't going to act until the police arrived, but from what I could see from the window, things were going down fast. We devised a plan to use the pizza box from Shavis's car to distract the gunman at the front door while I came at him from another angle. Sorry about the window, Elvis."

"No problem, dude. It was totally worth it. Thanks so much."

I looked at Elvis. "How did you know about the pizza thing? You didn't order a pizza."

"No, I didn't. But Slash motioned to me through the window. Well, I wasn't sure it was Slash at the time, but statistically the odds were high since I'd invited him over, too. I wasn't sure how much he knew of what was going on in the house, but I went with it because the situation was getting dire."

"That's no kidding. He was going to shoot my knee-cap."

"Yep. That totally qualifies as dire." Elvis blew out a breath. "It was close. Too close."

Slash pulled me into a one-armed hug just as two policemen entered the house. One of the FBI agents filled them in on the events before one of them led the intruder out in cuffs. The other policeman took brief statements from Elvis and me and left.

Once they were gone, Slash walked over to me. "So, what did the guy with the gun want?"

I glanced at Elvis, waiting for him to answer, but he wandered over to a small side table and stared at some plants that had been arranged inside a mini greenhouse with special lamps. I hadn't noticed the plants there before and it kind of surprised me because while Elvis was a genius at the keyboard, his gardening skills were on par with mine. Which meant we both had black, not green, thumbs.

I turned my attention back to Slash. "I don't know who he was, but he wanted a package Elvis's father had sent him."

Slash raised an eyebrow. "Elvis's father?"

I lowered my voice. "Yes." I couldn't say more because at this point I didn't really *know* anything else. I wasn't even sure if it were true. Maybe Elvis had said it just to keep me from being shot.

Finally, Elvis turned around. "The guy was right. My father sent me a package. Come here, both of you. That's why I asked you over. I want to show you something."

THREE

WE JOINED ELVIS at the mini greenhouse. For a moment we stood side-by-side, staring at the plants through the small greenhouse structure. I counted four plants, all looking green, robust and totally ordinary. Although given my miniscule experience with plants, they could be something extraordinary and I wouldn't have a clue.

After a moment of silence, I spoke. "Okay, Elvis, what the heck is going on? Why am I looking at plants?"

"It's kind of a long story."

I opened my mouth to tell him to spill when the doorbell rang. Slash slipped his hand beneath his jacket and approached the door warily.

"Maybe the police forgot something," I said.

Slash peered out the peephole. "No. It's a female in her twenties, shoulder-length ginger hair. She's carrying a lot of books."

Elvis spoke up. "Let her in, Slash. She's invited to the party, too."

Slash stepped back and opened the door. He stayed concealed in the shadows, his hand beneath his jacket. The young woman bounded in, her gaze instantly falling on me.

"Lexi Carmichael?" Her eyes widened. "Oh. My. God. I can't even."

"Can't even what?" I frowned. "Do I know you?"

I studied her face but came up blank. I was sure I hadn't met her before. The rare combination of red hair, lots of freckles and bright blue eyes ensured she was someone I would have remembered. Especially since red hair and blue eyes are a significant statistical anomaly, with less than one percent of the world's population having that combination.

"No, of course you wouldn't know me." Her cheeks flushed. It was especially pronounced on her pale skin. "I'm just not prepared for this meeting. Not that this is a meeting. It's a chance encounter. Totally unexpected. Well, not *that* unexpected seeing as how you're good friends with Elvis. But I didn't know you'd be here, as in right *now*. He didn't tell me. All of which leads to the fact I can't believe I'm finally meeting you in person and I don't know what to say."

She seemed to be talking a lot for someone who didn't know what to say. I glanced at Elvis for help, but he'd gone back to staring at the plants.

I searched for a response. "Apparently you have me at a disadvantage. You are…?"

"Gwen Sinclair." The young woman fumbled with her books, trying to shift them to one arm so she could shake hands with me, nearly dropping the lot. I grabbed one just as it slid out of her grasp.

She took it from me gratefully and then thrust out a hand, which I shook. "I'm sorry, Lexi. It's just…well, I saw you on television when you were on that reality show. Then you were trapped in the high school with my kid sister. Elvis told me about how you rescued him from terrorists in Somalia and then, OMG, the plane crash. I heard firsthand how you saved the microchip. My God, now I'm babbling. I'm a big fan. Not in a psycho-stalker kind of way because that would be too creepy. Just in a regular fangirl kind of way." The flush deepened. "I'm Elvis's microbiologist."

It took me several seconds to digest all that before I asked, "Elvis has a microbiologist?"

Slash closed the door behind her with a thump. Gwen whirled around, letting out a high-pitched screech and spilling her books across the floor. "Oh my goodness. You nearly scared me to death. You were so quiet I didn't even know you were there."

I bent to help her retrieve the books. "Gwen, that's Slash."

Her mouth dropped open. "Slash? OMG. I'm meeting Slash in person? I wondered if he even existed."

Slash lifted an eyebrow, but didn't say anything.

I rolled my eyes at him from across the room. "Slash, meet Elvis's…microbiologist."

Gwen seemed to come to her senses and knelt down next to me, trying frantically to gather the rest of the books and scattered papers. "I'm also his biochemist. Well, not *his* biochemist. Just *a* biochemist. I'm helping him out with this situation."

"What situation?" I tried to keep the exasperation out of my voice. As I straightened, holding an armful of her books, I glanced at the titles. *Pathological Diseases, Epidemic Modeling* and *Structural Biochemistry*.

Elvis finally spoke. "Gwen is helping me with an experiment. That's why I asked you guys over."

"You guys are totally going to freak out," Gwen said. "Wow. I get to freak out Lexi Carmichael *and* Slash. How cool is that?"

Honestly, I was already freaked out. Elvis was my

best friend. I usually knew *everything* going on with him. But for some reason, he hadn't told me his father had contacted him or that he'd started a mysterious experiment. But apparently, he'd shared all of these highly personal things with Gwen, a woman I'd never heard Elvis mention *once* in all the time I'd known him.

In turn, that made me wonder if Elvis's girlfriend, Bonnie, knew about Gwen, the experiment, and the recent contact from his father. I understood Elvis could tell his secrets to whomever he chose, but the fact that he had shared these sensitive matters with Gwen and not me, and possibly not even his girlfriend, seemed somehow significant.

I frowned, putting my hands on my hips and looking sternly at Elvis. "Okay. Spill already."

He had the decency to look a bit chagrined. "Let's all sit down first, okay?" He waved to the couch.

We headed that way when Gwen noticed the broken window. "Elvis, what happened to your window?"

"It's a long story," Elvis replied. "I'll fill you in later. Let's tell them what we discovered first, okay?"

Gwen nodded, then walked carefully around the glass on the floor.

After setting Gwen's books on an empty space on one corner of the coffee table, I sat down. Slash sat next to me on the couch, while Gwen and Elvis settled in two adjacent armchairs facing us.

"Gwen is a colleague from ComQuest," Elvis started, leaning forward and resting his hands on his knees. "She helped Xavier and me design the micro-fluid used in the development of the chip we recently deployed for manufacturing in Indonesia. The same one you helped deliver, Lexi."

I studied Gwen. "You're a microbiologist at Com-Quest?"

"Yes. It's been really nice working with Elvis. I've always wanted to meet you, too, Lexi. I've heard so much about you. And now I finally have. Yay." She gave a little squeal. "Except I wasn't prepared to meet you today, although I should have been because I know you often hang out here with Elvis and his brother. God, I'm babbling again, so you probably think I'm a total dork. It's cool being a part of your fandom, but it's a lot more nerve-racking to meet you in person."

I blinked. "My…*what*?"

"Didn't you tell her?" Gwen frowned at Elvis.

Elvis looked at me, suddenly nervous. "Ah, it may have slipped my mind."

"You have an online following, Lexi," Gwen explained. "A fan forum and group. It started out small—mostly kids from the high school you saved, but we now have two hundred and eleven members, including six foreigners. The network is putting out reruns from that reality television series you were on, so people have been joining your fandom left and right lately. Two members are from Canada, two from Australia, one from South Africa and one from Japan. The rest are American. It's pretty cool. We call ourselves the Lexicons."

I stared at her speechless and more than a little appalled.

Gwen fidgeted, apparently not expecting my reaction. "Well, anyway, that fandom stuff really isn't a part of this conversation and, apparently, it's totally awkward. So let's leave it behind."

"Forever," I suggested.

She smiled brightly. "Sure."

I squirmed uncomfortably in my seat. Holy cow. I had no desire to be the object of anyone's fandom. Ever.

Better to get things back on track. "So, Gwen, how does your work at ComQuest fit in with Elvis, those plants, and the secret experiment?"

"Well, that's the thing," Elvis said. "Just over a month ago I got this package from my father—"

"A month?" I interrupted.

His cheeks turned red. "Well, yeah. I, ah, didn't tell anyone at first because it was such a shock."

That's no kidding. I didn't know what exactly had happened with their father, but I did know their mother lived in a nearby health care facility with some kind of dementia. She and I got along great.

He avoided my stare, probably because he felt guilty. "Anyway, I needed help with the microbiology aspect, so I asked Gwen. She helped me figure out what my dad's package was all about." He gave Gwen a shy smile and she smiled back.

What the heck was going on? Was Gwen now fangirling on Elvis or was this something else? And was he liking it?

Elvis dared a quick glance at me and cleared his throat. Slash seemed to sense my tension, because he put a hand on my arm. I took a breath and told myself to take it easy. Talking about his father was obviously a difficult thing for Elvis and I needed to help, not hinder him, as he got through this.

Whatever *this* was.

"Anyway, when I received the package, it contained a letter and plastic vial," he continued. "The letter was in code written in my father's hand. I knew better than to open the vial before reading the letter—that's just the way my dad is. Regardless, it took me nine days to break his code and I was using pretty sophisticated software."

"Wait. You didn't ask me to help break a code?" Wow. I wasn't sure what to think about that except it hurt. A lot.

"I just thought I could handle it myself." His cheeks flushed as he swallowed hard and looked away. Unusual emotions crossed his face. Pain, embarrassment, discomfort. This situation was getting more uncomfortable with every revelation.

I took a deep breath and reminded myself this wasn't about me or my feelings. "How many years has it been since you spoke to or heard from your father?"

"Thirteen."

"So, after thirteen years he sends you a letter written in code completely out of the blue and a strange vial of something?"

"Yes."

"Where is he now?"

"That's the problem. I'm not sure." Elvis plucked at a thread on the knee of his jeans. "He's kind of nomadic. Last I'd heard, he was a tenured professor at Oxford."

"As in England?"

"That's the place."

I digested the information for a moment. "What does he teach?"

"Egyptology and advanced mathematics. That's his

bread and butter, at least. It's not his passion, though. That would be biblical archeology."

"Whoa. Biblical archeology?" I totally hadn't seen that coming. "Is that an Oxford-approved academic subject?"

"Actually, it is." Elvis leaned back in his chair. "The recovery and subsequent study of biblical artifacts can often shed light on the historical and cultural times of the Bible. It's a pretty popular subject."

I couldn't think of what to say to that. "Well, that's…unusual."

"Yeah, that's my father to a tee."

"So, is your father well-known for his work in biblical archeology?" Slash asked.

"I suppose," Elvis answered. "In certain academic circles, for sure. It's a small group to begin with, but it's pretty active. He's made some interesting finds over the years and has published extensively on them. He was the archeologist who discovered some ancient inscriptions in a cave in Jordan a while back. You might have heard of it. Anyway, he thought the discovery was going to be his big break but, instead, the academic world just yawned."

"You never told me any of this." I studied Elvis for a moment. "Why?"

He let out a long breath. "The truth is, Lexi, until I received the package, I didn't even know if he were still alive."

"But he knew your address," Slash said. "He kept track of you."

"Is that supposed to be significant?" Elvis's voice was bitter. "You know better than most that these days it isn't hard to track someone down if you want to."

Slash dipped his head in acknowledgment but didn't say anything.

Holy cow. I'd never seen Elvis like this. I don't normally notice things like body language and expression, but I knew Elvis well. His normally pale skin had taken on a gray tinge and the pulse on his neck visibly throbbed indicating high stress. Even worse, he was sweating and fidgeting in a way that indicated this was an extremely uncomfortable topic for him. It was awful to see him like this and not know what to do to fix it.

Elvis rubbed his right temple. "Look, I'll be honest. I'm not surprised he contacted me. If my father wants something, he'll find a way to get it. Even if he has to use the sons he hasn't seen in thirteen years."

Ouch.

The room was silent while we collected our thoughts.

"So, what does Xavier think of all of this?" I finally asked.

"I don't know." A shadow crossed Elvis's face. "He refused to look at the letter and wouldn't help me with the code. He doesn't want to have anything to do with him. Not that I blame him."

Ouch again.

Pretty harsh. Still, it was a bit strange, their father just popping up with a bizarre request after all these years.

"Okay, so you get a letter and a vial of some unknown substance from your father," I mused. "Why did he code the letter?"

"Not completely sure." Elvis settled in his chair. "My best guess is he didn't want the information regarding the possible nature of whatever was in the vial to fall into the wrong hands. Case in point, psycho guy just threatening to shoot us."

"What psycho threatening to shoot you?" Gwen's eyes widened in surprise.

I smiled sweetly. "Oh, didn't he tell you we're irresistibly attractive to homicidal maniacs and worldwide hardened criminals?" I was only half kidding. This past year had given us way more than our fair share of danger.

Gwen's gaze darted between us. At this point, she probably thought I was a nutcase.

Elvis gave me a bemused look. I couldn't decide if he was exasperated or exhausted with the conversation. Honestly I was feeling a little of both.

"She's teasing you, Gwen. Sort of. I'll explain it to you later." Elvis gave me a look that told me to take it easy on her. I wanted to comply, but I was still feeling hurt that I didn't know any of this, but Gwen did.

I wondered why Slash was keeping quiet. I looked over at him. His fingers drummed the top of his thighs as if he were typing on an air keyboard. His brows drew together, an indication he was deep in thought. "Any idea who your father might have been trying to outwit by using code?" he asked.

"Heck, no." Elvis shrugged. "Psycho guy didn't shed any light on that either. He was just going to shoot Lexi's kneecaps if I didn't turn the letter and vial over."

Thinking about it made me cover my knees with both hands. "What was in that package that made it so important?"

"Well, he said he'd found something big."

"Big as in…?"

"Historically big. A historically rare artifact sure

to put his name up among the archeology greats like Howard Carter, who found King Tut's tomb, and Heinrich Schliemann, who unearthed ancient Troy."

"So, what was the artifact?" Slash asked, his eyes lighting with interest.

"That's the problem. He didn't say. Not exactly anyway." Elvis clasped his hands in his lap. "He basically asked me and Xavier to analyze the material he'd found with the artifact. It was then he mentioned the tube contained actual biological material."

"What?" I said, flabbergasted. "He sent biological material through international mail? He *lied* to the post office? They always ask if the package contains anything perishable, fragile or potentially hazardous. Is he crazy?"

"Potentially, yes. Thank goodness I used common sense and didn't open the vial before decoding the letter. But I could have. What kind of father does something like that?"

Not a one of us in the room had an answer to that.

"So, what was in the vial?" Slash asked.

"Spores. I decided to run them by Gwen and see what she thought."

I glanced over at the plants. "I assume they have something to do with this."

"They do," Gwen confirmed. "Although not in the way you might think."

"I don't know *what* I think." I leaned forward, meeting Elvis's eyes. "Why would your father send you spores?"

"I think he didn't know for sure what they were." Elvis pushed his fingers though his hair. "He apparently thought, or hoped, Xavier and I would be able to figure it out."

"That's one hell of a request," Slash said quietly.

"I'm not surprised. It's typical of him."

"So, did you figure it out? What the spores are?" I asked.

Elvis exchanged a long glance with Gwen. "Yes. Luckily, Gwen took proper precautions before handling them. But this isn't like anything we expected. That vial didn't contain just any spores. They were ancient bacterial spores whose DNA is not on record anywhere. We believe my father unearthed them when he found this artifact. Now here comes the interesting part. Gwen's analysis suggests the spores might be the root of an ancient Egyptian plague."

FOUR

"PLAGUE?" I LOOKED at Elvis in astonishment. "As in, Black Plague?"

Gwen shook her head. I thought she looked a little disappointed. Like maybe she thought I should have known the answer. Ugh. I might be a geek, but that didn't mean I was an expert in everything. Great. Now she'd go back to the fan club and tell everyone I was a fake geek girl or something. On the other hand, maybe that was a good thing so they'd shut down the whole stupid club, whatever it was.

"Actually, the Black Plague came much later and is a different type of bacteria," Gwen explained. "In regards to the plague, scientists believe the very first widespread ones arose in populous hotbeds like ancient Egypt more than four thousand years ago. That makes sense because plagues evolve more quickly and spread faster where there are large concentrations of people. Ancient Egyptian cities were the largest in the world at that time."

Slash frowned at Elvis. His brow was drawn and his expression shuttered. I suspected he was both worried and intrigued at Gwen's revelation.

"So, you think your father discovered a sample of an ancient plague hidden in an artifact, woke up one morning and decided to send it to you?" he asked.

"I don't know what he was thinking." Elvis rubbed

his forehead. "Look, Gwen and I just figured this out over the past few weeks. We haven't told anyone *any-thing* yet. Certainly not the Centers for Disease Control. Unfortunately, we couldn't send them any of the spores to confirm. We only received a very small sample from my dad and we used them up by testing them. What we *can* confirm is we received bacterial spores of an unknown origin."

"While that is shocking, we don't have to panic, right?" I said. "Even if Elvis's father discovered spores for an ancient plague, so what? We live in the modern world. Plagues are derived from bacteria. Today we have antibiotics for that. End of problem."

"I'm afraid antibiotics won't work on this plague." Gwen's blue eyes darkened as she rested her elbows on her thighs. She looked at us one by one as if impressing upon us how important this was and imploring us to catch on quickly. "It's endospore-based. That means that it has a protective sheath that shields the bacteria from the usual body defenses, as well as harsh environments and sterilization techniques that would kill ordinary bacteria."

Okay. That changed things significantly.

She continued, "I'm not sure how familiar you all are with endospores, but an endospore isn't even technically a spore, but a case of bacteria cannibalizing itself into some kind of protective hibernation. They can survive in the harshest of conditions and live for millions of years. While these spores are not live like a virus, if ingested or inhaled, they could activate and cause lethal consequences. We both think that if Elvis's father uncovered more spores, they could be reactivated in the right environment and possibly retain their full toxicity. Unfortunately, given the gravity of this find, we have to assume that there are more of them in his father's possession."

"Tell me more about the endospores," Slash said, leaning forward, his elbows on his knees, watching Gwen intently.

"Well, endospores are fairly rare among bacterium. Most bacteria just can't change itself into an endospore. It's particular to a certain strain in the Firmicutes phylum. The interesting thing about endospores is they can live in both water and soil and are resistant to temperature extremes, hot and cold. They can survive most types of known chemicals and ultraviolet radiation. In addition, they're resistant to all antibiotics and antiviral treatments, at least the ones we have today. It's nearly impossible to destroy or control them."

"Okay, that's definitely scary," I said. "If we're talking about a plague made up of endospores, this isn't good."

"My point exactly."

Slash pointed at Gwen's lap. "What's in that notebook?"

"It's annotations from my testing, and excerpts from the unique DNA sequences we found. Though I haven't experimented with it yet, it also contains my professional assessment of the ideal environment for rapid reproduction of the bacteria." She held it up. "You can basically consider it a recipe to create a plague if you had the spores. And if you didn't, the DNA sequencing would potentially allow a competent scientist to recreate the bacteria from similar modern-day analogs."

"May I see it?"

"Sure." Gwen handed over her notebook.

Slash studied the material and I leaned over to look at it with him. I understood how she'd laid out the sequencing, but microbiology was not my strong suit. While I understood the pieces, I wasn't clear how they all fit together.

"What are the chances these endospores might be susceptible to protein disruption?" Slash finally asked.

"You know, I had that same thought," Gwen said. "But we won't be able to tell until we get our hands on more spores. The key is we need something to disrupt the protective sheath around the bacteria to allow normal defenses and antibiotics to work effectively. Now granted, I'm not an expert in prions or endospores. I don't even have a PhD in microbiology...yet. But I *am* sure we're talking about undiscovered, uncataloged, ancient endospores that may have caused a plague in ancient Egypt. That's pretty significant no matter how you look at it."

"Agreed," Slash said.

"If that's the case, we should turn over the information to the Centers for Disease Control immediately so scientists can be prepared," I suggested.

"And exactly how are we supposed to prove to the CDC our research is genuine and not a hoax?" Elvis said. "We don't have any of the spores left. Besides, the CDC is swamped with real diseases, not hypothetical ones. Sure, we could send them Gwen's analysis, but if they can't verify our research and assumptions, who will believe it? Even if they did believe us, they'll still want to know where we got the spores. Am I supposed to tell them it came from an unnamed ancient Egyptian artifact sent to me by a man I haven't seen in thirteen years and whose whereabouts we don't know at the present? That will surely convince them."

"Point taken," I said.

Elvis blew out a breath. "Look, I'm having a hard time with this. There are too many questions and not enough answers. Not to mention, my father is not the most reliable of sources."

"There's also the guy with the gun to consider," I said. "Given the possibility these endospores do have the ability of unleashing an ancient plague, how does this equal to him threatening to blow my kneecaps off? How and why does he figure into this?"

"*What* guy with a gun?" Gwen paled, making the freckles on her cheeks and nose seem darker. "Why were Lexi's kneecaps going to get blown off? Elvis, what aren't you telling me?"

Realizing she wasn't going to go any further until she knew what was going on, Elvis gave her a brief, sterilized version of the events. While speaking, he often patted her arm to soothe her. He was being awfully protective and attentive.

When Elvis was finished, Gwen leaned back in her chair. "Wow. This has gone from interesting to downright terrifying. What are we going to do?"

"We're going to figure this out. That's why I brought in Lexi and Slash."

I was glad he was finally bringing me up-to-date, but I wasn't sure how to approach this. Microbiology was out of my element. Still, despite her fangirling, Gwen seemed capable and smart. Plus, microbiology was her thing.

I looked over at the greenhouse. Guess it was as

good a place to start as any. "Okay, guys, so what's with the plants?"

"I was looking for plants whose material might affect the spores' sheathings," Gwen said. "Based on my research, I identified these plants as having the greatest potential to disrupt the bacteria. I was growing them here, hoping I could get my hands on more spore samples to test. Obviously, we never got that far."

"That was good thinking," Slash said.

"Technically, this is getting out of my realm of expertise. Epidemiology isn't my specialty. But based upon the research I've done since we started this, I believe it's possible that, back in ancient times, the endospores may have spread quickly through the population via plants. That may also be why the plagues were fairly contained at the time."

That was a pretty weighty statement. "You can't reproduce the plague without additional spores, right?"

"Right." Gwen shifted in her seat. "Besides I wouldn't have even attempted to analyze them if we'd known what Elvis's father had sent. Certainly I would have used far more sophisticated safety equipment than I utilized, including people with real expertise in this field and a special containment lab. I absolutely wouldn't have tried to make or reproduce them without a P-4 lab."

"P-4 lab?" I said.

"It's a biosecurity lab at the CDC. P stands for pathogen and the 3 or 4 depends on the pathogen level. A P-4 would be used to handle an unknown pathogen. But we can assess the potential risks another, safer way that doesn't involve the endospores."

Slash shifted on the couch, his eyes thoughtful. His

brow drew together like it always did when he was working something out. "Such as?"

"Modeling." Elvis tapped one of Gwen's books on the table. "Which is why I needed you and Lexi to help me. We need to put our mad math skills together and see if we can come up with a probable scenario for what might happen if this so-called plague is unleashed on the world today."

"We can do that?" I asked.

Elvis nodded. "We can sure try. You in?"

I glanced at Slash and he nodded. For the first time since we'd started this conversation, we were in my area of expertise.

I smiled. "You had me at mad math skills."

FIVE

SLASH SEEMED TO understand what Elvis had meant by modeling, but I was still unclear how it worked. I hated being the dumb one in the room.

"Um, while I'm happy to help, guys, how exactly do you mathematically model an endospore?" I asked.

Gwen grabbed her notebook from Slash and began scribbling. "We aren't actually going to model the endospore itself. We're going to use a mathematically based model to understand the spatial-temporal transmission of the plague if it went live. That way we can have a better idea of what we're dealing with. But my math isn't as strong as yours and there're a lot of complex calculations that need to be made. It would take Elvis and me a long time to do it alone. But with you two—and the power of the computers—we should be able to knock it off in several hours."

"I'm in," Slash said. "But I thought these kinds of models were used only for existing pandemics."

"Not only," Gwen replied. "I was an intern at the CDC in Atlanta for my junior and senior year at MIT. They use modeling as an epidemic forecasting tool, as well. I'm familiar with the software. We should be able to determine the plague's effect on animal and human populations with a fair degree of certainty if these exact endospores are activated."

"While that's cool, how are we going to get the software?" I asked.

"I've already got it," Elvis said. He didn't offer to tell *how* he'd gotten it, so I didn't ask. Slash didn't either.

"So, how are we able to model the plague's potential damage if we aren't sure how the disease will spread?" I asked.

"We do different models for each possibility," Gwen explained, showing me her sketch in the notebook. "The point is to identify spread ratios, possible epidemic cycles, and outbreaks. We should be able to figure, within a reasonable level of uncertainty, which populations will be at the highest risk and estimate mortality rates from that. Depending on what we come up with, it should help estimate the complexity and danger of the disease vectors. At the very least, we should have a scientific baseline for the level of public health danger we are talking about. We'll model both a best-case and worst-case scenario."

Science. Facts. Numbers.

This, I could get behind. It was exactly what we needed in this situation. My opinion of Gwen went a notch higher.

Slash crossed his arms behind his neck as he leaned back on the couch. "Okay, a few questions first. Elvis, do you have any idea where your father is now? What city was postmarked on the package? Did he provide a return address?"

"The package was postmarked from Cairo, but the address was bogus. According to Google Maps, the street doesn't exist. I followed up with a search of various online city maps of Cairo—old and new—and got nothing. I also ran the address against the code he used in the letter and came up empty again."

"Do you know what he was doing in Egypt?"

"A bit. I called Oxford University and they said he's been on sabbatical in Egypt for the past year. They lost touch with him about a month ago—right about the time he sent Xavier and me the package. According to the university, he was going to Cairo to do research for the Egyptology class he was teaching. His apartment in Oxford is being sublet, his phone number has been disconnected, and he doesn't have a cell phone, at least not one I could find. I truly don't know how to reach him. But after this encounter with the gun-wielding guy, I'm worried."

"Where's the letter from your dad?" I asked. "Is it in a safe place?"

"It is." He dipped his head toward Gwen. "I scanned it, so I have an electronic copy in a safe place, but I gave the original to her."

He trusted her that much? What was the deal with these two?

"Either way, I've got to warn my father," Elvis continued. "He could be in danger or already in trouble. He's got to know the seriousness of what we've found before someone else does. If this find is legitimate and we determine the endospores are real plague carriers, he'll be right about one thing—this is an extremely important, not to mention hazardous, find."

"How are you going to do that if you can't find him?" I asked.

"Well, I know he's in Egypt. His passport hasn't been used since he entered Cairo two months ago."

I didn't ask how he knew that. I didn't *want* to know

that he'd hacked into the State Department. Regardless I was impressed. That couldn't have been easy.

"So, other than the modeling, do you have a plan?" I worried about the strain around his eyes and the paleness of his skin. He didn't look well. This thing with his father was taking a toll. I really wished he'd talked to me earlier.

"I'm going to Egypt to find him, of course."

"*What?* You can't do that."

"Why not? Memorial Day Weekend is coming up and I've got nearly two weeks before the wedding."

"One week and five days," I clarified. "That's *so* not a good idea, Elvis. Guy with gun as my supporting evidence."

"I'm in full agreement with her statement," Slash said.

"Look, guys, I don't have a choice. I'm going." He crossed his arms against his chest and narrowed his eyes.

"Xavier and Basia will completely freak out," I warned.

"Can't be helped."

Gwen shook her head. "Lexi and Slash are right. You shouldn't do this alone, Elvis. I'll go with you."

Before I could express my utter astonishment, Elvis held up a hand. "Whoa. Time-out, everyone. Despite the embarrassing consensus I can't handle this on my own, I can."

"Of course, you can," Gwen said. "But you'll need me or at least my expertise. Questions or situations may arise that would require my microbiology or biochemistry knowledge. I'm willing to help remotely, but I'm sure I'd be more useful in a hands-on capacity. I don't mind going, Elvis, so if you'll let me, I'd like to accompany you. This is really important."

Elvis stood. "I don't want to put you in a dangerous situation, Gwen."

Uh-oh. Red-haired girl alert. Gwen's eyes fired and color rose in her cheeks. She stood from her chair and faced him down. "I'm already neck-deep in this situation, Elvis Alvin Zimmerman. So, don't think you have to protect me."

Alvin? Elvis's middle name was Alvin? Wait. How did she know that? How come I didn't know that?

Even though she was several inches shorter than Elvis, Gwen stood on her tiptoes and glared at him, hands on her hips. I wondered if it were true about redheads and tempers. Honestly, the way she was all fired up kind of intimidated me, even though I had a good eight inches on her.

"You need me. Don't say you don't," she said. "It would take way too long to explain this to someone else who might not agree to keep it quiet like I will. I understand the dangers and I want to come anyway. Besides, if those endospores are genuine, we're all in a lot of trouble anyway."

Elvis looked like he might argue, but then he sighed. "Fine. You can come if you want to. I'm not going to stop you. But let's not waste energy arguing about this. We need to get the modeling underway. You may change your mind after you see the results."

"I won't," she said firmly.

Slash walked over to Elvis's broken window and examined it. "I need to patch this up first. You'll need to get a window guy in here to replace the pane tomorrow."

"First thing in the morning," Elvis promised. "I'll fetch the tools from the basement."

"Don't worry," Slash said. "I can find them. You guys get the computers set up with the specialized software." He disappeared to the kitchen, where the entrance to the basement was located.

"Well, we'd better clean up the broken glass before we skewer ourselves." Gwen stretched. "You got a broom and dustpan anywhere, Elvis?"

Elvis went into the kitchen and came out with both. He looked a bit better, I thought. Planning, strategy and execution always made me feel better, too.

After handing it off to Gwen, he came over to me. "So, Lexi, I guess it's up to us to gather any materials we'll need and get the computers ready for some complex mathematical calculations."

"Guess so."

We started rearranging the laptops as Gwen began sweeping the glass. Slash returned shortly with a tool-box, a circular saw and a large piece of plywood.

I crawled under a table, threaded up a cable through a small space next the wall. "Here you go." Elvis got a hold of it and connected it to one of the laptops.

As I backed out, he held his hand on the underside of the table so I didn't bump my head. "Thanks, bud," I said as I straightened and stood.

"No, thank you. Seriously, what would I do without you…without my friends? And I can't believe I just said that. I've got *friends*. That's plural, in case you didn't notice."

"Oh, believe me, I noticed."

Near the window, Slash was freehand cutting the plywood with the saw, scattering sawdust everywhere.

Gwen, who had swept up the last of the glass and was carrying the dustpan toward the kitchen, turned as she heard the screech. As the sawdust wafted through the air and down to the floor, she did an about-face and began to redo her cleanup. Slash, however, seemed immune to the mess he was creating or Gwen's diligent efforts to clean it up.

He must be really deep in thought, I marveled. And who knew he could look so incredibly sexy with a saw?

I leaned my elbow on Elvis's shoulder. "You've got pretty cool friends, dude."

He looked at me and smiled. "I sure do."

SIX

GWEN QUICKLY TAUGHT us that modeling a potential epidemic was complex, but straightforward. Once I understood the parameters in which I had to work and the goal of the numbers I was crunching, I was in my element. I loved numbers and numbers loved me, which meant in spite of the dire scenarios we were modeling, I was enjoying myself.

We used a Monte Carlo approach so we could better model the probabilities. Elvis, Slash and I each worked on probabilistic calculations for different scenarios, while Gwen created and managed the different models on the computer. The software did the hard work; we just had to populate it with the environments and scenarios we wanted to evaluate. She walked back and forth between the laptops, entering data as we handed it to her.

It was after five o'clock in the morning when we finished the last of the calculations. I stood, stretching my arms over my head. Elvis groaned and massaged his lower back as he walked around trying to get the feeling back in his rear and legs. Slash stood, too, rolling his neck and shoulders. We all looked like we'd been through the wringer, which made me incredibly cheerful.

God, I loved math.

I walked over to the first laptop and peered at the

data scrolling across the screen. It didn't mean a thing to me.

"Don't touch that," Gwen warned.

"No worries," I said, lifting my hands in the air. "As fun as that was, I do not want to redo it."

"How much longer until they are done?" Elvis asked as he joined me at the laptop.

"Fifteen, maybe twenty minutes." Gwen was jotting something on a piece of paper. "Just go away and don't distract me."

We wandered into the kitchen, where Slash drank a glass of water and Elvis and I ate a couple pieces of cold pizza.

After we returned to the living room, I knew something was wrong. Gwen's already pale face had gone ashen.

"Hey, Gwen, you okay?" Elvis put a hand on her arm.

"Not really. I think everyone needs to sit down."

Once we were seated, Gwen took a deep breath and looked down at her notebook. "Okay, although we don't know as much as we would like about the endospores we're evaluating, if they operate in the same manner as the ones we know today and—factoring in the potential effects of the pathogenic capabilities of a few of the key DNA segments—we are talking about a pandemic. The critical determinant is how it's transmitted and whether or not an effective defense can be found."

"A pandemic?" Elvis said.

"Yes. All of the calculations and simulations we just did indicate this plague could be one of the most deadly in modern times. If an effective defense can't be found, it could be like the Black Plague all over again with the only defense being a quarantine. You can imagine what that would do to international travel, trade and commerce."

We all looked at each other grimly.

"In a worst-case scenario we could have an economic meltdown," she continued. "Even the threat of the disease without a means to stop it would cause things to grind to a halt as panic of potential infections spread. Look what happened in the US with the Ebola virus scare. We only had a few people infected and yet public fear was palpable."

No kidding. This was serious stuff.

"Can you give us some parameters, Gwen?" Parameters helped me make sense of things.

"Sure, but you won't like them." Gwen consulted her notes. "If these endospores are replicated and widely distributed somehow and meet the upper end of the possible transmission vectors, they would cause a global outbreak. Every country, race, age and gender would be at risk. Worse, if this plague is really unstoppable, then because of the endospores' nature and ability to survive for long periods of time, areas that are lost to the disease may never be recovered."

Slash murmured something in Italian under his breath. I felt sick and scared. What in the world had Elvis's father uncovered?

"Talk to me in actual numbers," Slash said.

Slash was a lot like me. Numbers always put things in perspective for us.

Gwen took a moment to compose herself and then looked down at her notebook again. "Given the absence of any known vaccine, effective prevention measures, or therapeutic intervention, the calculations indicate that if we assumed a deliberate worldwide release in a biological warfare or terrorist scenario, over seven hundred million people would be infected within the first twelve months worldwide. Two hundred million would be terminal as a result of a coexisting illness such as cancer, infections or diabetes. One hundred and eighteen million people would require hospitalization. Sixty-two million people would die outright. And that's a best-case scenario and the first year only. Depending upon the transmission vectors, medical and health care personnel would be disproportionately affected resulting in significantly reduced care in future years. You can only imagine what a worst-case scenario looks like."

"But the endospores would have to germinate." I was grasping at straws, but there had to be hope somewhere here. "Maybe after thousands of years they would have been damaged or won't work."

"Scientists have found endospores hundreds of millions of years old and were able to bring them to life," Gwen said. "I think it prudent to assume these spores could also be activated."

We all looked at each other, the gravity of the situation sinking in. Finally, Slash stood, a determined look on his face.

"Then it's up to us to make sure they aren't."

SEVEN

IT WAS DAWN by the time Slash and I drove to my apartment. We were silent, both thinking of the discovery. We were almost home before Slash finally spoke.

"Do you want to go to Egypt with Elvis?"

"Of course. Don't you?"

"*Si.* He's your friend and he's my friend now, too." He glanced over, his brown eyes assessing me thoughtfully. "Your strong bond with your friends is one of the reasons I love you so much."

It sounded cliché, but I never got tired of hearing him say he loved me. I wondered if I ever would.

"I'm really worried about him, Slash. Not only in terms of his physical safety, but his emotional safety, as well. Besides, given what we know in regards to the plague, the situation is even more dire than I thought."

"Agreed. So, why didn't you offer to go with him, if that's what you wanted? You held back. That's out of character for you. A month ago, you would have announced you were going to Egypt with him without another thought. Am I wrong?"

I leaned back against the seat and considered his words. "No, you're not wrong. It's just there's a lot of pressure on you right now with your new job, moving and the house." I reached over and took his hand, linking my fingers with his. "I didn't want to add to it."

He blinked. "You didn't volunteer to go…because of me?"

"That's part of the relationship dynamic, right? Thinking of your significant other as well as yourself. I had to weigh a lot of factors in this one. As much as I'm worried about Elvis, you came out on top this time."

After a moment, he squeezed my hand. "Thank you."

He pulled into a parking space in front of my apartment and removed the key from the ignition. I glanced over my shoulder and saw our FBI tail pull into a slot several rows over and turn off their lights.

He leaned over, kissed my cheek. "Let's go to Egypt with Elvis."

"What?" I couldn't have been more surprised than if he had said Windows 10 was a perfect operating system. "We're moving in two days. Plus, the wedding… How?"

"I'll hire someone to oversee the move of both our places to the new house and we'll make sure to get ourselves and Elvis back before the wedding."

While I wasn't thrilled with the possibility that someone would have to pack my underwear, it was a generous gesture. "You'd do that, Slash? For Elvis? For me? Just like that?"

"Just like that."

"What about your work? Will they allow you to go?"

"I'm not a prisoner. I work at the NSA of my own free will. If they make that increasingly difficult or uncomfortable for me to do, I'll leave the agency. I don't think that's what they want, so I presume they'll figure a way to be accommodating. That being said, this will require some special maneuvering. Egypt is not the safest place to be these days. But if I agree to stay in Cairo, I'll have a better shot. Since I understand their security concerns, perhaps better than most, I believe we'll be able to work it out."

"But you just became the Director of IAD."

"The key word being *director*, right? I'll delegate. Not to mention, it's a holiday weekend where historically, the largest number of employees at the NSA are on leave for the weekend and subsequent week. Hopefully, things will be slow. If not, they know, as well as you, I can do most, if not all, of my work virtually."

"But Egypt? All the forms you'll have to fill out and permissions to secure. Can you do that so quickly?"

"I'll try."

"What about visas? Do we need one?"

"Americans can get visas at the airport in Cairo. We can do this. It's important, *cara*. We have to help Elvis find his father. But perhaps more importantly, we have to help Elvis."

I stared at him for a moment. "Wow. Just wow. You're amazing." I unbuckled my seat belt and climbed across the cup holders, sliding my arms around him and squeezing between him and the steering wheel. "Thank you so much. This means a lot to me."

"It means a lot to me, too. I'll talk to Elvis tomorrow to make sure our travel arrangements sync with his." He wrapped his arms around my waist, anchoring me to him. I wondered fleetingly if the FBI was wondering what the heck we were still doing in the car.

"Do you need my credit card number for tickets?"

"No. I'll take care of it."

"But we'll work it out later."

"*Si*, we'll work it out later." He kissed me lightly, but his lips lingered against my mouth. I looked over his shoulder at the FBI car again.

"What about the FBI detail? Will they have to come?"

"Possibly not."

I looked at him in surprise. "Really?"

"Really. After the recent debacle with the FBI bungling my protection, along with others', they've been ordered to turn over their responsibilities for watching NSA employees to the Secret Service. Streamlining, so to say. They're starting the changeover this week."

"Well, wouldn't that mean the Secret Service detail would go instead?"

"Hard to say. I don't think they'd be ready yet to send a detail. Working this out won't be easy by any stretch of the imagination. I'll have to figure it out. But we'll make it work. I promise."

I cupped his cheeks with my hands. His stubble scratched my fingers. "Yes, we will. We always do." I gave him a kiss and his arms tightened around me.

"Come on. Let's get out of here." He reached beneath my leg to unbuckle his seat belt. He opened his door, slid out from beneath me and stepped out of the car, stretching out a hand to help me out. "However, before we go flying off on Wednesday, don't forget we have an important engagement to attend tomorrow evening."

I grabbed my purse and took his hand, climbing out of the SUV. "We do?" I racked my brain, but I couldn't think of it. "Oh, jeez, what did I forget?"

"Furniture shopping."

My stomach flipped. I hated shopping even more than I hated flying. I had really hoped we could hire an interior designer or something. But when I brought it up, Slash thought it was important we pick out several things we both liked, to make it feel more like our home. After considering it, I realized he was right. This was *our* home now. We had to work together to make it feel like it belonged to us as a couple.

Still I gave it another shot, just in case I could get out of the responsibility. "Are you sure my furniture, plus yours, isn't enough for the house?"

"I'm sure. It's a big house."

Crapola.

Since it had to be done, I sucked it up and smiled. "Well, then, I'm in. How hard can it be to buy another couch and a couple of tables?"

"We need bedroom, dining room and kitchen furniture, too."

"Right. Beds, dressers, tables. A walk in the park." I smiled, but my anxiety heightened. "What time does this shopping excursion take place?"

He put an arm around me as we walked toward my apartment. "Six thirty. Let's meet here after work and we'll go together in my car."

"Okay."

He chuckled. "Breathe, *cara*. Consider it an adventure." He pressed a kiss against my hair. "Furniture is inanimate. Remember, you've got the upper hand."

Easy for him to say. Didn't he know approximately six hundred and fifty people a year in the United States are crushed by furniture and die? That made the one-year odds of me dying at the hands of furniture 423,548 to 1, with lifetime odds of 5,508 to 1. While statistically unlikely, given my awkwardness, it wasn't completely out of the realm of possibility.

"Sure. I've got the upper hand." I repeated it a couple of times, as if I could make myself believe it.

I didn't.

EIGHT

I AWOKE TO sunlight peeking into the bedroom though a crack in the curtains pulled apart by a small tower of boxes I'd stacked underneath the window. The other side of my bed was empty. Slash was already up.

Yawning, I strolled into the living room, stretching my hands above my head. Slash stood in the middle of the room, eyes closed, balancing on one foot with his hands pressed against his chest in a praying position. He'd pushed my coffee table up against the couch next to several boxes I'd packed, giving him an open space. He was naked from the waist up and wore only a pair of loose gray sweatpants.

I stopped, watching him. The sun streamed in through the window, outlining his broad shoulders, taut biceps and abs. His breathing was deep, audible and rhythmed, his balance impeccable. Just standing there made me fall into sync with his breaths. I knew he was practicing qigong, the Chinese art of physical exercises and breathing control via tai chi. Lucky for me, I'd become intimately familiar with the principles of the practice…in the bedroom.

Breathe in. Breathe out.

Become one with each other. Master the energy and emotions. Move from being a prisoner of desire to the conductor of your own physical orchestra. Just thinking about it made me inhale sharply.

Slash cracked an eye open. In one fluid motion he changed his pose where he had one arm in front of him and the other to the side, still balancing on one foot. He smiled. "Coffee's on."

"Wow. Bless you."

He held the pose with ease even though it looked really hard. Too bad I had to go to work. If I had the time, I wouldn't mind watching him all day. "How's it going? Are your body's energetic anatomy and qi pathways blossoming?"

"That's the plan."

I figured he was working on outer dissolving—a tai chi technique that heightened mental and physical capability, improved stamina and dissolved any mental or emotional blockages that could interfere with free thought and pure sensation. I'd be the first to say I'd personally benefited from Slash's qigong knowledge. In spite of my awkwardness, but thanks to his careful guidance, I'd been able to access more than three times my personal qigong. As a result, I enthusiastically supported the art of tai chi.

Still, it mystified me how he was able to know when to switch poses. I studied him with interest. "Are you sure you don't you need music or something to keep the beat?"

"I'm sure."

He switched poses again. I watched him balance with one leg out behind him. He didn't even wobble once. "It looks hard."

"It's all about focus, *cara*."

"Despite your assuredness, I'm pretty sure focus isn't a viable substitute for a lack of athleticism or flexibility. Just saying. Please, carry on."

His smile widened as he closed his eyes and continued.

I drank an entire mug of coffee before taking my shower. Slash joined me in the kitchen for a quick breakfast of toast and orange juice before we headed out to our respective jobs. He kissed me in the parking lot as Mrs. Wolansky walked by with her dog and waved at us.

Happiness surged through me, taking me off guard. It was weird, but I'd almost forgotten what it was like living alone. I never imagined I'd be able to integrate my life so easily with his…at least, so far. It made the move seem that much more logical. My step lightened as I headed toward my car and got in.

Unfortunately, by the time I arrived in the office that happiness had evaporated. My blouse was stuck to my back with sweat, my butt had fallen asleep and my jaw ached from gritting it. There had been a backup on the Baltimore-Washington Parkway that made me more than thirty minutes late. After grabbing a fresh cup of coffee and settling at my desk, the first thing I did was pick up the phone and call Elvis.

"Hey, bud. Slash and I are coming with you to Egypt."

Silence.

"Elvis? Are you there?"

He finally spoke. "Look, you guys don't have to do this. Gwen is already coming, despite my strenuous efforts to talk her out of it."

"So, you don't want her to come?"

"No, I do. It's just I don't want to put her in danger. Not to mention it's kind of a mark on my man card that she feels like she has to go because I shouldn't be alone. Same with you and Slash."

I took a sip of my coffee. Should've added more creamer. "Your man card remains intact. We're your friends, Elvis. We aren't doing this because we feel obligated. We *want* to come because we care about you."

"You hate flying."

I really did. Even more so since the last flight I was on crashed in the jungle. But the odds of being in another plane crash on the very next flight I took were astronomical, which made me feel a lot better.

"What's going on with you and your father's discovery is inestimably more important than my fear of flying," I said.

He sighed because he knew I was right. "Gwen said the same thing."

"Yeah, about Gwen. What's the deal with her? How come you've never mentioned her to me before?"

"Well, because we're colleagues, that's all. It was all very professional…at first. But over this past month, she's helped me a lot. I think we may have crossed the colleagues-to-friends line."

"There's a colleagues-to-friends line?"

"I think so."

"How did you cross the line?"

"That's the thing. I have no idea. It's a bit baffling. Sometimes she texts me random things not even connected to the plague or my father. I respond because she's funny, smart and kind of pretty. She also uses a lot of emojis, though, which I think signals friendship. I'm not certain on that one."

"That's it? She uses emojis and that's how you can tell it's a friendship?"

"If you have a clearer parameter, please share. Seriously, I'm not sure how it happened, but I think we're friends now. She's been really nice helping me out with my father. I appreciate that. I appreciate *her*."

"I noticed." I tried to keep the hurt out of my voice, but it seeped in anyway. "You told *her* about your dad. Stuff you never told *me*. And I'm supposed to be your best friend."

"You *are* my best friend. I'm sorry, Lexi. I guess it was easier talking to her because she wasn't emotionally invested in me or my life. My situation with my father is rather painful and embarrassing. I won't lie to you. It was weird at first—spilling my guts to a stranger. But somehow, it was liberating, too. Gwen's a good listener."

"So, what does that mean? You like her?"

"Of course, I like her. I just said she crossed the line into friendship. Emojis, remember?"

"I mean like her—*like* her. As in a potential love interest."

"Oh." He was silent. "That I don't know. She just became a friend. Not to mention, officially I'm dating Bonnie."

"Does Bonnie know about Gwen?"

"Oh, God, no. You think I could manage that? Not that I'm hiding anything from Bonnie, because there is nothing to hide. Gwen just crossed the line into friends, after all. I can have friends that are girls, right?"

"Right. You've got me."

"Exactly." He sounded relieved. "Look, I can't expend any more energy thinking about women right now. I just can't. I'm too worried about my father, the plague, the trip to Egypt and the big fight I had with Xavier this morning when I told him I'm going to Egypt. Trust me, women are the last thing on my mind."

"You had a fight with Xavier?"

"Yeah. A pretty bad one. He doesn't want me to go for a number of logical and compelling reasons, including his upcoming nuptials and the fact that our father hasn't contacted us once in thirteen years. Yet, for some unfathomable reason, I'm still going to Egypt to hunt down a man who doesn't give a crap about me."

"The reason is he's your father."

"Biologically." He sighed. "Damn, this sucks. I might actually have reconsidered going if not for the plague."

"No, you wouldn't have. You've got this, Elvis."

"I know. You're right. Thanks, Lexi. I'm sorry I didn't tell you everything earlier."

"It's okay, Elvis. I understand. And, in spite of the fangirling, I'm starting to like Gwen. A little."

"She looks up to you."

"Ugh. No one should do that. Ever."

He laughed and I asked him for his travel details so we could fly together. He forwarded them to me in an email before we hung up. I glanced at them and forwarded them on to Slash.

Once all was settled with Elvis, it was time to take my Egyptian excursion to my boss, Finn Shaughnessy, sexy Irishman and onetime romantic interest. On the way to his office, I swung by the kitchen and added a bit more coffee to my mug. His secretary, Glinda, glared at me when I asked to see him. She'd been pursuing Finn for years without success. She'd never forgiven me for sort of dating him and then breaking up with no apparent hard feelings. Even worse, Finn still wasn't interested in her, which made her madder at me for some unfathomable reason.

Finn was sitting at his desk with some papers spread out and he waved me to a chair when I came in.

"Good morning, Lexi. What's up?"

"Well, remember how I worked two days of over-time on the DSC case last week?" I sat in the chair, taking a sip of the coffee and balancing the mug on my knee.

"I do. It was spectacular work, as always."

"Well, I'd like to take a couple of days off and make it a long Memorial Day weekend."

"Of course. You earned it. Last-minute preparations for Basia and Xavier's wedding?"

"Um, not exactly."

"Getting ready for your move?"

"No. I'm good on that front."

He was silent for a moment. "So, what's going on?" He sat back in his chair and regarded me with thought-ful green eyes. "Is the world ending again? Is the NSA, FBI or CIA asking you to jump from a plane?"

"Oh, God, no. Thank goodness. It's nothing like that. I just need to take a trip abroad."

"Abroad? Do I dare ask where?"

"Egypt."

His eyes widened. "Egypt? Why in God's name?"

I didn't want to tell him about Elvis's father. Not because I didn't trust him, but because it wasn't my story to tell.

"Well, I've always wanted to see the pyramids." That much was true.

He didn't buy it for a second. I could see that much

in his expression. I thought he'd call me on it, but instead he surprised me by asking, "Is Slash going?"

"Yes. Elvis, too."

He tapped his finger on his chin. "Okay, all of a sudden you, Slash and Elvis want to dash off to Egypt a couple of days before your move and just over a week before Xavier and Basia's nuptials? Need I remind you—you're the maid of honor and Elvis is the best man in said wedding?"

"Reminder not necessary. Trust me. Basia reminds me at least six times a day."

"So, what aren't you telling me?"

I sighed. "Look, Finn. I promise you I'm not going on a secret government mission. It's not my place to tell you why I'm going, but trust me when I say it's for a good cause. A very good cause."

"Is it dangerous?"

"Flying is always dangerous."

"True, that." He smiled, then sighed. "And good job avoiding the answer. Fine. Go to Egypt. As your boss, I have no reason to deny you time off you've earned. We've got nothing on the docket and the office will be mostly empty with everyone disappearing for the holiday weekend anyway."

"Thanks, Finn."

"But…" He reached out and took my hand, holding it tight in his. "As your friend, I'm worried about you. Lexi, whatever you're doing, be careful, okay?"

"Trust me. It's always at the top of my agenda."

"It bloody well better be."

I left his office, breathing a sigh of relief. Convincing Finn and Elvis had been the easy part. Telling my best girlfriend, Basia, would be way harder. As her wedding approached, she was becoming increasingly more nervous and worried about the details. Unfortunately, as maid of honor, I kept getting dragged into that weird bridal orbit. Seeing as how I sucked at social events like parties and weddings, this kind of thing was even more stressful for me than the average person. A trip to Egypt was attractive for that reason alone. But I had to be careful. Xavier would have certainly told Basia about Elvis going to Egypt and the contact from their father. I had to play this right.

Concerned friend, check.

Emotional support, check.

Making sure Elvis was back in plenty of time before the wedding, check.

After I rehearsed my argument a dozen times, I walked to her office. Unfortunately, or perhaps fortunately, Basia wasn't around. When I inquired as to her whereabouts, I discovered she was offsite with a client for the day. Apparently, it was my lucky day. It would be much more manageable to do this over the phone where I could easily have reception problems if the call got too dramatic or emotional.

Yep. Things were definitely looking up.

NINE

On the drive home to my apartment, I started thinking. In just a few days I would be moving in with Slash. Maybe that was a sign I should begin to explore my domestic side. Channel Betty Crocker. Release my domestic qigong in the kitchen. After all, I had an hour or so until Slash arrived for furniture shopping. Wouldn't he be surprised if I offered him a plate of warm, chewy chocolate chip cookies?

I wasn't sure I had everything I needed for cookies, but I figured I'd improvise. I'd always been pretty good at chemistry and cooking was just a step sideways to that. Walk. In. The. Park.

Yep. That was me. Suzy Homemaker.

As soon as I got to my apartment, I pulled up a cookie recipe on my phone and started taking stock of what I needed. Chocolate chips, flour, butter, sugar, eggs, and baking soda. I had the first five ingredients, but I was missing the baking soda. I could have substituted baking powder or potassium bicarbonate if I'd had either of those, but I didn't. However, I did know that the purpose of baking soda was to provide carbonation. While I didn't have baking soda, I did have a carbonated substitute. I went to the refrigerator and pulled out a beer. Chocolate chip cookies with a splash of beer sounded good to me.

After carefully turning on the oven to preheat (that

was the easy part!), I dumped all the ingredients except for the chocolate chips into my blender, since I didn't have a mixer. The blender groaned, probably because it was a little—okay, maybe a lot—thick as a result of the flour. After a few seconds the blender started vibrating so hard I had to hold it with both hands. I turned it off, added a splash more of beer to the mix to thin it out, then turned it on again.

The blender seemed to take on a life of its own, reminding me of a scene from *The Exorcist*. It started groaning and whining like it was going to explode. The vibrations were so hard my teeth were chattering as I valiantly tried to hold it in place on the base.

"Wh-what the h-heck?"

As I reached down to turn it off, the lid popped off, spraying cookie dough across me, the walls and counter. I yelped and took a step back. That was all the blender needed to lift off like a freaking helicopter and fly across the room before smashing into a lower cabinet.

I stood there in disbelief, covered in cookie dough. My kitchen looked like a murder scene and smelled like a bar. My ear felt sticky, so I pulled out a chunk of dough and dropped it on the counter.

Holy cow.

Time to go into recovery mode. I had to salvage what I could of the batter, so I scraped what was still left in the blender into a bowl, added the chocolate chips, and plopped dough balls onto a cookie sheet. I set the oven timer for fifteen minutes and spent those minutes using an entire roll of paper towels to clean up the kitchen and take a super quick shower. The timer was just going off when I returned to the kitchen. Black smoke curled out of the oven just as the smoke detector went off like a screeching banshee.

I snatched an oven mitt and reached in to pull out the cookies. Smoke filled the kitchen and the constant screech of the smoke detector hurt my ears.

"What the—!" I shouted in pain the second I picked up the cookie tray. I stumbled against the open oven door, flipped the tray five feet in the air and sent small, burned, beer-smelling projectiles sailing through the kitchen like a hail of bullets.

"Ouch, ouch! Damn!" Dancing on one foot, I yanked my hand out of the oven mitt with the previously unknown hole and stuck it under cold water. The cookie sheet landed with a clatter on the dish drainer.

I snatched the collapsible stool, climbed it and started waving a dish towel at the smoke detector. "The apartment is *not* burning down," I shouted at it. "I'm cooking."

I ran into the living room and opened the sliding glass door and then opened all the windows. After a few minutes of fresh air and my frantic dish towel waving, the detector finally stopped.

I climbed off the stool and looked around the kitchen in disbelief. Oh, yeah, I'd released my domestic qigong all right.

It took me twenty minutes pick up all the cookies, dump them into the trash, and wash the cookie sheet, blender, floor and counters. I'd just put the lid in the dish drainer when Slash strolled into the kitchen and gave me a quick kiss on the cheek.

I jumped. He moved so quietly, I hadn't heard him. "Oh, hey, Slash."

"Ciao, *cara*." He took a step back and studied me. "What's wrong?"

"Wrong? There's something wrong because I'm in the kitchen?" I smoothed down my hair and tried to look domestic, like I belonged there. I leaned my hand on the counter and the other on my hip. Casual, cool and collected. "I like hanging out in the kitchen."

He sniffed the air. "Were you cooking again?"

Dang it. He always knew. "Why do you ask?"

"Because it smells like smoke, your hair is wet from a recent shower, the windows and doors are all open, and the stove is still on. But I can't figure out why it smells like beer in here."

I threw up my hands. "That's *so* not fair. How can you be that observant in five seconds?"

He lifted an eyebrow but didn't say anything.

I sighed, then turned off the stove. "Fine. I was trying to make chocolate chip cookies for you."

He thought about that for a moment. "Okay. And that explains the beer smell how?"

"I didn't have baking soda, so I substituted a carbonated beverage to mimic the carbon dioxide present in the baking soda."

He chuckled and held out a hand. "Come here." I took his hand and he pulled me into his arms, resting his chin against the top of my head. "Must I try a sample?"

"Not unless you want to dig them out of the trash."

"Mio Dio." He blew out a relieved breath and murmured what sounded like a prayer in Italian. "I dodged *that* bullet."

"Hey!" I smacked him in the chest. "Who knows,

they might have been fantastic. You like chocolate and beer, right? It could have been a winning combination."

"*Could have* is the operative phrase here."

Secretly, I was relieved he hadn't tried one. Regardless of the cooking disaster, I was in a win-win situation. I could claim relationship points for trying to cook something special for him while maintaining the theoretical possibility—however slim—they might have been edible. Still, I was glad he hadn't eaten any of them. I loved Slash and didn't want him to spend the evening throwing up because he'd forced one down to please me. Plus, I was up for another attempt—reluctantly—if he really wanted freshly baked cookies.

I tried to summon as much enthusiasm as I could. Domesticity couldn't possibly be this hard, right? "I can try to make them again for you, if you'd like."

He looked so alarmed I almost laughed. He studied my expression carefully. "You really want to try again later?"

I sighed. "As much as I want to get every fingernail pulled out by someone using a toothpick. What do you say? Let's just buy a bag."

He stepped back, releasing me from his embrace. "We'll definitely eat out. Pack up the rest of your kitchen stuff. We won't need any of it until after the move. Need more boxes?"

"No, I'm good. How was your day?"

"Busy. I got your email. I'm glad Elvis is on board with us coming to Egypt."

"*On board* might be a bit strong. But despite an initial protest, I think he's glad he won't be doing this alone."

"Happy to hear that."

"Me, too. Finn gave me the time off, too. I worked a lot of extra hours last week on the DSC case, so it was good timing."

"Excellent. And Basia? What did she say?"

"Well, I haven't talked to her yet. That's going to be the hard one."

"I'm in full agreement with that. I don't envy you that conversation."

I sighed just thinking about it. "What about you? Were you able to get permission for the trip?"

"It wasn't easy, but I did. I made our reservations today. We're good to leave tomorrow evening."

"Hooray! Wait. Just kidding. It means more packing. Not my favorite activity at the moment."

He grinned and pulled something hard and black from my hair. He examined it with interest, then dropped it into the sink. "Ready for furniture shopping?"

I tried to smile. "As ready as I'll ever be." Which was never, but he didn't need to know that.

"Good. We can go to dinner after that."

I hoped it didn't take too long because all that cooking had made me really hungry. As we climbed into his SUV, a sedan in the parking lot started its engine and Slash lifted a hand in greeting at whoever was behind the wheel. Someone waved back.

"Is that your detail?" I asked, climbing into the car and fastening my seat belt.

"It is." He got in on his side and started the ignition.

"So is it the FBI or the Secret Service?" Not like I could tell the difference. It was still a nondescript black sedan and two guys sitting in the front.

"Secret Service. The transfer is complete."

"Wow. That was fast. Are they coming to Egypt with us?"

"Not this time. I had to promise to keep my internal chip activated and make certain accommodations regarding my safety, but we're cool."

If he thought he could slide that one past me, he was wrong. I narrowed my eyes. "What kind of accommodations?"

Slash backed out of the parking slot and headed onto the main street. "Security ones. I'll be fine."

"I'm not stupid. They aren't just letting you go, Slash. What kind of accommodations are we talking about? It's not something like the poison capsule in your tooth if you're captured by terrorists or spies, is it?"

He rolled his eyes. "God forbid. We are far more sophisticated than that these days, *cara*."

"So, what is it then? Some kind of microchip implant that will release potassium cyanide? A neurotoxin? Remote explosions? Spill."

He glanced sideways at me. "You can put your imagination at rest. It's nothing that dramatic. You know full well I can't talk about this. But I won't let myself get captured by terrorists. And if I do, I'd take care of it."

"What's that supposed to mean?"

"It means this discussion is closed." His voice was firm. "I'll be fine. The NSA trusts me to handle myself, so you should too. Don't worry. Nothing is going to happen to me."

I blew out a breath. I wasn't happy about it, but Slash had pulled the national security card. There wasn't much I could say or do that would cause him to admit to anything more. But I hated knowing that somehow, somewhere, he had something either implanted or hidden on him that he might use on himself in the name of protecting national security.

He smiled, trying to lighten the moment. "By the way, the police called me this afternoon."

"Really? Why?"

"Because I asked them to keep me apprised of what they found out about the guy that accosted you at Elvis's house," he said. "They gave me a brief update."

"And?"

"The guy's name is Merhu Khalfani. He's a thirty-six-year-old unemployed British citizen in the US, supposedly on holiday."

"He breaks into houses for his holiday entertainment?"

"Apparently. Perhaps of note, he's of Egyptian descent. His father was an Egyptian living in London, although he passed away about a year ago. His mother now lives in a small town outside of Cairo. Interestingly, the father worked for the British Museum as a curator."

"Let me guess, in the Egyptian exhibits."

"Correct."

"So, what was Mr. Khalfani's reason for breaking into Elvis's house?"

"He said he was hoping to make money off the computer equipment."

"Right. That's why he didn't even look once at the stuff." I mulled it over. "We can't consider it a coincidence that he has Egyptian ties and Elvis's father is in Egypt. Anything else?"

"Well, he claimed to have no knowledge of any letter or Elvis's father."

"That's a load of crap."

"Of course. But why did he want the letter or, more importantly, who gave him the directive to try and get it?"

"Good question. Do we know anything else about this guy?"

"Not yet. But we will."

Yes, we would. A few taps on the keyboard and a bit of sleuthing and we would know a heck of a lot about Mr. Khalfani. But right now I had to get my brain in the furniture shopping mode.

Unfortunately, that mode was significantly lacking, so, as a result, I was planning on totally winging it.

After about twenty minutes Slash pulled into the small parking lot of a colonial-style house. It had an impeccably manicured lawn with a lot of colorful flowers planted along the front sidewalk. A couple of giant pots filled with more flowers flanked the front steps. An old-fashioned sign hung from a signpost on the front lawn that said Marco's Italian Furniture and Antiques.

I shot Slash a surprised look. "I thought we were going to a furniture warehouse."

"My mother suggested Marco's. She thought we could probably find some nice pieces here. My family has been friends with the family for years. They used to live near my mother in London. I thought it might be less intimidating than a huge warehouse full of stuff. I called ahead and made an appointment for us."

My brain was stuck on the first thing he'd said.

"Your mother? You mean you told her we were going to be living together?"

"Of course I told her." He patted my knee. "She's really looking forward to meeting you. I invited her and my stepfather to visit as soon as we get settled and the construction is finished."

What the heck?

For a second I couldn't breathe. I would be sleeping in the same bed as their son while they were in the house. Why hadn't I fully considered the implications of that before?

"Slash, can we talk about this? Isn't that going to be weird for you? I mean, we'll be sharing a bedroom while they are in the same house at the same time. I could move to a mat in the exercise room, I suppose."

"You are *not* sleeping on a mat in the exercise room. We are adults. It will be fine as is."

Easy for him to say. They were *his* parents. To me they were complete strangers. I'd be sleeping in their son's bed, where everyone would rightly presume we were doing more than just sleeping. I had no idea how they would take to our living together arrangement in spite of Slash's assurances.

I hadn't even told *my* parents I was moving in with Slash, and I *knew* them.

I almost started to hyperventilate, but with supreme effort stopped myself. I couldn't stress about any of that now or I'd fall apart. I had to focus on one stressful thing at a time. Next up was shopping at some exclusive Italian furniture boutique for something to sit and sleep on. How hard could that be?

I climbed out of the SUV. Slash took my hand as we walked up the sidewalk. The Secret Service pulled up to the curb and turned off the engine. We climbed the front porch and Slash rang the bell. I looked down at my jeans and wrinkled green blouse. My hair was loose but hadn't been brushed since my shower. I did a quick finger comb, making sure there were no stray cookie pieces there, and wondering if one was supposed to dress up for furniture shopping at a fancy Italian furniture boutique. Heck if I knew. Slash hadn't said anything about it and now it was too late.

I took a step back when a giant man threw open the door. Without a word of greeting, he reached out his meaty hands and yanked Slash into a hug, smacking him on the back with enough force to shatter a brick wall.

"Buona sera!" He released Slash, grasping him by the shoulders, shaking him hard before kissing him on each cheek. "My boy, look at you now. You're a man. The last time I saw you, you were this high and about fifteen, I believe." He turned to me, his eyes widening. "And who is this *bella signorina*?"

Slash put a hand on my elbow. "Marco, meet Lexi Carmichael."

Black hair curled over his ears and his wide smile was framed by ruddy cheeks and a thick black beard. He looked like a cross between the Jolly Green Giant and Hagrid from the Harry Potter books. I sincerely hoped he didn't smack me on the back like he'd just done to Slash. I gingerly held out a hand.

"Una donna perfetta, è la coza più nobile della terra," he murmured, taking my hand. Instead of shaking it, he gently kissed my knuckles.

"Um, it's nice to meet you, too," I said.

Slash laughed. "Marco just quoted an old Italian

proverb. 'A perfect woman is the most noble thing in the world.'"

"Oh, that's nice, but I'm far from perfect."

Marco grinned as Slash put a hand on my lower back, guiding me into the house as Marco moved back to let us enter. We hadn't gone three steps when something huge and black shot out from behind Marco. Before I could even scream, it hit me square in the chest.

TEN

I WAS BEING crushed to death. I couldn't breathe. I couldn't speak.

Something wet was on my chin.

"Guido! Down, boy," Marco shouted. He grabbed the beast off my chest. "Sit."

I staggered to a more upright position, examining my attacker. It was a dog. No, it was a *big* dog. I swiped a hand across my chin, wiping off the dog slobber. Slash put a hand under my elbow to steady me.

Animals and I don't get along. At all. To me pets are a lot like people—invasive and unpredictable. I'm pretty sure animals sense my indecision and, as a result, try to dominate me.

There was an incident with my neighbor's pet garter snake in my shoe when I'd been in the third grade, and a hermit crab that had escaped his shell and found his way into my bed when I was eleven. In high school my brother's girlfriend's dog stalked me relentlessly and tried to hump my leg every time she'd bring him over. I'd also had a disastrous experience with Slash's grandmother's cat, Principessa, when I'd been in Italy. Then there was this fox in Djibouti I'd almost killed by accident after it pooped under my chair and followed me into my bedroom. Those were just a few excellent examples of why animals and I should *never* interact.

Right now Guido dutifully sat, but looked at me

with wide, mischievous brown eyes, his ears perked and tail thumping. The dog was huge even in proportion to his master.

"I'm sorry, Miss Carmichael," Marco said. "Guido usually has better manners."

"What kind of dog is it?" Slash asked, reaching over and scratching the dog under the chin. The dog's fur was black and it had a big head with a flat forehead and almond-shaped eyes. Guido wagged his tail happily and licked Slash's hands. Slash made the interaction look so easy, I felt envious. Although, let me make it clear, it wasn't like I was going to be touching the dog anytime soon. Or ever.

"Guido is an Italian mastiff," Marco said, patting him on the head. "He's just a puppy. They can get as big as one hundred and twenty-five pounds."

Holy canine! That was a puppy? It was already as large as a small pony. I edged slightly behind Slash.

Just then a woman with long black hair pulled back into a thick braid stepped into the foyer. She looked at Slash and clapped her hands to her chest. "*Oh, mio! The boy is a man.*"

Slash smiled and strode across the room to hug her, kissing her cheeks and then her hand. Putting one arm around him, she beamed and looked over at me.

"You've brought us a girl. Who is this?"

"Marcella, meet Lexi Carmichael. We're looking for furniture to fill our new house."

"Oh, how wonderful!" She pulled me into a hug and air-kissed my cheeks three times. "A girl. A new house. Your mother sent you to the right place. Come on into the kitchen. I will fix you some food right away."

"Oh, that's not necessary…" I started when Marco

swept a huge arm around me. "We are Italian. We don't do anything until we eat. Come, please, be our guest. It would be our honor."

Marcella still had an arm around Slash, so bundled like this we waded through a large room where all the furniture was arranged and into a cheerful kitchen located at the back of the house. I carefully watched where my feet were in relation to Marco's because I was pretty sure that one misstep of his giant foot and I'd have a broken toe or worse.

The kitchen was large, bright and cheerful. To my surprise, there were things cooking on all burners of the stove. The scents were heavenly. It made me wonder if Italians always had something cooking night and day. One thing I'd learned about Italians during my trip to Rome is they know their food. I typically abhor stereotypes, but in my experience, this one seemed to be consistently true. I'd never eaten better food than when I'd been in Italy. Slash's grandmother, Nonna, cooked meals so delicious I was convinced it was magic, despite the scientific implausibility of such a conviction.

Marco cleared the table and insisted we sit down. I'd barely planted my behind in a chair when Marcella placed huge glasses of red wine in front of me and Slash.

"It's Gaja Barbaresco wine," she said to Slash as if it would mean something to him. Apparently it did, because his eyes lit up. He swished it around in the glass before taking a sip. He closed his eyes and sighed.

"Eccellente."

He opened his eyes and saw me looking at him curiously. "It's a popular wine in Italy made from a first-rate winery in Gaja," he explained. "It's a rich and full-bodied flavor. I think you'll like it."

Everyone was waiting for me to try it, so I picked up my glass and cautiously took a sip. The wine exploded on my tongue in a taste burst with a slight tartness similar to that of cherries. It was unique and absolutely fantastic. Not too sweet and not too dry. Exactly how I liked my wine.

"Wow, that's really good," I said, taking another sip. "It's unlike any wine I've ever had before."

Marcella beamed and filled goblets for herself and Marco. Shortly thereafter, we were required to lift our wine in a toast.

"To old friends and new ones," Marco said in a booming voice.

As we sipped our wine, Marco told stories of when they had lived in London near Slash's adopted parents. I already knew that Slash's mother, Juliette, was a nurse, but I discovered his father, James, was a physical therapist.

Marcella put a tray of cheese and an assortment of olives on the table. I popped a couple of the olives in my mouth and found them soft and delicious. The food quickly disappeared, so Marcella put out another plate of food while Marco filled our wine goblets again.

Slash smiled as Marcella purposefully set the plate closest to him. "Ah, the antipasti. *Grazie*, Marcella."

I peered at the food, trying to figure out what it was when Slash leaned toward me. "It's salami, prosciutto, cheese and homemade, hand-crusted bread."

My mouth watered just looking at it all. It didn't take us long to devour it but more food kept appearing on the table. Slash informed me that the rice dish in front of me now was chicken risotto and the steaming stew to my left was *umbria*, a lentil stew with sausage.

After we ate all of that, Marcella brought out a plate of freshly cut tomatoes and mozzarella cheese drizzled with olive oil, followed by a huge bowl of seasonal fruit and another platter of assorted cheeses. By the time she brought out the dessert, a *panna cotta* with glazed raspberries, accompanied by cups of steaming espresso, I was beyond stuffed. How Italians could eat like this and not weigh a thousand pounds was well worthy of serious scientific study.

I glanced at my watch and realized we'd been eating and drinking for nearly three hours. Somehow, I'd actually enjoyed myself. What could I say? Italians clearly made the best food in the world and the conversation was interesting and lively. Plus, no one noticed I wasn't talking, since everyone else spoke at the same time and waved their arms around with great animation in support of whatever was being said.

Still, when it was all said and done, I felt like I'd eaten a fifteen-pound basketball. I was also pretty tipsy. My cheeks and ears felt hot, which always happened to me when I drank alcohol, which was rarely. I staggered to my feet, feeling my jeans pull tight across my stomach. I hoped I wouldn't pop the button on them.

I politely inquired about the bathroom and Marcella told me where it was located. As I wound my way through the furniture gallery, which had pretty cool stuff, I swayed a bit on my feet. Just then I heard the patter of steps behind me. Turning around I saw Guido behind me, his tongue lolling out, tail wagging.

His eyes sparkled with mischief, or something else. Hunger? Menace? Trouble?

Oh, dear God.

"Stay." I pointed a shaky finger at him with as much authority as I could manage. I had to be the alpha dog or he'd be all over me. "Don't mess with me, dude. I mean it. Clear?"

He seemed to grin at me just before he lunged.

ELEVEN

I LEAPED FORWARD with the skill of an Olympic jumper and the desperation of a woman not in sync with animals, and barely made it to the bathroom, slamming the door closed behind me just as Guido crashed into it. The door was antique wood with an old-fashioned crystal doorknob, but thank God and all the stars above, it held against the big dog. Panting, I flicked on the light and slid the small metal latch across the door to lock it. I leaned against the wall, my heart pounding.

Safe. At least for the moment.

As soon as I calmed down, I surveyed the bathroom. Small, but cute. It was painted pink with old-fashioned flowery wallpaper and had a small sink with antique brass fixtures. A bowl of floral potpourri sat on one side of the sink and the scent of dried roses and cinnamon wafted through the bathroom. The toilet was the old-fashioned kind with a chain pull instead of a handle to flush. It seemed to fit the house perfectly.

The steady patter of feet pacing sounded outside the bathroom. Jeez. Guido was waiting for me. I wondered how I'd be able to get back to the kitchen without shouting for help.

Perhaps because the door was antique and slightly warped, it didn't close completely. When I stepped away from it, I saw an eye pressed up against the small crack.

"Hey, bud, this is private," I said, bending close to the eye. "Beat it."

I heard Guido panting, but the eye stayed where it was.

Jeez. A peeper dog.

Sighing, I unfastened my jeans with a heartfelt sigh and started to sit on the toilet. I hadn't even had a chance to completely sit down before something tiny and furry shot out from a hole beneath the sink and ran right across my foot.

A mouse!

I screamed in surprise and fell backward, hitting the seat with my bare butt and the back of my thighs. I hit it so hard, I bounced off. My head banged against the wall as I fell sideways into the small space between the wall and the toilet. My jeans and underwear were tangled around my knees, my hands jammed between me and the wall.

Hearing me scream, Guido barked once and then leaped onto the door with the force of a tank. He brought the whole thing down in one ginormous boom. One more leap and he was on top of me, one paw stuck in the toilet, the other on me. He licked and slobbered on my face. I tried to scream, but I couldn't breathe.

At that moment, the mouse made another appearance, running across Guido's paw. The dog took one look at the mouse and yelped in terror. He scrambled off me, took two leaps and jumped straight into the sink with the force of a sledgehammer. He was ten times too big for it, so naturally it pulled from the wall and went crashing to the floor. Water sprayed out from a broken pipe, soaking both of us. Guido spun around in fear, his claws scrambling for purchase on the wet tile, hitting me in the face several times with a wet tail before finally dashing out of the bathroom. Still wedged between the toilet and the wall, I managed to hoist my jeans up to my hips just as Slash dashed into the bathroom with Marco and Marcella right behind him.

"*Cara*, are you okay?" Slash asked, eyes wide. He ran over to the sink, pressing a hand against the pipe, containing the water for the moment. "What happened?"

I was still stuck at an awkward angle. Marco took one step into the bathroom and extended a big hand, pulling me to my feet. I pressed one hand to my chest, trying to get my breath back. The other hand held up my jeans, which were still unfastened. I was soaked, smelled like wet dog and my blouse was torn on the sleeve. I looked like I'd been in a fight with a big dog and lost.

Badly.

"Mouse," was all I could get out.

Slash glanced between me and the sink. Of course, Guido was nowhere in sight, leaving me to deal with this on my own.

Figures.

"So, you smashed the door and sink trying to get the mouse?" Slash asked, clearly trying to figure out the chain of events.

"What?" I shook my head vigorously, my hair dripping. "No! It was Guido. He heard me scream when I saw the mouse. He broke down the door and then jumped on me. But as soon as he saw the mouse, he freaked out, then jumped into the sink to get away from it. He was too heavy for the sink and he brought

it crashing down, nearly killing me, the mouse and the house in the process of trying to get out of the bathroom."

Holy cow. I sounded like a character from a Dr. Seuss book.

For a second it was dead silent. Then Slash snorted.

Snorted!

I glared at him. He swallowed hard, pressing his lips together and avoiding eye contact.

Marco, however, coughed and hid his mouth behind his hand. I counted silently to five, but he'd already started a full-on laugh by the time I got to three. His laugh was as big as he was. He bent over completely and leaned against the wall outside the bathroom, howling.

That completely undid Slash. He started laughing as well. Their laughter, inside and out, shook the entire bathroom. At some point, Slash had to brace himself against the wall to keep from collapsing from laughter, which couldn't have been easy seeing as how he still had one hand containing the water.

Only Marcella came to my defense, admonishing the men and taking me by the hand. She led me out of the bathroom, dripping wet, leaving the men to laugh themselves into a coma before presumably figuring out how to fix the sink.

I was *not* amused.

Marcella took me upstairs and gave me a towel. I declined her offer to dry my clothes and wiped off the best I could before I returned downstairs. Everyone was waiting for me at the foot of the stairs. Marcella informed me Marco had apparently turned off the water to the bathroom, so all was fine. They apologized for Guido, who was wisely absent, but Marco still looked like he was trying not to laugh. His wet shoes squeaked on the wood floor when he walked.

Slash took one look at my face and lifted Marcella's hand to his mouth, pressing a kiss on the top of it. "I'm sorry, but we're going to have to make another appointment to come back to shop. I hope it won't be an inconvenience."

"Of course not." She patted his slightly bearded jaw. "You and Lexi are welcome here anytime, bambino. It was wonderful to see you again."

Then she approached me and kissed both of my cheeks. "Take care of our boy, okay? He's a good one."

I blushed. "Ah, sure. Thank you for dinner. I can honestly say it was one of the best meals I've ever eaten in my life. I'm, ah, sorry about the bathroom."

"Don't you give it another thought," Marco said. "Guido is the guilty party." I thought he might start laughing again, but somehow he held it together.

Marcella beamed and Marco squeezed me in a big bear hug. Finally, thank God, we departed the house without another sign of Guido.

I climbed into the SUV. "I'm sorry we didn't get any furniture, Slash."

"No worries. It will give us an excuse to come back. I shouldn't have waited so long to get in touch with them. I was busy, not that it's a viable excuse."

Any excuse to avoid social settings was viable in my book. But I wanted to be polite, so I didn't say anything along those lines. Still, I didn't want him to think it had been a total loss of an evening.

"They were really nice and the food was amazing. I liked hearing stories about you when you were young. But seriously, Slash. How can Italians eat like that and still be so amazingly good looking on the national average?"

He chuckled. "We work it off in other areas of our lives." He slid a hand to my knee and grinned meaningfully at me.

"Ha!" I grinned at him. "I bet."

We drove for a while before I noticed his hand on my knee was vibrating. I looked at his face. He was trying not to laugh. Again.

I crossed my arms against my chest. "Are you still thinking about the bathroom?"

"I'm not sure there's a safe answer to that question." He leaned over and plucked a big black dog hair from behind my ear.

I scowled at him. "Fine. Go ahead. Be amused. This is exactly why I hate shopping. It's a conspiracy. Shopping and the universe are aligned against me. This time it threw a dog in the mix. Totally unfair."

As if he'd been waiting for my permission, he burst out laughing. Finally, he swiped at his eyes with his hand. "I'm sorry, I can't stop thinking about it. *Cara*, your face when I came through that bathroom door… it was priceless."

"You're lucky I had time to pull my jeans up. That would have been a whole different level of 'Hi, I'm getting to know old family friends.' Why do animals hate me so much?"

"You're wrong. They like you. Guido likes you. Dogs can sense a good heart. It didn't surprise me at all that he went straight for you when we entered the house. It could have been the beer smell, but I suspect he just liked you. In the bathroom, well, he was just trying to protect you."

"Really? So, that's why he destroyed an entire bathroom, nearly suffocating me in the process?"

"He's just a big baby." He began laughing again. "*Mio Dio*, I can't stop," he said, holding up a hand. "Please, let's table all discussion of dogs, mice and suffocation until we get home. I'm going to drive us off the road."

"Forget it. The subject is closed anyway."

He laughed again and then drew in a deep breath. "Understood. But it's going to live in my memory always."

"I'm okay with that. As long as it lives there, and nowhere else."

TWELVE

SLASH AND I left an hour early for work the next day. We had a lot to wrap up before our flight to Egypt later that afternoon. While most of my work involved X-Corp, I did take time to do some digging on Elvis's father. Finding him had to be our utmost priority.

I started more than a year prior to when he'd started his sabbatical from Oxford. I counted three separate trips to Cairo. Two that lasted a week and one that lasted ten days. He'd also taken several longer trips during the summer break. He went to Israel on two separate occasions, Jordan, Saudi Arabia and Egypt again. He had hopscotched across the Middle East. But why? What trail had he followed to find that elusive artifact?

Since Egypt seemed to be his final destination of choice, and Cairo the city, I tried to determine what his connection to the city might be. There were a lot of choices, but, after short consideration, the Egyptian Museum of Antiquities and the Coptic Museum topped my list. Now that was settled, I'd have to do a little hacking. I closed the door and booted up my personal laptops. I took careful steps to hide my location and then began a penetration of the Egyptian Museum database. It was surprisingly easy. Not that it held national security secrets, but given the amount of world treasures located there, I almost felt compelled to offer my services pro bono to help protect the information on these priceless artifacts. Maybe someday I would.

Pushing that thought aside for the time being, I started my search for any mention of Arthur Zimmerman. Seconds later, his name popped up. He had been registered on dozens of occasions as visiting the museum in an academic capacity, examining various exhibits. I pulled up records from as far back as ten years earlier, which indicated he'd been coming to the museum regularly. I tried to find any rhyme or reason to the different exhibits he visited, but it was outside my area of expertise and I couldn't discern any particular pattern.

A penetration of the Coptic Museum showed only three visits in the past year, not nearly as many as to the Egyptian Museum.

I finally closed up those avenues of exploration and got back to my real job. I'd only been at it for just over a half hour when Basia strolled into my office, fire in her eyes.

"You are so *not* going to Egypt." She put both hands on the corner of my desk and glared at me.

I took off my computer glasses and set them next to my laptop. "I am. And so is Slash. We're looking out for Elvis. You want him to come back to the wedding on time and in one piece, right?"

"I don't want him to go in the first place. Talk him out of it."

"How exactly am I supposed to do that? He's a grown man. He'll do what he wants. This is between Elvis and his father. I can't stop him, Basia. The best I can do is help him."

She sighed and sat in my visitor chair. "Why does

Elvis even care? This is a man who hasn't given a damn about his family for fifteen years."

"Thirteen, but that's semantics at this point. What's important is their father has uncovered something potentially dangerous."

"Xavier told me about the man with the gun who accosted you and Elvis at the house. Is that a part of this?"

"It's exactly about that. I'm not saying any more. I don't want you to know the details for your own safety. My advice is for you and Xavier to avoid staying at the house while Elvis is gone. I know the guys will have every security measure in effect, but it would still make me feel better."

"This is all their father's fault. I think he just wants to wreck our wedding."

"I'm not even sure he *knows* about the wedding."

"But Elvis does and he's going anyway. The wedding is just over a week away. One week. How could this happen?" She looked close to tears and I fought back the panic.

"Basia, you've got to calm down. I really don't think this is an effort by Mr. Zimmerman to ruin the wedding. I promise I'll have Elvis back in time for the ceremony. You have to trust me. Neither of us is going to miss it."

She sniffed. "But if you're in Egypt, who's going to come with me for my final wedding dress fitting?"

"What about Bonnie? Or one of your cousins? Or better yet, your mom. Fly her out for the occasion. Besides, let's be honest with each other. Seeing as how this is the final fitting of the dress and absolutely nothing can go wrong, isn't it better that I'm not there?"

She smiled for the first time since she'd come into my office. "Maybe, but it wouldn't be nearly as exciting."

I LEFT THE office shortly after two and detoured to Elvis's house. I pulled up to the curb and hopped out, checking the shrubs for any lurkers. When all appeared clear, I rang the bell.

Elvis answered the door in frayed cutoff jean shorts and a white T-shirt. He looked over my shoulder and both ways down the street before letting me in. "Hey, Lexi. What's up?"

"I have a couple of questions."

"Sure. Go on into the living room. I've got to put in the last load of laundry and I'll be right back, okay?"

"Sure, okay."

I wandered into the living room and stopped when I saw a young girl sitting on the couch, a laptop balanced on her lap. Her red hair was pulled into a long ponytail and she wore shorts and a bright yellow T-shirt with something written on it. I couldn't see what it was because of the way she was hunched over the keyboard.

She looked up from the laptop and gasped when she saw me. "Oh, God."

"Oh God, what?" I looked down at my shirt. Had I spilled something? Was my bra strap showing?

"It's you. Lexi Carmichael."

I gave her a wary glance. "Yes. And who are you? Why are you in Elvis's house?"

"I'm Angel. Hasn't he told you about me?"

Of course he hadn't. Apparently this was becoming the norm. He hadn't mentioned Gwen, the letter from his father, or the Black Plague until now. So, why would he tell me about a red-haired teenager named Angel, who apparently had free roam of his house?

"No, he hasn't mentioned you." I studied her. "Is Angel your real name or a nickname?"

"Real name." She grinned. "Because I'm all angelic and stuff. Nice to meet you, Lexi Carmichael. In case you've heard of me, my online moniker is Arch-Angel007. Get it? 007—James Bond? I'm the leader of the Lexicons. We're based on Tumblr, but we also have a presence on AO3 and Instagram. Let me know if you ever want to stop by and say hi to your fan base. I'd be happy to arrange it. They'd love it."

I stared at her, horrified. "What did I do to deserve this?"

Elvis strolled in and put a hand on my shoulder. "Hey, Lexi. I see you've met Angel."

"Who's Angel?" I could feel my blood pressure rising. "And why exactly is she in your house?"

Elvis plopped down on the couch beside her and leaned over to see what she was doing on the computer. "She's Gwen's kid sister. Gwen dropped her off while she finished up some shopping at the mall for the trip."

I studied Angel and could see the resemblance now. The rare red hair and blue eyes combination. Not to mention the fangirling.

Ugh.

Angel tapped some keys and then shifted her laptop aside. She stood and stretched. I could see the writing on her T-shirt now. It said On the Third Day God Created the Undo Button.

"It's ace to finally meet you, Lexi." She gave me a big smile. "Actually, it's beyond ace. I was there at the high school when you, Wally, Piper, Brandon,

Elvis, and Slash saved us from those crazy terrorists. You were, like, so amazing. Girl power all the way. I bow to your geekiness. I kneel in front of your cyber knowledge. I prostrate—"

"Whoa." I held up a hand. "Stop. Seriously."

She grinned and her smile reminded me of Gwen, too. It also occurred to me that despite the fangirling, Angel might be teasing me…just a little.

"By the way, Piper says hi," she added. "She's a Lexicon, too."

Piper was one of the three students I'd worked with at the high school during the dangerous siege. She and two other students, Wally and Brandon, were currently my interns at X-Corp.

"Piper and I are going to have to have a serious talk," I said. "Wait. How is it possible that you even know Piper?"

"Duh. She's one of my closest friends at school. Geeks stick together. You should know that."

"You aren't in high school. You can't possibly be more than thirteen."

"Hey, I'm almost sixteen. I just look young for my age."

I understood that, having just posed as a high school student about six months earlier. But still, wow, she did look young for her age.

Elvis grinned. "Angel is finishing up her junior at Excalibur, which is how she knows Piper, Wally and Brandon. She has been pushed ahead a year. She's a pretty smart kid."

"Not pretty smart, *really* smart." Angel put her hands on her hips. "Not bragging, just keeping it real. I already have fifteen college credits at Georgetown."

She stretched out a hand to shake mine. I paused and then shook it reluctantly. Not because I wasn't impressed by her smarts. I was. It's just I'd met too many new people in too short a time, and some of them needed a definite redirection of their misguided fangirling. I needed quiet time to process and sort everything out in my head. Right now a headache was brewing behind my eyes.

Elvis cocked his head and glanced at me. "So, Lexi, why did you stop by?"

Before I could answer I heard a yipping noise from the stairs. A small white dog about the size of a shoebox came tearing down the stairs and slid sideways, paws scraping at the wood floor. The body straightened and headed like a projectile directly toward me. I'm not proud to admit it, but I put the fifteen-year-old girl between me and the dog.

Angel bent over and scooped the furry lunatic into her arms who was yapping like crazy. "Settle down, Mr. Toodles. You're a silly dog. I know you're excited to meet Lexi Carmichael. She's the one I've been telling you about." She thrust the dog at me. "Isn't he adorable?"

Oh, for crying out loud.

The dog growled and tried to snap at me. I backed up, knocking over the fireplace instruments with a clatter. So much for Slash's hypothesis that all animals loved me.

"Uh, actually, Elvis, I have to go. I'll talk to you later at the airport."

He glanced between Angel and the dog and nodded. "Okay, I'll see you out."

We walked to my car in silence. Before I got in the

driver's side, he put a hand on the driver's door, preventing me from getting in. "I'm really glad you came by, Lexi. I wanted to tell you something. Xavier and I aren't on speaking terms. We had another fight last night. Even bigger than the one before, leading to the no-talking thing. He wouldn't be reasonable about the endospore threat."

The revelation that they were fighting to this degree hurt me more than I would've expected. They'd always been a team—protective, supportive and watching each other's back. That an absent father could drive apart twins who were this close made me feel nauseous.

I froze as a revelation suddenly occurred to me. Somewhere along the line, Elvis and Xavier had become family to me. No, that wasn't quite right. I'd *made* them family. I'm not sure how it happened, it just did. That's why seeing the twins fighting to this level and going through such a painful metamorphosis was more upsetting than I ever imagined.

But this wasn't about me. Elvis needed a supportive friend, not another person falling apart on him.

"I'm sorry, Elvis." I jingled the car keys in my hand, wishing I knew just what to say to make this better. "I've discovered family relations are infinitely more complex than I ever imagined."

"I know. The crazy thing is, I get it. I really get it. Xavier's totally right on a number of important points. But the trip to Egypt wasn't the only catalyst. These fights have been a long time brewing."

"What? Why?"

He pushed his fingers through his hair. His hand trembled. "I'm not sure. I can't put my finger on it.

Maybe it's a twin thing. We've been growing apart for some time."

He looked so anguished, I put a hand on his arm. "Hey, growing apart is natural. Think of it this way. You and Xavier have been a dual processor system all of these years. You both knew the computer could operate on just one processor, and often it did. But it was a lot easier and more comfortable to share the load. As each year passed, the processors got upgraded and became more powerful. Looking back, just one of them is more powerful than both of them were just a few years ago. In fact, it's come to a point where each processor needs to have their own system to better serve the enterprise called life. It doesn't mean you won't still be closely networked—you will—but only that you won't still share the same housing. Does that make sense?"

"Absolutely. It's just harder than I ever imagined."

"Not just on you, but on Xavier, too. Change is mega. Keep in mind, Xavier is already living on the edge. He's getting married in just over a week. Emotions are high all around. That your father enters the picture at this exact moment is bound to open old wounds."

"Agreed."

I patted his shoulder. "You're going to get through this and so will Xavier, because no matter what happens, you guys are brothers. You'll always be there for each other, okay?"

"Okay." He gave me a hug. "Thanks, Lexi. See you at the airport in a couple of hours."

"Yep. Meet you there."

THIRTEEN

SLASH WAS ALREADY at my apartment when I got there. A black duffel bag and two laptop cases sat by the door. A black windbreaker was draped over the back of one of the living room chairs.

"Slash?" I called out, dropping my purse on the couch. "Where are you?"

"In the bedroom."

I walked down the hall and into the room. He'd stacked all my boxes neatly to one side of the room and had my half-packed carry-on suitcase open and on the bed, which had been stripped, ready for me to finish packing. He was dressed in black jeans, a short-sleeved T-shirt and no shoulder holster. He held out a hand, so I took it and he pulled me in for a kiss.

"You got off early," he murmured against my cheek.

"You, too." I leaned my head against his chest. "You smell good. You always smell good. How do you do that?"

"I shower?"

I wrapped my arms around his waist and closed my eyes. It felt nice to take a moment to appreciate the arms around me. "I'm really glad you're going on this trip, Slash."

"Me, too."

He ran a hand over my ponytail and rested his fingers against the nape of my neck. We stood there enjoying each other's company for a few beats longer.

Unfortunately, I couldn't stay there forever, because my suitcase wouldn't pack itself. Maybe I could ask Slash to invent something. He was good like that.

"Well, I guess I'd better get some things in my suitcase," I said.

"Don't worry about a laptop. I brought two sterilized ones, but loaded with software we may need."

"Perfect."

Slash loosened his embrace and I went into the bathroom to get my toilet kit. After rooting around under the sink for a minute, I peeked my head out the door. "Did you have time to find out anything about the financials on Elvis's dad today?"

"I did. But first of all, I did a little more digging on Mr. Merhu Khalfani."

"And?"

"He wasn't lying about one thing. He's unemployed. At least as of three months ago. He was fired from the British Museum."

"The British Museum? Wasn't that where his father worked?"

"*Si.* Like his father, he worked with the Egyptian exhibits."

"Interesting. Why was he fired?"

"He was caught handling exhibits he had no permission to touch. At least that's the official statement. Interestingly, it wasn't his first offense. He had a couple others before that. My guess is they cut him a break or two because of his father. But as it became a pattern, they cut him loose."

I stuffed in my toiletries and stepped out of the bathroom. "I wonder what we would come up with if we cross-referenced the exhibits he was caught touching with those Arthur Zimmerman was examining at the Egyptian Museum in Cairo? Maybe something would pop out at us."

"Good idea." Slash's eyes flashed with interest. "But I've got more on Khalfani. He's unmarried without any known family except for a sister, who lives in Jordan and does not provide him with financial assistance. Yet, for an unemployed man, Khalfani has an income, at least for the past few months."

"Then it's interesting he was able to afford a so-called holiday in the US."

"Agreed. Someone has been depositing money into his account for a few months."

I stared at Slash. "Who?"

"I don't know. Not yet. The account is hidden and I didn't have time for a thorough search. But it's another thread to pull."

"Wow. It sure is. Speaking of financials, what did you find on Elvis's dad?"

"First of all, he doesn't have a credit or debit card. He does, however, have a bank account at the Central Bank of Egypt. He made steady withdrawals from his account at one of the branches in Cairo until about a month ago. He made a sizable withdrawal of about seven thousand dollars and disappeared."

"Did he empty his account?"

"No. He still has several thousand dollars left."

"Was there any pattern to the withdrawals?"

"Funny you ask. There was. The first and fifteenth of every month."

I put my toilet kit in the suitcase. "It sounds like he was paying someone a salary."

"Or a bribe."

"Bribes are more irregular. Salary is consistent."

"Not always."

I stood in front of my closet, trying to decide what else to add to my suitcase. I'd put a couple of things in yesterday, including underwear, socks, pajamas, a pair of sandals and a sweatshirt for the cool desert nights.

"A hat," Slash reminded me. "Long pants or long skirts, lightweight material, if you have them. Modest tops. Shorts and low-cut blouses are out for women in Cairo unless you want to receive a lot of unwanted attention. I've got the suntan lotion."

I trusted Slash's judgment on the fashion front. "Okay. Hat first." I grabbed a floppy burlap hat I'd bought for a vacation at the beach I'd taken with Basia. I tried it on my head and looked at my reflection in the mirror. "I'm going to look exactly like an American tourist."

Slash rearranged it on my head. "It covers your entire face, but it's not discreet. Do you have a smaller hat or cap?"

I leaned over and rummaged in a box in the bottom of my closet. "How's this?" I pulled out a black cap that said Don't Drink and Derive. I stuck it on my head.

"It'll do," Slash said. "Better than the beach hat."

I tossed the ball cap into the suitcase. "So, want to know what I found?"

"I do."

"I think I know to whom Arthur Zimmerman might be paying a salary."

"Really?" Slash raised an eyebrow. "You're not going to say Khalfani, are you?"

"No, it couldn't possibly be that easy. It's someone else at the Egyptian Museum in Cairo."

"Who?"

"I don't know—a museum employee. I think he was working with someone while he was there. All I found was a name Z. Wahgdi." I grabbed a lightweight blouse from the closet and held it up against me. "That name was linked to Arthur's records during his examination of numerous museum exhibits and artifacts. At first I thought it might be a clerk who checks in and out artifacts for study. But a quick review of Wahgdi's file indicates he's a research assistant often assigned to help researchers at the museum. He's been there for about three years."

"Good work. That could be useful."

"Right. Mr. Wahgdi and the museum could be a good place to start when we get to Cairo." I put the blouse on the bed. "Wahgdi might have been the last person to see Arthur before he disappeared."

"Or, at the very least, can help us zero in on what he was doing before he disappeared."

I chose the rest of my clothes, pulling them from the closet and putting them on the bed. The blouse, an ankle-length cotton skirt, a couple of T-shirts and an extra pair of jeans. I folded everything and stuck it in the suitcase. "Done."

"Quick, efficient and light." Slash nodded approvingly. "Impressive."

I closed the suitcase and Slash carried it to the door.

We stood by the door examining our pile of luggage. "You ready to go?" Slash asked. "We can catch a bite to eat at the airport."

"Perfect. Do you want to take your car or mine?"

"Mine." He put a hand on my shoulder. "Time to say goodbye to your apartment, *cara*. This is it."

I looked around at the furniture and stacks of boxes. My apartment was small and cramped, but it had been mine—my first home as an adult. I'd paid for every cent of my rent and I'd been happy here. The walls had served as my matrix of safety, the one place where I could retreat when the real world became too much for me. Now it was becoming a symbol of my past. I didn't want to dwell too long on that.

I turned around and grabbed the handle of my suitcase. "I'm ready."

Slash covered my hand on the suitcase handle with his, stilling me. He'd sensed something in my voice. "It's not the end, *cara*. It's a new beginning. I felt the same way when I left Italy."

I lifted my eyes to meet his gaze. His brown eyes were sympathetic and warm. "I know, Slash. It just feels like I'm leaving a little part of myself behind."

"You will. That's inevitable with change. But you'll also find a new part of yourself. I'll miss this place, too. It's where I fell in love with you."

Somehow, that made me feel better. I managed a small smile. "At least I can take my memories with me."

"There's that." He patted my shoulder once more. As if sensing I needed a moment, he shouldered both his laptop bag and mine and wheeled his suitcase out in the hall, leaving me alone for one final look.

"Goodbye, apartment," I whispered.

I slid my purse on my shoulder, then pulled my suitcase out the door and walked into a new chapter of my life.

FOURTEEN

WHEN WE ARRIVED at the airport, Slash didn't head for the main terminal.

"Um, Slash, you do realize you just missed the turn-off to the long-term parking area."

He didn't deviate from the road. "I know. We're not going out of the main terminal."

"We're not?"

"No. I've chartered a plane for our trip." He drove along a side road ringing a runway and turned onto a road leading to a two-story glass building. There was a parking lot in front with several trucks and cars already parked there.

"You did? Do Elvis and Gwen know?"

"They do. Elvis is bringing Gwen. They should be here in about an hour and a half."

After we checked in at the terminal, Slash took me by the elbow and directed me toward a restaurant. It was a small setup with a handful of tables. A waitress led us to a table by the glass window so we could look out at the planes.

"It was nice of you to charter a plane for Elvis," I said as I sat. "I guess this is why you didn't ask me for my credit card number."

"It was the easiest arrangement for everyone and gave us the most flexibility."

"That was thoughtful. Thank you."

He reached across the table and took my hand. "Look, *cara*. I know you are nervous about flying again so soon after the accident. But I'm with you this time. About fourteen hours until we are there. Okay?"

"Okay." I squeezed his hand. "I won't lie. It means a lot that you're here."

We ate, sipped our wine and talked. When the waiter cleared our table, Slash pulled out his laptop and opened it.

"Something you said earlier made me curious," he said. "I'm going to download the exhibits Khalfani was caught examining at the British Museum, cross-referencing them with those Arthur Zimmerman was viewing at the Egyptian Museum in Cairo. Once I've downloaded the data, we can examine it on the flight."

"Great idea," I said. It helped to think I'd have something to do other than just look at the window and remember the last time I'd been on an airplane.

The entire operation took him twenty minutes, just about the time Gwen and Elvis joined us.

The two of them walked into the restaurant, dressed in jeans, T-shirts and tennis shoes. Elvis's hair was windblown, his glasses askew. Gwen's sweatshirt was crooked and she looked around the terminal with wide eyes. Both were carrying laptop bags over their shoulders. They looked more like teenagers than brilliant young scientists.

Gwen set her laptop bag on the floor next to me and pressed her nose against the window. "Wow! Is that a Gulfstream?" she asked staring at one of the airplanes. "I've never been on one. I saw one in the movies once, but it's hard to say what is real and what is added as an extra prop for the purpose of the script."

Slash pointed to the one of the left. "That one is our plane."

"This is going to be so cool. A Gulfstream! I'm going to cross something off my bucket list today."

Both Gwen and Elvis declined Slash's offer to get something to eat, so Slash put away his laptop. We stood and headed for the exit. I almost wished I hadn't eaten anything because my stomach jumped. No question about it, despite Slash's assurances, I was nervous.

I knew Slash had come early to the airport for that very reason. He'd set me in front of the airplane, giving me time to look at it and process. He'd then wined and dined me in an effort to relax me. I appreciated the effort. Statistically, the chances of being in a plane crash two times in a row was unlikely to a point of nearly being impossible. But the universe was funny and I did have a little black cloud that liked to follow me around. Still, walking with my hand in his, I felt safe.

I could do this. I *would* do it.

Accompanied by a young man who greeted us when we entered the terminal, we exited the building and walked onto the tarmac. We headed for the plane Slash had pointed out to us from the restaurant. As we boarded, a young, male flight attendant with short brown hair and a wide smile greeted us. He was dressed in a crisp blue uniform with a white shirt and blue tie.

"Welcome aboard. I'm Peter and will be your flight attendant for the duration of the trip to Cairo. It's my pleasure to serve you."

Everyone found a seat in the leather recliner-type seats. Slash led me to the back to a section with four seats and a folding worktable. Along the left side was a large flat-screen television and a glass credenza that held crystal, real plates and silverware. I had a flash-back of myself rooting through the broken glass of a similar credenza looking for something to help me and my friends survive after the crash. My fingers crept up to touch the faint scar on my forehead—my reminder I was a survivor. I took a deep breath to calm myself and slid into my chair.

The pilots came back to introduce themselves and before I knew it we were taking off. I gripped Slash's hand as we rose into the air, but as the flight contin-ued without incident, I began to relax.

Gwen, however, was the picture of excitement. Smiling, oohing and aaahing over everything in the cabin. She examined every inch of the plane, taking pictures of everything with her smartphone. Despite my protestations, she somehow snapped a selfie with me and her.

"Perfect," Gwen said, tapping. "Angel will love this. In fact, she'll probably blow this up, and use this as the cover photo. Before we left, she texted we have twenty-seven new Lexicons since yesterday. We're really becoming a small fiefdom."

I winced. "Just. Stop. Talking. I beg you."

Elvis and Slash seemed amused. I tried not to be too cranky about it because at least it took my mind off my nervousness about the flight.

After a while Gwen finally settled down and she and Elvis started playing cards. Slash booted up his computer. At some point Gwen laughed loudly, throw-ing down her cards and slapping Elvis on the shoulder. Elvis grinned at her and gave her a big goofy smile.

I leaned over toward Slash, lowering my voice. "What do you think is the deal with those two?"

He didn't look up from the keyboard. "Don't get involved."

"I'm not getting involved. I'm asking a question."

"Asking questions is getting involved."

"That's not true. I'm asking *you* the question, not Elvis or Gwen. If I were asking them, then I'd be getting involved. Technically, I'm just expressing my curiosity to my boyfriend."

"Those are not the kinds of questions you ask your boyfriend."

"They aren't? Why not?"

"Because those questions are none of our business."

"Of course they are. Elvis is our friend, right?"

"Right." Slash looked up from the screen. "Which is exactly why we leave him alone, *cara*. You like Bonnie, right?"

"Of course."

"Well, how would you react if she asked you if you knew something was going on between Elvis and Gwen?"

I considered. "She'd do that?"

"She might."

"Well, even if she asked, that's the problem. I don't know anything. That's why I'm asking you. Is something going on? I can't tell."

"If we don't ask, we don't know, right?" He went back to tapping on the keyboard. "Honest deniability."

I pondered his words for a bit and decided Slash was a wise guy, indeed. I figured Elvis would tell me if he wanted me to know.

After a while Slash became absorbed in what he

was doing and Gwen fell asleep. I went to sit on the other side of Elvis.

"How are you doing?" I asked him.

He set aside his book and hooked his glasses on the front of his T-shirt. "Okay, I guess. Gwen is doing a good job of keeping my mind off the task at hand— confronting my father."

"Do you know what you're going to say to him?"

"Not really. What do you say to a man who has been absent and unemotionally unavailable to you pretty much all of your life?"

When I remained silent, he sighed. "That's not even the worst part. You know what I worry about the most, Lexi? That I'll turn out like him. That I already *am* like him. Xavier…he's always been more like my mom in terms of temperament and personality. He's not afraid to say what's on his mind and open himself up to others. Look at him. He's getting married in a week to the girl of his dreams. I'm both thrilled and horribly envious of him. I… I can't do that kind of thing so easily."

"Being cautious in relationships is a lot different than being emotionally unavailable."

"I know. It's just that I don't even know my father anymore. Maybe I never knew him."

I put my hand over his and squeezed. "I don't know the answer to that, but I *do* know you. You might have been shaped in part by your father, but you aren't defined by him. I don't subscribe to the theory of tainted blood. I think it's pretty simple at this point. You hold the cards to any kind of reconciliation with your dad. Either you'll forgive him…or you won't."

We sat for a few more minutes in companionable silence before I returned to my seat. Turning down the light over my chair, I reclined and drifted off to sleep. Despite the fact that I was flying on exactly the same type of airplane that I had crashed on several weeks prior, I didn't once dream of falling out of the sky.

FIFTEEN

I MAY HAVE survived the flight to Egypt, but there was a good chance I was going to die on the streets of Cairo.

After we disembarked from the plane, gathered our luggage and went through customs, we rendezvoused in front of the terminal where Slash had secured a van to drive us to the hotel. A quick glance at my watch indicated it was just after eleven, approaching the hottest time of the day. The heat was thick and oppressive even though we were standing in the shade. I almost cheered when the van pulled up, even though the sides had so many dents and craters, it reminded me of an asteroid. It did not, however, have air-conditioning. At least the driver was cheerful and spoke some English.

Unfortunately, he drove like a freaking lunatic.

As we left the airport, we watched in horror as he weaved through traffic without slowing or adjusting his speed even once, nearly hitting a half dozen cars in the process before pulling onto a crowded bridge. Gwen clapped a hand over her mouth after several small shrieks.

"Cairo is beautiful city," our driver said in heavily accented English. Apparently he was oblivious to our terror. "It has thousands of mosques. See there?" He nearly sideswiped a black sedan as he took his eyes off the road to point at the numerous minarets dotting the city skyline in the distance. Since all the windows were open, I could hear the muezzin calling the faithful for afternoon prayers. I could also hear screams from what I assumed were other tourists in taxis. But before I could comment, our driver squeezed between a bus and a Mercedes with barely an inch to spare.

I sat in the back, sandwiched between Gwen and Elvis while Slash sat in the front. He had his hand braced against the dashboard while Elvis, Gwen and I had resorted to holding hands and murmuring prayers. My foot kept pushing an imaginary brake every time we barely avoided a collision, which was about every three seconds. Gwen finally just closed her eyes. Elvis's skin took on a faint green tinge.

"In case you didn't know, Cairo was built more than one thousand years ago," Slash suddenly said.

I exchanged a confused glance with Elvis. Why in the world had Slash decided to play unflappable tour guide when our lives were hanging by a thread?

The driver swerved to the right and pulled alongside a large truck, sandwiching us between the truck and the concrete side of the bridge. As the van shot forward, the door handles scraped the concrete, shooting off sparks. I held my breath and tried not to scream my head off.

Slash continued to point out the sights of the city as we hurled along as if we weren't moments from impending death. "Cairo has resided on the same spot since its inception. It was perhaps the most prosperous city in the world for many centuries until a plague ravished the city in 1348. Its location is prime since it sits at the juxtaposition between the Nile Valley of Upper Egypt and the delta of Lower Egypt."

I was about to tell him where he could stick his juxtaposition when Elvis screamed, "Look out! That's a red light!"

We exited the bridge and shot through an intersection without slowing down, barely avoiding a dump truck and another cab. Additional cars followed right behind us, riding our bumper and screeching past us without staying in their lanes or showing any kind of road courtesy. It occurred to me that no one in the city was obeying *any* of the traffic signals or signs whatsoever.

The driver suddenly slammed on the brakes, hit the horn and let loose a stream of what I had to assume were swear words. He stuck his head out the window and shouted at the car in front of him, making several hand gestures. Before I could catch my breath from the sudden whiplash, he slammed on the gas again, streaked around the offending car, shot over the curb and into the city.

"Other than the pyramids and museums, one of the best-kept secrets of Cairo is the Khan al Khalili open market," Slash said calmly, pointing out the window in a vague direction. "There are a collection of old-time shops, selling anything from soap to soup. Most of them are folded into small courtyards and presented in a style quite similar to what you might have seen in medieval times."

I lifted my hand to smack him when our driver careened around a corner, slamming all of us to the left. Elvis's head bounced off the window as we came within inches of flattening a pedestrian, two dogs and a café table with two patrons. We straightened and I gasped for breath as Elvis gripped my shoulder to steady himself. Then the driver took a hard right and my stomach bottomed out. The green tinge to Elvis's face turned purplish.

"I'm going to be carsick," Gwen said, her eyes still closed. "Right now."

"Me, too," Elvis added.

"Slash, tell him to slow down," I begged. "Gwen and Elvis are going to throw up and I'm a sympathetic vomiter. Things could get ugly back here."

Our driver took two more hard rights and the van abruptly squealed to a halt next to a large black gate manned by several security guards. After I recovered from the whiplash, I stared out the window at the red stone building flanked by two large red towers on the other side of the gate.

The Cairo Marriott.

The guards at the gatehouse stuck their head through the windows and asked for our passports. While checking them against our reservations, another guard examined our luggage in the back. A German shepherd walked around the van sniffing. Other guards used mirrors to look under our van. When we were cleared, the gate was opened and we pulled up to the front of the hotel with a screech. A bellman leaped forward to help us remove our luggage from the trunk.

We staggered out of the van on shaky legs. Gwen clutched her stomach and leaned over, resting a hand on my shoulder to brace herself. "That was the worst car ride I've ever been on. I don't mean to be rude, but who drives like that?"

My own stomach was still roiling around and I'm pretty sure I'd left my tonsils on the bridge. "Apparently everyone in Cairo. At least we got here in one piece, so that has to count for something."

Slash paid the driver, then put an arm around me, lowering his voice. "Sorry for that. I had to take over as tour guide or our driver would have insisted on doing it. I felt as if it were a better idea to let him focus solely on the driving. Short of knocking him unconscious and taking control of the wheel, which I admit I was seriously considering, there wasn't much else I could do until we got to the hotel."

"I would have voted for knocking him unconscious. Seriously."

Slash patted my shoulder. "For the record, we survived."

"Barely." I blew out a breath and glanced up at the hotel. "It's beautiful. It looks like a castle."

"It was built as a guest palace in 1869," Slash said. "It's a historic landmark."

We walked into the hotel holding hands. Elvis walked beside Gwen and the bellhop with our luggage on a cart trailed behind us. We were met by even more security guards and a magnetometer machine inside the entrance.

"Welcome to the Marriott. Please place your purses and bags on the machine. Empty your pockets of keys, jewelry, cell phones and any other assorted items that might set the machine off."

We did as he said and each of us walked through a machine while we were checked for weapons or illegal contraband.

"All clear," the guards declared. We were permitted to retrieve our items, bags and luggage. A bellman loaded them onto a cart and led us to registration.

"Wow. I didn't expect that level of security," I said in a low voice to Slash.

"The price of safety these days."

Not that I didn't appreciate it, but it made me wonder how Slash had been permitted to come. What exactly had he told his bosses at the NSA? Had he given them a hint about the danger of the endospores? Had this become another secret mission for him?

"By the way, the Marriott is a five-star resort," Elvis said coming up to walk beside me. "The Wi-Fi connection isn't what we're used to, but it will have to do. I brought several Wi-Fi enhancers, so hopefully that will help. By the way, I've already paid for everyone's rooms in advance."

I opened my mouth to argue when he frowned at me. "Don't argue, Lexi. Slash paid for our transportation here and you and Gwen took time off to come to help me out, so the least I can do is pay for the accommodations. I think everyone will be comfortable. There are fifteen restaurants, an outdoor pool, a Jacuzzi, six acres of gardens, a fitness center and tennis courts. Not like we're going to have any time for any of that, but by God, we've got them if we want them."

I wasn't sure how to respond, so I just snapped my mouth shut. Slash looked around the lobby and nodded as if satisfied. "Security is good and there are plenty of exits."

"Wait," I said. "You checked out the security and exits in the short time it took us to walk into the hotel?"

"I did." He grinned, leaving me to believe that he might have also checked things out in advance, too.

We headed to registration. The bellman motioned to us, so Slash and Elvis took Gwen's and my passport and went to check us into our rooms while we stayed with the luggage cart. After a few minutes the guys and the bellman returned, handing us our key cards and passports.

"We got the Executive Suite with two connecting bedrooms," Elvis said. "Slash and Lexi can have the suite bedroom, and Gwen and I will each take one of the adjoining rooms. Our suite is situated in the Gezira Tower, fifth floor. It's air-conditioned."

"Oh, thank goodness," I said, fanning myself.

"The suite has a large living room with multiple desks and tables where we can set up our computer equipment. It also has a safe where we can store said equipment. Best yet, there are ceiling-to-floor windows with an excellent view of the Nile."

"It sounds perfect." Gwen was looking around with so much excitement and enthusiasm, it was hard not to smile.

We rode the elevator up and entered the suite. The bellman removed our luggage from the cart and left as soon as we tipped him. The setup was just as Elvis had described with a large joint living space and adjoining bedrooms. The hotel had left a large and lovely basket of fruit and dates on the coffee table with a warm message welcoming us to Cairo. The dates looked inviting, but I couldn't help but recall the last time I had seen a similar basket. In that movie, a poor monkey saved the hero by eating a poisoned date from the basket. Suddenly, they didn't look so appetizing.

While Gwen and Elvis took their bags to their respective rooms, I went over to the window and looked out. "Slash, come see the view. It's spectacular."

He joined me at the window and we stared down at the ancient river framed by large buildings on either side of it. The sun glinted off the water, creating a golden shimmer and making it look ethereal. It was humbling to realize the river had been here for thousands of years, surviving all the wars, conflict and economic growth that had happened on its shores.

"The Nile, forever new and old," Slash murmured. "Among the living and the dead, its mighty, mystic stream has rolled."

When I looked at him questioningly, he put an arm around me. "Henry Wadsworth Longfellow."

Before I could respond, Gwen and Elvis returned. We turned around just as Elvis took a deep breath and spread his hands. Guess he wasn't wasting any time getting the ball rolling. Not like we had any time to waste.

"Okay, we're in Egypt, so here's my plan," he said. "Yesterday I made an appointment with Mr. Haji Saraf, the Director of the Research Department at the Egyptian Museum. He's the museum's contact for Oxford University. My father would have been required to go through him to get approval for access and research at the museum."

"Sounds good to me," I said. "Especially since Slash and I have been doing some research on your father's activities at the museum."

I caught him and Gwen up on what Slash and I had found about his father having a possible assistant from the museum helping him out.

"Good idea," Elvis said. "We can ask Mr. Saraf about this Wahgdi guy. Are you guys sure you're feeling up to accompanying me to the museum?"

Slash nodded. "Time is critical. We must find your father as quickly as possible and determine if he has any more of the endospores in his possession. That has to take priority in terms of our activities."

I agreed wholeheartedly. Arthur Zimmerman's whereabouts were paramount. "I'm good to go, guys." I meant it. Jet lag hadn't caught up with me…yet.

Gwen leaned a hand on the back of the couch. She looked a lot better now than when she had been in the van. "I'm in, too."

"Good," Slash said. Now that the decision was made, he was all about logistics. "It's about a half hour walk to the museum. Anyone vote for a cab?"

Not a one of us was ready for that, but the thought of trudging for a half hour in the hot desert sun at midday had me reluctantly voting for a cab. Gwen and Elvis finally came around to the cab idea, so we returned to the front of the hotel and waited while hotel staff summoned one. Maybe we'd become inured to the crazy driving, because it didn't seem that bad this time around. We arrived at the museum inside of ten minutes, mostly because the streets were so jammed no one could move at hardly more than a crawl.

The museum was an imposing building with gaggles of tourists congregating in whatever shade they could find. We went through security—another magnetometer and a bag search—before Elvis informed one of the guards we had an appointment with Mr. Saraf. We were instructed to wait a few minutes in the entrance area before the guard returned.

"Follow me, please."

We followed him down a hallway filled with fascinating exhibits. Despite the urgency of our mission, it took everything I had not to stop and look at each of the displays. I saw Slash and Gwen were having the same problem. Gwen was looking sideways when she ran into the back of Slash, who had stopped to examine something. Only Elvis seemed oblivious to the ancient treasures on either side of us, his mind solely on his father.

We went up a flight of stairs to the administrative offices before the guard stopped in front of a nondescript brown door with a clouded window. He rapped twice on the window and someone called out in what I presumed was Arabic. The door opened and the guard motioned for us to enter.

As we entered, a thin man with a mustache wearing a white shirt and blue tie stood up from behind a cluttered desk. "Greetings. I am Haji Saraf. I didn't realize there were so many of you. I will get more chairs."

"No, it's okay," Elvis said. "The ladies can sit and we'll stand. I'm Elvis Zimmerman, the one who sent you the email." He stepped forward and shook Haji's hand. "Thank you for agreeing to meet with me on such short notice."

"It is my pleasure. I hope your journey was satisfactory."

"It was fine. Thank you."

Elvis motioned for Gwen and me to sit, so we did. The men remained standing. It felt like an old-fashioned arrangement, but we had more important matters on which to focus so I didn't say anything.

"You said you are here about your father," Haji said. "You actually look a lot like him."

Elvis stiffened, but I don't think anyone but me noticed. "Did my father come here often?"

"He did, indeed. We have a very good arrangement with Oxford University and, of course, the British Museum. Your father is quite well regarded. I was alarmed to hear he is missing."

"Well, he may not be exactly missing. I'm just not sure how to find him. I hoped you might help. I believe he is still in Egypt. When was the last time you saw him?"

He thought for a moment. "I think it was about four weeks ago. Maybe a bit longer, I'm not sure. We had a brief discussion on a royal chariot, of all things."

"Really? Do you happen to know what my father was studying?"

"Many things. He taught a course at Oxford on Egyptology, so naturally his interests were varied."

I leaned forward in my chair. "You wouldn't happen to know a man named Merhu Khalfani, would you?"

He thought about it. "No, I'm afraid I do not know that name. Should I?"

"No, I just wondered. We're trying to put together as many pieces as we can with Mr. Zimmerman's disappearance and what he was studying. Do you know anyone named Z. Wahgdi?"

He brightened. "Oh! Now *that* name is familiar. Please, wait a moment, I will be right back."

He stepped out of his office and we looked at each other.

"Okay," I said. "That was odd."

A minute later, Haji returned, carrying a chair. "Your father's assistant will be here momentarily."

"Thank you." Elvis gave me a hopeful glance. This was a promising lead.

"Mr. Saraf, do the researchers, by any chance, pay the assistants?" I asked.

"No, it's part of their studies. We assign student

interns to assist the researchers and fetch items they require. However, if the researcher would like to use the time of the intern outside of their hours at the museum, they are welcome to do that and could conduct their own arrangements, including payment."

Haji set the chair next to me when there was a knock on the door. Haji rushed to open it. The most beautiful woman I'd ever seen stepped in. She was taller than me—and I'm five eleven—and was dressed in a silky white blouse and teal skirt that fell just below her knees. Thick, shiny black hair spilled down to her waist, covered by a teal scarf that matched her skirt. Her striking green eyes were offset by long, dark eyelashes, perfectly applied eyeliner and arched eyebrows.

Holy modern-day Nefertiti.

"Hello," the woman said with a smile. As she spoke, I noticed dazzling white teeth, heart-shaped lips and a small mole at the corner of her mouth. She carried a cell phone in her hand, as if we'd just interrupted her in the middle of a call.

Haji stepped to her side. "Ladies and gentlemen, I'm pleased to introduce Zizi Wahgdi, one of our best research assistants here at the museum."

SIXTEEN

THIS IS Z. WAHGDI?

I slid a glance at Slash and saw he was mesmerized. He stood leaning against the wall with his arms crossed against his chest, but his eyes were locked onto her face. She noticed him, too, because her eyes lingered on him while they swept over the rest of us.

An unfamiliar sensation tugged at my stomach.

Jealousy.

"You're…a she," I blurted out. Thank God for my high IQ.

She turned those remarkable green eyes on me. I felt myself blush under her scrutiny.

"I am. And you are too, I see."

Wow. This was getting off to a real awkward start. "I'm Lexi Carmichael. I'm here with Elvis Zimmerman. He's looking for his father." I swept my hand toward Elvis, who still stood staring at Zizi, his mouth slightly agape. I tried to get his attention, but he wasn't looking my way. I slid my foot out and kicked him lightly on the ankle. He blinked and closed his mouth.

Gwen was glaring at Elvis, not that he noticed. Was she jealous, too?

"Uh, nice to meet you, Ms. Wahgdi," Elvis said. He put a lot of emphasis on the *Ms.* and then glanced at me as if it were my fault she wasn't a he.

"Please, call me Zizi." She looked around the room,

her gaze again noticing, then settling on Slash. "All of you."

"Sure, okay, Zizi." Elvis's face turned bright red. "You call me Elvis. I mean if you want to. You can actually call me anything you'd like. I'm good like that."

Jeez.

I was just about to kick him again when Haji insisted Zizi sit. She slid into the chair, crossing her long, smooth legs and leaning back. No one in the room, including me, could take our eyes off of her.

"You're Arthur's son," Zizi said to Elvis. "Arthur never said anything about a son."

"I'm not surprised. We aren't close. And he has two sons. I'm a twin."

"Oh. I'm sorry. I didn't know." She studied Elvis. "But you do look like him."

Again he stiffened. "I understand you've been working with my father."

She smiled again and the entire room seemed brighter for it. "Yes, Arthur and I have worked together. He's quite a hardworking man and so dedicated to his study."

"Do you happen to know where he is?"

"I'm sorry, no." She frowned. "I presumed he returned to England. Did he not?"

"No. He didn't."

She thought for a moment, then sighed. "I did think it odd he didn't say goodbye. I do hope he is okay."

"That's why I'm here," Elvis said. "To find out."

"Of course. Then please consider me available to help as required. I truly consider Arthur a friend."

"That's good to know," I said. "By the way, did

Arthur specifically ask for you when he started his research here?"

"This past time, he did, indeed."

"Why?" I asked. As soon as I said it, everyone in the room stared at me like I was an idiot.

Duh, Lexi. The woman is freaking gorgeous.

My cheeks heated. "I mean, do you have a particular background in some field?"

"I'm a microbiologist, which I believe is why he specifically requested me to help with his research. Here at the museum I support archeological research through the analysis of pollens, grains and mummy DNA found in and on the artifacts."

Haji beamed proudly. "Zizi is one of our few microbiologists on staff, which makes her a valuable addition to the museum, as well as highly sought after by the researchers. She's also quite accomplished, having published several articles in the *Egyptian Journal of Microbiology*."

"Wow. That's cool." Gwen's face lit up. "I'm a microbiologist, too. I don't typically examine ancient artifacts, though. I'm more of a microbiology-technology girl. I work at ComQuest in Baltimore with Elvis."

Zizi smiled. "How fascinating. I hope we will have a chance to talk before you leave. I do enjoy meeting people in my field. I'm finishing up my PhD. My thesis is on infectious diseases. I hope to work at the Global Disease and Detection Regional Center here in Cairo someday."

Jeez. She was a doctoral candidate, too?

Slash spoke up. "Are you able to provide more detail as to what Arthur was studying here at the museum?"

"Of course." Zizi cocked her head, studying him. "And you are?"

"Slash." He stepped forward, kissed her hand adeptly, murmuring something to her in Arabic.

I looked at him in astonishment. I'd had no idea he spoke Arabic.

Zizi seemed impressed as well. "Pleased to make your acquaintance, Slash."

The way she said his name was the same way I said chocolate cake. Like I was ready to dig in and eat it all up.

"I'd be happy to offer whatever assistance I can," she continued. "Arthur was searching for a specific artifact."

"Which was?"

"I don't know. Truthfully, I think he'd already found it, but he refused to confirm that or speak of it at all. The last few weeks here at the museum, he became quite secretive and, I'm sorry to say it, a bit paranoid. Then, one day, without warning, he asked me to separate some spores he'd found."

"Found where?" Slash asked.

"I don't know. He didn't say. He said it was an experiment. Since separating spores is a simple activity for a microbiologist, I assisted him as requested."

Elvis crossed his arms. "You had to think that was an unusual request. Had he asked you to do anything like that before?"

"Never. But Arthur had been acting a bit erratically, so I wasn't as surprised as you might think."

"Do you know what kind of spores they were?" Slash asked.

"Truthfully, I'd never seen anything like them before. At first I simply assumed they were from a plant he'd been growing in his room. I took precautions, naturally, but after he presented me with the container holding the spores and I'd conducted the separation, I was concerned I hadn't taken *enough* precautions."

"Why?"

"Because I suspected the sample wasn't recent. I'd never seen anything like those spores. I confronted him about the origin of the finding, but he was evasive in his answer. I also found it strange that he had stored the spores next to some leaves from a plant."

Elvis and Gwen exchanged a glance. Gwen leaned forward, her eyes lighting with interest. "What did the plant look like?"

"Oh, I don't know. It wasn't special, if that's what you're asking. It was a common plant from the Nile. I didn't know why he was growing it or where he came across it, but I suspected it had something to do with his research and the spores. My professional opinion is that those spores did not come from that plant. I'm not sure of the association or if there even is one. He never explained it."

"And he never said where he'd found them?" Elvis asked. "In or on an artifact, for example?"

"Absolutely not. If Arthur had confirmed they were from an artifact, especially one from the museum, I would have alerted Haji immediately. Arthur didn't give me any indication whatsoever where he'd found them, but I had my suspicions. Still, without evidence, I couldn't prove it."

"Is there anything you can think of that might help us pinpoint the origin of the spores?" I asked.

"Maybe. I must think about it."

Slash pushed off the wall. "It might help if you could show us some of the exhibits or items he was studying shortly before he disappeared."

"I could do that." She lowered her eyelashes at him. "Even better, I'll make a list for you. If you are willing to wait, I'm off work in an hour and a half. I'll even take you to where he lived before he stopped coming to the museum."

Slash smiled. "Thanks. We'd be most grateful, Zizi."

I wanted to protest that she didn't have to go to that much trouble, but I was pretty sure I'd be the only one on that ship. Everyone else seemed riveted by her. Personally I didn't like the idea of Zizi hanging around us. Especially not around Slash. But if it helped us find Arthur Zimmerman sooner rather than later, I had no choice but to suck it up.

As she swept out the office, she shot Slash a final glance. There was no mistaking her interest. I only saw the back of his head, so I had no idea how he responded. I tried to ignore the bad feeling creeping through my stomach.

We'd just gotten to Egypt and I already wanted to leave.

SEVENTEEN

ELVIS THANKED HAJI for his time and we filed out of his office.

As Slash and I walked side by side, I lowered my voice. "We already have the list. Why do we have to get it from her?"

"Let's see what she gives us. If she omits anything, it might be significant."

"Why would she omit anything?"

"Why, indeed?"

Slash steered us toward the ticket booth. "No sense in wasting the opportunity while we wait for Zizi. Let's look around."

We were all in agreement with that, so we purchased four tickets.

"I can't wait to see some of the artifacts here." Gwen excitedly waved her ticket in the air. "It's been a life-long dream to see the treasures and artifacts from King Tut's tomb."

"You came to the right place, then," I said.

"Come on, Elvis." Gwen grabbed his hand, pulling him toward the stairs. "Let's not waste a minute."

After they left, I carefully studied the museum map, determining what I would like to see first. I calculated approximately how much time I would have per exhibit within the hour and a half we had allotted before Zizi met with us.

I looked up from the map and saw Slash smiling at me, amused.

"What?" I asked.

"Are you done mapping out our course of action?"

"Why? Are you going where I'm going? You aren't going to just wait here for Zizi?" I don't know why I suddenly felt so cranky. Jet lag had never affected me so adversely before.

"I'm going with you, of course. But perhaps we should start sometime soon?"

I studied him for a moment. "You're implying that I'm wasting time. I'm not. Planning is never a waste of time." Still, I folded the map and put it in the back pocket of my jeans. "But it so happens I'm ready. Are you sure you don't want to know what I'm going to see before you commit to accompanying me?"

His smile widened. "No."

"Oh. Because you've already been here, right? You've already seen everything."

"Actually, I haven't been to this museum before."

"But you speak Arabic."

"I do *not* speak Arabic. I know a few phrases, that's all."

"Have you been to Cairo before?"

"I have. For work."

I looked at him for a minute, but he wasn't offering any more information. Instead he just looked at me as if he didn't have a care in the world.

"Fine. Well, this is my thinking. I know the big draws are the artifacts from King Tut's tomb and the mummy room. That's where Elvis and Gwen are starting. But I'd rather take a look at the pre-dynastic and

Old Kingdom objects first. I mean we are talking seriously ancient—as far back as 10,000 BC. There are only a few places in the world you can see artifacts that ancient. This is one of them."

He pulled me in for a hug and kissed my hair. "That would have been my first choice, too. Let's go."

We walked around, examining the fascinating exhibits. I viewed spectacular royal sedan chairs, hieroglyphics taken from numerous tombs, and several exquisite statuettes of ancient pharaohs. I quickly got lost in the fascinating history. It felt like only five minutes had passed when Slash tugged on my arm.

"We're getting close to the time to meet Zizi."

I glanced at my watch. "Already?" Had my calculations been that off or had I just lost track of time?

"Unfortunately, yes."

I really didn't want to leave the exhibits, I had no desire to see Zizi again, and I'd only seen a tiny part of the entire museum. Disappointment swept through me. "Can we come back sometime?"

"Absolutely."

We headed back for the lobby, passing several giant and imposing statues. "This place is really incredible."

"That it is. It could, however, use a serious update on several fronts, though. The exhibits are rather cluttered and not always well identified. It could also use a thorough cleaning and paint job. Security is awful."

"Leave it to you to notice the security. I heard they're building a new museum closer to the pyramids in Giza which will house a lot of these exhibits. Maybe that's why this place is getting so run-down. They are spending all of their money on the new museum."

"So I've heard. I am curious to see it when it's finished. From what I've heard, it's expected to be state-of-the-art with a lot of technology upgrades. It should be finished soon."

"That's pretty amazing."

We waited five minutes before Elvis and Gwen showed up. Gwen was practically jumping up and down, she was so excited.

"OMG. Lexi, Slash, I can't believe it. I saw mummies, scarabs, gold statues and ancient tablets. It was like a dream come true. Way cool, right, Elvis?"

"Totally."

"What did you see, Lexi?"

I started to tell her when I spotted Zizi making her way toward us. The museum lobby fell mostly quiet as everyone stopped whatever they were doing to watch her. Again, the comparison to Nefertiti leaped out at me. It seemed illogical that she could command that kind of attention based on her beauty alone, but she did.

Zizi held a folder in her hand which she gave to Elvis as she reached us. "I made a list of the most recent exhibits and items he was studying. I hope it will help."

"Thank you." He took the folder. "I appreciate your assistance."

She looked around at us, her glance resting on Slash. Her gaze always seemed drawn to him. Not that I noticed. Much.

"Are you ready to go to Arthur's place or at least where he used to live? He occasionally asked me to drop off copies of documents to his room so I know where it is."

"How far is it?" Slash asked.

"Not far. We can walk."

Slash spread out his hand. "Excellent. After you."

EIGHTEEN

"THERE'S A SHORTCUT this way," Zizi said, taking us into a narrow alley. Luckily, the way offered a bit of shade. Elvis's cheeks were red from the heat and Gwen's bangs were stuck to her forehead. I was pretty sure I was getting sunburned in spite of the enormous amount of sunscreen I'd slathered on my skin.

Only Slash and Zizi looked cool and collected.

Once in the alley, some kids ran past, laughing and pushing each other. They bumped into us, giggling. As they ran past, Slash caught one of the boys by the back of the collar and lifted him off his feet in one easy motion.

The boy screeched, feet dangling, while his friends dashed off without a backward glance. As I looked on, I saw a strange expression on Slash's face. He was staring at the boy, but his focus was far away. For a moment, it actually scared me.

"Slash," Elvis finally said. "What are you doing?"

I hurried over and put a hand on Slash's arm. The little boy was still kicking his legs, struggling to get free.

"Slash?"

He blinked and then looked at the boy. He held out a hand. "Give it back."

The boy shouted something as Zizi joined me at Slash's side.

"Good catch," Zizi said. She faced the boy and lifted a finger under his chin. Forced to look at her, she said something softly to him in Arabic. He stopped struggling and reached under his robe, handing her a green wallet.

"Hey, that's mine," Gwen said.

Elvis and I quickly checked to see if our wallets were still with us. We both sighed when they were. Elvis showed me his wallet was chained to the belt in his jeans.

"Smart," I said, and he smiled.

Zizi tossed the wallet to Gwen. "Zip your purse and hug it tight."

Gwen did as she said and Slash set the boy down. The kid streaked down the alley faster than I'd thought possible. I held my purse under my arm a bit tighter.

"Street rats," Zizi murmured and continued leading us toward our destination.

I slid up next to Slash. "How did you know?"

He paused for a moment, as if considering the question. "I'm not sure. But lucky for Gwen, I did."

"No kidding," she said. "All my money and credit cards are in there. Thanks, Slash."

We came out of the relative shade of the alley into the heat of the street. "This way," Zizi said. We went about two more blocks and stopped at a small gray building.

"It's a hostel." She pushed open the door. "It's popular with many of the researchers."

We entered the building. While it didn't have air-conditioning, it felt good to be out of the direct sunlight. Zizi headed for what looked like a small reception area. An elderly woman rose from behind the counter and they spoke for a few minutes.

Zizi returned to us with a copper key dangling from her fingers. "She knows me. She said we could go take a look at the room. No one has rented it since Arthur left."

We climbed a set of stone stairs to the next floor. She led us down a hallway and stopped at a door with a small plaque that said 202. She inserted the key and we entered the room. It was small with a single bed, dresser and two desks backed up to each other to make one large working space. There was no air-conditioning, but a large fan stood on the floor next to the bed. I peeked my head into a tiny bathroom. Dingy and dark. There was no balcony and Slash was not able to open the window.

Elvis was looking through the drawers in the dresser, but they were all empty.

Gwen examined the closet. "Nothing in here."

"Did he pay his full rent and check out?" Elvis asked Zizi. "Or did she have to clear his things out?"

"She said he paid until the end of the month. When she came to check on him, the room had been cleared out. He didn't tell her he was leaving. He didn't tell me either. He just stopped showing up at the museum."

Elvis got on his knees and looked under the bed and dresser, but found nothing of significance. After a few minutes we filed out of the room and Zizi locked it up.

Slash walked next to Zizi as we headed down the hallway. "Can you ask the lady whether or not Arthur had any regular visitors during his stay or has anyone come around asking about him since he's been gone? Ask her, too, whether he had any habits, such as always eating at the same café or restaurant for breakfast or dinner or taking walks along any particular paths."

"You're worried something has happened to him?" she said.

"I think we need to explore every avenue."

"Of course."

Zizi returned the key and spoke for a few more minutes with the lady. When she returned, we walked outside.

"She said no one asked about him other than me, and he had no visitors that she saw. Her grandson often works the desk, so she said she'll ask him later and let me know if she hears of anyone."

"Good."

"She did say one other thing. He liked to frequent a café not far from here for breakfast and dinner. Come on, I'll show you which one."

We trudged along the sidewalks, and when there were none, the street.

"Here," she said, stopping in front of a small café.

I raised an eyebrow. "The Ramses Café? Really?"

"Can't speak for the food, but the coffee is good." She pointed to an empty table. "Sit down and I'll have a chat with the owner."

We sat at a table beneath an old, faded umbrella. Gwen's chair was uneven and she kept rocking back and forth in it. A young guy came out and took our order for something to drink. It was too hot to eat, so we stuck to liquid. We all got cold drinks except for Slash, who ordered coffee.

"Don't expect ice," Slash warned us.

"Bummer," Gwen said, lifting her red bangs off her forehead.

In a surprisingly short time, the waiter brought our drinks. Slash took a sip of the coffee and closed his eyes. "Excellent."

For Slash, excellent coffee meant you could start your car with it. I wasn't brave enough to try even a small sip.

After a few minutes, Zizi came back out. We'd saved her a seat at the table and she slipped into it. All the guys instinctively sat straighter. I tried not to roll my eyes. I had no idea how she looked so cool and lovely, but she did. Maybe after living here for so long her body had adjusted. Mine had not. Sweat pooled around my hairline and dripped down the back of my neck. It felt like every pore was oozing moisture.

"I've got interesting news," she said.

Elvis pushed his Coke aside. "Good or bad?"

"Both. The bad news is another man was here two days ago looking for your father."

I exchanged a worried glance with Slash. "Who was it?"

"They hadn't seen him before, so they didn't know. But they indicated he was of a disreputable nature."

Elvis glanced at Slash with a worried expression. "And the good news?"

"Your father was spotted here."

"What?" A slight hitch caught in Elvis's throat. "When?"

"About one week ago."

NINETEEN

"ONE WEEK?" ELVIS leaned forward. "They're sure?"

"They're sure."

"So, he's alive," Gwen said. "Or at least he was a week ago."

Elvis took a moment to digest that. A parade of emotions crossed his face. Relief, concern, anger and despair. It occurred to me that he might have been seriously prepping himself for the news that his father was dead. Now that we knew Arthur wasn't dead—at least not as of a week ago—he had to consider the alternative. He'd have to confront his father.

"Was anyone with Arthur?" Slash set down his coffee.

"No. Apparently he was alone. But they passed on that same information to the man who came before us."

"So, someone else knows he's alive and still in Cairo," I mused.

We pondered that for a moment until Zizi stood. "I'm sorry, but I have to get home now."

Slash stood as well. Feeling the gentlemanly pressure, Elvis came to his feet, too. "Thanks for helping us out."

"You're welcome. Where are you staying?" Zizi asked, but directed the question to Slash.

"The Marriott."

"Nice place."

"It really is," Gwen interrupted. "We have a gorgeous view of the Nile. And they gave us a basket of food, including dates, which happen to be my favorite."

"Egyptians are known for their friendliness." She reached into her purse for her cell phone.

"Shall I hail a cab for you?" Slash asked.

"No, thank you. I'll walk. It's not far. I'm just going to call my family to tell them I'm on my way. Will you come by the museum tomorrow?"

I wasn't sure if she were referring to all of us or just Slash. It was hard to tell.

She glanced down at the table where the folder she'd given Elvis sat. "You may have questions after reviewing the material I provided for you."

"We might," Slash agreed. "If so, we'll call ahead to the museum to let you know we're coming. Would that be acceptable?"

"Of course." She turned to the rest of us. "It was nice to meet you."

"We appreciate your assistance," Elvis said. "Really. Thanks."

"It was my pleasure."

She walked off and everyone watched as she disappeared down the street, her hips swaying. A couple of guys walking past stopped to watch her. After a minute, I nudged Elvis with my elbow and he cleared his throat and picked up the folder.

"Uh, let's get back to the hotel."

I agreed with that plan one hundred percent. I was hot, hungry and jet lag was starting to catch up with me. "We need to review what Zizi provided in terms of the exhibits and put together everything we know so far. It might help to have a big picture view at this point."

Slash nodded. "Agreed."

We caught a cab back to the hotel. The hotel air-conditioning felt so good I almost cried. Everyone disappeared to their respective rooms to shower and change clothes. Slash let me have the shower in our room first. I stood under the cold water for several minutes before shampooing because it felt so good.

After our showers, we assembled in the living room. Slash suggested ordering room service so we could get to work. He had begun setting up and networking our computers while I was in the shower. Elvis sat down and began taking extra precautions to protect us from any potential Wi-Fi hackers at the hotel. Since I had spent too much time in the shower, I got tasked with getting us food.

I stared at the menu Slash had handed me. "Um, what do I order?"

"Something authentic," Slash suggested from under the table.

Like I even knew what that meant.

I studied the menu and, after listening to a couple of Gwen's suggestions—she knew even less than me about Egyptian food—I ordered the *mulukhiyah*, a leafy green soup and chicken, a main dish of *ful medames*, which was mashed fava beans with sliced eggs and vegetables, and a thick Egyptian pita bread. Personally, I felt like a hamburger, but when in Rome, or in this case, Cairo, I had to do as the Egyptians do.

To drink, Slash suggested the *Cru des Ptolémées*, a dry, white Egyptian-made wine, and for dessert, a couscous and a milk pudding called *mihallabiya*. He also made me order a large carafe of coffee. He was probably in some kind of coffee heaven.

The showers seemed to have rejuvenated us, but I was hungry, so I hoped the food tasted good and didn't take too long to arrive. We each sat in front of our respective computers, except for Slash, who was still under the table connecting us to each other, and waited for Elvis to orchestrate our plan of attack.

"I can't emphasize enough that time is of the essence," Elvis said. "Especially since there is someone else looking for my father. We must find him and the endospores, if there are any more, as quickly as possible."

No one disagreed with that. But we had little to go on other than the letter he'd sent to Elvis. "Where do we start?" I asked.

"We need to focus on breaking the code to his address. That bogus address on the envelope has to mean something. It's not the same code he wrote the letter in, I already tried that. I ran it through a few other ciphers, too, but I came up empty. I didn't devote a lot of time to it, so maybe we can come up with something better."

"I'm on it," I said. Finally, something I could do well.

Slash stood, brushing off his jeans. "And me?"

"Stay on the code with Lexi. Gwen, can you run some probabilities on what this mysterious artifact might be based within the parameters of the time frame he seemed focused on, the historical significance of that time, and the curriculum of my father's courses at Oxford, which I've already forwarded to you."

"Sure," she said, sitting in front of her laptop.

Our assignments given, we started our work. After

finding out what ciphers and codes Elvis had already run against the address, I got started. Once my fingers hit the keyboard, I went into the zone. I barely even heard the knock on the door when room service arrived about forty-five minutes later. Slash answered the door and the waiter wheeled in the cart of food. We ate while we worked. I sipped my wine as I tried different things, but so far I had exactly nothing. Slash, Elvis and I compared notes, but we got nowhere. Worse, the food and wine were making me sleepy. Jet lag had caught up with me.

A glance around the table indicated everyone else was completely absorbed. I hated to be the first to give up, but I was fading fast. I decided to give it one more crack before I folded.

I needed a fresh approach. Elvis's dad was a trained mathematician, so I started with the most common and interesting math ciphers. But that got me nowhere. There were dozens more ciphers I could try, but they were pretty complex and this was a one-line address. A street name and some numbers. A complicated math cipher seemed overkill to me. Of course, I could be wrong, but what would be the point? It was much more likely to be something simpler.

But what?

I put my chin on my hand as I stared at the screen and suddenly had an idea. "Elvis, can you shoot me the key you used to decipher your dad's letter?"

"Sure. But I already told you I tried it on the address and it didn't work." He tapped on some keys.

"I know. I just want to see it."

When I got the key, I opened it up. I studied it for

a minute and then sat back in my chair. "It's a hand cipher."

Elvis looked up from his monitor. "Yeah. So?"

"How old is your dad?"

"I don't know. Fifty-eight. Maybe fifty-nine. Why does that matter?"

"You said he liked to code. He taught you and Xavier to code when you were younger, right?"

"Sure, but what does that have to do with anything?"

"It means he grew up during the Cold War. Hand ciphers were popular then."

Slash looked up from his laptop. "Hand cipher. Cold War. I see where you're going with this, *cara*."

I tapped a bunch of keys. "Bingo. It's a VIC."

"What's a VIC? What's a hand cipher?" Gwen looked between us like we had lost our minds. "What are you guys talking about?"

"A hand cipher is a code for which encryption and decryption can both be done with a pen and graph paper," Elvis explained. "It's pretty simple, actually. It's not as secure as computer-operated stream ciphers, but you don't need a calculator or computer to do a hand cipher. You don't even need mad math skills. VIC is one of the most well-known hand ciphers in the world. It's based on a Fibonacci generator and is short for VICTOR. It was used by Soviet spy Reino Häyhänen during the Cold War. The NSA wasn't able to decrypt it until Häyhänen defected in 1957."

In the short time Elvis explained that to Gwen, I'd broken the code on the address. "Got it," I said. "47 El-Falaky Street. Let me see if I can find it on Google Maps."

Both Slash and Elvis stood and came behind me while I pulled it up. "It's ten minutes from here, across the Nile." I pointed at the map. "It's the Cecilia Hostel."

"Do you have a room number?" Gwen asked.

"Not yet," I said. "Besides, if he's trying to hide, I doubt he would have used his real name or passport to check in. Elvis, didn't you already do a search of Cairo accommodations for him?"

"I did, but came up empty."

"Then he isn't using his passport as his ID."

Slash returned to his computer. "Give me a few minutes and I'll pull up a list of all guests registered at the Cecilia. Maybe something will pop for you, Elvis."

"Good idea. Thanks."

I closed my laptop. "Well, it's getting dark and we're exhausted. My suggestion is we call it a night and start fresh in the morning. There's not much else we can do at this point anyway."

Gwen closed her laptop and stood, yawning. "I'm all over that."

"As soon as I finish compiling the list, I'm turning in, as well," Slash said. "We'll have clearer heads in the morning."

While Slash finished up his work on the list I took a quick shower and brushed my teeth before crawling into bed. He came in shortly thereafter and took his turn in the bathroom before sliding into bed next to me.

"How are you holding up, *cara*?" He rolled to his side, propping his head on his hand and looking at me as I lay on my back staring at the ceiling.

"Good, I guess. I'm worried about Elvis and about what we might find if we do locate Arthur. What if he's dead? How would Elvis deal?"

He traced a circle on my arm with his fingertip. "Elvis is a lot stronger than you think. We'd help him, of course. Because that's what friends do."

"You're right. I just don't get it. What kind of father just takes off and leaves his family behind?"

The circles on my arm stopped and Slash lay back on the bed, tucking one arm behind his head. "I don't know. And I say that from firsthand experience."

"Slash. Oh, crap." I rolled over, leaning close. My hair spilled onto his chest. "I'm sorry. I didn't think before I said that."

"Don't be sorry. I don't know what my biological parents' circumstances were. I don't blame them. I'm happy where I ended up."

I leaned forward and pressed a kiss on his mouth. "I'm happy for where you ended up, too. Still, have you been wondering about them lately?"

He reached out and twirled a strand of my hair around his finger. "Why would you think that?"

"Well, sometimes you get this look on your face when Elvis talks about his dad. It's hard for me to read you exactly, but it's like you understand where he's coming from. You get his struggle because…well, maybe you wrestle with it, too."

"I suppose all of this has caused me to reflect deeper on my own beginnings."

"Speaking of which, what happened today in the alley? After you caught that kid stealing Gwen's wallet, your eyes were miles away. Where were you?"

He was quiet for so long I wasn't sure he'd answer. I wasn't even sure he was breathing.

"I've told you how I don't remember anything from the first seven years of my life," he finally said. "It's a blank slate. My memories start when I woke up in the hospital in Sperlonga and saw the nurse who would become my mother. But there are times…"

I took his hand and threaded my fingers together with his.

He inhaled and held it for a moment before speaking. "There are times I have nightmares—several of which you've witnessed—but I can't remember anything when I wake up. Lately I've started to have some unusual flashbacks. At least I think that's what they are. They're not a whole picture or even a memory, just a quick glimpse into something."

"Into what?"

"I don't know. This is going to sound strange, but today in the alley, I knew that kid. When I lifted him off the ground by the back of his shirt and I looked at him, *really* looked at him, his face was mine."

TWENTY

WE DIDN'T TALK much more after Slash's revelation. We were both too exhausted and I sensed Slash needed time to process his thoughts. Instead, I offered the comfort of my arms and that seemed enough to help him drift off to sleep.

I awoke first and quietly got dressed so as not to wake him. Today I chose a tank top with a light blouse and a long, loose skirt and sandals. Loose and light-colored clothing seemed to be the smart thing to wear in the desert, along with lots of sunscreen. When I went out into the common area of the suite, Elvis was already up. He sat behind his laptop typing away and drinking coffee.

"Hey, Lexi," he said. "Coffee's ready."

"Thank goodness." I went and poured myself a cup, adding all but one of the creamers that were left. I hoped Gwen wasn't big into cream in her coffee.

"What are you doing up so early?" I perched on the arm of the couch and blew on my coffee.

"I could ask the same of you."

"My body is messed up from the time change. You okay this morning?"

He looked up from the screen, his blue eyes troubled. "Not really. I'm trying to pretend I'm not freaked about possibly finding my father today."

"You've got this."

"You think?"

"I do." I blew on my coffee some more and dared a sip. Even with all the creamer it was really strong. I returned to the coffee pot and added three bags of sugar, stirring it in the best I could.

"How do you think he'll react when he sees me?"

"I don't know your father, Elvis. But I'm pretty sure it's safe to assume he'll be surprised to see you in Egypt."

"Do you think we'll really find him? What if he's not there? What if we discover he's not even alive?"

"Speculation at this point doesn't help anything. Don't work yourself up, Elvis. Let's take it one step at a time, okay?"

He nodded. "Okay. You're right. Let's just find him first."

"Exactly. So, what are you working on over there?"

"I'm reviewing the list Slash created from the Cecilia Hostel to see if a name pops at me. So far, nothing. He could be registered under any of the names. Or he might be long gone."

"Can I see?"

"Sure. A second set of eyes never hurts."

We'd only been reviewing the list for a few minutes when there was a soft knock on the door. I looked through the peephole and then opened the door.

Zizi stood there, dressed in a short-sleeved white blouse, a yellow skirt and sparkly yellow sandals. A white scarf with golden threads was draped over her thick black hair. She smelled like flowers.

"Hey, Zizi," I said in surprise. "What are you doing here?"

"I hope you don't mind. The registration clerk is an

old friend and he let me know where you were staying. I have the day off and I'd like to help, if I can. I'm as anxious as you to find Arthur. I thought perhaps you could use a guide."

"Hey, that would be great," Elvis called over my shoulder. "Thanks, Zizi. Please come in."

I stepped aside and she entered the suite. The scent of flowers drifted past with her.

"Would you like a cup of coffee?" I asked.

"That is most thoughtful of you. I'd love one."

I made her a cup and brought it over. Thankfully, due to the lack of creamer, Zizi drank it black like Slash, who showed up shortly after she arrived. He walked into the suite in jeans and a tight white T-shirt. He was barefoot and his hair tousled.

He lifted an eyebrow when he saw Zizi on the couch sipping coffee. "This is a lovely surprise. What brings you here?"

"Good morning. I'm offering my assistance in helping you find Arthur. I figured you could use a local guide."

"We could. That is kind of you."

Just then, Gwen wandered into the suite. She was still in pajamas, her red hair tangled and a sleepy look on her face. "What did I miss?" She yawned and stretched her hands above her head. She blinked when she saw Zizi on the couch.

"Oh, hey, Zizi. What's up?"

We quickly brought Gwen up to speed, letting her know that Elvis hadn't had any success while reviewing the names of those registered at the hostel. While she changed and Slash finished getting dressed, Elvis ordered breakfast from room service.

When Slash came back out, he sat down at Elvis's laptop and started working. I went to stand behind him.

After a few minutes, I asked, "What are you doing?"

A few more taps and he angled the laptop toward me. Arthur Zimmerman's passport photo filled the screen.

I took a moment to study him. Easy to see the Zimmerman resemblance. He had a mop of black hair streaked with gray, black-rimmed glasses, a heavy beard and the same intense blue eyes as his sons. It was uncanny. I could pretty much see what Xavier and Elvis would look like in thirty years.

Gwen and Zizi had come up beside me and were looking at him, too.

"He didn't have a beard when I knew him," Zizi observed.

"Me neither," said Elvis.

Slash stood. "Let's keep that in mind. For now, Elvis and Lexi, you'll watch the front door. Zizi and Gwen, you'll be in the back, if you're in, Zizi."

"Of course, I'm in."

"Good. I'll go inside and see if I can do some reconnaissance inside the hostel. Maybe someone will know of a single American man living there."

We ate a quick breakfast of bread, cheese and more coffee before packing up. Gwen, Elvis and I slathered on suntan lotion and made sure to bring our hats. Elvis was really nervous. His hands kept shaking and he dropped the suntan lotion twice while he was putting it on.

The second time he dropped it, I reached down and handed it to him. "Take it easy," I said in a low voice, not wanting to embarrass him. "You've got this."

We decided to walk to the hostel since Zizi insisted it was a lovely morning. Personally, I felt like I was walking around in a furnace. I clearly didn't understand her definition of lovely morning. I also didn't get what people meant by a dry heat. Fourteen steps from the hotel and I was sweating like I'd just run a marathon. Not that I could actually run one, but still.

Regardless, it was pretty exciting to stroll along the streets of Cairo, taking in the sights and smells of the busy city while dodging cars, motorcycles and bicycles. Zizi knew the streets, so she helped us find a less traveled route to the hostel.

When we arrived, we all took up our stations outside the entrances to the hostel. Slash disappeared inside. Elvis had a good view of the front entrance from a nearby café and Zizi was sheltered by a rare tree in the back. Gwen and I made sure they had water and we settled in to wait.

Gwen bought an English language newspaper and I read it while sitting across from Elvis, who was surreptitiously watching the front door. I was experiencing firsthand the monotony that was surveillance. No wonder Slash had to practice tai chi. Patience was hard.

Minutes stretched into hours and soon it was nearly midday. Slash came and went. Gwen wandered around to the back entrance to talk microbiology with Zizi. I walked around, stretching my legs and trying to ignore my impatience, but I was getting hotter and more uncomfortable by the minute.

I knew Elvis felt worse. Despite sitting in the shade, the strain of watching the door and his nervousness was taking a toll. He had a lot more at stake than me, so I shelved my discomfort and did what I could to keep him hydrated and engaged without distracting him from the mission.

"Have you seen the latest developments in adaptive security software from AdaptTech?" I asked him casually. "It's pretty cool how it can predict the next strain of malware by determining how hackers will form their next attack."

"I know, right?" Elvis perked up. "It's based, quite correctly, on the fact that black hatters can be lazy and like to recycle techniques."

"Yeah, it's a good approach since—"

I didn't get to finish because Elvis abruptly stood up, pointing at a dark-haired man in khaki shorts and a white polo shirt who had just exited the apartment complex.

"That's him, Lexi." His voice was strained. "That's my father."

TWENTY-ONE

"Text Slash and the others that you've spotted him," I said, moving out from behind the table. "I'm going to follow him to make sure he doesn't get away. Follow me when you can."

Elvis's hands were shaking as he pulled out his cell phone. I patted him on the shoulder. "Remember, you've got this."

I darted off, leaving him texting the group. I made sure to keep my eyes focused on the white shirt. I followed at a discreet distance, trying to keep at least one or two people between us at all times. When he took a hard right onto a small street, I picked up the pace, nearly running to catch up to him. I rushed around the corner and was nearly brained by an iron pipe. It missed my head by a quarter inch and smashed into a brick wall next to my right eye.

"Holy crap!" I yelped, stepping back.

"Who are you?" He brandished the pipe. "Why are you following me?"

I was still a bit stunned I'd almost been killed by Elvis's father. I took a couple of steps backward, out of the alley just in case, and took a moment to find my voice. "Are you Arthur Zimmerman?"

He narrowed his eyes and advanced, still holding the pipe. "Who wants to know?"

"Me." Elvis stepped around the corner and put a

hand on my shoulder. He'd been running because he was out of breath. "Put the pipe down. She's with me."

The surprise on his face was visible. He dropped the pipe to the ground with a clatter. "Elvis? What are you doing here?"

It surprised me that after thirteen years, he could tell Elvis apart from Xavier so quickly. That he *could* had to mean something, although I wasn't sure what.

"What do you think? I'm looking for you, Arthur."

Not Dad or Father or anything like that. Just Arthur.

He looked over Elvis's shoulder. "Where's your brother?"

"He didn't want to come."

Arthur considered for a moment, but didn't ask why. Guess he could figure that one out for himself. "Dammit, if I had wanted you to find me, I would have told you where I was."

I recoiled at the anger in his voice. Thirteen years of not seeing his son and this is how he greeted him?

Elvis remained calm. "You *did* tell me. The return address on the letter?"

"Well, yes, but that was in case of emergency."

"This *is* an emergency."

Arthur narrowed his eyes. "Your time would have been better spent on doing what I asked you instead of traipsing to Egypt to find me."

"I *did* do what you asked. Stop pissing me off. That's why I'm here."

Arthur blinked in surprise. "You broke the code and figured out what the spores are? Already? Was it significant?"

"Yes."

"That can't be right. I calculated it would take you

and your brother at least three months to crack the code in the letter, let alone study the spores. Are you sure you did it right?"

"I'm sure." Elvis gritted his teeth. "I'm not fourteen anymore, Arthur. I happen to be good at codes, not to mention, I've got a lot more computing power these days. Plus, I have friends who are willing to help me even if it means coming to Egypt to get assaulted by my father."

Arthur paused a moment and then looked at me. "Sorry about that. You startled me. But, Elvis, why are you chasing me down now?"

"Because I've got something important to tell you. Would it have been so hard to leave a phone number where I could reach you? It might have saved me the trip."

Arthur's face flushed. "I didn't want to be found. I'm being watched." He jerked a thumb at me. "Speaking of being watched, who is she exactly?"

"Arthur, this is Lexi Carmichael. My best friend."

"Your best friend? Why did you bring her along?"

"Because I needed help finding you."

I heard pounding feet behind me and saw Slash, Gwen and Zizi all running toward us. I raised a hand to flag them down, but they'd already seen us. They came skidding to a stop behind me and Elvis. The girls were breathing heavily, but Slash didn't even look as if he'd broken into a sweat, despite the heat. Guess all that working out and tai chi was paying off.

It wasn't a surprise that Arthur noticed Zizi first. It was hard to notice anything else when she was around.

"Zizi?" He looked stunned. "What are *you* doing here?"

"Arthur, where have you been?" She came up beside him, panting a bit. She adjusted her scarf and pushed her hair off her shoulders. "There are a lot of people worried about you."

"You shouldn't have been worried. I just needed to disappear for a while."

"You should have trusted me to help. I thought I was your friend."

"You are my friend, and I do trust you. It's just… I thought it was better this way." He noticed Slash and Gwen. "Who are they?"

Elvis spoke on their behalf. "That's Gwen Sinclair and Slash. More of my friends."

"You involved more people, as well as Zizi?" His expression was incredulous. "Good Lord, Elvis. What exactly have you told them?"

"Pretty much everything I know, which isn't much." He glanced apologetically at Zizi. "Except for her. We just met."

Arthur staggered back. "How could you divulge such sensitive information? You could have jeopardized the entire situation."

"*What* situation?"

"I uncover perhaps the most significant biblical archeological find of the past four thousand years—one that dwarfs my vastly unappreciated caves inscriptions—and you show up here with a bunch of your friends, presumably to help? I suppose if I had found the burial place of Moses you would be asking me for a tour right now." Arthur threw up his hands and then sighed in exasperation. "You probably led them right to me."

"Who is them?"

Honestly, I was starting to get mad on Elvis's behalf. This guy had nerve. We'd flown halfway around the world to warn him about something he'd sent to his own sons with little to no instruction as to the danger, and all he could think about was himself?

To my surprise, Elvis remained poised, which was more than I would have been if this was my father. "Do you want to know what I found out or not?"

Excitement flashed in Arthur's eyes. He glanced furtively around the alley. "Don't say a word more. You never know who might be listening. Let's return to my room so you can fill me in on what you discovered. Come on. Hurry."

He pushed past us and headed toward the hostel. I exchanged a glance with Elvis, who sighed, but—without any other recourse—followed his father.

TWENTY-TWO

When we got back to the hostel, we squeezed into Arthur's small room. Zizi and Gwen sat on the bed while Slash leaned against the wall next to a tiny desk with a laptop on it. I stood against the back of the door so that Elvis and Arthur could have center stage, facing each other.

"Okay, Arthur, enough of the cloak and dagger." Elvis had his hands on his hips, and his eyes narrowed. "Why did you code the letter you sent to me and Xavier?"

"Why do you think?" Arthur replied. "I didn't want it to fall into the wrong hands. What did you and your brother discover?"

"For the record, Xavier didn't want any part of this."

Arthur shrugged. "I'm not surprised. He was always the rebellious one. So, what did you find?"

"Well, despite the inanity of you sending an unknown biological substance through the mail, I had enough common sense to proceed carefully with it. What were you thinking, Arthur? What if the vial had broken en route? What if Xavier or I had opened it before we decoded and read your letter? Didn't the danger posed to us ever occur to you?"

"What danger? I raised you boys with more sense than that. Obviously nothing happened, so let's not dwell on what could have happened and focus on what you've found."

Elvis drew in a breath and I could tell he was trying hard to keep his cool. It couldn't have been easy. My blood pressure was rising exponentially and Arthur wasn't even my father.

"I'm not even sure why you sent the vial to Xavier and me in the first place," Elvis said. "We're not microbiologists. You had to know that once we decoded your letter, we'd have to bring in a specialist to help."

"Of course, I knew you would. But I figured you would be discreet."

"I *was* discreet," Elvis said.

"See? Excellent."

"Arthur, I'm a microbiologist," Zizi interrupted angrily. "I separated those initial spores for you. I could have assisted you without you having to send the spores to America. Why didn't you consult further with me on this? I could have helped you."

"Zizi, my dear, as much as I appreciate your expertise and thoroughness, your loyalty lies with the museum. I couldn't risk you going to Haji until I was ready." He glanced back at Elvis. "So, what did you find?"

Gwen stood up. "I believe that's my cue to speak. Is that your laptop?" She glanced at the desk.

Arthur nodded. "It is. Who are you again?"

"Gwen Sinclair. I work with Elvis at ComQuest in Baltimore. I'm a microbiologist on staff and the person Elvis consulted with regard to the sample you sent him in the vial." She reached into her purse and pulled out a flash drive. "I've got the information you need right here on this drive, so if you'll permit me to load it to your computer, I'll pull it up. I think it will help you to have a visual."

Arthur glanced at Elvis, who nodded. He shrugged. "Be my guest. Let me get you in the system first." He booted up the laptop and typed in his password. As he vacated the chair, he motioned for Gwen to sit in it.

"Thanks," she said. She plugged in the flash drive and transferred the contents onto his desktop. "I've just downloaded the annotations from my testing and excerpts from the spores. It also contains my professional assessment of the ideal environment for its rapid reproduction."

Arthur peered at the screen as she opened the first of her documents. Zizi joined him, trying to see what Gwen had pulled up on the screen.

"What's your analysis?" Arthur asked.

"The analysis is they are ancient and uncataloged endospores."

"Endospores?" Zizi said, stunned.

Arthur looked surprised as well. He placed a hand on his forehead. "Endospores," he murmured.

"If I'd known what you'd sent had been found in an ancient artifact in Egypt, I never would have tested them myself. As it was, my test results were astonishing, not to mention scary. Mr. Zimmerman, you basically found seeds for a virulent plague. Even worse, the subsequent DNA sequencing I generated could potentially allow a competent scientist to re-create the plague from synthetic material and modern-day analogs using the spores. Unfortunately, I destroyed the endospores you'd sent during testing so I had nothing to pass on to the authorities for further examination."

"Authorities?" Arthur's voice rose. "You would have had no right."

"She would have had *every* right." Elvis stepped between her and Arthur. "We're talking about spores that could reignite an ancient plague in today's world."

"A plague," Arthur breathed, his eyes now taking on a faraway look. "That makes perfect sense."

"What makes sense? Where did you find the spores, Arthur?" Elvis asked.

But Arthur was in his own world. "An instrument of destruction created by God to be used against those who would harm His chosen people."

"What are you talking about?" Elvis said. "Just tell me where you found the spores."

Arthur snapped back to focus. "Not yet."

"What? Didn't you just hear what Gwen said? The endospores could ignite a pandemic. Where did you find them and where are the rest?"

Arthur studied Gwen. "I need to know more of what this young lady found before I say anything more. Please, Ms. Sinclair, start at the beginning and explain it to me clearly."

Elvis blew out a frustrated breath and stalked out of the room, letting the door slam behind him. Slash exchanged a glance with me, pushed off the wall and followed him.

Gwen twisted around in the chair, looking to me for guidance. Like I knew how to sort out this mess.

I sighed. It wasn't like I had a lot of options. "Go ahead and tell him what you know."

Gwen turned back to her research and began explaining in greater detail. Arthur and Zizi interrupted her often, asking questions and requiring clarification.

An hour passed. I was lost about fifteen minutes into the discussion with all the talk of microbes and bacteria. Finally, Gwen stood up, stretching. "I'm famished and dying of thirst. Where's Elvis?"

He hadn't returned and neither had Slash. I shrugged. "I guess we could get a bite to eat. They might be out front. Is there someplace close by we can catch a bite?"

Zizi nodded. Her eyes were lit and her face flushed with excitement. Who knew microbiology could be so thrilling? "There's an excellent restaurant on the corner. Let's go."

Arthur locked up his room and we exited the building. Elvis was sitting at the same café table where we'd been sitting earlier watching for Arthur. Despite the fact an hour had passed, he still looked extremely angry at his father.

Slash was nowhere in sight.

"We're going to get something to eat and drink," I said to Elvis. "Gwen has told them everything she knows."

He stood, looking at Gwen. "Thank you."

"Sure. No problem."

"Where's Slash?" I looked around.

"He left a bit ago to take care of something," Elvis said. "He didn't specify."

"Oh." I glanced at my phone, but there was no text and no message. "Okay. He knows how to reach us if he needs us."

We walked to the restaurant which was about a block away. Apparently being with Zizi had its advantages. We were seated immediately after she flashed a smile and some leg at the maître d'.

Zizi provided some menu recommendations, so we ordered food and drink. Since no one else was talking, I decided I needed to get the ball rolling.

"So, Arthur, by any chance do you know a guy named Merhu Khalfani?"

Arthur blinked in surprise. "How do you know him?"

"I don't *know* him, per se. He just broke into Elvis's house, tied us up and almost shot my kneecaps looking for the letter and spores you sent Elvis."

To his credit, he looked shocked. "My God, I *knew* he was involved in this."

"Involved in what?" Elvis asked.

"Mr. Khalfani worked at the British Museum. He was a shifty character, always nosy and snooping around me. Anyway, the inscriptions I found and translated in the cave in Jordan led me to a stone tablet located in the Egyptian section of the museum. In turn, it provided an important clue to the discovery of the artifact I was seeking. One of the inscriptions in my caves gave me the insight to realize the import of the reference on the tablet. Only I was able to put the pieces together. After I'd left for Cairo, I heard he'd been fired for handling the same stone tablet without museum permission. It wasn't a coincidence. He was onto me."

"Is that why you disappeared?" I asked.

"Partly." He paused while the waiter brought us our drinks. As soon as he walked away, Arthur resumed. "You see, all these years I've been following a trail of clues—all leading to what promised to be an archeological find of historical and religious significance to sixty percent of the world's population. The quest for this artifact required me to piece together clues from three continents. And I did it. It's been decades of dedicated scholarship, but my work has paid off. Finally, I will be recognized among the pantheon of elite archeologists. Here's the most exciting part—I've even held the artifact in my hands. In doing so, I found and solved a puzzle on it that allowed me to recover a treasure unseen since before Moses parted the Red Sea. But there are many others who lack my knowledge and who are trying to steal my discovery from me at my moment of greatest triumph."

My phone vibrated and I saw I had a text from Slash asking where we were. I typed in the name of the restaurant and the general location, figuring he'd find it easy enough.

"Arthur, we can't help you because you aren't sharing details," Zizi cajoled. I could hear the irritation in her voice. "You can't expect us to see those spores as anything but dangerous."

Elvis nodded, leaning forward on the table. "If nothing else, you have to tell us where they are."

Arthur sighed and reached into his pocket, withdrawing a sturdy leather pouch and setting it on the table. We all stared at it like it was a bomb.

"That's not what I think it is, is it?" Elvis asked.

Arthur ran his fingers across the pouch. "Unfortunately, yes. It's the rest of the spores."

TWENTY-THREE

A HAND CLAMPED down on my shoulder and I nearly jumped out of my chair. Slash slid into a chair next to me.

"I've got bad news," he said. "We can't go back to Arthur's hostel. It's being watched."

"What?" Elvis exclaimed. "By whom?"

"I don't know."

"How is that possible?" Gwen asked. "There was no one watching when we were trying to spot Arthur. Or was there?"

"Who is he again?" Arthur pointed at Slash.

"A friend," Elvis said firmly. "But if Slash says we can't go back, we can't."

Arthur took the leather pouch with the spores, returning it to his pocket. "I *have* to go back my room. My laptop is still there."

"What about your notes?" Zizi asked.

"They're on the laptop, too, along with the material Gwen just loaded."

Slash looked around the table at us. "First priority. We need to find a safe place to stash Arthur."

"And the spores," Gwen added. "He's got them in his pocket."

"Where they are perfectly and safely contained," Arthur insisted. "I do have a Bachelor's Degree in

Applied Science, not to mention a PhD in Egyptology. I'm a scientist. The spores are contained. Trust me."

Considering we were talking a plague of epidemic proportions, I wasn't reassured by his personal guarantees. But we had more pressing problems at the moment.

Slash gave me a look that said he was not on board with any of this whatsoever. I fully agreed. But first things first.

"Can't we just take Arthur back to the Marriott with us?" Gwen asked.

"No." Slash shook his head. "Arthur would have to use his passport to enter, and then once there, anyone who wanted to could find him."

"But the security…" Gwen said.

"Is good, but not impenetrable. If the goal is to keep Arthur's whereabouts a secret until he leads us to the artifact, the Marriott is too high profile."

"They may have already spotted us with him," I said.

"I know. Which is why we need to disappear for a bit, too. Zizi, do you think you could find us all temporary quarters somewhere that wouldn't require our passports?"

"What?" Gwen looked disappointed. "We have to leave the Marriott?"

"For now."

"Figures. It was a pretty sweet setup."

"I have an idea where we can take Arthur and where you can all stay safely." Zizi stood up.

"Good." Slash pointed at us. "You all go with Zizi. Once you find a place, text me the address."

I looked at him in surprise. "Where are you going?"

"I'm going to get Arthur's computer."

"Alone?"

"Alone." He held out a hand to Arthur. "The key to your room, please?"

Arthur stared at Slash and then turned to Elvis. "Why should I trust him? I don't even know him. How long have you known him? He could be with them, and making this all up just to steal my laptop."

Slash was working hard to contain himself. I saw the twitch of his jaw, which meant he was probably clenching his teeth. Even though Arthur hadn't spoken to him directly, Slash said, "If I'd wanted your laptop, sir, I would have taken it as soon as you led us into your room."

"But you wouldn't have had my password."

"I don't need your password to get into your computer."

Elvis rolled his neck as if that could ease the tension of the moment. It didn't. "For God's sake, he's telling the truth, Arthur. Give him the key."

"Only if you go with him. I don't know him, but I know you. You're my son. You wouldn't steal from your father."

"No one is going to steal anything." Elvis's voice had taken on a hard edge. "Need I remind you, we're here to help. Slash is my friend. And I'm staying with you. No way am I letting you out of my sight until this is finished."

I stood, offering a compromise. "I'll go with Slash." Truthfully, I needed my own break from Arthur Zimmerman.

To my surprise, Arthur agreed. "Elvis said you're

his best friend. If you go with Slash and promise to return my laptop to me, he can have the key."

I glanced at Slash, but his lips were still pressed together tightly. He said nothing. At least he didn't argue and his hand hadn't moved. It remained steady and stretched out to Arthur for the key.

I glanced uneasily between Slash and Elvis. Neither was looking my way. They were both staring daggers at Arthur. "Um, I promise. So, ah, okay, it's settled, then. Right?"

Arthur remained focused on me for some strange reason. "I'm holding you personally responsible for having my laptop returned to me. Are we clear, young lady?"

"Perfectly." At this point, I wasn't going to argue semantics with him.

Arthur reached in his pocket and handed a silver key to Slash. "I hope you all understand why I'm not telling you everything. Without me and my knowledge, none of the pieces you have will come together. You need me and my research and that's the way I intend to keep it until I can reveal my discovery to the world."

Without a word Slash pocketed the key and strode to the restaurant door. I ran to catch up.

"So, what's the plan?" I asked as we left the restaurant.

"The plan is I have to stop imagining the six different ways I'm torturing Arthur Zimmerman in my mind and focus on the task at hand."

"I'm with you on that one. I feel sorry for Elvis. Xavier, too."

We walked back toward the hostel. Slash came to a stop on the sidewalk across the street. People and animals streamed past, no one giving us the time of day. "See that guy over there in the gray shirt and black pants? The one with sunglasses and a blue cap?"

I followed his line of vision and saw the person he described. The guy was walking back and forth, staring at the hostel entrance and talking on his cell. "Yeah, I see him."

"Good. Look to the left now. See the guy with the red T-shirt and khaki shorts?"

I did. He was a pretty muscular guy. He was talking on his phone, as well. He was closer to the entrance, as if planning to stop anyone who exited.

"My guess is they have someone in the back and someone on the inside trying to figure out which room is Arthur's. It won't take them long to pinpoint it."

"How can you be sure they are looking for Arthur?"

"Because I noticed them immediately. They are watching the place. So, I maneuvered behind the guy talking on the cell and heard him say Arthur's name. Not exactly professional, which leads me to think they are a bunch of thugs along the line of Merhu Khalfani."

"Why are they trying to find Arthur?"

"There are a number of possible scenarios, none of them good. Especially since Mr. Khalfani was armed and ready to shoot people to get his hands on the spores."

"Agreed. What are we going to do?"

He pulled me into a space between buildings, trapping me against the wall, then started unbuttoning my blouse.

"What in the world are you doing?" I asked.

"You've got a tank under the blouse, right?"

"Yes, but…" Before I could finish, he unbuttoned the rest of my blouse and slid it off my shoulders.

"Drape it over your arm." He bent down toward my feet.

I frowned, but did as he said. Still, I felt half-naked in just my tank top and I hadn't put suntan lotion on my shoulders or back, so I hoped this new look wasn't going to be for long.

Suddenly there was a ripping noise and my legs felt a rush of air.

"Hey, what was that?" I yelped, looking down.

Slash straightened, holding most of my skirt in one hand and a pocketknife with small scissors in the other. "I think it's short enough."

"Why did you do that?" I peered over my shoulder. "I think my butt is showing."

"Perfect." He snapped the pocketknife shut and then released my hair from its ponytail, spreading it about my shoulders.

Stepping back, he surveyed me. "You look more cute than sleazy, but it will have to do. Try to wiggle your hips a lot when you walk."

"What?"

He motioned to the hotel entrance. "Haven't you noticed the clientele going in and out of the hostel?"

I glanced over at the entrance. I'd been watching it all morning and hadn't noticed anything unusual. But now that I paid more attention, there were more couples going in than coming out.

"Wait. Are you saying Arthur is staying in a brothel?"

"I don't know if it's a brothel proper, but if the shoe fits…"

"They have brothels in Cairo?"

"There are brothels everywhere, *cara*."

"Oh. Okay, I guess I just never thought about it. I see where you're going with this. You want me to pose as a prostitute and you're going to be my john. We're going into the hostel to have sex."

He chuckled. "Unfortunately there will be no sex this time. But if we're going to stroll into the hostel and look like we belong there, this look is a good idea."

He took off his jacket and put it over his arm and pulled a black cap out of the pocket. He turned the bill of the cap around so it was on backward.

"Those guys may have spotted us earlier when we weren't looking for anyone looking at us. This should change up our look enough that we can get in and out without raising suspicion or having anyone follow us to Arthur's door." He hooked his sunglasses on the front of his T-shirt and voila, he had a totally different look. It was amazing to me how he could so effortlessly change his appearance without doing much.

"Well, I'd feel a lot better about this charade if my butt wasn't showing."

He turned me around. "It's not showing…completely." He grinned. "Although I may have cut it a bit short."

I hit him on the arm. "You did it on purpose." I straightened, trying to suck in my stomach in hope it would provide a tiny bit more material to cover my rear. "The things I do in the name of national security."

He leaned over and kissed me on the cheek. "Ah, *cara*, welcome to my world."

TWENTY-FOUR

THE WALK FROM across the street to the hostel was the longest of my life. It felt like every eye in Cairo was on my butt, even if it wasn't. It was probably one of the most self-conscious moments in my life, and I'd had many. Slash had his arm around my waist, clearly indicating I was with him, but it was uncomfortable to say the least. I was pretty sure this wasn't a common look for Cairo, even if it might not have been an unusual sight in front of this particular hostel in the middle of the day.

"You're waddling like a duck," Slash said out of the corner of his mouth. "Sashay. Use your hips."

"You trying walking in a skirt this short," I hissed. "And we'll see who looks like a duck."

He smiled and we strolled into the lobby. It was packed with guys and a few girls strolling around talking to them. He headed straight for the stairs and to the second floor. A guy exited room 210 fastening his pants. He looked our way and gave a thumbs-up to Slash. I tried not to throw up.

We reached room 202 and Slash inserted the key. He motioned for me to wait in the hallway and pushed open the door. A quick glance indicated no one was there. The laptop still sat on the small desk.

I came in, closing the door behind me. Slash unhooked the laptop from the electrical cable and bent to one knee, looking under the bed. He dragged out a soft laptop bag and slid the computer inside.

"Check the desk drawer for any important papers," he instructed.

I opened the drawer and pulled out a passport, some other loose papers and a gun. I held the gun out to Slash.

"Look at what Arthur was hiding."

Slash rolled his eyes and tucked it in his waistband at the small of his back. He took the papers, passport, and cables I handed him, stuffing them in the bag as well.

I quickly checked the dresser drawers, but found only clothes and more toiletries.

"There's nothing else here." Slash looped the laptop bag across his shoulder and then put on his jacket. "Let's go."

He didn't have to tell me twice. I was all for getting the heck out of this place. He opened the door and we stepped out into the hall just as a guy walked down the hall directly toward us.

Slash pulled me toward him and starting noisily kissing me on the neck. I was so surprised by his actions I nearly tripped, but it occurred to me that he wanted the guy to think we belonged there, just part of the scenery.

Not knowing what a prostitute would do in such a situation, I did the first thing I could think of. I licked the side of his face. It was more like a dog lick than a sexy, prostitute lick, but as I wasn't practiced at either, I did the best I could in the heat of the moment.

I tried not to wince since the guy looked more freaked out than turned on by my licking. He passed us—giving us as wide a berth as he could—stopping in front of Room 202. He glanced at the number on the door and then at us before he made the connection we'd just left that room.

Thankfully we were already at the stairs.

"Hey!" he yelled, followed by something in Arabic. Slash yanked on my arm as we flew down the stairs.

Instead of going out the way we'd come in, Slash pushed me toward the back door. We pushed through people who gave us annoyed looks as we slipped out the back entrance.

A guy with a black shirt, black pants and a cell phone across the way spotted us as soon as we exited. He shouted something, shoved his cell in his pocket and started running our way.

Slash already had a plan. About five feet away a de-livery guy had just pulled up on a motorcycle in front of a door and was carrying a box toward an unmarked entrance at the rear of the building. Slash ran in that direction with me hot on his heels.

He swung his leg over the motorcycle and took hold of the handlebars. "Get on."

I hesitated. "I don't see any helmets."

"Get on or we're dead."

"If you put it like that." I had barely even swung my leg over the motorcycle when Slash took off. I caught his waist with my hands as I lurched back-ward, barely hanging on. My skirt was hitched up to my waist, which meant my undies were on full display. Not like that was the most pressing of my problems, but there you have it.

I may or may not have screamed like a girl as we tore off down the street. The guy whose motorcycle we'd stolen dropped his box and ran after us yelling, along with the black-clad thug who'd spotted our exit.

Slash sped around a corner when I heard a noise behind us. I twisted my head to the side and saw there was another motorcycle hot on our tail.

"Bad news," I shouted in Slash's ear. "We've got company."

"We'll lose them," Slash said. He took a hard left. We listed so low I nearly scraped my knee on the pavement. Before I could panic, Slash straightened the motorcycle and we rocketed down a busy street.

I swallowed a scream as people leaped out of our way. Intellectually I understood his strategy. The more people on the street the better the chance we could blend in or slow down our pursuers. The bad news was that there were a lot of people and it was only a matter of time before we hit someone or something.

"Oh jeez." I clutched his waist as tightly as I could, hoping I wouldn't throw up or fall off.

We barreled down the street, jumping over curbs and swerving around pedestrians, tables, animals and lampposts. Each mile brought its share of teeth-crunching jolts and bumps. The motorcycle shook, as if it might simply fall apart beneath us given the speed Slash was pushing it. My eyes were watering from the lash of the wind, so things were blurry. Maybe that was a good thing. I didn't dare reach up to wipe my eyes for fear of falling off if Slash took a corner unexpectedly.

Slash ripped into an alley. A gunshot hit the brick right above my head. I pressed closer to Slash.

"They're shooting at us," I shouted.

Slash took the next right at a breakneck speed and

plunged onto a smaller street. I didn't know how he hadn't hit anyone or anything yet. Cairo's congested streets, even the smaller ones, teemed with cars, motorcycles, bikes and pedestrians weaving around in chaos. He, along with everyone else, never once obeyed a stop sign or traffic signal. I guess that meant we fit right in with the flow of things. But my jaw was sore from clenching it and my hair was whipping my face like a hundred stinging bees.

Another shot rang out and I tensed, waiting any moment to feel a bullet in the back. Slash rocketed around another corner and directly forward into what looked like an underground garage of a building.

"Hang on," he shouted.

He hit a couple of bumps that caused my bottom to completely leave the seat before he slid sideways into a parking spot, tires squealing. Slash was off the motorcycle before it had fully stopped. He yanked me off toward a set of stairs.

We ran up the stairs and around the back of a building before going down an alley and coming out on another busy street. Slash took a quick glance up and down the street before pulling me across it and into a store.

It was a women's clothing store. A couple of women looked at us in surprise. I tried to push down what little skirt I had left.

"Good. We lost them." He wasn't even breathing hard.

I, on the other hand, was hyperventilating like a freaking racehorse.

"How did you learn to drive like that?" I asked.

A quick glance in a nearby mirror indicated my hair looked like a dozen birds had nested in it.

"I had a motorbike in Italy," he said with a grin. "Used to race them with Anthony Dioli around the streets of Sperlonga when I was sixteen. I also had some training at the Vatican, but this was pretty prime."

He steered me toward a rack with skirts. "Pick out a skirt and a new blouse. And make it quick."

I don't know how he could transition so effortlessly from a motorcycle chase to skirt shopping, but I needed a freaking minute.

After trying to smooth down my hair, I pulled a light blue skirt with an elastic waist off the rack. It looked like it might be a bit too short, but I wasn't worried about that for the moment. The waist looked about right and it was far superior to what I was currently wearing. A matching blue blouse hung nearby, so I grabbed that, too. Slash reappeared next to me with a gold scarf in his hand. He shoved it in my hands.

"Go put everything on. I'll pay for it."

"Okay."

I found a tiny dressing room in the back and changed clothes. The skirt was too short. It barely fell to my knees, but it would have to do until I could retrieve my other clothes. I abandoned what was left of my other skirt in the room and carried only my tank top and blouse rolled up in my hands. When I exited the dressing room, Slash was waiting. He took a quick look up the street and then, apparently satisfied the coast was clear, motioned for me to follow.

"We got a text from Elvis," he said as we fell into

the pedestrian traffic. "They found a place for us to stay and they've secured Arthur."

"Good. Now what?"

"Now we get this laptop to Arthur. He's got to tell us what the hell is going on before anyone gets hurt— starting with us."

TWENTY-FIVE

WE TOOK A cab to the Dabab Hostel, which we found out later was run by family friends of Zizi. Elvis told us Zizi had found us two rooms, one for the men and one for the women. I guess that meant Gwen was going to be my new roommate. If Slash was bothered by our new arrangement, he didn't say so. It wasn't like we had a lot of choice in the matter.

Elvis texted me that everyone was in room 101, so we knocked and waited. Elvis opened the door and we went in. Gwen and Arthur sat on one of three twin beds. There were some drawings scattered on top of one of the spreads, so I assumed Gwen had been giving Arthur a lesson on the spores.

Arthur rose when he saw us. "Thank God. Did you get the laptop?"

Slash pulled off his jacket and removed the laptop strap from across his shoulder. "We did." But instead of handing the bag to Arthur, he handed it to me.

"You know what to do, *cara*."

"On it." I took the bag.

"Excuse me," Arthur said. "That laptop belongs to me. Just what do you think you are doing?"

"Protecting it, Arthur." I sat on the bed and pulled the laptop out of the bag. I connected the cable to the outlet and balanced it on my lap. "Slash and I were almost killed trying to get this. You've got a lot of valuable information stored on here. It needs to be better protected until we can get to a spot where we can offload the material to a more secure location." I looked over at Elvis. "Any idea if this place has Wi-Fi?"

He shook his head in the negative.

"Oh, well. I don't have a SIM card on me, but I can still make some modifications." I reached into my purse and pulled out my keys. I had a flash drive attached to the ring where my apartment key was. I plugged it into the side of Arthur's laptop.

"Where's Zizi?" I asked no one in particular.

"She had to check in with her family," Gwen said. "Hey, did you hear that you and I are going to be roommates? Angel is going to be so jealous. Is that a new outfit?"

I had no idea how or why she could even notice such things in times like these, but we are who we are.

Before I could respond—not that I wanted to—Slash reached beneath his jacket and pulled out a gun. "This was in your room, too, Arthur."

"My gun. Thank God you found it. The way things are going, I might have to use it." He reached for it, but Slash didn't hand it over.

"You have a gun?" Elvis asked in astonishment.

"Of course."

"May I ask what you're doing with it?" Slash asked.

"Personal protection. People are following me, remember?"

"Guns are very difficult to obtain in Egypt," Slash said.

"I have my ways."

Slash lifted an eyebrow but didn't comment. "Do you know how to use it?"

"I do." Arthur frowned. "Now hand it over, please."

After a moment of what seemed like internal debate, Slash handed it over. Arthur took it and stuck it in an empty dresser drawer.

I looked up from the keyboard. "Arthur, what's your password?"

When he hesitated, Elvis gave his father a stern look. "Tell her."

"Why can't I just type it in?"

"We're trying to help you," Elvis said. "And you're making it damn hard."

I adjusted the laptop on my knees. "Mr. Zimmerman, I promised you I'd bring you the computer and I did. Giving me the password helps me enhance your security. I just want to protect your information and make it hard for anyone to access your files if your laptop got stolen."

"Even if they get the laptop, I coded that file," Arthur protested.

"If your files are not electronically encrypted, they aren't safe. And even if they are encrypted, it's *still* not safe." I tried to keep my voice even, not irritated, even if that's exactly how I was feeling right now. "The file needs to be specially encrypted and protected in ways that would take a hacker, even a good one, a long time to get in. Can you please trust me on this?"

Arthur sighed. "Do I have a choice?"

"No." Elvis frowned. "Now give Lexi the password and let us do our work."

WHILE I WORKED on Arthur's laptop, Slash disappeared and came back with bottles of Coke, water, orange Fanta and three giant pizza boxes, of all things.

"Domino's Pizza?" I said when I saw the writing on box. The smell of pizza wafted through the room and I realized I was ravenous. We hadn't eaten lunch and breakfast had been a long time ago.

Slash handed out napkins and the five of us devoured the pizzas in record time.

"Wow. I can't believe I came to Egypt for Domino's Pizza." Gwen wiped tomato sauce off her chin. "But it was good." She burped. "Oops, excuse me."

Slash tore off a bite of his pizza and chewed. He motioned at me, the pizza still in his hand. "How's the security upgrade going?"

"Slow. Without Wi-Fi, there's only so much I can do. But I've done my best for now."

"Your best is always good enough," Slash said, taking another bite. "But we need to talk. All of us. Arthur, you must give us a better idea of what we're dealing with here."

During dinner Slash filled him and Elvis in on our earlier escapade, so they knew about the guys chasing us and our close getaway on the motorcycle.

Arthur sat back, drinking Fanta and studying us. "Okay. Fair enough. I'll give you a bit of background. But I'm not putting all my cards on the table, just so we're clear."

Slash and Elvis exchanged a glance before Elvis nodded. "Fine. Just give us *some* idea of what's going on."

Arthur set his drink on the table. "Well, for the past thirty years I've been traveling across the Middle East tracking the lost treasures of the Jewish Temple during the sacking of Jerusalem in 925 BC. This particular destructive campaign was led by Egyptian Pharaoh

Shishak. Apparently Shishak had his forces cart off precious Jewish treasures from the temple and brought them back to Egypt for his own palace."

"That's a version corroborated by the Bible," Slash offered.

"Yes, it is." Arthur looked at his hands. "Well, apparently one particular treasure was believed to contain a special power."

"What kind of power?" I asked.

"A holy one."

Gwen leaned forward excitedly. "Whoa. Like the spiritual power of the Ark of the Covenant or the Holy Grail?"

"Something like that."

"That's awesome. It's like I'm in an Indiana Jones movie or something."

Slash rolled his eyes, but I felt the odd urge to giggle.

"So, what treasure was it?" Elvis balled his napkin and tossed into an empty pizza box.

"At the time, I didn't know," Arthur said. "But I got a lead to this unnamed holy treasure from the inscriptions on the cave in Jordan. They pointed to the existence of a stone tablet which held the story of the treasure. I eventually tracked down the tablet to the Egyptian section of the British Museum in London."

"The same tablet Merhu Khalfani was manhandling at the British Museum?" I asked.

"Exactly. That tablet spoke of an Egyptian royal chariot that either carried or held the treasure. The search for that chariot led me back to Cairo."

"So, that's why you were looking at so many chariots and chariot-related items," Slash mused.

"How do you know that?" Arthur demanded.

"Stand down, Arthur," Elvis said irritably. "Zizi provided us with a list of things you'd been studying when we were trying to track you down. Chariots was on the list."

Arthur didn't look happy, but he kept talking. "Anyway, I examined the chariots on display in the museum, but didn't see what I was looking for. Then one day I came across an interesting display in what is affectionately called by researchers the Archive Museum. It's basically a museum in the basement of the Egyptian Museum. It's open to researchers and scholars only."

"There's a museum in the basement of the museum?" I said in surprise.

"You'd be surprised what's down there. Large statues, thrones, jewelry, pottery, ancient scrolls, jeweled scarabs and, yes, chariots, just to name a few. They don't have room to display everything in the museum, so they are building a new museum. The sheer number of artifacts they have harvested from the tombs and surrounding areas is staggering. Right now, a lot of it remains boxed, uncataloged and poorly preserved."

"So, you found what you were looking for in the basement?" Elvis prodded, clearly trying to keep his father on track. "The holy object you'd been seeking?"

"I did." Arthur lowered his voice. "I held it in my hands."

"What is it?" Elvis asked.

"Sorry, that's one card I'm not playing," Arthur said. "Not yet."

Slash sighed, clearly exasperated. "Where's the artifact now?" He was nearing the end of his rope with Arthur's games. "Is it still in the Archive Museum?"

Arthur shook his head. "No, that's the problem. If it were still in the basement, it would be easier to access. Shortly after I found the vial and sent a sample to Elvis and his brother, I realized I was being followed. Then I heard about Mr. Khalfani trying to decipher or steal the stone tablet. I decided it would be prudent to disappear for a while. I figured he, or someone else, was onto me and my discovery. Later, I heard the chariot went on display. That means researchers like me are no longer able to have access to it without specific permission. If I had to request permission, I'd have to say why, fill out special paperwork and be questioned by the museum board. I wasn't ready to do that yet. That's where you come in. I need you to go to the museum and take pictures of all the chariots on display, so I can see exactly where the artifact is now located and decide what to do next. I'd go myself, but as you have witnessed, there are people out to hurt me and steal my life's work."

"Why can't Zizi just get it for you?" Gwen said.

"Once an artifact is on display, not even museum employees can touch it without special permission. Permissions take time, require forms, interviews and a vote by the museum board. It's a lengthy process because it's expensive to move exhibitions around or remove them for examination."

I frowned. "Okay, let me get this straight. Because you can no longer access the artifact and aren't sure where exactly it's located in terms of display, you want us to go to the museum and take pictures of various chariots without even knowing what we're looking for?"

"Yes." He looked at me as if making sure I comprehended. "Then, after I determine its location, I'll decide whether or not you can help me with the rest of plan to reveal the artifact to the world."

Slash abruptly stood and picked up the empty pizza boxes. "I'm going to find a place to dump these." He strode to the door.

I rose and followed him.

"Wait, Slash." I jogged to catch up with him. "What do you think about Arthur's revelations?"

"You have to ask?" Frustration tinged his words. "I think he's beyond eccentric. But we're stuck. The biggest threat at the moment is the endospores. I could take them from him, but we still won't know where he got them and whether or not there are any more. Add to that, we don't know who's after him or why. Merhu Khalfani, or whoever he's working for, is obviously tracking Arthur's steps and is willing to shoot or kill people to get those endospores. We don't know why, and we can't even speculate, because Arthur isn't giving up any information. All of that means we are operating in the dark. Not to mention, we're running out of time."

We walked outside and the heat hit me like a fist to the stomach. I pushed my hair off my neck and fanned myself with my hand. Not far from the building, Slash found a trash container and dumped the boxes in it.

"You're right. We can't take or steal those spores from him," I said. "He's barely trusting us as it is. If he notices them missing, there's no one else to blame but us. He'd clam up for good."

"I know. Which means we have to treat Arthur like he *is* the endospores. He has to be protected. Which, I suspect, is part of his plan. What we are protecting him from, I don't know. But until we can get more information, we have to play his game."

"Which means taking pictures of chariots until he finds what he's looking for."

"Unfortunately, *si*."

Slash leaned over and kissed me on the cheek. "I'm going back to the Marriott. I want to do some more research on Mr. Merhu Khalfani and pick up our laptops."

"You really think we're safe here?"

"I do. For the time being at least."

I paused. I wanted to say this in a sensitive way, but I wasn't sure how. "I hate to raise the issue, but do you trust Zizi that much? What if she's in on this?"

"What motive would she have?"

"Oh, I don't know…money?"

Slash put a hand on my shoulder. "I already checked her out. Her finances are clean, as is her record. A review of her cell records for the past six months shows no calls to any known felons or criminals. She appears to be an intelligent, hardworking and reliable woman. She still lives with her parents and younger siblings in Cairo and helps support them. I also think she's smart enough to understand what's at stake with those spores. In fact, she's worked hard to get ahead in a field that isn't kind to women in this part of the world, which reminds me a bit of someone else I know."

I don't know why I felt worse after hearing that, instead of relieved, but I'd have to figure that out later. "You've certainly been busy."

"Always. I'd better go."

"Okay. By the way, can you look in the front pocket of my toilet kit? I've got a couple of SIM cards in there.

Would you bring me those? At least we'll be able to connect from here, even if it is slow."

"Absolutely. Good thinking. I'll see you later." He gave me one more kiss, this time a lingering one on the mouth, before disappearing down the street.

Frowning, I went back inside.

I knocked lightly on the guys' door. Elvis opened it and looked over my shoulder. "Where's Slash?"

"He'll be back in a bit."

I walked into the room. Arthur was at the desk pouring himself more orange Fanta.

"Where's Gwen?"

"She went to take a shower and hit the sack. By the way, here's your room key."

"Thanks." I took it and slipped it in my pocket. "Are we done for the night?"

"Yeah. We're done. Tomorrow morning, we head to the museum to take random photos of chariots to satisfy my father's wishes. We just have to figure out who's going and how to do it without getting spotted and trailed back here."

"Don't think I can't hear the note of derision in your voice," Arthur said, turning around.

"Note?" Elvis crossed his arms against his chest, facing his father. "Try a whole symphony. Your behavior has been inexcusable, not to mention embarrassing. We came here to help and this is how you treat us."

"How *dare* you speak to me in that tone!"

"How *dare* I not?"

I cleared my throat. "Well… I, ah, really need to take a shower, too, so I'll just be going…"

Elvis reached out, put a hand on my arm. "Stay, Lexi. Please."

The urge to bolt was strong, but how could I say no? If he wanted me to stay, then I had to stay no matter how uncomfortable the situation became. Swallowing hard, I nodded and pressed my shoulders back against the wall.

Elvis turned his attention to his father. "There are things that need to be said between us. I swore to myself a thousand times if I ever saw you again, I wouldn't say them. But they aren't going to stay locked inside anymore. So, here goes." He pushed a shaky hand through his hair. "Why the *hell* did you leave us, Arthur? I deserve to know."

Arthur took a few steps forward until he faced his son. They glared at each other like two gunslingers in a Western movie. Except the only bullets that would be fired here were verbal, although I suspected just as deadly.

"I didn't leave. I had to work." Arthur's frown deepened. "When you, your brother and mother could no longer accompany me on-site, I had to find a good home base for you. I chose a spot near your mother's parents and saw you settled."

"That's what you tell yourself? You settled us?"

"I had to work. There were bills to pay. It's not my fault your mother and grandparents shut me out."

"Maybe because you *left* us."

"I'm an archeologist. My work requires me to be in the field."

"You're a teacher, Arthur. A professor. You could have found a job in the same damn country as us, even if it were just for a little while. We needed you."

Arthur pushed his hand through his hair in a gesture eerily similar to the way Elvis did it. "I admit the timing was terrible. It's just I was onto something big, Elvis. Those inscriptions in the cave in Jordan—while it wasn't the significant find I'd hoped for—it was the clue I needed. It eventually led me to the artifact…and the spores. This is the one, Elvis. I swear."

"So, you abandoned us when we needed you most because your search for some stupid artifact buried for thousands of years was more important to you than your family?" Elvis's hands shook badly, so he pressed them against his side. I wanted to close my eyes, pretend I was anywhere but here listening to this intensely private and painful conversation. But he had asked me to stay, so I stayed.

"You don't understand." There was a defensive note in Arthur's voice. "I did this for you. For our family."

"No, Arthur, you did it for *you*. In the meantime, Xavier and I had to finish high school without the assistance of a responsible adult when Grandma and Grandpa died. We had to take care of Mother, too, pretending she was fine so we didn't get stuck in foster care. Do *you* understand how hard that was when we were just two scared teenage boys?"

Elvis enunciated each word with small intakes of breath, as if it were strangling the life out of him. I wanted to put a hand on his arm as a measure of support, but I was afraid the slightest touch would cause him to fall apart and I knew he had to get through this.

Arthur looked shaken. He sagged into a chair. "I thought I was doing the right thing. It took me longer than expected. I thought if I could find the artifact, it would save our family, not hurt it. It would make all the effort worthwhile."

Elvis shook his head. "That's just an excuse, and a lousy one at that."

"You're right." Arthur pressed his hand to his forehead. "That's not the whole truth. A part of me believed you were better off without me…after what happened."

Anger flashed across Elvis's face. "Don't you dare say that. You don't have the right. Maybe it was better for *you*, but we needed you, especially after Sadie. What kind of man leaves his wife at such a time? What kind of father just…*leaves*?"

Arthur closed his eyes and then seemed to steel himself. "None of this is going to get settled tonight and it isn't the time to rehash old family matters, especially not in front of her. I reached out to you and your brother, Elvis, because we're family and the discovery of this artifact is bigger than me. Bigger than you. It's history in the making. The impact on humanity could be staggering."

Elvis exhaled, steadier now. "Make no mistake, Arthur. That's the only reason I'm here. If you think I came because I wanted some kind of family reunion, you couldn't be more wrong. I deserve better, and so do Mom, Xavier and Sadie."

With those words, Elvis turned sharply and left the room, closing the door hard behind him.

I stood alone in the small room facing Arthur Zimmerman. I had no idea who Sadie was and what exactly had happened to this family that had torn them apart so terribly. Daring a glance across the room, I saw there were tears shimmering in Arthur's eyes.

He took a shaky breath and looked at me imploringly. "I tried to do the right thing by my family, by him, Lexi. I really tried."

I met his gaze evenly. The anguish was palpable in his voice, but that didn't excuse his actions.

"You're his father," I said. "You better try a lot harder."

TWENTY-SIX

I WENT IN search of Elvis.

There was no sign of him, which told me he wanted to be alone. I figured he knew where I was if he needed me. I went to my room and found Gwen already in her bed dressed only in a T-shirt and underwear, her hair wet.

"No clean pajamas and no hairdryer." She lifted a strand of her limp hair. "The shower was basically a handheld sprayer and there was no shampoo or soap. But it's better than nothing."

I took off my sandals and sat on my twin bed with all my clothes on. "Oh, well."

She yawned. "How's Elvis?"

"He's dealing."

"It's tough. Dealing with an absent father sucks."

There was something in her voice that made me look over my shoulder. "You sound like you know something about that."

She shrugged. "My dad split when Angel was six months. Haven't heard from him since. I don't miss him because I didn't really know him. But I kind of miss the idea of a father, if you know what I mean."

I didn't know—thank God—but the revelation she had an absent father made me wonder if that had helped Elvis feel more comfortable sharing the details of his father with her.

Gwen let out a huge yawn and raised her arms above her head. "While it's really cool being your roommate, Lexi, I'm just too tired to chat. I hate to say it, but do you mind if I go to sleep? We can have a meaningful girl-to-girl conversation tomorrow night. It will be a true slumber party. Afterward, I'll blog about what it's like to sleep in the same room as Lexi Carmichael."

Oh, God, no! What had I done to deserve this? I made a mental note to schedule a hack on her website to make sure that blog never went up. "Go to sleep, Gwen. We've got a busy day tomorrow."

To help things along I turned off the overhead light for her. In less than five minutes, she was asleep. Unfortunately, I wasn't sleepy in the slightest. I sat in the dark, my head resting back against the headboard, my mind playing and replaying the painful scene between Elvis and his father.

About an hour later I heard a soft knock on the door. I went to the door and whispered, "Who is it?"

"Me. Elvis. Are you decent?"

I opened the door. He smiled tiredly when he saw I was fully dressed.

"Where's Gwen?" he asked softly.

"Asleep, thankfully. Is Slash back?"

"I haven't seen him. Where is he?"

"At the Marriott. He wanted to do some more research on the guy who held us at gunpoint at your house." We didn't have to wonder whether he'd be careful in returning to our location. Slash was a pro.

Elvis nodded and then paused. "You got a few minutes to talk?"

"Of course. Let me get my shoes."

I put on my sandals and locked the door behind me

as we left. The building had a small terrace with a single iron table and four chairs. No one else was around.

We took a seat at the table and I leaned back in the chair. The night was hot, the air scented with the rich, intoxicating aroma of jasmine. The moon shone bright.

I'm not sure how many minutes we sat in silence. It could have been five, it could have been thirty. I had taken off my watch, so I had no idea.

"I hate him," Elvis finally said. "I absolutely, totally hate him." He fell silent for another minute before sighing. "Well, I want to hate him. He deserves it. But somehow I can't. So, who I really hate is myself for that weakness."

There wasn't a question involved, but he paused as if waiting for me to make a comment. This was clearly an emotional statement and since there was no logical way to address this, I said, "You just used *hate* four times in six sentences. I'm sensing a pattern here."

"Of course, there's a pattern. He abandoned us. He left his wife, who was ill with grief, and two teenage boys, who didn't have a clue how to deal with it. How could he do that? How can I not hate him for that?"

The agony in his voice caused a physical reaction to me. He hurt, so I hurt. I spoke gently. "I don't know the answers to those questions, Elvis. I don't even know if there are answers to those questions. Who is Sadie?"

Elvis looked down at his hands. "My sister."

My mouth dropped open. "You have a sister?"

"*Had* a sister. She passed away while we were living in Jordan. That's where Arthur had made his so-called big discovery. The ancient inscriptions in the back of the cave. Sadie was four. She was the sweetest, happiest child. She was special, Lexi. Really special." His voice shook. "She contracted some kind of airborne sickness. It happened so fast. One day she was there and the next day she wasn't. We didn't even have time to take her to the hospital."

My heart twisted at the anguish in his voice. I put a hand on his forearm. "I'm so sorry, Elvis. I had no idea. You never talked about her."

"I should have. That's on me. I dishonor her memory by not talking about her. But it's hard because it still hurts. Even after all these years, it's still an open wound for me, Mom and Xavier. People say time heals wounds, but they are wrong. It doesn't heal at all. You just learn to live with it. When she died, we lost a part of our hearts. Then we lost Mother. And without Mother to hold us together, our family collapsed."

"Your mother…what happened to her?"

"I don't know," Elvis said. "She just…changed. Grief. Loss. Depression. I can't say for sure."

I'm not an overly emotional person, but I had to blink back tears. I couldn't even begin to imagine what the Zimmerman family must have endured. I didn't know what to say, or if I could say anything that would help, so I squeezed his arm to let him know I was listening.

"Yet, here I am in Egypt, having traveled halfway around the world to find him." Elvis rested his chin on his hand and stared at the moon. "He sends one damn letter, without an apology or a care for his family, and I do exactly what he asks. No wonder Xavier is furious at me. Why did I come, Lexi? Nothing has changed. Nothing will ever change."

I finally found my voice. "You're wrong, Elvis. Something did change. *You* changed. You came because you didn't let your father's actions, or inaction, define you. You're a good person, a decent man. Despite your father's dysfunction, you were mature enough to make a decision to help. I know you can argue you came because your father uncovered something that put millions of people in danger. But I also know you well enough to say you also came because Arthur is still your father. And because you knew it was the right thing to do."

Elvis closed his eyes and sat in silence. I leaned over and took his hand, squeezing it, knowing there was nothing more I could say or do that would help.

We sat there in sadness and friendship, connected to each other by nothing more than our hands. At that moment, while I understood life was better lived outside of virtual reality, this was one of those times I longed for the safety and anonymity of that world.

TWENTY-SEVEN

MORNING CAME EARLY. Especially because I'd had a difficult time falling asleep in a strange place, in a strange bed, and without the warmth of Slash's arms. It was funny how accustomed I'd become to sleeping beside him.

A soft knock on the door woke both Gwen and me. When I answered it, Slash was there looking handsome, fresh and completely rested.

"What time is it?" I asked, my eyes barely open.

He stepped inside, giving me a kiss. "Eight o'clock. Did you sleep in your clothes?"

I smoothed my blouse. "I didn't have pajamas and I don't know Gwen well enough to sleep naked. Where did you sleep?"

"Next door with the boys, of course."

"How can you look so good? The beds are lumpy and the shower is more like a trickle of water from a handheld showerhead. I couldn't even brush my teeth."

"I showered and changed clothes at the Marriott before I returned."

"Good thinking. No one followed you back?"

"No." He handed me two laptop bags. "Yours and Gwen's. The front pocket of yours has the SIM cards, your phone charger, a change of clothes and a toothbrush. Gwen's has a change of clothes, too."

I kissed the bag, hugging it to my chest. "Wow. Mr. Laptop. I can't tell you how much I've missed you."

"You're making me jealous," Slash said.

Gwen sat up in bed, raising her arms above her in a big stretch. "Good morning, Slash. Lexi is right. You do look good in the morning."

"Don't give him a big head," I warned.

Slash chuckled. "What happened next door while I was gone? Elvis and his father aren't talking and it's pretty frosty over there."

I rubbed my eyes and sat on the side of the bed. "A family thing. Can we get coffee?"

"At the museum." He motioned to the door. "Come next door when you're ready, okay? Make it quick. We've got a lot to do today."

I nodded. "Okay."

I changed clothes before going to the bathroom, splashing water on my face and brushing my teeth— essentially completing my morning routine. After grabbing my purse and phone charger, I waited for Gwen to get ready before we knocked on the men's door.

To my surprise, Zizi opened the door.

"Hey, Zizi," I said. "What's up?"

She opened the door wider, letting us in. Today she was dressed in a light green skirt, a white blouse and plain white sandals. The green of her skirt matched her eyes and it was a stunning look. And I wasn't even a fashionista. A museum identification card hung around her neck.

"I came by to see if I could help. I've got a light load today at the museum, so I can shift things around as necessary. I thought this is much more important.

Elvis and Slash have already caught me up on what the plan is for today."

"Oh. Okay." Seeing as how I didn't know what the plan was yet, I looked over at Elvis for guidance.

He shrugged. "Well, it looks like we're chariot hunting today. The only questions are who goes, who stays, and how do we ensure we aren't followed back here?"

"I'll be the guide," Zizi said. "I think I know the location of all the chariots currently on display."

"I'll go, too," I volunteered.

Slash looked around the room. "I'd stay with Arthur, but someone has to ensure we get back here without being followed. I'm the best person for that. Elvis, can you and Gwen stay with Arthur?"

Slash's eyes moved to the dresser drawer where Arthur had put the gun. Elvis understood and nodded.

"Great," Gwen said cheerfully. "This will be fun. We can play cards or charades or something to pass the time. I've even got a deck of cards in my purse."

Thank God. I exchanged a small smile with Elvis. He knew, like I did, Gwen would unwittingly serve as a buffer between him and his father. It made me feel better about leaving.

"Can we take pictures in the museum?" Slash asked Zizi.

"Yes, but you have to buy a photography ticket and there's no flash allowed. There's also no photography whatsoever permitted in the mummy room. But that shouldn't be a problem since there are no chariots on display there. Do you have a camera?"

Slash pulled out his phone. "This should do."

I dug mine out and held it up, too. "I got one, too. It needs to be charged, though."

"There are outlets at the museum," Slash said. "Let's go."

We said our goodbyes and were halfway down the corridor when Arthur suddenly stepped into the hallway. "Excuse me. Lexi, can I talk to you privately for a moment?"

I exchanged a puzzled glance with Slash and then nodded. "Sure, I guess."

Zizi and Slash continued down the hallway as I returned to Arthur. "What's up?"

"Are you really Elvis's best friend?"

I wondered why he asked, but I simply said, "Yes."

"He said you saved his life. Is that true?"

"It's true. But Elvis saved mine, too, in more ways than one. Your son is an extraordinary man. So is Xavier. What's this all about?"

"Do you know how to keep a promise?"

I stared at him. I had no idea where he was going with this. "Yes."

"Good. Then if I tell you what you're looking for on that chariot, it stays between you and me until I say otherwise."

"If it's so important, why don't you tell Elvis?"

"He's not going to the museum, is he?"

Guess he had a point.

"On the other hand, I like you," Arthur continued. "You play it straight and you've been a good friend to my son. So, if you want to know what to look for on that chariot, give me your promise."

I sighed. I didn't know whether to humor him or not, but if we could pin down that artifact sooner than later, I'd make that promise.

Still, there had to be limits.

I kept my gaze steady on his. "If there comes a time where I need to divulge information to save a life, I will, whether I give you my promise or not. So, don't tell me unless you can live with that."

Arthur studied me a moment and then put a hand on my shoulder, lowering his voice. "It looks like a pole. It has elaborate markings on it and will be attached to the chariot and the horse's reins. It will differ from the other pole. That's what you're looking for. I found the spores in one end of it."

I digested that for a moment. "That's it?"

"That's it."

Slash stuck his head back in the hallway. "You ready, *cara*?"

Arthur looked at me for a long moment before returning to the room.

I exhaled and walked toward Slash. "Yeah, I'm ready. Let's go."

TWENTY-EIGHT

"How many chariots are there on display at the museum?" I asked Zizi.

She and I sat in the back of the cab. Slash was in the front. I was thinking about what Arthur had told me and trying to take my mind off the fact we'd just missed sideswiping a bus, two bicyclists and a table at an open café. Zizi didn't seem bothered in the slightest by the drive, but I did notice Slash had his hand braced against the dashboard in the front.

She seemed preoccupied and stared out the window. "Hmm? Oh, I'm not sure. Five? Seven? I'll check the online catalog and cross-reference when we get to the museum."

Slash had the driver let us off about a block from the museum. I climbed out and tried to get my feet steady beneath me after the wild ride. Zizi strode quickly toward the museum, so we hurried to keep up.

She stopped us at the entrance. "It will be faster if we split up. Slash, you take the lower level. Lexi, you take the upper floor. I'm going online to see what I can find."

I exchanged a look with Slash who shrugged. Zizi expedited our entrance through security and they let us in without having to pay for a ticket.

"I'm going to get you two photography tickets," she said. "If the guards see you taking pictures, they'll ask for it. Slash, I'll meet you in the east wing in about five minutes. Lexi, I'll find you upstairs."

Slash headed directly toward the east wing while Zizi moved toward the ticket booth.

Left alone, I walked past the giant statues in the atrium and up the stairs to the second floor. This floor held many fascinating exhibits, including King Tut's excavated find. I headed for Gallery A. That's where Zizi found me about five minutes later.

"Here's your ticket," she said, thrusting it into my hand. "Good luck."

"Thanks," I said, but she'd already headed for the stairs.

I returned to scouring the exhibitions. My brain screamed at me to slow down and enjoy the opportunity to see such amazing historical discoveries, but I had to focus on the mission. If I didn't see a chariot, I forced myself to move on.

It took me forty-seven minutes to clear the upstairs, even after giving myself ten minutes to charge my phone. I found only three chariots on display and took multiple pictures of them. As Arthur had suggested, I studied the poles and zoomed in on several of them. Some had markings and some didn't, but since I didn't know what I was looking for, it was hard to tell if I'd found what he wanted or not.

I wandered down to the lower floor and headed toward the west section in search of Slash or Zizi. I found Slash first. He was taking several photos of a chariot. He straightened when he saw me. "Finished?"

"Yeah. I found three. How about you?"

"Three, too, so far. But I just started this room. Want to help?"

"Sure. I'll start at the door and work toward you."

He tipped his head. "Perfect."

A few minutes later I found a chariot on display next to what was identified as a queen chair carrier. I tried to imagine Nefertiti sitting on it while her servants carried her, but all I could picture was Zizi. I stepped sideways to get a better angle and waited until a tourist group of what sounded like French nationals passed before snapping several shots of the chariot.

I was studying the poles the best I could from my position when Slash came up behind me and put a hand on my shoulder. I nearly jumped out of my skin.

"Sorry," he said.

"It's okay. Guess I'm a bit jumpy these days."

"It's understandable. Looks like you found one more."

"I did. Just taking some photos now."

I glanced over and saw Zizi in the doorway. She saw us and strode our way.

"How many did you find?" she asked us.

"I found three upstairs, Slash found three, and then there's this one here," I said. "That makes seven."

Zizi nodded. "Perfect. The catalog states seven chariots. I downloaded the list onto my phone, so we can cross-reference with Arthur. Did you get pictures of all of them?"

We nodded.

"Good." Zizi's face was grim. "Then let's get them back to Arthur right away. We need him to tell us where that artifact is located."

"Everyone has their walking shoes on, right?" Slash asked. "We're not taking a direct route home."

I dug in my purse for suntan lotion and put some

on my face, chest and arms. I didn't have my hat, but such were the state of things. "I'm ready."

Zizi nodded her readiness, too, so we headed out. Slash took us across streets, through alleys and into cafés and out their back doors until even Zizi wasn't sure where we were. My shirt was soaked with sweat and stuck to me in embarrassing places. When I shook my head, droplets of sweat trickled down my temples and nose.

Ugh.

"How do you know how to do this kind of thing?" Zizi asked Slash while we paused in the shade of a building. "Are you in the military or something?"

Slash grinned at her easily, but never stopped looking around. "Nope. Just had too many married girlfriends, I guess."

I rolled my eyes. I don't think Zizi bought it, but there wasn't time for further discussion, not that Slash would have told her anything.

When Slash was convinced we weren't being followed, we headed for the hostel. When we were close, he made us wait about a block away while he reconnoitered the outside to make sure it was clear outside the building.

He returned shortly, assuring us the building wasn't being watched. It felt good to step inside even if it wasn't air-conditioned. At least we were shaded from the sun and that had to count for something. I wiped my sweaty brow as he slid his key into the knob and opened the door.

Gwen sat in a chair in the middle of the room, her arms tied behind her and a gag in her mouth.

TWENTY-NINE

"Gwen!" I started to rush to her when Slash held out an arm stopping me, practically shoving me into Zizi.

"Stay," he ordered tersely.

We both froze. Slash disappeared silently into the room, going in at a crouch and leaving the door ajar behind him. Despite his order to stay, I peeked into the room after him. He didn't have a weapon and I was worried about him.

To my surprise, Slash hadn't gone to Gwen. Instead, he appeared to be checking the closet, and under both beds. He looked over at the door, saw me peeking into the room and rolled his eyes in exasperation. Thankfully, he was too busy to chastise me. He motioned for us to enter.

As we walked in, he knelt next to Gwen.

She was clearly terrified. Her skin was so pale it was nearly translucent. Tears leaked out of her eyes and she was gagged with what looked like duct tape. Slash sliced the cloth ties holding her arms behind her, then gently tugged at a corner of the tape on her mouth.

"I'm going to pull it off quickly." He spoke softly. "I'm sorry. There is no easy way to do this. It's going to hurt, but it will be over fast. Curl your lips inwards as much as you can to protect them. Okay?"

I knelt down next to her and took her hand. "You've got this, Gwen. Be strong? Okay?"

She nodded and then blinked hard a couple of times as if steeling herself. Her freckles stood out on her cheeks and nose. I squeezed her hand as she closed her eyes. In one quick gesture, Slash pulled the tape off her mouth.

She gasped in pain and then threw her arms around Slash's neck, pressing her face in his shoulder.

He held her, patting her back. "It's all done. You did great, Gwen."

She kept her face hidden. "I've never been so scared in all of my life. They took Arthur and Elvis." Her voice was muffled. "They had guns."

"Who had guns, Gwen?" Slash pulled back, holding her shoulders. "Who took them?"

"Three policemen. At least I think they were policemen."

"Why do you think they were policemen?" I asked.

"They were dressed in uniforms. They didn't even ask us who we were or ask to see our passports. They just surprised us, pulled out their guns, grabbed Arthur and Elvis, then tied me up. Elvis tried to protect me, but…" She put her hand against her mouth. "One of them hit him and he went down. They hurt him."

I pressed my lips together and glanced over at the desk. The laptop was gone. "They took Arthur's laptop?"

Gwen nodded. "Yes. And worse, they found the endospores in a vial in Arthur's pocket. They took those, too."

Zizi paled. "So now they have Gwen's sequencing of the plague *and* the endospores?"

"Technically, they don't have the sequencing or her notes," I said. "Not yet anyway. I encrypted the document. Besides, unless Arthur tells them what it is or those guys are microbiologists, they aren't going to figure out it's a plague."

"But what if Arthur talks? What if he does tell them what it is?" Zizi seemed really panicked. I actually understood because I didn't have a lot of faith in Arthur myself. But panic wasn't going to solve anything at this point.

"I don't know, Zizi. Arthur is a dangerous variable, but it's what we have. The first step is to figure out where they are. The fact they took Arthur's laptop is actually a stroke of good luck for us."

"What?" Zizi looked at me in surprise. "How can that possibly be good?"

"I installed a tracking program on Arthur's laptop that uses his GPS card so I could monitor his whereabouts in the future. I didn't actually anticipate this use, but as soon as they connect to a network—any network—I'll be able to pinpoint their location."

"Is that possible?"

"It is." I spread my hands. "A lot is possible with the marvels of technology."

Slash yanked open the dresser drawer and pulled out Arthur's gun. "Lucky for us, they didn't find this. Another break for us and an indication that this was a grab-and-run operation." He tucked it in his waist at the small of his back. "First order of business. I need to know how they found us. Gwen, did either Arthur or Elvis do anything out of the ordinary? Make any calls? Go anywhere?"

"Arthur was hungry. He was complaining so much that Elvis went out for food." Gwen pointed at a wrinkled paper bag and some bottles of water that were on the bed. "Maybe they spotted Elvis and followed him back here. I don't know. They came about thirty minutes after he returned."

Slash shook his head, probably blaming himself for not staying instead of Elvis. But we had needed help getting back undetected from the museum and he couldn't be in two places at one time. I didn't bother trying to make him feel better about it because I knew it wouldn't work.

"Do you still have your laptop in your room, *cara*?" he asked.

"I hope so."

"Mine should be there, too, unless they went in after they tied me up," Gwen added.

Slash held out his hand. "Give me a key and wait here."

I rooted around in my purse and gave him the key. Minutes later he returned with Gwen's and my laptops.

"Break number three," he said. "We're on a roll."

"Let's hope it stays that way," I added.

"Grab your stuff. We're moving back to the Marriott." Slash started gathering items. "They obviously know who we are, so concealing our connection to Arthur is no longer necessary. Besides, it's safer there and we need the Wi-Fi, such as it is. Move out."

Gwen grabbed her purse and laptop bag, slinging them over her shoulder. She looked remarkably stronger than she had just minutes ago. In fact, if I weren't mistaken, I'd almost say she looked angry.

"So, what are we going to do about finding Elvis? They weren't policemen, were they? Real policemen, even in Egypt, wouldn't have tied me up."

"I don't know who they were," Slash answered. "But

I doubt they were policemen. Regardless, I'm sorry, but we can't risk going to the police until we know more. Zizi, it's unfortunate you had to be dragged into this. Are you coming with us?"

"Of course, I am." She moved toward Slash, put a hand on his arm. "What do you need me to do?"

"Once we are live, I'll need you to translate what they are saying."

"Live?" Her expression was puzzled.

"In addition to the tracking program, I also created a backdoor," I explained. "As soon as the guys that stole Arthur's laptop connect to a network, we'll have not only their location, but I should be able to activate the camera and microphone without them knowing. We'll be right there in the room with them."

She looked surprised. "You can do that?"

"I can."

"That's...amazing." She gave me a long look and then nodded.

Slash pulled out Arthur's gun. "I've got to leave this here. I can't take the gun with me to the Marriott. They'd catch it when we went through security. You okay if I keep it in your room?"

"Sure." I handed him my key. "Put it under my mattress."

Slash stowed the gun and we took a cab back to the Marriott. Despite the wild ride, I felt calm, almost as if I were getting used to Cairo driving. Or maybe I was just too worried about Elvis to care. Gwen, too, was unusually quiet.

As soon as we got to our suite at the Marriott, Gwen, Slash and I each set up our respective laptops and waited.

And waited some more.

"What's taking so long?" Zizi asked. She'd been circling the room like a lioness for the past forty minutes.

I scanned my computer. "We can't do anything until they connect to a network."

"What if they don't connect?"

"They will."

I tried to keep the panic out of my voice, but it seeped in anyway. I didn't want to imagine Arthur or Elvis getting tortured or hurt, but it kept playing in my head anyway. Why did Elvis have to be the one getting kidnapped all the time? Was that my fault or his? If I'd stayed behind, I would have been the one to be kidnapped. But no, while I was the trouble magnet, he seemed to attract kidnappers.

A glance at Gwen indicated she wasn't doing so well. Her momentary surge of strength was now being tested by seemingly endless waiting.

She'd left her laptop open on the table and perched on the edge of the couch, pressing her hands together in her lap. She was clearly trying to hold it together, but I doubted she had ever been in a situation like this. The strain was showing. I imagined the same scenarios of torture that were playing through my head were playing through her head, too. Unfortunately, there wasn't much I could do to alleviate that.

Slash's impatience was showing, as well. He drummed his fingers on the table next to the keyboard. Waiting was agony for all of us, even worse than watching the latest Microsoft patches download. I was becoming increasingly terrified that the kidnappers wouldn't connect to a network and we would be helpless.

After ten minutes and no sign of activity, Slash

pushed back from his computer, picked up the hotel phone and ordered two carafes of coffee, a plate of sandwiches and some *basbousa*, which Zizi informed us was an Egyptian pastry. I didn't feel like eating and I'm not sure anyone else did either, but at least it might temporarily break the monotony of waiting.

In twenty minutes the coffee arrived, as did the food.

We all sipped on coffee, mine with a lot of extra cream, but no one touched the food. Not one bite.

Sixty-seven minutes after we'd arrived at the hotel, my laptop dinged.

I rolled the chair over my toe as I pulled it up to the table and my laptop, but the pain barely registered. "Thank God. They finally connected. Let's see where they are."

THIRTY

SLASH LOOMED BEHIND my chair, peering over my shoulder. Gwen and Zizi maneuvered beside him to look at the screen, too. I was absolutely certain they'd have no idea what I was doing.

"What's going on? What do you see? Where are they?" Zizi demanded.

"Give me a freaking minute, people." I pinpointed the network signal and in a separate window pulled up Google Maps. From what I could see the location looked like a tall apartment complex. "Mostafa Ragab. It's a street near Al Qubbaah Palace."

"Where's that?" Gwen sounded excited.

"That's not too far from here," Zizi answered. "Ten, fifteen minutes away."

"So, let's go." Gwen grabbed her purse. "What are we waiting for?"

"Whoa, Madame SWAT Commander." I held up a hand. "First of all, we have one gun and one guy who knows how to use it. Not to mention we have no idea how many of them there are. We aren't even sure Elvis and Arthur are in the same location as the laptop. We need a lot more information before we go anywhere."

"Let us do our work, Gwen," Slash said gently. "I promise you, we'll get them back."

I didn't know how he could make such a promise, but that he did made me love him even more.

Gwen clutched her purse, her hands trembling. "You promise?"

"I do." He turned his attention to my screen and put a hand on my shoulder. "Do we know anything else?"

My fingers flew across the keyboard, my brain processing and compartmentalizing the information as the data flew past. "Yes. You want the good news or bad news?"

"Good first."

"Okay, it appears our kidnappers are not cybersecurity experts. They haven't found any of my security measures yet, haven't bothered to run a single diagnostic, and have no idea that we know their location."

"That *is* good. What's the bad news?"

"They're in the system. They got into it legitimately and went straight for Gwen's document."

"What? How did they get in legitimately?" Zizi said.

Slash and I exchanged a glance. "Arthur," I said.

"Arthur?" Gwen looked at me with stricken eyes. "What does that mean?"

Slash straightened, sighed. "It means Arthur talked. He gave them the password to open the computer."

"Just like that?" Gwen said.

"Just like that."

"We can't blame him." My heart squeezed. "We don't know what's happening over there."

"Do you think they're still a-a-live?" Gwen could barely speak the word, her teeth were chattering so badly.

"Yes." I spoke reassuringly, partly because I was trying to convince myself. "They may be in the computer, but they'll have a harder time getting into the document. I encrypted it. Plus, if they do get in, they'll need Arthur to explain the technical details." I just hoped whoever had kidnapped them was smart enough to know that. I wasn't getting a good feeling about which end of the IQ bell curve these guys might reside on.

"What about Elvis?"

"He'll be okay, too." I didn't add that he would be useful alive as an incentive in case Arthur refused to talk, which is why I suspected they took Elvis in the first place. There was no telling how fast he'd tell them the decryption password to open the document. That being said, I hadn't placed all my eggs in one basket.

"What do we do now?" Zizi asked. She was visibly anxious.

"Let's see what we're up against." I zoomed in through the back door and activated the camera. "Stand by, everyone."

A photo of a dark-haired man sitting in front of the computer suddenly filled my screen. He was leaning close to the keyboard, typing, his dark eyebrows scrunched together tightly.

Zizi gasped.

I looked over my shoulder at her. "Have you ever seen this guy before?"

She peered at the screen, then shook her head. "No. I've never seen him before. But how did you do that? Just bring him up on your screen."

"It's pretty easy, actually." I opened a log of his keystrokes in one corner of my screen and studied it. He was trying to open the document. Thank God, he wasn't having any success. Yet.

"Can he see us?" she asked.

"No. He doesn't even know the camera is on. I prevented the red light on the camera from coming on."

Zizi peered closer. "He's wearing a policeman's shirt, just like Gwen said."

I nodded. "He sure is. Stand by and let me turn the audio on." A few keystrokes later, I heard a voice. I adjusted the volume and we all leaned closer to listen as the guy at the keyboard said something in Arabic.

Zizi leaned even closer. I could smell her perfume and her dark, thick hair spilled onto my keyboard. I carefully pushed it aside and used my keystroke logger to watch what he was doing on the keyboard in real time. He was still trying to open the document. His expression was pissed and he was yelling something to someone behind him. I strained to hear Elvis's or Arthur's voices, but I heard only the tap of his fingers on the keyboard.

"He's mad," Zizi confirmed. "He's said the document won't open."

"Good," I said.

"Can you hear Elvis?" Gwen asked. "Is he there? What about Arthur? Are they hurting them?"

"Sssssssh." Zizi waved her hand at Gwen in annoyance and we all remained quiet.

After a couple of minutes, the guy at the keyboard stood and disappeared from view, so we had a better view of the room. Now I could hear men talking. People were walking back and forth. I couldn't see either Elvis or Arthur so I couldn't confirm if they were there.

After a few minutes had passed, Slash glanced at Zizi. "Can you make out anything they are saying?"

She straightened and pushed her hair off her shoulders, arching her back in an attempt to stretch it. "They are walking around, so I can't hear them clearly. But from what I can hear, they're talking about how to get the document open."

"No sound of Arthur or Elvis?" I asked.

"Sorry. Not yet."

"I've seen three men so far," Slash said.

"Yes," Zizi confirmed. "There are three different voices."

"Wait." I lowered my head closer to the screen. "I hear Elvis now. Oh, thank goodness. He's talking loudly, which means he's probably hoping we've hijacked their computer and is trying to give us some clues to his whereabouts. Since he suspects we might be monitoring them, we need to listen carefully for any clues he may drop."

"He's alive? Oh, that's wonderful." Gwen looked ready to cry, which didn't make sense since I'd just confirmed Elvis was alive, but I didn't have time to ponder that at the moment.

"What about Arthur?" she asked. "Do you hear him, too?"

"I don't hear him yet. Zizi, do you?"

"No. Not yet."

"Well, if Elvis is aware we're listening, he'll be ready," Slash said.

Zizi lifted her head to look at Slash. "Ready for what?"

Slash didn't answer. He was staring intently at the screen as the same guy who'd been there earlier came back into view and sat down. I watched his keystrokes as he started typing. As he was typing, he started talking right into the microphone, so we got clear audio.

After a minute of talking with someone, he fell quiet.

"What just happened?" Slash asked Zizi.

I already knew. The guy had just typed in the password to decrypt the document.

Zizi paled. "Arthur…he told them the password to unlock the document. They…" She paused, pressed her hand against her chest as she listened to a voice holler from the back of the room. "They're now going to upload Gwen's notes on the plague to a website and hope someone can figure out how to create it. They want to broadcast the plague as a jihad on the Western world."

My mouth dropped open. *"What?"*

Before I could say another word, the guy opened the content management system for a website. I scrambled to pull up the website in another window. I angled the computer so Slash could see.

As soon as Slash saw who ran the website, he swore. "This is bad. Really bad. We've got to stop them. We can't let them upload the document contents."

"Don't worry. They can't." I tapped on a few keys and then clarified. "Not yet anyway. I just activated my basic security program I installed with my encryption program. It will prevent them from uploading or downloading anything on that laptop. It also disables the USB ports and blocks the Bluetooth and all the ports used by email protocols. So they can't copy, transfer, mail or broadcast the details of the document to any devices or even to the cloud so long as my program is in place. That means, for the time being, that document is being held hostage on that laptop. Neither Arthur nor Elvis knows anything about this or how to disable it, so we may have a little bit of breathing room. But as I wasn't anticipating this scenario, I used my basic program. It's good enough to hold against a novice or even a power user, but it won't last long if they find someone with legitimate hacking skills."

"That's what they're doing." Zizi turned her green eyes on me. They were filled with concern. "They were arguing with Elvis, but he said he didn't know anything about this and they seem to believe him. So, two of the men are leaving now to bring over a friend who has some skill at hacking into computers and networks."

That was not a good development.

"What's happening with Elvis and his father?" Gwen asked. She had unknowingly crumbled a pastry to bits as she walked around, leaving a trail of little crumbs. "Are they okay?"

Before I could respond, I heard yelling in the background.

"That sounds like Arthur." Slash leaned closer to the screen. The guy at the keyboard stood and disappeared from view again. The shouting stopped, but the guy didn't return.

"Oh. My. God. What just happened?" Gwen asked.

Honestly, I had no idea. I hadn't heard a gunshot or screams of terror, though, so that was something positive.

"Don't we have to do something?" Gwen spoke in a rush, clearly terrified.

I exchanged a glance with Slash. "Yes, we've got to do something. If they're going to get hacker-level help, we're in big trouble. What I planted on the computer isn't going to stop anyone who knows what they're doing. They'll break through it in a matter of hours, maybe sooner, depending on how good they are. If they are any good at all, it won't take them long to find my camera and audio hacks."

"What can we do?" Gwen's voice became shrill. "We don't have weapons. We can't go to the police. How are we supposed to save them?"

Slash stood, his expression grim. "We save them ourselves."

THIRTY-ONE

GWEN LEAPED TO her feet. "Thank God. We're *finally* going to do something. Let's go."

"Whoa," I said. "What are you going to do?"

"Whatever it takes. I'm not totally useless. I have a purple belt in karate, you know."

Despite the gravity of the situation, a smile touched Slash's lips. "I appreciate your offer of backup, Gwen. But I need you monitoring events from the camera right here. If something happens to us, I want you to go to the American Embassy and tell them everything you know, okay?"

"Wait, who is us?" I interrupted.

"You, me…and Zizi." He turned to face her. "If she's willing."

Zizi stood looking at Slash in disbelief. "You can't possibly be serious. You're just going to rush over there and take on a guy with a gun and two hostages with no backup other than two women?"

"*Si.* But we need your help. You're the only one of us who can speak Arabic. If I'm able to capture the guy, I may require your assistance…asking him questions."

"Who *are* you?"

"Just a guy with a desire to help two of my friends. I'm also more than interested in making sure that the specifications for that plague don't get loaded onto a jihadist site. Are you in?"

She hesitated. I could see her weighing her options. Her career, her position at the museum, her future—all of that would be in jeopardy. On the other hand, she knew better than most, better than me, what it would mean to the world if Gwen's notes and structural analysis on the plague were uploaded to the website.

She took a deep breath. "I don't like this, but we've got to get that laptop back. And Arthur is in danger, too. Fine. I'm in."

I felt the knot in my stomach lessen a little.

"Thank you, Zizi." Slash handed me his laptop. "Then let's go. We're operating on borrowed time."

He gave Gwen quick instructions on how to monitor the laptop and made sure his number was programmed into her cell before we left.

As we were leaving, Gwen gave me a hug. To my surprise, I didn't shrink away. One thing I'd learned so far about Gwen during this trip was that she was genuine. A little excitable and impressionable, but—despite the fangirling—she was smart and surprisingly resilient. Seeing as how she'd held up under difficult circumstances, I felt that warranted a hug.

When we got to the front of the hotel, the bellman secured us a cab and we climbed in. We swung by the hostel to pick up the gun and then headed toward the apartment building. I sat in the back with my laptop balanced precariously on my lap. I say precariously because the driver was racing like Dale Earnhardt Jr. on steroids. We were sliding around in the backseat as he swerved and screeched around corners. I inserted a SIM card that gave me Wi-Fi access, and, after some quick maneuvering, I managed to pull up the apartment complex layout. Thank God it was publicly available so I didn't have to spend time on a hack.

The driver let us out about two blocks from the complex. We walked one block and found an outdoor café with an empty table. I sat down and resumed my work on the laptop, while Zizi and Slash watched to keep prying eyes from seeing what I was doing. I quickly reviewed the GPS location data and eyeballed the apartment layout.

"The GPS elevation data is not as accurate as the coordinates, but my guess is that they are on either the second or third floors." I switched windows. "My best guess is the third floor. The coordinates peg the third window from the right. That would be apartment 304. I guess if I'm wrong, we're going to need Zizi to explain to the surprised occupants of 304 that we are looking for a jilted lover."

I returned to the window with the apartment building website. "I think it's a one-bedroom place. The layout is such that you walk right into the main living room. The kitchen is to the right, the bedroom to the left side of the living room. There is one bathroom adjacent to the bedroom."

Slash nodded. "That's all I need. I want you two to follow me, but wait out in the hall. If it sounds like I am in trouble, I'm going to need you to make sounds while you are there, so he thinks I have backup. He might be more susceptible to surrendering without incident if he thinks he's outnumbered. If we can resolve this peacefully, that's the way to go. Okay?"

Zizi looked at Slash, more than a little afraid. "Do I even want to know how you guys know how to do all this?"

"No."

"That's what I thought."

Zizi looked extremely nervous. I was nervous, too, but compared to some of the past situations I'd been in, this wasn't nearly as intimidating.

There was no security on the entrance to the complex, which was a stroke of luck for us. We strolled right in. There were no elevators, so we took the stairs. The third floor hallway was empty as we approached the apartment.

Zizi and I pressed back against the wall as Slash withdrew his gun. He wasn't going to announce his arrival and ruin the element of surprise—he'd go in hard and fast. He nodded at us and paced a step back from the door. Moving forward—by my estimation exactly six inches—he hovered his foot slightly above the floor and then, with an explosive, precise kick just left of the lock, he smashed the door open.

It was perfect technique, which I had come to expect from Slash. Yep, I was lucky to have a guy with perfect technique.

When I snapped out of my reverie, I noticed Slash was gone and there were shouts coming from the apartment. As instructed, Zizi and I started stomping our feet and banging on the wall in the hallway.

There was another shout, a couple of loud crashes, and then silence. It was over in less than thirty seconds.

I peeked around the corner of the door and saw Elvis and Arthur cuffed and gagged in chairs in the living room. They were blessedly alive. Zizi pushed me inside and followed. She closed the door behind her as best she could, given the doorjamb was now broken.

"People are looking out into the hallway," she whispered.

Slash came out of the bedroom, tucking his gun into the back of his pants. I breathed a sigh of relief when I saw him unharmed.

That relief faded when I saw his face was grim. "We've got trouble. The guy took one look at me and hightailed it for the bedroom, locking the door. Before I could break through, he'd gone through the window and down the fire escape. I didn't dare shoot—too many people—and he got away with the laptop."

Slash knelt behind the chairs and cut through the plastic cuffs on Arthur and Elvis with a knife while I removed their cloth gags.

"Look out!" Elvis shouted.

A guy dressed in a policeman's uniform burst into the apartment, his gun out.

Slash angled himself in front of us as the policeman shouted something in Arabic at us. Although we didn't understand the words, we got the message. We straightened slowly, our hands raised.

"Iisqat bunduqia!"

Zizi, who'd been standing behind the door, suddenly appeared behind the guy and poked him in the back with…a cane. He froze, unsure of the threat and most likely surprised the voice was female. Regardless, his eyes remained locked on Slash, the biggest threat in the room. I could almost hear him thinking. He had no idea what she held in her hand, but if he turned to fire at her or take a look, Slash would be on him instantly. It put him in a difficult situation.

"Nnafeal dhlk alan." I had no idea what she was

saying, but Zizi's voice was cold and calm. No doubt about it, the woman had guts.

The policeman came to his decision and dropped the gun. Slash retrieved it, then with one hard movement, chopped at his neck. As the policeman dropped to the floor, I wondered at the science of where to place the blow and how hard to apply force to ensure unconsciousness, but I couldn't let myself dwell on that, seeing as how our current situation was still rather precarious. I also wondered about the advisability of giving him an extra whack with the gun, just to make sure he stayed down.

Slash saw my look. "Don't worry, he'll sleep for a bit."

Zizi, who'd stood frozen as the action unfolded, suddenly dropped the cane and held a hand to her heart. "There. I did my part."

Slash took a few more steps and put a hand on her shoulder. "You did, indeed. Thank you, Zizi. We owe you a great debt." He wedged a chair against the door to hold it shut for the time being so we weren't surprised by anyone else, then turned to face Arthur and Elvis.

Arthur coughed. "For the love of all that's good. Zizi, my dear, you were magnificent. I had no idea you were so capable. All of you. I should have trusted you from the beginning."

"You think?" Elvis glared at his father.

Arthur sighed, rubbing the top of his head. "However, I'm sorry to report that not only do they now have the laptop—they also have the endospores. They found them in my pocket."

Jeez. Things had gone from bad to worse, except at

least we had Arthur and Elvis back and alive. To me that was worth a thousand vials of endospores, even if that was an emotional and not a scientific response.

For a moment, we just stood there, trying to figure things out. The rescue had been successful, but we'd failed to secure the laptop. I wasn't sure what to do next.

Slash glanced at the apartment door. "We've got to get out of here before anyone else returns. Let's go through the window and down the fire escape like he did. It will give us more anonymity than walking out through the hallway."

No one argued. Slash put a hand under Arthur's elbow, helping him out of the chair while I gave Elvis a hand. As we shuffled toward the bedroom, Slash quickly rooted through a couple of backpacks left by the kidnappers, but came up empty.

"No identifying information," he said.

I shrugged, not that I was surprised.

Slash checked that the area was safe before climbing out the window first. One by one, he helped us out. I was the last to climb down. Slash insisted we walk a few blocks before he managed to hail two cabs. I wondered how it was possible that whenever he or Zizi wanted a cab, they had only to lift their hands once and one magically appeared. Whenever I needed a cab, there wasn't one in the same half of the city. In fact, I was pretty sure I couldn't attract one like he did even if I were willing to run naked and shouting through the streets.

Life just wasn't fair.

Slash put Arthur and Zizi in one and climbed in the front. Elvis and I took the second cab.

We were silent during the cab ride. When we finally entered our suite at the Marriott, Gwen rushed to greet us. Well, technically she greeted Elvis. With a squeal, she threw her arms around his neck.

"Oh, thank goodness. You're okay. You're really okay."

He hugged her back. "I'm fine. Just have a bruise on my left cheek and a couple on my ribs where the guys hit me. Not too hard, thankfully. I'm glad you're safe, too. Did they hurt you?"

"No. They just tied me up and left. Slash, Lexi, and Zizi released me."

"You're sure you're okay?"

"I'm fine. Really."

For a moment they stood there, embracing in silence. I looked away. Arthur leaned against the table, looking old and strangely frail. The kidnapping had certainly been an ordeal for him.

I pointed to a chair. "Why don't you sit down, Mr. Zimmerman."

He nodded and sat. Elvis released Gwen and walked over to stand in front his father. For a moment he just stood there in silence. Then he held out a hand.

"Thank you for saving my life."

Arthur looked up. "What?"

"I said thank you. You gave them the password to save me. You didn't have to do that. I didn't expect you to do that."

Arthur studied his son and then took his hand. "You're welcome."

They shook and Elvis turned to face me. "I assume you had a GPS locator on the laptop."

"Yep."

Slash clapped a hand on my shoulder. "She also had the foresight to plant a back door so we could monitor audio and visual."

Elvis looked at me with pride. "Good work, Lexi."

My cheeks may have turned pink. "Aww, it was nothing. Standard operating procedure, that's all. The real question is what do we do now?"

I glanced at the laptop Gwen still had running. "They haven't connected to the network yet. When they do, at least we'll know where they are."

"They'll be better protected this time," Slash said. "And if they get a decent computer guy, the first thing he's going to do is turn off the GPS. So, while we wait for them to reconnect, we've got to focus on finding, or at least confirming, if an antidote even exists. If they release the information on the plague, the antidote will be more important than ever."

"I understand what's at stake here," Gwen said, "but isn't now the time to finally bring in the police? If these guys are impersonating policemen, the real authorities should know."

Slash shook his head. "We can't risk that. They might indeed be policemen and this could even be government-sanctioned. We can't be sure. However, I do agree we'll need the real police's help at some point, but not yet."

"So, what's the plan?" Elvis asked.

"First, I need to contact someone at the…office so they can alert the CDC. I'll use Gwen's name in the correspondence so they know I'm backing this up with at least some expertise. I can't hold off on this any longer. They need to be aware of this potential threat."

"Will the CDC take this threat seriously?" I asked.

"They will if I connect my name to it."

"But they won't have the endospores to test," Gwen said. "How will they prepare themselves?"

"I don't know. But we're giving them a head start anyway. I think we can all agree the threat is real and potentially imminent. The fact that the request for their review comes from me should be enough to get them started."

Slash held out his phone. "Right now we need Arthur to look at the photos of the chariots we took and let us know where the antidote might be located. We don't have any more time for games or secrecy. Which chariot has the artifact with the antidote, Mr. Zimmerman?"

Zizi dug in her bag. "Here's the online list of all the chariots currently on display." She swiped her phone to the document and then handed it to Slash. Something about this moment seemed significant, but I couldn't put my finger on it. Yet.

"Lexi?" Slash said, snapping me out of my thoughts.

I blinked and reached into my purse, pulling out my phone. "I can save us time." I held it up. "I think I've already found it."

THIRTY-TWO

EVERYONE TURNED TO me in surprise except for Arthur. He simply held out a hand for my phone.

"Show me," he commanded.

I opened my phone, pressed my finger to the button and swiped until I found the photo. I magnified it so the part I wanted him to see was clearly visible before handing it over. He took the phone and eagerly examined the photo.

"Yes." His eyes lit up. "This is it. Excellent work, Lexi. I was right to trust you."

Elvis marched over and stood between us. He stood with his hands on his hips, his glasses half-perched on his nose. But his eyes were blazing with anger. "Just what the hell is going on?"

I looked meaningfully at Arthur. "Am I permitted to speak freely?"

Arthur didn't answer. Elvis stared at the both of us, his left eye starting to twitch. That seemed to happen when he was furious. He reached out and snatched my phone from Arthur's hand.

"I asked you a question." His eyes narrowed at his father. "Why does Lexi have to get permission from you to speak freely?"

Arthur sighed and then dipped his head at me. "Fine. Go ahead and tell him."

I steeled myself as I turned to Elvis. "Your father

gave me some information, Elvis, but he made me promise not to share it with anyone. When I went to the museum, he told me to look for a pole with ornate carvings on the chariot. He said that's what I should pay attention to, so that's what I did. All of the chariots I saw had matching poles except for this one. On this particular chariot, one pole was plain and the other pole had a bunch of intricate carvings on it. I only had a partial view of the pole because of the way the chariot is arranged in the exhibit, but this one was different. Really different."

Elvis whirled on his father. "Why didn't you share this with all of us? With me? Why did you swear her to secrecy?"

"Because she was going to the museum and the less people who know the details of my find, the better."

You don't even trust me." Elvis's cheeks were flushed with anger. "I'm your son, dammit."

"I do trust you, Elvis. I sent you and your brother the spores, didn't I?"

Elvis looked at his father in disbelief. "You don't even care that you could have killed us. Did you ever even consider what might have happened if the package had broken open en route?"

"Don't be so dramatic." Arthur waved a hand. "Great science always embodies some risk. It's not like I could get the spores tested locally and have someone ask me where I got it."

Elvis threw up his hands. "Listen to yourself. Your great discovery is basically a new way to kill thousands, perhaps millions, of people. And now it is in the hands of some jihadists who won't have any hesitation to use it."

"You can't blame that on me," Arthur insisted. "You were the ones who led them to me."

"Stop. Please." My head and heart hurt. "We have to figure this out."

Without a word Slash strode across the room and took my phone from Elvis. He examined the picture, magnifying it so he could see the carvings better.

"Are you confirming this is the artifact, Arthur?" Slash's voice was cool. He was pissed, too. Not that I blamed him. Arthur was playing games, moving us around like chess pieces on a board. Slash didn't like it one bit and neither did I.

"Yes. I am confirming that. That pole connected from the base of the chariot to the horse's harness is the artifact from which I extracted the plague endospores."

Slash studied the picture again. After a moment, he raised his eyes and met mine. "It's the chariot from the last exhibit you were examining. The one when we were in the room together. Right?"

I swallowed. I could see it in his eyes. He was hurt, maybe even angry, I hadn't told him what Arthur had revealed to me. That moment in the museum when we were alone would have been the perfect opportunity to bring him up to speed. But I hadn't. Originally I'd gone along with Arthur's insistence on secrecy because we were desperate for information. Perhaps that had been a mistake. It's just that things had moved so quickly after we'd left the museum, I hadn't had time to weigh the consequences of that promise. But I'd given my word to Arthur, so I'd kept it.

The words stuck in my throat, so I just nodded.

Slash turned away from me, but not before I saw the expression on his face. Betrayal and hurt. Arthur had now effectively driven a wedge between all of us. That guy was some piece of work.

Zizi moved next to Slash. There wasn't even a nanoinch between the two of them. "Show me the artifact, Slash."

Slash angled my phone so she could see the photo.

"That's it?" Her eyes were alight with excitement. "That chariot pole? That's where you found the plague endospores, Arthur?"

"Yes." He motioned to my phone. "Take another look, Zizi. Do you see the end of the pole that's connected to the horse's reins? That's where I extracted the spores. The pole is hollow and apparently compartmentalized. The cavity from which I extracted the spores was quite small."

I glanced at Elvis, but he wouldn't meet my eyes. In fact, he'd moved to another part of the suite, as far away from me as possible. He walked back and forth, his hands clasped behind his back. I felt sick. It hadn't occurred to me that Elvis, too, might feel hurt by my promise to his father. But clearly he was.

I pressed a hand to my forehead. This is exactly why I sucked at relationships of all kinds. There were too many hidden variables I didn't know how to calculate in advance, so I couldn't figure out the potential cost or the risk. Things needed to be black and white for me. The gray was a nebulous, scary place.

This situation was getting worse by the minute.

Slash leaned back against the table and crossed his arms across his chest. His demeanor was one of frustration. "Now is the time to tell us everything, Arthur. No more games. Lives are at stake. What exactly do you know about that pole?"

Arthur hesitated, looking around the room at us. Elvis turned around and faced his father, his expression upset and hurt. I had no idea of all the thoughts— good and bad—that were running through his head.

Zizi stood next to Slash waiting for Arthur's answer. They looked good together. Two impossibly beautiful people certain to turn heads wherever they went. She tucked her arm into his, her eyes brimming with excitement. I forced myself to look away.

Arthur sighed. "I guess I have no choice at this point than to tell you." He looked directly at me even though I hadn't been the one to ask the question. "I believe I have found the staff of Moses."

THIRTY-THREE

HOLY BURNING BUSH.

"Moses?" Disbelief coursed through me. "As in the Ten Commandments guy?"

"Yes. That guy. Moses's staff. The Rod of God. Call it whatever you'd like."

"The same staff that parted the Red Sea?" I asked. "Made water from stone? Blood from water? Wood to snake? *That* Rod of God?"

Slash glanced over at me in surprise.

"What?" I lifted my hands. "I've read the Bible."

"The staff, according to Jewish legend, was created at the beginning of the world, on the sixth day," Arthur continued. "It's said the power of the staff is endless. Moses used it when he brought the plagues on Egypt to force the pharaoh to let the Jewish people leave their bondage in Egypt. Later it was used by Moses to work more miracles and even smite the armies of the enemies of the Jews. It's not clear, but some biblical scholars believe after Moses died, his brother Aaron took possession of the staff. Aaron then left the staff to the family of David, who supposedly carried it with him along with his sling when he slew Goliath."

I was having a hard time wrapping my head around this one. "Okay, is it just me or is this mindboggling stuff?"

"Totally mindboggling," Gwen agreed. Her blue eyes were wide.

"In fact, it could be the most significant find of the past thousand years." Arthur sat back in his chair. "Add to that, the staff may have powers we can't even comprehend. Now I hope you understand why I've been so secretive."

"Are we talking Ark of the Covenant powers or something else?" Gwen asked.

"I have no idea. But one thing I'm sure of—this find is extraordinary. You can understand why I've been reluctant to bring others in."

"I don't understand why the Rod of God would be on an Egyptian chariot," Elvis said. "Explain that to me."

"Well, David supposedly left the staff to his descendants, who used it as a holy scepter in the temple until the Pharaoh Shishak captured and pillaged Jerusalem, as well as looted the temple in 925 BC. As an insult to the Jews, the pharaoh purportedly took it back to Egypt and used the staff as an ordinary part of the royal chariot."

"Why didn't he just destroy it?" I asked. "Wouldn't that have been a bigger insult?"

"Do you think they didn't try? Legend says those in the pharaoh's employ who tried to break or destroy it failed and then died horrible deaths. Apparently the rod is indestructible. It's an instrument of God, after all."

Guess he had a point.

"How did you find it?" Slash asked.

"Thirteen years ago I uncovered a series of ancient inscriptions in a cave in Jordan. After the destruction of Jerusalem, many Jews fled the city and hid in caves in nearby regions. Inside the caves, they inscribed specific details to the sacking of the city. Once I translated them, the inscriptions led me to a particular stone tablet that had been important in the temple. I tracked that tablet to the British Museum. Together, those two historical accounts enabled me to piece together a story. It told of an important Jewish relic that the pharaoh placed on the royal chariot after all attempts to destroy it had failed. He brought it back to Egypt. The stone didn't describe the artifact or its size. So, archeologists assumed that meant they carried it back to Egypt on the chariot. I believed that was an incorrect interpretation because they didn't understand the artifact."

"But you did?" Slash asked.

"Yes. As a result of the inscriptions from the cave, I had a leap of insight. I decided to take the translation literally and assumed that it was actually attached to the pharaoh's chariot. I began examining all royal chariots I could find. You can't imagine my excitement when I found a chariot awaiting display with unmatched draft poles." His voice rose with excitement. "When I found the chariot and examined the rod closely, I noticed there was ancient Hebrew writing on it. That alone was odd on an Egyptian chariot. Then, one phrase carved on the staff convinced me the artifact was indeed Moses's staff."

"What was the phrase?" Elvis asked.

"Roughly translated from Hebrew it is 'I am that I am.'"

Slash looked surprised. "Exodus 3:14."

Arthur turned to Slash. "Yes. The full passage reads: 'And God said unto Moses, I am that I am.'

Then God added, 'This is what you are to say to the Israelites: I am has sent me to you.'"

The expression on Slash's face was thoughtful. For me, it was all a lot to take in. Personally, I wasn't sure *what* to think. This was so far out of my realm of expertise I was struggling to keep up.

"So, you're saying Moses's staff has been on an Egyptian royal chariot for all these years?" Elvis said.

"That's what I'm saying." Arthur shifted in his chair. "Given a relatively ordinary appearance and unexpected location, it has remained hidden in plain sight all this time."

"So, where do the spores come in?" Gwen asked.

"Do you remember the plagues that Moses brought down upon Egypt to convince the pharaoh to let his people go?"

"Yes," said Gwen. "There were six or seven of them."

"Ten," Slash said quietly.

"Correct." Arthur rubbed the back of his neck. "The last and the greatest of the plagues suddenly killed all of the firstborn of Egypt. It was so horrible and devastating the pharaoh relented and let the Jewish people leave."

The scenario Arthur was portraying was really starting to convince me that there are some things better left buried in the sand.

"Do you believe the spores were the source of the final plague?" I kind of wished he'd get to the point. I worried we'd have to sit through a two-hour history lesson before he explained the bottom line. Not that I didn't like history—I did. But now wasn't the time for that.

"I certainly wasn't looking for a plague," he said. "In fact, I had to disguise my interest in the staff and could only view the chariot in short intervals. But I was able to take a picture of the bottom of the staff where there were more ancient Hebrew symbols. It took some time to decipher them, but they roughly translated to 'home of the death seeds.'"

"Death seeds?" Gwen repeated.

"I puzzled for a long time as to what that meant," Arthur said. "Underneath those symbols was a line that went around the staff and more symbols that said 'death moves as the sun.' I first assumed it to be a reference to the angel coming in the night and slaying the first-born of Egypt. But it didn't make sense. I think it would have been more appropriate to say the moon instead of the sun. But then, I had an *aha* moment and twisted the bottom of the staff in the same direction as the sun and it moved and eventually came off. Inside I found a small clay tube with what turned out to be the spores."

"There were spores inside the tube?" I asked.

"Yes, but I didn't open the tube there. I slipped it in my pocket and brought it home to study. The death seeds and plague references had me scared a bit. So, I asked for Zizi's help. She suited up with a respirator, gloves and disposable gown and opened the vial. She separated a few samples of spores for me. I later sent those spores to the boys to figure out what they were. And here you are."

"Here we are." Elvis's voice was void of emotion. "Amazingly enough alive, considering you *knew* the spores might contain dangerous death seeds and still you sent them in the mail to me and Xavier without proper safety protocols or warning."

"We've been over this." Arthur sighed. "I was careful how I mailed it. The vial didn't break, did it? Besides, I knew you and your brother were smart enough to decode my note before examining the spores."

Elvis looked like he might argue, but then he just shut his mouth, realizing debating the issue was futile at this point.

"The bottom line is, my research led me to the staff. I followed every clue and found it. This will go down as one of the greatest archeological finds of all time."

I didn't necessarily agree with that, especially if his discovery released a plague on the world, but I had already made enough people mad at me for one day, so I kept my mouth shut.

"Arthur, what else can you tell us about the properties of the staff?"

Arthur took a deep breath before picking up his water bottle and taking a swig. "I think it holds a possible antidote also hidden within the rod at the top end. There's a rounded knob there with markings that translate in ancient Hebrew that read 'life from death.' The knob spins but won't come off. There are four rotating sections underneath the knob with special markings. The sections have hieroglyphics of the pyramids and some dots. I believe it's an ancient puzzle or code."

"Why do you think there's an antidote?" Gwen asked. "Given its age and apparent lethality, how would Moses have known about an antidote? I would think back then they barely understood the idea of poison. For that matter, how did Moses know how to use the bacteria to kill the Egyptians and not the Jews?"

"God told him?" Slash suggested softly.

Hard to find a way to argue with that.

Arthur smiled at both Gwen and Slash, as if they were his best students. "Well, Exodus 12:8 speaks of Moses insisting that the Jews that night eat their dinner with *bitter herbs*. He said *all* must eat the herbs. Then, that night, the death came and passed over all those who ate the herbs. I believe there was some property in those bitter herbs that protected against the bacteria and acted as a natural antibiotic against the spores. We just have to get our hands on the staff and figure out the combination to open the other end. Then we can analyze the antidote and broadcast it to counter the plague. It's really quite simple."

"That's simple?" I asked.

"Of course. If you only knew what I've already done to get to this point, you'd understand."

I rolled my neck, trying to work out the tension. I was wound tighter than a hacker one keystroke away from a crack into the CIA. "What if there isn't an antidote?"

"There is. There *has* to be."

"Why didn't you tell Haji any of this?" Zizi asked. "The museum would have helped you."

"Maybe. Maybe not." Arthur held up his hands. "Besides, I wasn't sure what I'd found at first. Haji could have taken the staff and the endospores, pretending it was *his* find. It would have been his word against mine. Who do you think people would believe? The Director of Museum Research at the Egyptian Museum or me—a nobody?"

"You're hardly a nobody, Arthur." Zizi dropped into

a chair and crossed her long legs. "You're an Oxford professor."

"Who has spent his life in pursuit of this artifact. You think I'd turn it over just like that? When I am so close?"

Gwen had moved to her laptop and held up her hand like a student. "Um, excuse me, Mr. Zimmerman. Supposedly the staff of Moses has already been found. It's in Topkapi Palace in Turkey. Pictures from the museum make it look like it's a wand, versus a staff."

"That's not Moses's staff," Arthur said firmly. "I've examined it myself."

"Agreed," Slash said.

It surprised me how quickly and assuredly Slash spoke. Then I remembered the little gold cross he always wore under his shirt. He'd worked at the Vatican and probably had as much access to religious secrets as the Pope. Maybe he knew something we didn't. I waited, but whatever it was, if anything, he wasn't sharing.

Slash pushed off the desk. The movement caused Zizi to drop her hand from his arm. I sighed an inward breath of relief.

He walked to the window, leaning a muscled forearm against the pane and stared out. "So, now we know exactly where the staff is…what's next?"

Zizi shifted on her feet. "We have to get the staff into safe hands. It's imperative."

"Exactly whose hands are those?" I asked.

"The museum, of course. The staff belongs to them."

"The staff was stolen thousands of years ago from

Jerusalem," I said. "How does that make it the property of the Egyptian government?"

Zizi narrowed her eyes at me. Wow, if she could have stabbed me with that look, I would have been toast. Great. Now I'd pissed her off, too. I was batting a thousand today in terms of wrecking relationships.

"Moses was an Egyptian," she said coolly.

"Not originally. He was born Hebrew and adopted by the Pharaoh's daughter," Gwen spoke up. "Besides, he was exiled by the time he received the staff from God, which means technically he was no longer an Egyptian."

I almost smiled, but out of respect for Zizi, didn't. Still, the fact that Gwen was the only one in the room coming to my defense didn't escape my notice.

"Ladies, let's not argue," Arthur said. "We have to work together on this. I found the staff. It's my decision to whom we turn this over. But we have to be careful. This is far more dangerous than I realized."

"What do you mean it's your decision?" Zizi strode in front of Arthur. "What's to stop me from telling Haji where the staff is?"

"The endospores." Slash spoke quietly, still facing the window. "You're a microbiologist, Zizi. You understand what's at stake. Those men have the endospores and they're going to upload Gwen's structural analysis and notes on how to create this plague to a jihadist website. I can't speak to your personal beliefs, but that plague isn't going to ask about religion before it kills. If that staff has an antidote, it's imperative we get it. Ownership of the staff and who gets credit for the find is secondary to that. Otherwise, thousands, maybe even millions, of innocent people are going to die."

Zizi let out a deep breath, pressed her fingertips to her temples. "Fine. You're right."

Elvis exhaled heavily. "Okay, while that's not even close to settled, the next question is—how do we get our hands on the staff?"

"Zizi, is there any way you can get it?" Slash asked.

"No. Only certain museum officials are permitted to touch the exhibits. I'm not one of them."

"We don't have time to request permission either," Elvis said.

"No we don't." Slash shoved his fingers in his hair. "But we have to examine it. We must. We have to determine if there's actually an antidote. Divinely made or not, one thing is certain—no living soul should ever be harmed by this plague again."

Zizi picked up her purse, a tired expression on her face. "Despite my reservations in regards to ownership of the staff, I agree with Slash. Still, it's getting late. I must go check in with my family. They'll be worried about me. I need time to rest and think. I'll come back later."

I was certain Slash would protest her departure. At this juncture she knew too much and could completely jeopardize the situation if she decided to spill our find to the police, the museum, or any one of a dozen people.

Instead he turned away from the window. "Good idea. I'll walk you home."

My mouth dropped open. Gwen and Elvis looked surprised, as well. Only Arthur sat quietly, most likely thinking of his monumental discovery and how to secure the glory for himself.

I watched as Slash strode to the door and opened it

for Zizi. She went out and Slash followed her, the door closing behind them. Neither looked back.

I felt strangely close to tears. Blinking hard, I stood and sat down in front of my computer. There was no movement on any front. No signal from Arthur's laptop. Nothing appearing on the jihadist website.

Nada.

Gwen came up behind me and handed me a water bottle. "Here, Lexi," she said. "You should stay hydrated."

I took the water and unscrewed the top. "Thanks, Gwen."

"Sure. No problem."

She sat down at her computer and Elvis came and sat at his. We stared glumly at the screens.

Arthur stood up, apparently hoping to energize us. "Why are you just sitting around your computers? We have to go get that staff."

"We're trying to figure out how to do just that," I said, more than a little annoyed. "If you have any ideas, I'm open to hearing them."

Apparently he didn't have any because he picked up the remote control and turned on the television and started watching.

About forty minutes later, Slash returned to the suite. He was alone.

His eyes met mine across the room as he entered, a slight smile touching his lips. I watched him warily, wondering what had put him in a good mood. I hoped it hadn't been a passionate kiss from Zizi or something.

Elvis stood up. "Slash, are you sure you did the right thing leaving her? What if she goes to the police?"

"She might. But we can't keep her against her will. And I don't think she will go to the police, because we aren't completely sure those jihadists weren't really policemen who have a side business. Besides, we need to retrieve the staff without her."

"We do? How are we going to do that?" I asked.

He reached into his jeans pocket and pulled out a plastic card, the size of a credit card. He held it between two fingers. "With this."

I squinted. "What is it?"

"Zizi's key card to the museum."

"She gave you her key card?" My eyes widened in surprise.

"No. I lifted it from her."

I hate to admit the first thing that crossed my mind was a mental calculation of how close he had to be to standing next to her to steal the card or how he might have distracted her.

Gwen looked shocked. "You…stole it? But, she's on our side."

"She's also a museum employee and an Egyptian citizen. We have to do this without her. I'm afraid we're out of options."

It sounded more like he was protecting her. "Isn't she coming back later?" I asked. "How will we keep this from her?"

"I told her not to return until the morning and we needed time to think things through."

Arthur clicked off the television, his full attention now on Slash. Gwen stood next to Elvis, slipping her hand into his. He seemed to stand taller when he was next to her.

I studied Slash's face. "So, what does that mean?"

He turned his gaze on me. "It means I steal the staff. Tonight."

THIRTY-FOUR

EVERYONE STARTED TALKING at once.

"What?"

"Are you crazy?"

"Steal it from the museum?"

"What if you get caught?"

Slash held up a hand, quieting us and our questions. "Listen, if we do this right, we won't get caught."

"What if we do it wrong?" Gwen asked.

"That option is not on the table," Slash said.

"I think *all* scenarios should be on the table," Gwen said. "We're talking about stealing a priceless artifact from one of the world's most well-known museums. Moses's staff, for heaven's sake. What if we get caught? I don't want to live out the rest of my life in an Egyptian prison."

"Give Slash a chance to explain," I said. "I think we all should sit down."

Those of us who weren't seated found a place to sit, but Slash remained standing. It was a position of power, a position of leadership.

Right now, that's what we needed.

"Okay, let's put all of our options on the table," Slash said.

"Maybe it's time to risk going to the police," Elvis said quietly. "This is getting too dangerous."

Slash shook his head. "We can't do that, Elvis. What

if those guys who kidnapped you really *are* police-men? What if the government or some people in the government are supporting this? They might even be in on the jihadist plot. Worse, if they discover there is an antidote in the staff, they may try to destroy it."

"Well, according to the legend, the staff would take care of that problem," Gwen pointed out. "Curse, re-member?"

She had a point, but we had to deal in facts, not curses. "What about Haji Saraf?" I suggested. "If we explain everything to him, maybe he'll see our side."

"He'd be obligated to contact the authorities," Slash said. "That would bring in the police and the govern-ment, and we're back to a worst-case scenario."

"What about the Egyptian government?" Elvis said. "Can't we have our government talk to their govern-ment?"

"In theory it's a good idea, but you know better than most that governments move with the speed of a gla-cier. We are running out of time. If the jihadists upload Gwen's data, the antidote becomes vital. These are my thoughts. First of all, we need someone to keep moni-toring the laptop whereabouts," Slash said. "We have to get that laptop back. But equally as important, we must verify if there is a viable antidote. There's only one way to do that. We have to let Arthur examine the staff and see if we can find that antidote."

Arthur nodded vigorously. "Finally. I've been say-ing that all along."

Elvis looked at his dad and sighed. Exhaustion and exasperation were etched on his face. Probably on all of our faces. "While that may be true, Slash, we can't just walk in to the museum and waltz out with the staff. How do we do this?"

"We use our brains." Slash walked about the room while he spoke, which meant he was thinking on his feet. "The museum security is antiquated. They are using an electronic security card swipe as access control. No biometric systems to defeat."

"Which is why you stole the card," I said.

"It will help. But there are guards and alarms and a variety of other more complicated problems even if we were able to get in using Zizi's card. Despite their shoddy ingress security, they do have cameras in every exhibition room of the museum based on our recon of the museum. There are also physical alarms to contend with, except they are present on only a few of the exhibits, none of which concern us. Getting in electronically and shutting down the power, alarms, and cameras remotely will be the easy part. As the museum is old, they make up for their lack of sophisticated security with security guards. Guards are much more unpredictable and dangerous to our success. But since we only need one thing and it is not in the highest security area, we should be able to get in and get out without detection if we do this right."

He made it sound easy, but I knew it wasn't.

"What are you thinking, Slash?" I asked.

"I'm thinking I slip in, after hours, using Zizi's card. You or Elvis hack into their access control system and wipe it clean once I'm in so no one knows her card was used. I enter through the administrative offices and then I watch the museum areas for a bit to determine the location and rotation of the guards before I move. You can help me by monitoring the guards through the cameras once we take control of them. Elvis takes down the cameras as I go through the rooms, maybe even before, filling in a static scene so all looks quiet to any guard who is monitoring it. I take the staff and go out a side entrance. If I run into trouble, someone takes down the electricity or sets off a fire alarm. I'll handle the rest. The downside is we will be blind to the guards in any area once we take that camera down, so we will have to be on our toes anticipating their movements."

"There's a problem with that approach," I pointed out. "That chariot is heavy and the staff is facing the back wall of the exhibit. Since the rod is likely attached to the chariot in the same way it's attached to the harness, it means you'll have to get behind it in order to cut through the binding. Bottom line—you're going to have to move the chariot in order to get the staff out in one piece."

"She's right," Arthur said. "It can't be done by one man. By chariot standards, the Egyptian design is light, but it is too heavy and awkward for one person to move. Especially if you have to do so stealthily. To move it quietly, you'll probably need three people and that's simply to move it enough to slip between the wall and the chariot."

"That's unacceptable," Slash said.

I went to my purse and retrieved my phone, swiping until I found the photo. I handed it to Slash. "Here, take a better look at how the chariot is arranged."

As Slash studied it, Elvis came to look over his shoulder. "They're right, Slash. You're going to need help to move it."

"I'm going in with him," I said.

"No." Slash's voice was firm, harsh. "You are not."

"I agree. She's not." Elvis stepped up next to Slash. "I will. I got everyone into this mess. I will see it through myself. Lexi will handle the computer."

"Whoa." I held up a hand. "Despite this amazing show of testosterone, I intend to be the voice of reason. Despite your noble intentions, Elvis, your desire to go is totally illogical."

"It is not." Elvis narrowed his eyes at me.

"It is," I insisted. "I'm not nearly as good as you with cracking security cameras and systems and you know it. Look how seamlessly you did it when we were trapped in the high school. If we want this to go off without a hitch, we need the *best* people in the *right* places. That means *I* go with Slash and *you* keep your hands on the keyboard where they need to be. I'm strong enough to help him lift the chariot."

"I could go," Arthur said.

"No!" Elvis, Slash, and I yelled at the same time.

Elvis took a breath and clarified. "We need to get in and out fast, Arthur. You don't have any experience with this kind of thing."

"And you do?"

"Actually, I do."

Gwen lifted her head and crossed her arms against her chest. "Okay, no one has addressed the elephant in the room. Even if Lexi and Slash were able to move the chariot a foot—which is doubtful they can do that alone—neither of them would be small enough to slip behind the chariot and free the staff. I'm the best choice for that. So, the job of releasing the staff from the harness is mine."

Elvis looked at her aghast. His face paled. "Oh, hell no."

Gwen gave him a fierce stare. "Elvis Zimmerman, this is not your decision. Lexi is right. That's just the testosterone speaking. I can do this. I may be small, but I'm also strong. I can bench-press eighty pounds at the gym. That may not seem a lot to you, but it's not bad for someone my size."

I didn't even know *how* to bench-press any amount, so it seemed pretty darn impressive to me. Still Elvis was glaring at me like somehow it was my fault I'd inspired her to risk her life.

I sighed. "Elvis is right to be worried. It's going to be dangerous, Gwen. Really dangerous. We could get hurt, arrested, even killed. Any number of bad outcomes could occur."

"I'm not going to sit on the couch and do nothing," she said. "You need me, so I'm in. End of discussion."

Slash handed me my phone back and then turned away, rubbing the back of his neck. "There has to be another way."

I wished there was. I truly did. There wasn't one iota of me that wanted to carry out a heist from the Egyptian Museum, but sometimes—okay, maybe a lot of times—we had to do what was necessary in order to save the world.

Again.

"There is no time for another way, Slash." I spoke quietly. "If we had more time to plan, we might be able to come up with a better solution. But if you want to do this tonight—and I fully agree we *must* do it tonight—this is the way it has to be. We all have to pitch in and play to our strengths."

Slash sighed, glanced over at my laptop where the signal remained silent. "They haven't connected to the network yet?"

I shook my head. "No. Not even to fire it up enough to disable the GPS, if they even know that's how we found them."

"And no sign of the plague being uploaded to the extremist's website?"

"Not yet. But if they get help—which we have to assume that's what they're trying to do right now—I'd give us less than twelve hours before it's cracked and that's probably a generous estimation."

He let out a heavy breath and then nodded. "As much as I don't want any of you involved in this kind of danger, we do need each other to do this right. Please take a minute to consider this fully. If you back out now, we can adjust the plan accordingly. You are in no way obligated to do this."

For a moment we just looked around the room at each other, taking the time to acknowledge the danger and difficulty of what we were going to do. What we *had* to do.

Rob one of the most well-known museums in the world.

THIRTY-FIVE

GWEN STEPPED FORWARD FIRST. "Well, just so we're all clear, I'm not backing out." She put her hands on her hips, her eyes flashing. "I say, let's do this."

I decided at that moment I had to stop underestimating her. This fearless, redheaded General Patton was pretty impressive. In fact, I thought she might possibly have more audacity than the rest of us put together.

"That's pretty brave of you, Gwen," I said and looked at Slash. "I'm in, too."

"Me, as well," Elvis added. "The Four Musketeers."

Arthur watched us quietly and finally spoke up. "I will do what I can for my part to assist. Please assign me accordingly."

Gwen blew out a breath. "Well, that was intense. I want you to know that even though I'm still committed to going, I'm so scared I may pee in my pants."

I rolled my eyes. "Okay, Slash, now we're all on board, what's next?"

Slash sat down at the table, chin in his hand. We waited, letting him sort it out. *Needing* him to sort it out.

Finally, he leaned forward, his brown eyes thoughtful. "Let's aim for a one thirty break-in. Before that we've got work to do. Elvis, you need to take a closer look at the museum's security system. Get in, figure out how everything works, determine the level of effort we need. See what you have to do to adjust the security cameras, disable any alarms and wipe the entrance log so Zizi's card can't be identified."

Elvis nodded and sat down in front of his laptop and started to type.

Slash glanced at Gwen. "You—little weight lifter—are responsible for watching to see if those guys with Arthur's laptop connect to a network again."

"Got it," she said.

He looked at me. "I'll need the last laptop to do my work, so see if you can use your phone to do some research and pull up any useful information or background on the chariot. Arthur, I want you to work with her to fill in any blanks. I want to know everything there is to know about it, and the staff, that you haven't already told us. After that I'll need to ask you some questions about the interior of the museum."

"Of course, I will assist in any way I can."

"What are you going to do, Slash?" Elvis asked from behind his laptop.

"First, I'm going to pull up the layout of the museum, the location of the exhibit, and figure out an ingress and egress strategy."

I started to move to the couch with my phone when Slash reached out and grabbed my hand. "But first, may I speak with you in private?"

I looked around the room but everyone seemed unusually busy except for Arthur, who was watching us with interest.

I tried to act casual even though my heart had kicked up a notch. "Sure."

Still holding my hand, he tugged me into our bedroom, clicked on the light and kicked the door shut behind him. I wasn't sure what he was going to say, but I wanted to be on equal footing to hear it, so I didn't sit. Instead I untangled my hand from his and leaned against the wall, crossing my arms against my chest. It was a defensive posture. My heart was pounding so hard, it felt better to be holding my arms against my chest. My throat was dry and tight.

Was he going to break up with me? Had he realized he was in love with Zizi? What guy wouldn't be in love with a woman that practically oozed gorgeousness and sexuality? Especially if she were interested in him, which it seemed abundantly clear to me that she was. How could he resist that?

Okay, now I wasn't breathing.

Slash paused for a moment with his back to the door. After a moment, he strode across the room, pulling me into his arms. He rested his chin on the top of my head and held me in silence.

I stiffened, confused by his actions. Was he trying to comfort me before he dumped me? Was this how couples broke up? It wasn't like I knew since Slash was my first and only boyfriend.

He stroked his hand down my hair. "I don't like being at odds with you."

I didn't say anything. I didn't know *what* to say. This was all new territory for me. Hurt. Jealousy. Fear. Not to mention, feelings of relationship inadequacy and insecurity.

I inhaled a deep breath, summoned my courage. "I'm sorry I hurt your feelings, Slash. I tried to do the right thing. I gave Arthur my word I wouldn't tell anyone."

"It's okay." He pulled back, held my cheeks between

his warm hands. "I understand and respect the fact that you held yourself to your promise."

His answer surprised me. Of all the things I'd mentally cataloged as a possible response, that hadn't been among them. "You understand?"

"I do. When you say something, you mean it, *cara*. You stand behind your word. It's your promise. That's a rare commodity in a world where people will say or do anything to get ahead…or get what they want, regardless of the cost."

"You're not mad at me?"

"Hurt a bit, perhaps. Regardless of your honorable intent, you purposefully excluded me. That stings. But on greater reflection, I understand why you did it. Arthur's motives, however, are another story. He's been manipulating us from the moment he met us. I'm pretty sure I know his endgame. Still, for now we're stuck in his game. We have to let it play out the way he thinks it should. But that doesn't mean I don't have a few surprises of my own planned."

I felt the squeeze of my heart ease a bit and I closed my eyes. "I'm glad you're not angry. It was never my intention."

He kissed my forehead. "I know. We'll get through this, okay?"

We stayed there in that position, his lips pressed against my forehead. I could have ended the discussion there, but something still bothered me. I wavered between indecision to bring it up and a need to know. Finally, I decided I didn't want to leave it inside me to fester.

I opened my eyes, looked directly at him. "Do you think Zizi is pretty?"

He blinked in surprise, his expression suddenly guarded. Apparently he hadn't seen that one coming. "Why are you asking me that question?"

"Why are you avoiding the question?"

"I'm not avoiding it. I'm trying to figure out what motivated it."

I studied his face. I'd clearly caught him off guard. I wasn't sure if that was a good thing or not. "It's just a simple question, Slash."

He fell silent, thinking. I could imagine him weighing potential answers and discarding them until he found the one he wanted. Finally, he exhaled. "*Si*, Zizi is a beautiful woman. I also find the sunset beautiful, as well as the moon on the ocean and a mother cradling an infant."

"That's not what I meant."

"Then it wasn't just a simple question."

It was my turn to fall silent, thinking.

Slash slid a finger under my chin, tipping my head up to look at him. "Why are you asking me that, *cara*? Really?"

"No reason. Never mind."

"You're not the kind of woman who asks a question for no reason."

I still didn't say anything.

"If I didn't know you better, I'd think you were jealous."

"Me? Don't be ridiculous." Unfortunately, I said *ridiculous* with a bit too much emphasis. My cheeks got hot. "Okay. Maybe a little."

My answer seemed to both amuse and baffle him. "Why? There's no logic, not to mention basis, for thinking that."

"Why not? You two look perfect together."

"What?" Startled, he took a step back. "You think… Zizi and…me?"

"Why shouldn't I? You guys are both gorgeous, poised and smart. Besides, she…likes you. I can tell."

He lifted an eyebrow, but his expression was pained. "You can tell?"

My cheeks got hotter. I was handling this all wrong, but I had no frame of reference, no experience with jealousy. All I knew was that I didn't like how it made me feel—irrational and upset. "Yes. She's always looking at you in that womanly way. Fluttering her lashes and crossing her legs whenever you are looking at her. She also likes to touch you. Little touches. Your arm, your shoulder, your leg. I think she wants you to notice her."

He sighed and put his hands on my shoulders. "I'm not interested in Zizi. Not in that way. You don't have to worry about me leaving you for her or for anyone else, *cara*. That's my promise to you."

I swallowed hard. For some reason, I felt close to tears. I couldn't remember ever feeling so emotional and vulnerable. Was love really this hard? I tried to get a grip on my feelings, but it wasn't easy. "I suppose this is what happens when logic is overtaken by emotion. I'm not confident in my role as a girlfriend yet, let alone future roommate. It's hard for me not to let my insecurities get the best of me."

Slash brushed his knuckles across my cheek, let his fingers slip into my hair, pulling me close. "You don't have to explain. I understand jealousy all too well. I've felt it myself with you."

"You have?" I stared at him in surprise. "With me? How is that possible?"

"You have no idea how special you are to me and to others. I'm still in a learning curve regarding our relationship. This is new for me, too. I'm used to being in control, *needing* to be in control. Perhaps that's been ingrained in me from a time when I felt helpless. Yet I have to share that control with you to make this relationship work. I'm still a work in progress on that front. But there's one thing I'm sure of. Jealousy is an ugly path. I don't want either of us to go down it. I trust you and I hope you'll trust me."

"I do, Slash. It's just…an adjustment."

"We're going to have to sort through a lot of adjustments in the coming months. But it'll be worth it because we're building from the ground up. I love you, *cara*. We'll get through this, because it's important. *We're* important."

My heart filled as he tucked a strand of loose hair behind my ear. "And, just so we're clear, I'd take one of you over a thousand Zizis."

"Really?"

"Really." He curled his arm around my waist, pulling me against him. "Despite that cute little mole next to her mouth."

I hit him on the arm. "Hey!"

He laughed. "I'm just kidding. I can barely handle you, let alone another woman. Besides, there will only *ever* be one girl for me, thank God."

He slid a warm hand down my arm, resting it in the small of my back. A firm press and I was against him. Keeping his eyes open, he bent down to press his lips against mine.

Although he'd kissed me a hundred times, somehow this kiss was different. He sighed in pleasure against my mouth, as if this was the one place for him where the world was right. I understood that, because lately I felt the same way, too. "You opened a future I never saw for myself," he murmured. "For that, I thank you."

I pressed my face to his chest and wished we could stay like this forever. But we couldn't. Because now, we had work to do.

THIRTY-SIX

WE WERE JUST into an hour of planning our heist when trouble hit.

"It's official. I'm not going to be able to do this on my own." Elvis looked up from the notes he was jotting on hotel stationery. We were all working hard, making notes, comparing ideas and making suggestions.

Slash strode over to his side. "What's wrong?"

Elvis tapped his screen. "There's no way for me to jump back and forth between the security grid, the electrical grid and the key card access. Nothing is integrated. When things get moving fast, I'm going to need another set of hands."

"I'll help," Arthur said.

"Do you know anything about hacking?" Elvis asked him.

"No. But I can learn."

We all looked at each other. It was like someone offering to fly a rocket to the moon without knowing the first thing about how to drive.

Elvis sighed. "Thanks, Arthur, but that won't be possible."

"Xavier?" Slash suggested.

"No. He won't help. He made that abundantly clear."

Slash glanced at me and I shook my head slightly, confirming Elvis's words. The sick feeling in my stomach was back. I hated the reminder that Elvis and Xavier were still fighting. I couldn't even begin to imagine how Elvis felt right now. To think that at a moment of great need, he could no longer rely on his brother had to be agonizing.

Suddenly I had an idea. "Hey, Gwen, can you get your sister, Angel, on the phone?"

Elvis glanced over at me and smiled, knowing where I was going with this. "Good thinking, Lexi. That's an excellent idea."

ELVIS AND I spent an hour on the phone with Angel before we were satisfied she could handle the task at hand. I would have asked one of my interns, Wally, Piper or Brandon, for an assist, but I happened to know firsthand that all of them were on vacation with their families for the holiday weekend. Since we were out of options, I went with what I had. To my delight, Angel proved more than capable. Even though she had no idea what we were doing, just the thought of working with me was enough to excite her.

"Are you sure she won't be in any danger?" Gwen asked me for the eleventh time.

I glanced over at Elvis, who was furiously typing on the laptop. "I'm positive, Gwen. She is reporting to Elvis and Elvis only. She has no idea what is going on. She thinks we're testing her. In no way will any-one be able to trace her connection or assistance on this. She'll just be doing some real-time monitoring to help Elvis out, and that's it."

"Okay. I just want to be sure."

"You're pretty protective of her," I observed.

"Yeah, well, she's my kid sister." That apparently explained it all. "Besides, she doesn't have a lot of friends to watch her back. That's my job as her older sister. Except when it was your job at the high school when those terrorists came in. You saved her, Lexi. I'll never be able to repay you for that."

"Hey, there's no payment necessary. Besides, I didn't do it alone. Slash and Elvis were critical in that effort. But look, I understand what it means to be the outsider in high school, without many, or in my case, any friends. Angel's skills are impressive for a fifteen-almost-sixteen-year-old. She's got a real future in computers if that's where she's headed."

"That's where she's headed. She aspires to be like you."

"Jeez, she shouldn't. No one should. She should aspire to be herself."

"I know." Gwen looked down at her hands. "What I mean is that you're a hero to her. She's a young girl who looks to you as a role model in a field that doesn't have that many women. Yet. Whether you realize it or not, you're an example of what you can achieve if you follow your dreams, regardless of stereotypes or glass ceilings. You're fearless."

"Whoa. I am *not* fearless. I fear a lot of stuff. Actually, I fear *most* stuff."

"But you try anyway. I'll admit, that's why I'm part of the fan club, too. You always give it your all, Lexi. Angel's like that, too. There is no stopping her when she sets her mind to something. She'll find a way."

I sighed. "You do realize all of this means I may have to bug Finn to add another intern to my cadre."

"You'd do that for her?" Gwen's eyes lit up. "At X-Corp? Wow. She'd be totally floored."

"I wouldn't have *done* anything for her. She'd have

earned it. But there won't be anybody to intern for unless we get it right tonight. So, we all need to be on our game."

"We will." Gwen threw her arms around me and gave me a big hug. Slash looked over at me and lifted an eyebrow while I just shrugged. I'm pretty sure I hadn't been hugged so much in a week.

Minutes ticked past while we continued our planning. We ate a light dinner in the room. Arthur and Gwen took a nap and Slash disappeared for nearly two hours. He came back with black clothing for Gwen and me, a couple of burner phones and other assorted items. I didn't ask where he got them. Slash and Elvis briefed Gwen and me on exactly how we would get in, where we would go and how we would get out. Slash made us repeat the instructions several times to make certain we understood.

"Just remember, stick to the plan and all will be well," he said.

My stomach was doing butterflies by the time I got dressed in the clothes. When I returned to the living room, Gwen sat on the couch looking a bit paler than usual, but holding up better than I expected.

"You good?" I asked her.

She nodded. Her blue eyes locked onto mine. "If I get scared, I'll just do the WWLD thing."

"What's the WWLD thing?"

"WWLD—What Would Lexi Do? I try to imagine what you would do and it helps me figure out what's the best course of action. Angel was thinking about getting it printed on those little rubber bracelets and handing them out to the Lexicons."

I was aghast at the mere thought. "Oh, God, no, Gwen. Please, I beg you."

"You have to admit, though, if we pull this off, it's going to be epic. Well worth a WWLD bracelet."

"If we pull this off, I'm going to fangirl *you*, Gwen. Okay?"

"Really?" Her face broke into a smile.

"Really."

Just then Elvis announced he and Angel were ready with the setup. It was time to get the show on the road.

Slash stood, giving us one last pep talk. "We go in without any identification whatsoever. We'll have money and small flashlights only. I'll carry the knife for Gwen to cut the binding. Lexi, you'll have the only burner phone to communicate with Elvis. If we get separated, we rendezvous here." He pulled out a map and showed us a spot about six blocks from the hotel. "Check in here on the hour. If no one shows, don't go back to the hotel until at least three hours have passed. After that, return with caution."

Gwen and I nodded our heads to indicate we understood. Finally, the hour was at hand. Elvis asked my opinion on a few of the virtual details before he got Angel on the phone. My stomach churned with nerves. I couldn't imagine how Gwen was feeling, but to my surprise, she still didn't show outward signs of nervousness despite the fact we were about to conduct a heist at one of the most renowned museums in the world.

I patted my pockets. I had four hundred and fifty Egyptian pounds, which was roughly equivalent to fifty United States dollars, a flashlight, a burner phone and a pair of black latex gloves. The gloves were to keep fingerprints at bay, but also to protect the staff when we had to touch it. I assumed Gwen had the same items. I wasn't sure what Slash had in his pockets, and since he didn't volunteer the information, I didn't ask.

Gwen stood in front of me, inspecting my look. "You know, Lexi, you look a little like Angelina Jolie in *Tomb Raider* just before she breaks into the tomb. Of course, except for your hair, body and the guns."

I rolled my eyes. "Jeez. Thanks, Gwen."

"Sure. I really wanted to take a picture of us right before the mission for our forum, but Slash put the big X on that idea. So, it will just have to live on in my imagination."

"Thank goodness."

When it was time to go, we walked to the museum, forgoing a cab. The museum itself was dark, but a few people were still out and about in nearby Tahrir Square. There was a roving patrol outside the museum, but it was only two guys and they didn't seem too interested in maintaining security.

Slash timed their rotation. It was inconsistent, but within a twelve-minute window. Plenty of time to get past them.

I called Elvis on the burner phone as they passed. "Okay, we're heading in. Take down the security camera at the east-end staff entrance and any outdoor cameras in this area."

"The outdoor cameras have already been adjusted, and…" I heard him tapping on the keyboard. "I just put the staff entrance in a loop. You're good to go. The entire first floor interior cameras are already in a loop. You're good to go the whole way in case we lose contact."

"Thanks, bud. I'll be texting from now on."

"Understood. Good luck."

We quickly walked to the entrance door, acting like we were supposed to be there. I didn't see anyone about, but I checked just in case. Slash swiped the card through the access control panel and the door popped open. I held my breath waiting for some kind of alarm, but nothing happened. We slipped in, with Slash going last and quietly closing the door behind us.

We're in, I texted to Elvis.

Cleaning entrance log now, he texted back.

I turned off the phone and slipped it in my pocket. Slash motioned for us to put on our gloves, as he'd put on his before we'd entered. We did as he instructed and he nodded in satisfaction when we were done.

He took point, peering down a corridor and motioning for us to follow. The lights had been dimmed to a night setting, presumably to waste less energy and also keep the museum cooler. That worked in our favor. We quietly moved along the wall behind him, past dark offices. A guard walked past along a perpendicular corridor and we pressed into the doorways, hopefully melting into the shadows.

No alarm was raised, so we continued on. Surprisingly, we hardly encountered any guards in this area. Apparently they were instructed to stay mostly with the exhibits, which was good luck for us. We made it all the way down to the front entrance without incident. To our left was the security center. There were a couple of guards talking and another one sitting behind a desk viewing what looked like the footage from the security camera. Everyone seemed completely relaxed. That was good except my body thrummed like a live wire. I desperately hoped the gallop of my heart wasn't audible from across the museum floor.

Slash leaned over, pressing his mouth against my ear. "We can't get by those two guards over there without crossing their line of sight. We need a distraction at the security center. See if Angel can find the museum security number and call it. Tell her to be careful she isn't traced. She needs to think of something to ask to keep them occupied for at least three minutes."

I slipped the phone out of my pocket and texted the request to Elvis. He replied with an okay.

We waited. And waited. We weren't really exposed where we were, but with every minute we faced the random chance of someone coming down the hall behind us. I couldn't decide whether I should watch the guards ahead of us or behind us to give us some warning of trouble. I noticed that Gwen was staring intently back the way we came and was quivering slightly.

It seemed like eons, but when I checked my watch only six minutes had passed. When the ring of the phone finally reverberated through the museum, I nearly jumped out of my skin. Gwen stiffened next to me. One of the guards answered the phone and then shouted for someone, probably one of his English-speaking colleagues. Moments later, the guard who had been summoned strode into view and started talking on the phone.

"No, we can't look it up for you," he said in heavily accented English. "Museum closed."

Silence.

"Yes, of course, I'm Egyptian. I know who the kings were. Who are you trying to find?"

The other guards had perked up and slowly wandered over to see what was going on. They were laughing as they listened to the guard try to answer whatever ridiculous questions Angel was posing for them.

"Now," Slash hissed and motioned for us to move. We slipped past the center, hiding behind several giant statues on our way to the western side of the museum. When we got to the west wing entrance, Slash took a peek and indicated for us to follow him inside.

Since I'd just been there in the afternoon, I was familiar with the layout. It seemed a lifetime ago. It was eerie in the dim light and shadows with the musty smell of ancient objects permeating the air.

Slash headed straight for the exhibition with the chariot and we followed. Before going in, he took a moment to study the setup of the exhibition, presumably looking for any special alarms that hadn't been noticed before. Satisfied he didn't see any, he waved us forward. We stepped over the velvet-roped stanchion and slipped behind a queen carrier chair to the other side of the chariot. I reached out and brushed my fingers against the staff and felt a tingle go through my finger and up my hand.

The staff of Moses. Could it be true?

Slash pulled on my arm, whispering in my ear. "You were right. I can't fit back there. We're going to have to move the chariot forward about two feet in order to give Gwen space to release the rod."

I motioned to Gwen and she nodded. Slash did a quick review of the chariot and motioned where we should stand. We took our positions and in the dim light waited until Slash nodded before we lifted.

The chariot barely moved. It might have gone an inch before we gave up. Holy cow. Had my calculations been off that badly? Now I wasn't sure three of us could move it two inches let alone two feet.

Slash motioned for us to try again. Knowing what to expect this time, I braced myself for a heavier lift. We moved it slightly more this time, but nowhere near enough. The chariot wasn't that heavy. Couldn't be. But they had partially anchored it for the exhibit and that made lifting it a royal pain. My heart was racing. Time was ticking by, every moment putting us in greater danger of being discovered.

Inhaling a breath, we tried again. This time it moved significantly farther, but the cost was a screech as the ancient wooden wheel scraped across the stone floor on the side Gwen and I were lifting. We quickly lowered the chariot back to the floor and froze in place. I realized I no longer heard the soft murmur of the guards' voices from the security center.

That couldn't be good.

Thankfully, we'd moved the chariot far enough for Gwen to wiggle behind it. Slash withdrew the knife from his pocket and handed it to her and she disappeared behind the chariot.

Footsteps clicked on the floor, coming our way. Slash ducked behind the queen's carrier, pulling me with him. We squatted as low as possible. We covered our faces so that nothing white would show in contrast to the black shadows. We were hidden in the dim light, but if one of the guards stepped across the rope for a better view with a flashlight, we would be exposed.

I held my breath as the footsteps paused. The guard stood listening. My heart sounded overly loud in my ears. Finally, the guard took a few more steps, closer in our direction. The beam of a flashlight shone over the exhibition, but thankfully from a distance. We still had a chance.

I closed my eyes, wishing I could teleport somewhere, anywhere, from here.

The guard lowered the flashlight and paused, listening. After an agonizingly long time, I heard his footsteps moving away, apparently deciding nothing was amiss. I let out a quiet breath, feeling lightheaded from nerves and fear.

After a minute, a tiny movement caught my eye. Gwen moved partially out from behind the chariot. She had the staff in her gloved hands.

I started to stand, but Slash held my arm, keeping me down. He murmured against my ear, "Tell Elvis we need a distraction in one of the rooms on the back east side."

I slipped the phone out of my pocket and texted Elvis.

A few seconds later the message came back. Stand by.

We waited until we heard someone shout and the sound of running feet toward the back of the museum. Gwen held out the staff with shaking hands to Slash, who motioned to me to take it. Presumably he wanted to keep his hands free to handle any potential confrontation. I handed Gwen the burner phone and motioned for her to keep an eye on the text response from Elvis.

She nodded while I crouched there next to Slash, holding the Rod of God in both hands with extreme nervousness. Given my tendency to clumsiness, I wasn't the best person in the world to hold one of the most significant artifacts of all time, but we didn't have time to debate the wisdom of the placement. I wasn't sure how to hold it. Did I put my hands together in the middle with my wrists facing each other or did I spread them apart and hold it like it was a hotel railing? What would Moses do?

I was debating this and working hard not to drop the rod from my trembling hands when Gwen bumped my shoulder and angled the phone toward me so I could see Elvis's text.

Sprinklers.

It was a clever distraction on Elvis's part. Sprinklers meant the fire department would arrive, which meant a lot of people coming and going. Great cover for us, *if* we could pull this off and get out of here undiscovered.

I leaned over toward Slash and murmured, "Sprinklers."

He nodded and stood, stepping across the rope held by the stanchions, motioning us to follow. Gwen and I didn't waste any time and followed closely on his heels. I held the rod gingerly in my hands, being careful not to bump or knock into anything. It was almost a head taller that I was.

Calculating the height of the average man in Moses's time by using a backward regression from today's average height and the standard growth rate, I determined that Egyptian men probably averaged about 5'3" in height. That meant Moses must have been a tall man.

Turning with the staff almost vertical, I still narrowly missed the post upon which an ancient priceless jar sat. Oh, jeez, it would *not* be good if I knocked over a half dozen priceless exhibits before we left the museum.

After Slash made sure the immediate wing was empty, we darted into the entrance hall and crouched behind a statue. This one wasn't wide enough for three of us, so Gwen hid behind an adjacent display. I rested the staff vertically against the statue beside me to better hide it, my back pressed up against the stone, trying to make myself as small as possible.

Slash peered out to check if the coast was clear, when footsteps abruptly headed our way.

Holy pharaoh! Had we been spotted?

Slash crouched back down, his gaze meeting mine. He seemed remarkably calm given the fact that it sounded like at least one guard was coming right toward our position. My stomach flipped. Why had I ever thought this was a good idea?

Slash didn't seem to be having any doubts. Instead, he seemed to ready himself for a potential confrontation. The footsteps walked right up to the statue where we were hiding. At the last second, Slash tugged on my arm, pulling us both around the other side of the statue and out of the guard's view.

He looked at my hands and his eyes widened. I realized I'd inadvertently left the rod standing up against the statue when he unexpectedly pulled me to the other side. I lifted my hands in a silent *oops*, and he rolled his eyes in exasperation.

Thankfully, the guard's footsteps went past us without slowing. That had been way too close. Since no alarm had been raised, I assumed Gwen had done the same thing on her side. She had to be terrified and yet she'd kept her head.

I scuttled back around the statue to retrieve the staff. Unfortunately, my hands weren't as nimble in the gloves. I fumbled it. My mouth opened in a silent gasp as it toppled toward the ground. Slash caught it with one hand when it was about a half inch from the floor.

I closed my eyes in relief. I needed to calm the heck down or I'd expose us all.

The wail of sirens was right outside now. Guards were rushing to the front door to let the firemen in. Slash tugged on my arm motioning toward a side entrance between the west and southwest wings. Since Elvis had disabled the alarms, we should be able to slip out of there unnoticed with all the action at the front of the museum. But we couldn't leave without Gwen.

I came to a half crouch and looked around the statue myself. No sign of her.

Slash tugged on my arm again, motioning toward the exit. I vigorously shook my head and mouthed *Gwen*.

We couldn't leave Gwen. I *wouldn't* leave Gwen.

Slash leaned over and murmured in my ear. "We *have* to get the staff out. I'll come back for Gwen."

I looked down at the Rod of God, wondering if it truly held an antidote to the plague. If it did, Slash was right, we had to get it out.

Reluctantly, I nodded and followed him.

The scream of the sirens was deafening. The front doors of the museum had been thrown open and the sound echoed in the great chamber. I imagined Elvis had his hands full, monitoring all the entrances, exits, cameras and alarms. I was glad he had Angel to help.

Slash and I dashed across the floor in a half crouch, darting between displays. We were almost to the side door when Slash skidded to a halt. He opened a display case and picked up a small gilded statue of the god Majdet, according to the sign below it. He slipped the statue into a collapsible bag that he pulled out from beneath his jacket while I watched openmouthed.

"What are you doing?" I hissed.

"I have an idea."

"That involves stealing the Egyptian God of Justice?" If karma existed, it wasn't going to be on our side.

He didn't answer and instead put a hand on the door and pushed it open without hesitation. No alarm went off. No one stood on the other side with a gun pointed at us. No guard yelled at us from behind.

We just stepped out of the museum without incident—me, Slash, the Rod of God and a pilfered Egyptian God of Justice.

Yep, that's the way we felons roll.

"Walk calmly," Slash murmured to me. The door closed behind us as we took several hurried steps before colliding with a figure stepping out of the dark.

Gasping, we stepped back. A shard of moonlight shone down as we looked right into the surprised face of Zizi Wahgdi.

THIRTY-SEVEN

"You!" ZIZI EXCLAIMED in astonishment. Her eyes first fell on the staff I was holding and then between Slash and me.

Slash didn't waste time with explanations. "Gwen is still trapped in there. Undiscovered so far, I think."

"What were you thinking?" she hissed.

I held up the staff. "This. We've got it. But Slash has to go back for Gwen."

"What about the security cameras?" Zizi asked.

"Not filming," Slash said. "Can you help us?"

Zizi let out a breath and stared at Slash for a long moment. Despite her initial shock, she seemed to come quickly to a decision. "Where was the last place you saw her?"

"Entrance hall. Third tomb, left side."

Zizi nodded. "Where do I bring her?"

"Gwen knows the spot," Slash said. "Hurry."

"Fine. Get out of here." Zizi gave us a final look and swept past us.

Slash took my elbow, guiding me down the empty sidewalk before taking a hard left into an alley. He moved us away from the entrance of the museum and Tahrir Square.

After we'd gone a little way, I turned on him, forcing him to stop. "How can you just trust Zizi like that? She could turn Gwen in. She could turn us in."

"*Si*, she could. But I think she understands what's at stake. I don't believe she will. Since she has the best chance of getting Gwen out unnoticed, I made the decision to trust her to handle it."

"How can you be so sure that's the right decision? What is she doing out here at this hour anyway? She's probably furious at us. We stole her card. She could betray us."

"She could. It was a calculated risk and one I had to take given the circumstances. Let's trust it will work out for the best." He took my arm, pulling me into movement again.

I sure hoped he knew what he was doing. No matter which way I looked at it, the odds were low for this playing out in our favor. Honestly, I felt sick about leaving Gwen and even sicker we'd left her fate up to Zizi. But I had to trust Slash and his instincts. It wasn't like we had a lot of choices at this point.

"Relax, *cara*." He patted my shoulder. "I fully expect to see them both at the rendezvous spot."

I wished I shared his optimism, but I didn't. "Elvis is going to be freaking out, especially now he can't reach us. Gwen has the burner phone."

Slash stopped and looked at me. "She does? That's an unexpected variable."

"Well, when you handed me the staff, I handed her the phone. Given my proclivity to awkwardness, I figured I had better hold the staff with two hands. Gwen had to check for Elvis's texts." I glanced down at my gloved hands where they held the rod in a death grip.

Slash thought it over and shrugged. "It's okay. The phone is untraceable if she's caught. And Elvis is good. Very good. He'll hold it together."

"I hope you're right. That might not be true if Gwen gets caught. He might lose it."

"I'll handle it if Gwen gets caught. I promise she'll be okay. Let's just focus on what's within our control at this moment, okay?"

He was right. There were so many variations of what could go wrong, I would drive myself crazy trying to calculating the odds. Better to stay on task and do the best we could with those circumstances under our control.

I tried to regulate my breathing. No sense in passing out from stress. "Okay. What next?"

"We have seventeen minutes until the rendezvous. We need a quiet place to examine the staff."

We headed down the sidewalk, Slash making sure to vary our route, when we stepped into an alley. A huge guy stepped out in front of us, blocking our way. His biceps were the size of tree trunks, his torso three sizes bigger than mine. He had to be nearly six foot six.

Slash stepped in front of me as the guy smiled, showing a row of broken and rotted teeth. "I take that," he said in broken English. He pointed to beneath Slash's jacket where a small piece of the golden Majdet statue was visible from the bag.

Crap. I *knew* karma was going to bite us for that.

"I don't think so," Slash said calmly.

"Yes. You give me. See." The guy reached behind his back and withdrew a big, honking scimitar, a sword with a curved blade, from a sheath strapped to his back.

Oh. My. God. What kind of guy carried around an enormous sword on his back?

"Give it to him, Slash," I said in a low voice, stepping back against the wall.

Instead of being afraid of being carved up like a fish, Slash sighed. "We don't have time for this."

He reached at the small of his back where he usually had a gun but this time he didn't have one. Instead, he smiled at the guy, murmured something in Italian, and set the bag with the statue on the ground at my feet.

I looked at him incredulously. "What are you doing?" I hoped I didn't sound as panicked as I felt, but I was pretty darned stressed at the moment.

"I'm taking care of this so we don't miss the rendezvous."

"In case you didn't notice, he's got a sword. A really big one. And you've got…your fists."

"Even odds, *cara*."

Before I could provide a statistical analysis of the odds of winning a fight against a hulk with a ginormous sword, Slash engaged the guy. I pressed a hand to my mouth as the big guy swung the blade and Slash barely danced out of the way.

After my initial terror passed, I began to watch them a bit more carefully. Although I'm not an expert at fighting by any stretch of the imagination, the guy with the sword didn't really seem to have any skill other than sheer brute force and strength. Not that he needed anything else. Slash was dancing in and out around him, staying largely out of reach, until I realized he was trying to get a feel for what kind of skills the guy had.

The guy sliced again at Slash. It missed him by a hair's breadth. I swallowed a yelp. This was intolerable. I had to figure some way to help.

The good news was the guy readily assumed I was a helpless female. So, he had no problem turning his back on me. I gripped the staff in my hand and waited until the next time he turned around. When he did, I took a couple of steps forward and swung the rod like a baseball bat.

Boom.

The staff connected with the guy's head with a hard crack. The force of the hit vibrated all the way down the staff to my arms and body, causing my teeth to chatter. I had only hoped to distract him long enough for Slash to get a couple of hits in, but to my utter shock, the guy dropped like a stone. He hit the street face-first, the sword clattering out of his hand and sliding across the asphalt, clanging against a trash can.

Slash ran to my side. "Are you okay, *cara*?"

"I'm fine. What about you?"

"I'm untouched. What did you do?"

"I brained him with the staff."

Slash's face was incredulous. "You did what?"

"I took him down. You're welcome."

"You used the staff?" He snatched the staff from me and started examining it. "What if you'd broken it?"

"I was trying to save your life. But technically, isn't it supposed to be indestructible?"

He looked at me, the staff and the guy lying in the alley as if he couldn't believe it. "There's not even a mark on the staff. But he's out cold. How hard did you hit him?"

"As hard as I could. I imagined his head being a baseball and me the one girl who'd never hit a home run."

After a moment, he shook his head and handed me

back the staff. He knelt down next to the guy, feeling his pulse. "Definitely unconscious."

Straightening, he jogged over to the trash can, picked up the guy's sword and dropped it down a street drain. I heard it clatter as it hit the bottom.

"Come on, we've got to go," he said returning to me and picking up the bag with the statue. "We've ten minutes until rendezvous time."

Slash grabbed my hand and we started walking. His eyes never stopped scouring our immediate environment. How he managed to take in and process so much information at once was truly mystifying. His posture remained tense and coiled as if ready to engage in battle at any moment. He was in full survival mode. Dangerous and primed for a fight.

We exited the alley onto another sidewalk. There was no one around, but it felt awkward holding the staff. I felt self-conscious, like I was wearing a neon sign that flashed Thief of Ancient Artifact.

"What are you going to say if someone asks us what this is?" I held up the staff. "I mean, who walks around with a six-foot staff in the middle of the night?"

"If we run into anyone brave enough to ask, I'll tell them it's a *bō*."

"A what?"

"A *bō*. It's a martial arts staff. It's used in bojutsu—a Japanese martial art. It's a fairly popular sport in Cairo. I've used a *bō* before, so I can handle one, at least on a rudimentary level. It takes a pretty specialized skill to use it properly. I had a fight once with Haruto Muiro that did not end well for me. Thankfully, he hurt my pride a lot more than my body. But he could have done real damage if we weren't on the same side."

"The same side as what?"

Slash smiled, but didn't answer. "However, if we encounter any more unsavory characters, I'm just going to step back and let you wield that thing yourself. To hell with my bojutsu skills. Just remind me never to anger you while you're holding a sharp or heavy object."

"Okay, I'll keep it in mind." I smiled a little to myself. Who was the alpha girl now? Of course, I'd had the Rod of God on my side, so that had helped. But still. I took care of business.

Slash detoured into a tiny park with a couple of benches and a few trees. "Let's sit here. I want to examine the rod for a few minutes." He sat on the bench, taking the staff from me and placing it horizontally on his lap.

"What if a policeman walks by? It's the dead of the night."

"I'll tell him I'm sitting here in the dark talking with my girlfriend. If he asks about the staff, I'll tell him it's from my martial arts class. It's dark and it's possible he'd buy it."

"And if he doesn't?"

"Then I'll take care of it." He sat and patted the bench next to him. "Let's not play the what-if game, *cara*. Relax. Stay on the operational need of the moment. We need to take a good look at the staff, so let's do it."

Relax. Easy for him to say. I wasn't nearly as calm about what had just happened, but his refusal to get ruffled did have a soothing effect. The extreme adrenaline rush that had surged through my body at the museum had started to subside just a little.

Slash took a flashlight from his pocket and handed it to me. I turned it on and angled the light so it landed on the middle of the staff.

"Can you aim it at this end?" he asked.

I adjusted the angle to the spot he wanted. It appeared to be the top of the staff with a rounded knob and some intricate carvings.

Slash ran his gloved fingers gently across the wood. "It's beautiful."

"It really is. Do you think it's Moses's staff?"

"It's possible."

"What are those markings down there?" I asked, shining the flashlight closer.

"Egyptian hieroglyphics." He pointed to the lower part of the staff. "This is Hebrew writing down here."

I pointed my finger at some shapes. "That must be where it says 'I am that I am' in Hebrew. Just like Arthur said it would."

He looked at it and nodded. "It does make a compelling case for this being the true staff."

I leaned over, resting my chin on his shoulder.

"So, what do you think those dots are for?" I pointed at the spots where there were small clusters of dots.

He examined them for a moment. "I'm not sure, but I think they are significant. I'm going to see if the top will come off." He gently turned the rounded knob. It rotated, but didn't come off.

"Interesting," he murmured. "Several sections of the staff rotate at both the top and bottom." He slid his fingers down to the flat bottom. "This must be where Arthur found the plague endospores."

I leaned against him. "I can see the Hebrew markings and the line around the bottom. Look, the lid isn't even on tight. Arthur didn't put it back on very well. Sloppy."

"Agreed."

Slash gently eased off the lid and I shone the flashlight into the small cavity. It was empty.

"So, Arthur was able to open that end, but he had no idea how to crack the end with the dots at the top," I observed. "It must be a different puzzle to crack in order to retrieve the antidote, provided one actually exists."

"It's definitely a puzzle." Slash returned the lid to the staff and then ran his fingers over the dots on the other side. "I'm not sure how to start looking for a pattern."

"Maybe it would help if we could determine the purpose of the rotation."

"That's a good idea." Slash began rotating the section closest to the top. "My guess is it's some kind of ancient combination lock. I think we have to line up these figures and writing just right."

I leaned over, nearly putting my nose to the staff to get a better look. "You did notice that the top panel are hieroglyphics of pyramids, right? When you rotate them, you get a different configuration of how the pyramids are laid out."

"Giza," Slash said. "There are this exact number of pyramids at Giza."

"Minus the Sphinx."

"The Sphinx isn't a pyramid. But that's an interesting angle, *cara*."

We studied the markings for a bit more until Slash's watch suddenly beeped. "Time for the rendezvous."

We stood and walked back to the sidewalk. After going a few blocks, we stopped in front of an outdoor café that was closed for the night. He pointed to a chair and table. "Stay here. Give me five minutes. If something happens and I don't return, take the staff and get to the American Embassy as quickly as you can. Tell them everything." He handed me the staff and rattled off an address.

I grabbed his arm. "Wait. What? You think something is going to happen at the rendezvous?"

"No, I don't. I'm going to be too careful for that. But I'm giving you a contingency plan, just in case. Be careful, *cara*. Look at the time." I glanced at my watch. "It's three forty-two. Five minutes. Mark."

Giving me a quick kiss on the cheek, he melted into the shadows. I watched him go, my mouth open. I hadn't expected to be separated from Slash and left alone with the staff.

Oh. My. God. Literally.

I looked down at the rod. No pressure at all.

Since my legs were shaky, I sank into the chair and waited. My pulse was kicking. I sincerely hoped I didn't see anyone.

I glanced at my watch. Wow. A whole thirty seconds had passed.

A couple more minutes passed. My hands gripped the rod so tightly I was pretty sure the blood wasn't flowing to my fingers. I wanted to relax, but I felt hyper alert and kept searching for anyone, or anything, lurking in the shadows ready to leap out at me.

I had just started to relax a fraction when I felt a hand on my shoulder.

THIRTY-EIGHT

I YELPED AND jumped up, wielding the staff like it was a weapon.

Slash stood there, amused. "Good reflexes."

"Slash. Jeez. You scared the beejeebies out of me."

"I'm sorry, *cara*. I had to make sure you were alone." He put an arm around me, pulling me to his side.

I closed my eyes, willing my heart to get back to its normal rhythm. "Where are Gwen and Zizi?"

"I don't know. I didn't see either of them at the rendezvous and I didn't get the right feeling. We won't be going back."

"What do you mean you didn't get the right feeling? Did they capture Gwen?"

"I don't know. I simply didn't get a good feeling about the site. That's it."

"But Gwen…the plague…the website. What are we going to do?"

He stroked my cheek. "We can't do anything about Gwen right now. If she's in custody, we'll have to sort it out later. I assure you, we will. On the other hand, if Zizi has her out safely and we don't show for the rendezvous, Gwen knows to wait three hours and go to the hotel. If the guys with Arthur's laptop have logged in by then, we can be sure Elvis will be tracking them and doing whatever he can to stop them from uploading the plague to the website."

"He can't stop them once they break through, though. You know that."

"I know. But he'll do whatever he can to slow them down. He's good and we have to trust him. Us being there wouldn't change any of that."

"They are going to be so worried about us."

"They will. But they'll have to trust us to do the best we can."

I looked at the staff in my hands and took several calming breaths. Slash was right. We could only control our own movements at this point. "So, what do we do now?"

"We go somewhere private."

"Where? We can't use our passports. We don't even *have* our passports."

"Money speaks volumes. I'll find us a place. Come on."

We walked past several small hotels and hostels, but all looked dark and closed up. Finally, we came upon one that appeared to be open 24/7.

"Wait here," he instructed and then disappeared into the building.

I leaned against the building wall, looking in through the glass in the door as Slash spoke with a man behind a desk. After a few minutes, Slash came back out holding a silver key between his fingers.

"You got a room?"

"Yes. We've got two hours."

"Two hours? How did you pull that off?"

He lifted an eyebrow. "I said I needed a couple hours alone with my woman. I promised we'd be out before morning. I paid him well enough that he graciously agreed."

"Oh, jeez." I couldn't help it, I blushed. "He agreed to it without asking for our passports?"

"*Si*. This is between him, me and a roll of cash. We're good. Come on."

He angled me behind him, so we mostly hid the staff as we walked in through the lobby and down a dark corridor to a room with the number six on it. It wasn't necessary as there was no one awake, but Slash wasn't taking any chances. He inserted the key to the room and turned the knob. It opened and we stepped into the room, closing the door behind us.

Slash flicked the ceiling light on. It was a dark and dismal room that smelled of food and unusual spices. There was a single bed, a dresser and a nightstand that held a lamp with a faded shade. A small bathroom with a toilet and small sink was to the right. No shower. Slash set the staff on the bed, turned on the light in the bathroom, then picked up a desk lamp that was on the nightstand near the bed. He removed the shade, which gave us more light, then set it down on the bed next to the staff.

"Let's take a better look. See if you can find some paper."

I checked in the dresser drawers but came up empty. The nightstand had two pencils and a pen, but no paper. I went into the bathroom and since I was there, used the facilities. I came out with a roll of toilet paper. It wasn't soft and mushy like American toilet paper, but firmer. I could speak with firsthand experience that it was a *lot* less comfortable. It wasn't ideal in terms of writing material, but it was sturdy enough that it would work.

Slash raised an eyebrow when I handed him a roll, but he tore off a piece without comment and placed it on the nightstand where the lamp had been.

"I think the key has to be in these dots," he said. "Let's see if we can determine a pattern to them."

"This would be a lot easier if we had our laptops," I said.

"It would. But since we don't, we'll have to use the old-fashioned hard drive—our brains."

I sat down next to him on the bed. "Okay, then let's take a look at what happens to the dots when we rotate the staff."

Slash did a full rotation while I carefully sketched the pattern of the dots. After we had gone one rotation, I looked at the dot configurations to see if anything jumped out at me. It didn't.

I handed it to Slash. "I've got nothing."

He looked at it and then shook his head. "Of course not. It wouldn't be that easy."

"It never is. Why can't saving the world be easy for once? It's totally unfair."

He rolled his eyes.

We sketched, calculated, tried to discern patterns. After an hour, we had exactly nothing. I pushed my hand against my forehead in frustration. "It isn't working."

Slash tapped his pencil against the nightstand where he had his notes. I leaned over to read what he was doing and noticed he was no longer focused on the dots.

"What are you doing?" I asked.

"Something you mentioned earlier at the park about

the placement of the pyramids is bugging me. The placement seems significant. Watch. When I rotate the staff, their configuration changes." He demonstrated by rotating the staff an entire circulation. The pyramids changed positions. During one rotation, I noticed a small hieroglyphic showed up beneath one of the pyramids.

"What's that?" I asked, tapping my finger next to it.

Slash picked up the lamp and angled it closer to the staff for a better look. "I think it's the Egyptian Sun God Ra."

I squinted at the picture. "Is that supposed to be the sun next to him?"

"I think so, thus my conclusion that it's the Sun God."

"Are there any other pictures of Ra on the staff?"

"Excellent question. I don't know." Slash marked a spot in the center of the staff. "You take that end and I'll take this one. Let's see what we find."

We each examined our sections of the staff, but came up empty.

"Okay, so there's the only one. Think it's significant?"

"It might be." I examined the hieroglyph again. "It's smaller than the other pictures and it's placed oddly. It's the only hieroglyphic at this end of the staff. That alone implies it's important."

"Agreed. But what does it signify?"

Something was tugging at my mind, but I just couldn't put my finger on it. "You said earlier there are the same number of pyramids on the staff as there are at Giza."

"Exactly." I pressed my hand to my forehead. It was

hard to keep my focus on the matter at hand when there was so much to worry about. Gwen, Elvis, the plague, Arthur, Zizi, and the jihadists.

Had the museum noticed the staff was missing yet?

Were the police looking for us?

Had Zizi turned us all in?

What could be happening with any *one* of those things was cause for enormous stress, let alone all of them together. I stole a sideways glance at Slash. How did he compartmentalize everything so easily? It seemed effortless for him, but I knew better. It must take a toll. What had he said to me earlier? We had to focus on what we could control and do what was needed operationally in the moment.

Everything else had to wait.

He was right, but it seemed a heck of a lot easier said than done. A wicked headache was already brewing behind my eyes.

I focused on the staff. There were multiple configurations of the pyramids. A small hieroglyphic of Ra the Sun God under one of them. In sum, what did it mean?

My eyes flew open. "Slash, what if these pyramids actually represent the ones at Giza?"

"That would be logical. I considered that, but what would be the significance?"

"Well, it might be why the configurations are different when you rotate the staff."

Slash shook his head. "I'm not following you."

"Direction. The configurations look different depending upon what direction you are facing them. So, say we're standing to the west of the pyramids, the configuration will look differently than if we're standing and viewing them from the north."

Slash's eyes lit. "That's good thinking, *cara*. If that's true, how are we to know which view is the right one in order to line up the configuration properly?"

"Ra. The Sun God."

Slash snapped his fingers. "South. He's facing the sun. So, we have to see the pyramids as they look from a southern view and then line it up the same way on the staff. That might be the first part of the combination. Perceptive, *cara*. But what about the dots? We must figure out what they represent."

"I don't know, Slash. Maybe when we look at the south view, something will present itself. It's worth a shot."

"It certainly is." Slash stood, held out a hand to me. "You know there's only one way to find out."

"Yep." I took his hand and rose from the bed. "We go to the pyramids."

THIRTY-NINE

AFTER A SHORT walk from the hostel we managed to catch a cab. Since Cairo is a big city, there was no shortage, regardless of the hour. Giza was thirteen miles from Cairo and, thankfully, the roads were mostly empty.

Fortunately, the cab driver didn't ask why a couple of foreigners—one of them carrying a six-foot staff—were catching a cab in the middle of the night. Unfortunately, the mostly deserted streets didn't stop him from driving like a maniac. I closed my eyes, sat near an open window in case my stomach revolted, and hoped for the best.

The night air was hot and arid, making it hard to draw in a deep breath. Within two minutes of being outside, I was thoroughly sweating.

Slash sat up front, saying something to the driver. When we stopped, I opened my eyes. I was surprised to see the cab driver had halted alongside the curb of a quiet neighborhood of tall apartment buildings. I thought perhaps the driver was checking a map or something, but Slash looked over his shoulder at me in the backseat and motioned for me to get out.

"This is our stop."

I wondered why this was our stop, but I dutifully climbed out of the cab holding the staff. Slash paid the driver and the cab sped away.

I looked around. This neighborhood didn't look like the best part of town, especially in the dark, but Slash didn't seem worried. He took my elbow, directing me down a street, confident in our direction.

"Why exactly did he drop us here?" I asked.

"It's on the south side of town. The pyramids are less than a mile in that direction. I didn't want to let him know exactly where we were going."

"Okay, understood." Our footsteps echoed loudly on the streets as we walked. Glancing around, I saw a couple of lights coming on in a few apartments. I looked at my watch and realized we were nearer to dawn than I expected. I adjusted the staff in my hands.

"We'd better hurry," I said.

"Agreed. Walk briskly."

Haste was important. It was one thing to be walking around with a staff in the dark, but it was much more dangerous in the daylight, especially if the theft had been noticed by the museum.

We walked behind an apartment complex and onto the base of a hill. A small row of trees screened us from the building behind us, so we continued walking up the hill, climbing until we hit the top of the small rise.

I gasped in surprise at the sight that greeted me. Although I had seen numerous photographs, pictures, and documentaries of the great pyramids I was not prepared for the spectacle and majesty of seeing it in person. The view was far grander than I'd ever expected. They were situated on a flat plateau, surrounded by tombs and stones and other small pyramids that were falling into disarray. Amid all of this, the Sphinx rose proudly into the desert sky, its body partially buried in the sand. The sheer stateliness and splendor of that monument alone commanded respect and was breath-taking in its own right.

The pyramids and Sphinx were still lit up by artificial lights, but those were muted by the faintest hint of dawn on the horizon. Although every second of time was precious, we could not move, both of us utterly riveted by one of the most incredible sights in the world.

"It's beautiful," I whispered.

Slash put an arm around my shoulder and we stood there for a few minutes staring at the exceptional sight. It seemed surreal, yet I felt blessed to be viewing the pyramids with my boyfriend while possibly holding the same staff Moses had once wielded to part the Red Sea.

"The view is extraordinary," Slash murmured. "The pyramids, the Sphinx, they are unparalleled mathematical masterpieces born of exceptional human effort and ingenuity."

I liked that his thoughts mirrored mine exactly. The finished product was remarkable, but my mind lingered on all of the breathtakingly hard work that had been done by the engineers and the excruciating cost in lives when the pyramids had finally been raised and finished. While they were truly fantastic examples of engineering precision, technical innovation and pure genius, the human cost of creating such lasting monuments was inestimable.

I could have stood there taking in the view and letting my mind wonder about the life of an ancient engineer, but we had work to do.

I tore my gaze away from the view and held up the staff. Slash pulled his flashlight out and aimed the beam at the top. We both took a long look at the way the pyramids lined up in the view, before I replicated it on the staff. I gently tugged on the top, but it held firm.

"We have to finish the combination," Slash said. "Those dots have to signify something."

"I agree. But what?"

"It's got to be some kind of code."

I frowned. "I think at this point the code means straight up mathematics. Since some of the most advanced engineering took place at this time, we have to also assume that this will be a sophisticated code."

"Agreed." Slash leaned over, tipping one end of the staff toward him with his gloved fingertips. "At this end, the spot where Arthur retrieved the plague endospores, I don't see any dots. Only Hebrew characters which Arthur said he used to open that end."

"The dots are clearly the clue on this end."

"Do you have the paper?"

I pulled out the long wad of toilet paper from my pocket and two pencils. "Here you go."

He laid the paper across the staff and began to gently create a rubbing of the dots.

"That's a good idea," I said. "It will give us a flat, non-skewed look at how they are arranged in their entirety."

Slash finished the rubbing and laid it out atop a flat boulder a few steps away. We crouched around the rock, looking at the layout by the beam of the flashlight.

"Anything leap out at you?" I asked after a few minutes. "I've got nothing."

Slash studied it and sat back on his heels. "Me neither. Maybe this isn't the right way to go about this."

"Let's try some basic ciphers to make sure. Just to rule them out."

He nodded and we spent the next thirty minutes calculating the possibilities. Finally, Slash stood and tossed his pencil aside in frustration. "Nothing. We're no closer to opening this staff than when we started. We're out of time."

I rubbed my temples. He was right. We were getting nowhere fast. We had no parameters, no baseline, no starting point. Without those, we couldn't determine a rhyme or reason for the layout of the dots.

I still sat cross-legged on the ground. I arched my back, staring at the pyramids in the distance. Dawn was in full bloom now. The night lighting of the pyramids had been turned off and now they were cloaked in the first bloom of the pinkish orange hue of the dawn. These amazing structures had lasted thousands of years. How many more puzzles and mysteries did they hide?

I looked at Slash. He was pacing, which he always did when he was thinking.

"Let's go back to the basics," I said. "We have only one certainty here. Those dots are not randomly placed on that staff. They are precisely and carefully carved."

Slash scuffed his foot, stirring up some sand. "You think I don't know that? Damn it, *cara*, we need more information. Something to start with." The fact his voice held a note of desperation concerned me. Maybe he wasn't as calm as I thought about the fact we had no idea what had happened to Gwen, was happening with the plague, or what Zizi had done or said. That he wasn't his usual implacable self was worrisome.

"Maybe we should just try to break it open," Slash suddenly said.

"What?" I looked at him appalled. "Did you just suggest we try to break the Rod of God?"

"If we can't open it, at this point, it may be our only recourse."

"Did you not hear of the legends about what happened to the people who tried to do just that? They died horrible deaths."

He raised an eyebrow. "Are you, Lexi Carmichael, suggesting myth and legend might be well heeded in this case?"

"Maybe I am. Look, Slash, religious, spiritual or woo-woo concerns aside, I don't want anything to happen to you. I don't want anything to happen to me. We are running on fumes with no food or sleep. But it doesn't mean we have to abandon common sense. Even though I don't believe in superstition, we just can't break this staff. In addition to the fact that it's clearly an ancient artifact, it could also be holy."

Wow. I couldn't believe I was the one taking a sacred stand here. But here I was, standing up for the holy relic like I was the Pope or something.

"Did you just say woo-woo?"

I rolled my eyes. "Secondly. We can't break the staff because we might damage whatever is inside. You know that. It's not worth risking."

Slash blew out a breath. "I know. It was just frustration speaking."

I got a cramp in my lower legs from the way I was crouching, so I sat on my bottom. I was still uncomfortable, so I stretched out on my back, one arm behind my head, the other hand balancing the staff horizontally across my stomach. I stared up at the disappearing night sky and tried to clear my mind. The answer had to be within our grasp, we just needed to know how to find it.

Hey, God. If you're up there and this is your staff, a little help here would be great.

Wonderful. Now I was talking to God like we were long-lost friends or something. I took a couple of deep breaths to relax my mind and body.

"Okay, Slash, let's go back to Egyptian times and think like Moses or the person who wrote this code on the staff to protect the endospores inside. What do we know about Egyptian mathematical techniques? What resources did they have that they might have relied upon to create this puzzle?"

Slash kept pacing. The steady fall of his footsteps calmed me. I wondered if he even realized he paced when he was worried. "It's no secret the Egyptians were math geniuses. You want me to list some of the overall practices of the time?"

"Yes, please. I remember some, but I'm tired. Give me a refresher, if you would."

There was a pause in his pacing before he resumed. "Well, their number system was based on ten and was additive. They were the first people to use unit fractions and develop a sophisticated measurement system roughly based on the cubit. Multiplication for them was a binary sort of arithmetic, a constant doubling of those things that needed to be added. They used algebra, geometry and quadratic equations, surprisingly, much in the same way we still do today. How's that for an overview?"

"Good. How did they tell time?"

"Sundials. Obelisks. Merkhets."

I leaned on one elbow, looking up at him in surprise. "Merkhets? Are those the devices used by early astronomers to tell time at night?"

"*Si*. A merkhet had a weight with a pointed tip that was suspended from a string and used as a vertical reference line. In order to tell time, two merkhets had to be in operation at the same time. One was the base measurement and was aligned with Polaris, the North Star. They created a north-south meridian."

"That's right. I remember now. How did they measure time from that?"

"They observed certain stars and constellations as they crossed into the meridian and became aligned with the merkhets. There are some merkhets on display at the Egyptian Museum. It's thought they were likely used in the construction of the pyramids."

I stared at the sky, trying to imagine how that worked when suddenly I sat up. "Slash, I think I've got it."

Slash knelt down beside me, careful not to knock the staff. "Got what? *Cara*, what are you thinking?"

I smiled up at him. "The stars, Slash. The dots are the stars. It's a celestial map."

FORTY

SLASH STARED AT ME, clearly not quite seeing the whole picture yet. "How does the merkhet play into that?"

"They used it to tell time. The dots are the location of the constellations and the stars from the southern perspective at a certain time. When those are aligned properly on the staff, it should open."

He sat on the ground next to me, taking the staff from my hand. "It's as good a theory as any. It might work, except how do we know at what time we're supposed to calculate the position of the stars?"

"That... I'm not sure." I rested a hand on his shoulder and looked down at the staff, clicking on the flashlight. In a few minutes we wouldn't need it. Dawn would be in full bloom by then.

I pointed at the small figure of Ra. "Look where the sun is situated in comparison to Ra."

"It's not above his head like it would be at midday," Slash observed. "It's lower."

"Sunset, then?"

Slash turned his head and looked at me intently. "Or sunrise."

I glanced up at the sky. We could still see the stars, but not for long. "Let's map it and see what happens. But we have to hurry."

Slash grabbed his rubbing of the dots and smoothed it out on top of the boulder. He looked up at the stars and then down at the rubbing. "Let's start with the first dot sequence. Polaris is here." He did a few rotations and stopped, glancing between the stars and the staff. "This is the one." He clicked it into place behind the southern configuration of the pyramids.

I had worked ahead and was ready with the second dot configuration. "This one looks like Argo, the boat. Well, at least it was called Argo by the Greeks. I'm not sure what the Egyptians called it."

"As long as it lines up, I don't care what it's called."

"Agreed."

There were four more configurations. Aries, Cassiopeia, Eridanus, and Leo, at least those were their Greek names. Slash and I each worked two and then rotated the correct configuration into line.

I slid the final one into place under the others. "Done. Fittingly, and perhaps not coincidentally, the last constellation was Leo, better known as the Sphinx to the Egyptians." I glanced over at the real Sphinx that had started to shimmer golden in the exploding dawn sky. "It seems fitting somehow."

I glanced over at Slash. "Do we try to open it now?"

Slash nodded, but first he slipped the gold cross out from beneath his shirt and kissed it. My hand rested on the knob on top of the staff. Slash placed his hand over mine. It was warm, strong and determined.

My rock. My partner in crime. Literally.

"As we open it, hold your breath, okay?" he said.

"Why?"

"I don't know what's in there and I don't want either of us inhaling spores if they are loose."

"Okay. Shall we do it?"

He leaned forward and pressed a kiss on my forehead. As he pulled back, he murmured something in Italian.

"What did you say?" I asked.

His cheeks and chin had dark stubble, and his brown eyes were shadowed and tired. Yet, as he looked at me, he smiled. "I thanked God for bringing you to me in case He's watching right now. Ready?"

"Ready."

I inhaled a deep breath, holding it. Together we turned the knob and gently tugged upward. Nothing happened. Slash glanced at me and nodded. We tugged a little harder and this time the knob at the top popped off right into my hand.

A strange whooshing sound that sounded like a sigh, or perhaps an exhale of breath, released just as a weird sweep of static electricity shot through me, causing my hands and toes to tingle. At that same moment, bells started going off across the town although it was far too early for a call to morning prayers.

I released the staff, leaving it in Slash's hand. Still holding the top, I staggered back a few steps, then bent over and gasped in air. After a few seconds, I straightened. Nothing was on fire, I was breathing normally and I hadn't broken out into oozing pus-filled sores.

Alive and in one piece...at least for the moment.

The bells had stopped. I glanced at Slash. "Did you hear those bells or was it in my head?"

"I heard them."

Slash tipped the staff sideways holding out his gloved hand. After a few gentle shakes, something fell into his hand. Our eyes met and then he lightly prodded the item with a fingertip. It was a long, thin bundle wrapped in something white.

"What is it?" I murmured, moving closer again.

"I don't know and I don't dare unwrap it here. But I think we've found the antidote."

I stared in wonder at the object cradled in his gloved hand. "You think there are spores in there?"

"I have no idea."

I took a closer look. "What's that white thing?"

"It looks like a papyrus. It's sealing whatever is inside. But look here, *cara*, there is something on it."

Even though the sun had started to rise, I trained my flashlight on it. "It's a leaf."

"What kind of leaf?"

"I don't know. Take a closer look."

Slash peered at it and shook his head. "It's not familiar to me. But it must be part of the antidote."

I considered the significance. Was that small bundle the answer to preventing a global pandemic?

Who had put it in the staff? God? Moses?

Did it really matter?

A swell of protectiveness rose inside me. No. It didn't matter who had placed the endospores in the staff. It was up to us to make sure it was well protected. That meant getting whatever was inside that bundle into the hands of people who could use it in the way it was intended—to save lives.

Slash and I watched as the sun peeked over the horizon, bathing us, the bundle and the rod in a golden glow. As the rays of the sun fell upon the staff, it seemed ablaze with an inner light.

"What are we going to do now?" I asked Slash in a hushed voice.

Slash looked down at the hidden treasure. "Make sure we protect it."

"ARE YOU SURE about this?" I asked for the millionth time as we stepped into the lobby of the Marriott Hotel.

"I'm sure. We hold all the cards at this point."

I was grateful for his patience as he answered my repeated questions. But it didn't make me any less nervous. I looked around expecting someone to jump out at us any second and drag us off to prison.

Thankfully, no one had—yet—so I followed Slash to the elevators, trying not to look as nervous and guilty as I felt.

We climbed into a waiting elevator and went to our floor. When we got to our suite, Slash knocked a few times on the door. I slid my hand into his and he squeezed it. I heard movement on the other side of the door and presumed someone was looking out.

A squeal and then the door was flung open. I was tackled into the hall wall behind me with Gwen throwing her arms around me, crying. "You're okay, Lexi. Oh my God. You're alive."

Relief flooded through me that she was unharmed and obviously not in police custody. I tried to untangle myself from her grip. "I'm fine, Gwen. I'm just glad you're okay."

Gwen stepped back, pushing her red hair from her shoulders. A relieved smile crossed her face. "I knew it. I told them you'd be fine. Lexi Carmichael is always fine. It says so on your forum."

Slash shot out a hand and grabbed us both by the upper arm. He pulled us into the room and closed the door behind us. Elvis rose from behind the laptop looking at us in relief. Arthur rose to his feet as well, his appearance gaunt, his expression distraught.

"Lexi," Elvis said, coming around the desk to pull

me into a hug. "Slash. Wow, am I glad to see you. Are you guys okay? What happened in the museum? We were so worried."

Before I could answer, Zizi stepped out of the bathroom. Her eyes fell immediately on Slash and then me. "It's about time. What took you so long?"

Slash walked over to Zizi, took her hand and kissed it. "We had some things to take care of. Apparently, I owe you a debt of gratitude for rescuing Gwen. Were you detected?"

"No." Zizi's eyes flicked over our shoulder. "Where's the staff?"

I didn't give Slash time to answer as I stepped up beside him. "How did you get her out?"

"She found me crouching behind the statue where you guys left me," Gwen interrupted. "I was lucky no one had discovered me yet. When Zizi found me, I almost passed out I was so frightened."

Slash put a hand on Gwen's shoulder. "I'm sorry to have put you through that. You did great. You've got the temperament of a field agent. I would have come back for you, but I wanted to get the staff out first. Running into Zizi was a stroke of luck. I knew she was in a better position to help you. It looks like I was right."

"You were right," Zizi said.

Gwen beamed, still stuck on Slash's compliment. "Thank goodness, Zizi is on our side. Hey, Lexi, did you hear that? I've got the makings of a field agent. Gwen Sinclair 007. I may have to change my online moniker."

Slash grinned and turned toward Zizi. "How did you do it?"

"I waited until there was enough distraction inside the museum to remove her from a side entrance—the same one you exited from, to be exact. She was not discovered. Elvis assures me the cameras will not reflect my participation whatsoever in that effort. That apparently is also true for the entrance card you stole from my purse." She gave Slash a long, hard stare.

He bowed his head. "Please accept my deepest apologies, Zizi. It was done for the greater good and in a good faith effort to protect you." He reached into his pocket and handed her back the card. "You have been an invaluable partner in this rescue."

She took it and stuck it in her purse. "You'd better be right." She frowned. "I don't like that you excluded me on this."

"We didn't want to put you in a position that could compromise you in any way."

She narrowed her eyes. "Don't you think it's too late for that?"

"Well, now it is," Gwen offered.

Arthur muscled between us. "Who cares about all this stuff? Where's my staff?" He shook his finger at me. "Zizi said you had it."

"The staff is safe for the time being, Arthur." Slash strode across the room to Elvis. "We couldn't just stroll through security carrying it. But right now we have more pressing matters at hand. What's happening with the plague, Elvis? Did they connect yet?"

"Yes. About an hour after the heist. I got a location from the GPS when they initially fired up the computer, but unfortunately, the first thing this IT guy did was close Lexi's back door, shut down the audio and visual and then turn off the GPS. My guess is they would have been smart enough to move once they noted the GPS was on. Anyway, here is the address where they were when they first connected to the network, but I sincerely doubt they are there anymore." He held up a scrap of paper with an address on it.

Slash took it and glanced at it.

"Zizi said it's a heavily populated area with a lot of apartment buildings," Elvis continued. "They could have moved anywhere in that area or heck, in that apartment complex and we wouldn't know. It's possible they could have left Cairo altogether. Without the GPS tracking them, they might as well be on the moon. I don't know how we'd even start to find them."

Slash ran his fingers through his hair and started pacing. "So, you're saying the only way we're monitoring them at this point is by watching the jihadist site to see if the plague shows up?"

"Unfortunately, that's what I'm saying. This hacker guy seems pretty competent. My guess is they have to be very close to cracking Lexi's protection."

Slash swore under his breath.

I walked over to the desk and patted Elvis on the back. "All is not lost yet. Let me take a look. There may be a way for me to reactivate my back door to sneak in again."

"He closed it, Lexi."

"My door is ever revolving. Have faith, my friend."

Elvis nodded. "Faith given. But even if you do get in, Lexi, this guy will notice. I assure you of that."

"Not if I'm fast to get in and even faster to get out. May I?"

Elvis abandoned his seat and I sat down. Slash tossed me a bottle of water and I drank nearly the entire thing without putting it down. I'd no idea how thirsty I was.

Setting the mostly empty bottle beside me, I got down to work. As time was against us, I decided on speed versus stealth. I wanted in quickly, so that's what I did.

Seven minutes later I was in. I typed the last keystroke with a flourish. "Done."

"I'm in awe of you, geek princess." Elvis looked over my shoulder while Gwen hung on his arm with an awed look on her face, too.

There was no time for gloating. I needed to check a couple of things. Luckily Gwen wandered over to the couch, Arthur was asleep in a chair and Zizi and Slash were in one corner of the room talking quietly.

Elvis watched me for a minute. "What are you doing?" he hissed.

I lowered my voice to a whisper. "Something important. Trust me, okay? Keep the others away for a minute."

He stared at me and then left to join Zizi and Slash in conversation.

Once I'd quickly checked something, it was back to the matter at hand. I needed to discover how close they were to breaking through.

As soon as I saw it, my heart sank. "Guys, unless they change tactics, they should crack in within the hour."

Slash strode to my side, and Elvis, Gwen and Zizi all came to look over my shoulder. "Hurry, *cara*."

My fingers poised over the keyboard. "Okay, here goes. I'm going to turn on the GPS. I don't want to keep it on longer than twenty seconds because I'm hoping he's too immersed in the crack to notice. So, here I go."

I turned on the GPS and several seconds later I got a hit. "Here." I took a quick screenshot of the address then switched it off, leaning back in my chair. "Well, I sincerely hope that went undetected."

I opened the screenshot and examined the address. Elvis typed it into Google Maps on his laptop and zoomed in on the location.

Slash peered at Elvis's screen. "Another apartment complex. Looks like the signal is coming from the southwest corner. First floor."

Elvis pulled in closer to the apartment in question. Slash pointed at something on the screen. "This spot. This corner apartment has three windows. The front windows—two of them—face the street. There's one more window around the corner. That's probably the bedroom window. There are shrubs and decent-sized bushes around the complex. That's good."

"Why is that good?" I looked at Slash over my shoulder. "What are you thinking?"

He straightened. "We go get the laptop and the spores. And this time, we don't fail."

FORTY-ONE

"CAN I ADMIT I'm really nervous about this plan?" I walked next to Slash as we approached the apartment complex. He was carrying a small, lumpy bag I didn't recognize. This morning the streets were bustling and alive with people, noises, traffic and pollution. In the one block we'd walked, I'd nearly gotten hit by a bicycle, brained by a soccer ball and slipped on a large pile of poop from an indeterminate animal.

Luckily I'd avoided everything so far, but I was pretty sure I wouldn't have been so lucky without Slash, his eagle eyes and a guiding hand beneath my elbow.

"It's going to be fine, *cara*. Just stick to the plan."

I hated when people told me that, because invariably it meant I would deviate from the plan. And when I did, it would be my fault, no matter how good a reason I presented. Or maybe it meant they thought I would deviate from the plan, because I often did, though it was more like improvisation than a deviation. It was like I was jinxed or something. While considering the relative fault probabilities if I did or didn't adhere to the plan, I almost bumped Slash into a careening car.

"Stay with me, *cara*. Keep your head in the game. We are going to need you at your best."

I really, *really* hoped the plan worked exactly as we had outlined it, because I was tired of improvising. Just once I wanted the plan to work as it was supposed to. I didn't think it was too much to ask of the universe.

The apartment complex came into sight and my stomach filled with butterflies. I couldn't even remember how long ago I'd eaten anything. I'd had a couple of cups of coffee, but it hadn't settled well on my empty stomach. It had been more than twenty-four hours since any of us had any sleep. We were operating on fumes, which meant we were ripe to make a mistake.

Sighing, I willed myself to focus and kept my head down with the scarf tied tightly around my hair.

We walked directly toward the apartment building before taking a detour to the side. Slash glanced around. When the coast was clear, he yanked me into the bushes and crouched directly underneath a window.

My hair got tangled in the branches, but since I was wearing long sleeves and jeans, my body was protected from major scratches. That was the upside. The downside was that because I was wearing long sleeves, jeans and a scarf, it was hotter than heck hiding in those bushes. Sweat started to slide down my temples and back. My hands began to shake as I wondered if there were snakes, spiders or scorpions hiding in there with me. I pressed my lips together and started reciting Fermat's Theorem to calm myself. Better not go down the snake/insect road or I'd go screaming for the hills at any moment.

Lucky for us, it seemed for the moment we were pretty well sheltered from the street even without the shrubs. This side of the building wasn't getting any pedestrian traffic, at least none yet.

Slash leaned close, whispering. "We've got a break.

The window is partially open. I'm going to take a look."

I nodded and he stood, coming at the window from the side and peering in. I watched to see if anyone was walking by, but we were still clear.

He crouched down beside me again, keeping his voice low. "One guy in what looks like a bedroom, working on a laptop."

"Arthur's?"

"*Si*. Confirmed."

"That's another break for us. Thank God. Now if we could just magically wish it and the spores into our hands and go home."

"The third break is the charm. Arthur's pouch with the spores is sitting right next to the laptop."

"Wow. Could God still be watching over his stuff?" I asked.

Slash's mouth curved into a smile. "He does work in mysterious ways." He looked back at the window. "I have to open it farther. I won't fit through the opening as it is now."

"Okay. Let's do it." At this point, I just wanted to get it over with, go home and eat six cheeseburgers.

"Agreed. Tell Elvis we're ready."

I slipped the burner phone out of my pocket and texted. In position.

Elvis responded. Roger. Three minutes.

He hung up and I slipped the phone back into my pocket.

I glanced at my watch. Two minutes and fifty-one seconds later I heard a loud screeching noise from in front of the apartment complex. Shouts, screams and the screeching of cars rent the air.

"Right on time," I breathed.

I could hear movement in the room above us. Slash stood and peered in the window again. "He's gone to see what the fuss is all about."

He shoved at the window, but it didn't budge. I stood and tried to help him. No matter how hard we pushed, it wasn't going anywhere.

I stopped trying and turned to Slash. "Lock your hands together. You won't fit through that window, but I will."

"*What?* No."

"Don't argue with me. We don't have time. Just give me your hands."

He wavered for a moment and finally locked his hands together. I stuck my right foot in his hands and he boosted me up. I braced myself against the wall with one hand while wiggling sideways in through the opening. It was tighter than it looked, so I held my breath and sucked in my stomach. After a few hard maneuvers, I suddenly popped through the window like a greased pig. I fell hard onto my right shoulder, making a loud thump.

Uh-oh.

As I rolled to my feet, the wail of sirens sounded in the distance. Heavy footsteps were returning to my location. I ran to the bedroom door and locked it. Barely a second later, someone yanked on the knob and started shouting. I grabbed the laptop from the desk, unplugging it as I shoved it out the window to Slash's waiting arms. I stuck the pouch with the spores down my bra, as I was sure it would break in my pockets. Slash tossed me up the Egyptian statue he'd stolen from the museum. I caught it, gently rolled it under the bed and turned to the window.

My breath was coming in hitches as a series of shots popped at the door.

Holy bullets.

Someone was shooting his way in. Time for a hasty exit.

Without even trying to be quiet, I jammed myself into the window opening headfirst, holding out my hands. I was halfway out when I had a panicked vision of the clay bottle filled with horrific plague spores shattering in my bra and raining down on Slash as I fell out of the window. Slash dragged me out with one hard yank. My feet had just cleared the sill when I heard the door bang open.

I'd never moved so fast in my life. My feet scrambled for purchase on the ground as Slash tucked the laptop under one arm and dragged me along with the other. I tensed for a shot in the back, but Slash hauled me around the corner with surprising speed and moved us directly into the large crowd that had gathered in front of the complex. No one even spared us a glance.

I soon saw why. Two attractive women were engaged in a catfight. Clothes were torn, hair was disheveled, shoes were off. The crowd was huge and growing exponentially, made up of mostly guys who were laughing, whistling and cheering the girls on. The distraction was epic. No one noticed us at all.

Slash slipped the laptop under his light jacket and pushed his way to the front of the crowd, making sure Zizi could see him. She gave him a slight nod, before turning back to Gwen, presumably to alert her that we were clear.

Just then several police cars screeched to a halt and the crowd, including Zizi and Gwen, quickly dispersed even as they began to redress themselves. We were the first to clear the area as Slash led me down a sidewalk, then into an alley.

"You've got the spores, right?" he asked.

Dear God, in the terror of falling out the window, I had forgotten to see if I still had them. I reached slowly into my bra…and couldn't find the pouch.

I looked at him in horror. "Slash, I…" I couldn't finish the sentence. My voice choked up. After all this, I'd lost the spores. I had screwed up the plan. This time it *was* all my fault. I could feel the tears coming and I hated that. I was about to scream, apologize, cry, or all of them at the same time when Slash leaned forward and kissed me. I kissed him back because it was better than explaining how sorry I was. When I felt him reaching down my shirt, I pulled back. He smiled as he raised his hand with Arthur's pouch.

"It was sticking out the side of your bra. I could see the outline of it against your shirt. Forgive me?"

I was so happy he had the vial, I threw my arms around his neck. "Oh, I do. Thank God."

"*Si*, we should. Thank God, that is." He lowered his voice further. "Now ask Elvis if we were in time. Did they upload the document?"

I pulled out my phone and texted the question to Elvis. He sent back one word. Negative.

I looked up at Slash, relief flooding me. "We did it."

Relief crossed his face. "Excellent." He steered me down a sidewalk, then into an alley.

"Are you sure Gwen and Zizi are going to be okay?" I was out of breath, still shaking a bit from my close escape and completely lost in terms of where we were in relation to the hotel. But I trusted he knew where we were going. He was good like that.

"Zizi and Gwen should be able to slip away safely," he said. "Luckily, the police are not there to arrest the girls anyway. The jihadists will assume that the police are coming for the catfight, when in fact they are coming on an anonymous tip to arrest those responsible for a major art heist from the Egyptian Museum."

"Do you think the police will find the artifact under the bed?"

"I guarantee you, they will tear that place apart until they find something. The Egyptians are pretty serious about antiquity thefts and these guys won't have much of an alibi. If nothing else, they will be detained for some time while they sort it out, I suspect."

I stopped and then leaned over to kiss him again. "You're amazing, you know that, right? I never would have thought ahead to planting that statue on those guys."

"You're not so bad yourself." He lifted an eyebrow. "I seem to recall someone other than me shimmying in through that window and saving the day."

"You're right. We make a good team."

He kissed the top of my head as we started walking again. "We certainly do."

I slid an arm around his waist. "So, now that we have a bit of breathing room before the next crisis—and I sincerely hope that's true—there's something important I have to tell you. No more secrets between us. It's something I discovered."

Slash paused and looked at me with thoughtful brown eyes. "What is it, *cara*?"

Without hesitation, I told him.

FORTY-TWO

WE MADE A couple of important detours before returning to the Marriott, which meant we got back about
two hours after Zizi and Gwen had already arrived.

As soon as we entered the suite, Gwen barreled
over, giving me a huge hug while Elvis high-fived me
and Slash. I didn't even mind. Much.

Arthur grabbed his laptop from Slash in happiness,
hugging it tightly to his chest.

"You retrieved the laptop." Arthur's smile was huge.
"You really did. What about the spores?"

"We got those, too, thank goodness. It was true
team effort." I tapped on the laptop case he was still
squeezing. "However, I'm afraid you're going to have
to turn that over to me again for a short time. I have to
offload and then delete that file as a precaution. You
okay with that?"

"Are you sure no one was able to download my or
Gwen's notes?"

"I'm sure."

Arthur handed back the laptop to me without protest. "Then good work, team."

I glanced over at Gwen. "So, how was the fight?
From my vantage point, it looked like you guys were
really going at it."

"We were." Gwen put her thumb out toward Zizi.

"She's an incredible actress and almost made *me* believe we were fighting."

Zizi smiled. "You did just fine."

Gwen beamed. "You know, Zizi. I wasn't sure about you at first. But you're not only gorgeous, you're pretty darn smart. All of which means I may have to start a new fan forum for kick-ass women microbiologists."

To my surprise, a faint blush crossed Zizi's cheeks. "Well, I do have to say this has been, by far, the most exciting week of my life. It was my pleasure, not to mention civic duty, to assist you in this important endeavor." She glanced over at Slash. "But where's the staff and the spores?"

"In a safe place for the moment," he answered. "We couldn't stroll past security with the staff. But what's more important is what we discovered *in* the staff."

Arthur's mouth dropped open. "You managed to open it?"

"We did. But the discovery is yours, Arthur. As a result of your work, Lexi and I were able to figure out the coded puzzle on the top of the staff."

"And the antidote?" His voice lowered to a whisper. "Was it there?"

"It was there."

A collective gasp went up before everyone started talking. Arthur blinked rapidly, clearly stunned.

Slash held up a hand, quieting everyone. "Please sit down and we'll tell you everything."

Everyone quickly sat. Arthur's hands trembled as he folded them in his lap. He pressed his lips together and his cheeks quivered with emotion. It wasn't hard to understand why. The culmination of his life's work was in front of him. I almost felt badly that Slash and

I had cracked the final code instead of him, but the truth was, we wouldn't have been able to do it without his work leading us to the staff.

"How did you open it?" Arthur asked in a hushed voice.

"We figured it out somehow. Made educated guesses." Slash lifted his hands when Arthur looked at him in disbelief.

"It's possible we had a little divine intervention," I added.

Slash's mouth curved into a smile. "It's hard to say why exactly we got lucky."

"I am stunned and humbled," Arthur said. "But where is the antidote now? Did you leave it in the staff?"

"No. I brought it." I reached into my purse and pulled out a small wooden box Slash and I had purchased at the hotel gift shop. "It was a small bundle wrapped in a papyrus. We enclosed it in this box for the time being for added defense until we can get it properly protected. Slash and I think it's the antidote, but obviously we can't confirm that. We have to leave that to the experts."

Arthur reached out and reverently touched the box. "That has to be it—the antidote to the first known plague. Everything I've studied has led me to this conclusion."

Slash nodded. "I strongly agree. It would certainly make sense."

"Do you guys think it contains more spores?" Elvis rested his hands on his knees.

"It's hard to say, seeing as how we didn't dare open

it." I picked up an unopened water bottle on the table and unscrewed the top. "But we're thinking no."

"No?" Arthur's gaze rose to me, puzzled. "Why not?"

"Because we think it contains leaves."

"Leaves?" Zizi repeated in surprise.

"Yes." I touched the top of the box. "On that small papyrus wrapped around the bundle, which we think may be a clay container, there's a drawing of a leaf. Without unrolling the papyrus, we couldn't see the full picture. But from what we *could* see, the leaf looked quite unusual. I took a couple of botany courses in college and Slash took a class in plant anatomy, but neither of us recall ever seeing a leaf that looked like this."

"Can we see the papyrus?" Gwen asked excitedly. "I've had several advanced botany classes. Maybe I can figure it out."

"Sorry, Gwen. For obvious reasons, we're not going to unwrap the papyrus, expose it to the air or open the container for fear of contamination."

"I understand." Still, she looked disappointed.

"Could you at least draw the leaf?" Zizi suggested.

I exchanged a glance with Slash and lifted my shoulders. "I guess I could try."

I rose and grabbed a piece of hotel stationery and pen from the desk and returned to the couch. I did my best to sketch it, but I'm not an artist, so it wasn't the best rendition.

I handed it to Zizi, who took the paper eagerly. Gwen stood and went behind the couch, looking over her shoulder at my drawing.

"I've never seen anything like that before." Zizi's expression was thoughtful.

"Me, neither," Gwen agreed. "It may be from a plant that's extinct."

Arthur and Elvis also took a look at it, but it didn't mean anything to them either.

"Okay, I'm just not getting how a leaf equals an antidote," Elvis said. "Someone needs to spell it out for me."

"Well, if there's any of the leaf left, or even part of a stem, scientists can extract the DNA from it," Gwen said.

"Why would you need DNA from a leaf to make an antidote?" Elvis asked.

"Because..." Zizi's eyes lit up. "Because the properties of the leaf could contain a special kind of protein disruptor or a specific biological marker that could break down the endospore's sheath, leaving it vulnerable to being destroyed by antibiotics, ultraviolet light, or other immune system defenses. It's an extraordinary possibility."

I nodded. "Yes, that's one possibility. The leaves could have any kind of special properties. It does make a strong case that this is indeed an antidote."

Arthur ran a finger lightly across the top of the wooden box. "The implications are staggering. We've unlocked a thousand-year-old secret hidden in the staff of Moses—the first ancient plague and its antidote. It's not only a significant archeological find, it's a scientific and medical treasure as well."

"You were right, Arthur," I said, standing. "It's an extraordinary find. You're sure to get into the books for this one. Congratulations."

"Yeah, good work, Arthur," Elvis said. "You found your prize. You'll be famous now. Possibly rich, too."

Arthur stared at the box.

Slash cleared his throat. "Well, I think this calls for a celebration. Food, champagne, dessert and wine. Who's with me?"

Gwen jumped up. "I'm totally on board with the food part. You people eat so irregularly, that between being famished and scared out of my mind, I've already lost three pounds."

"I'm all for a celebration as long as we stay right here in the room," I said. "I don't want to go out in that heat again for at least the next eight hours, possibly more."

Slash grinned and looked at Zizi. "I hope you celebrate with us. This wouldn't have been possible without your help."

"Please do stay, dear," Arthur said. "It would be an honor."

Zizi leaned back against the couch and pulled off her scarf. "I agree the discovery is well worth a celebration and if nothing else, a toast or six in Arthur's honor."

Slash ordered the food, champagne and wine. We toasted Arthur, each other, the antidote, and whatever else came to mind. We talked and laughed—old friends and new—until the hour was late and we were all more than a little tipsy.

"Well, I'm heading to bed," Gwen said, standing and nearly toppling over Arthur. "Oops, the room is spinning a bit."

Elvis rose as well. He didn't look all that steady on

his feet either. "Come on, Gwen, I'll get you to your room."

"It's just over there, silly," Gwen said, pointing at the window and then giggling. "Nope. It's over *there*." She swayed a bit to the left. "Wow. Who knew there was so much furniture between me and my door?" She took a step and would have face-planted on the coffee table if Elvis hadn't been holding her elbow.

"One step at a time," he said.

They staggered toward her room while I took the empty dishes and glasses and stacked them outside our door. Slash walked around cleaning up the trash and piling it in an overflowing trash can. Guess we'd have to leave a big tip for the cleaning crew.

Arthur rose from his chair, looking tired. "I, too, will say good-night. Lexi, Slash, you are perhaps two of the most fascinating and capable people I've ever met. Zizi, my dear, in addition to your grace, beauty and mind, you have been a pleasure to work with. I salute you and your invaluable assistance. Thank you."

Zizi smiled. "It was my pleasure, Arthur."

He disappeared into Elvis's room where he'd been sharing one of the two queen beds just as Elvis exited Gwen's room.

Elvis shot a rueful grin at me. "She passed out. She's going to have a bit of a hangover in the morning. Personally I'm taking ibuprofen before I call it a night."

"Good idea," I said as he entered his room, closing the door behind him.

Slash stretched his arms over his head. "Well, would you like me to see you home or to a cab, Zizi?"

"At this hour?" I said. "It's too late and we all drank too much. Zizi is welcome to stay here until morning, if she'd like."

Zizi looked at me in surprise.

"You can sleep here." I pointed to the couch. "We've got extra pillows and blankets. It's only a few hours until morning anyway."

Zizi looked toward the door and sighed. "You're right. It's late. I'll text my family and let them know I'm staying with friends for the night."

"Great." I collected the blankets and pillows and made a bed for her on the couch while Slash disappeared into our room. I went in to get into my pajamas and retrieve an additional pillow for her before I came back out.

Zizi looked at me curiously. "You changed in there. Are you two together?"

"Yes, we are."

"Oh." She considered for a moment. "I thought you were like his sister…or something."

"Something," I agreed. I pulled back the blanket so she could climb in easier. I turned off all the lights except a soft lamp on the table where the laptops and antidote now sat. "I hope you'll be comfortable."

Zizi removed her sandals and wiggled her toes. "I'm sure I will. You know, I'm pretty good at reading people, but I just never quite figured you out."

I shrugged. "That's okay. I'm horrible at reading people, but I think I've figured you out."

"Really?" She seemed amused by my declaration.

"Maybe. Good night, Zizi. Thanks for your help."

"*Tusbih ealaa khayr*, Lexi. That's good night in Arabic. May fortune smile upon you always."

"Trust me, if fortune is smiling at me for a change, it's a good day."

FORTY-THREE

"Lexi. Get up." Someone was shaking me, so I cracked open an eye.

"Arthur?" I blinked both eyes open. "What time is it?"

"Nearly ten o'clock. Hurry."

Slash sat up next to me rubbing his eyes. Sunlight streamed in from a part in our curtains. The day was well underway. "Hurry for what? What's wrong?"

"The antidote is gone."

"What?"

"The antidote is gone and so is Zizi. Did you put it somewhere safe?"

"I left it on the desk last night." I swung my feet over the bed. My oversized T-shirt didn't quite hang to my knees, so I snatched my robe off a chair and padded to the living area with Slash right behind me. Sure enough, the makeshift bed on the couch was barely tousled. Zizi, her purse and the antidote were gone.

"I've looked everywhere for the box," Arthur said. Panic flared in his eyes. "It's not here. She had to have taken it. But why?"

Elvis walked into the room, squinting and shielding his eyes from the sunlight with his hand. His dark hair was sticking out and he wore a loose white T-shirt and shorts. "Can you guys keep it down in here? People are trying to sleep."

"The antidote is gone," Arthur said, his voice one step short of hysterical. "And so is Zizi."

Alarm crossed Elvis's face. "What? Zizi took the antidote? Why?"

"Before we jump to conclusions, let's just make sure it was Zizi." I walked over to the laptop and typed a few commands. A video pulled up.

Elvis walked over next to me, looking at me in astonishment. "You filmed last night? Why?"

"Let's just say I had a hunch. Guess we're about to find out if it paid off."

A grainy feed from the video came in. Everyone pressed around me to get a look at the screen. The laptop camera wasn't the greatest and it was dark except for the soft glow of the lamp on the desk. I fast-forwarded to forty-seven minutes into the video when a dark shape arose from the couch and approached the desk. As the person reached out to take the antidote, a side view of her face came into view just as her fingers curled around the wooden box. I paused the video.

Zizi.

Arthur gasped and took a step back. I resumed the video as Zizi took the box and moved too far out of range to be seen anymore. About two minutes later we heard the unmistakable click of the door opening and then closing.

"Why?" Arthur whispered, stunned. "Why would Zizi take the antidote?"

"I think we're about to find out," I said.

WE DEBATED GOING to Zizi's home or to the museum. A quick call to the hotel concierge made our decision for us. The museum was currently closed, apparently due to a sprinkler malfunction.

"They aren't making the theft public yet," Elvis observed.

"That's not a surprise. They need time to do a full inventory," Arthur said. "They must determine exactly what's missing."

"As an employee, couldn't Zizi be at the museum anyway?" Gwen asked. To my surprise, she didn't show any sign of a hangover other than being really thirsty and having little dark smudges under her eyes. I had previously thought it biologically impossible to be cheerful with a hangover, but apparently Gwen had found a way.

"It's doubtful," Slash said. "It would be a crime scene. My guess is if we are to find her, it will be at home."

Arthur stood up. "Then what are we waiting for? She must have a good explanation for this."

I exchanged a glance with Slash, but said nothing. In front of the hotel, the bellman secured us two cabs. Slash, Gwen and Elvis went in one cab, while Arthur and I took another.

Slash told us Zizi lived on the second floor of a two-story commercial building right above an Indian restaurant. It was about a ten-minute ride from the hotel. Gwen looked decidedly more green after our usual wild cab ride. She pressed her lips together and put a hand to her stomach while she climbed out of the cab. As the cab sped away, Slash asked Arthur, Gwen and Elvis to wait by the café while he and I went to knock on Zizi's door.

Zizi opened the door. A television played in the

background and the scent of something cooking wafted out. She pretended to be surprised to see us, but even I—potentially the most non-astute person in all of Egypt—could see she wasn't. She had showered and changed into a light pink blouse and blue jeans. Her feet were bare, thick hair loose and face makeup free. But even casual like this, she was breathtakingly beautiful.

"Slash. Lexi." She widened the door and stepped out. "What a surprise. I'm sorry I slipped out this morning without saying goodbye. I didn't want to disturb you."

Slash held out a hand. He had no intention of wasting time. "The antidote."

"What?" She pressed a hand to her chest. "What are you talking about?"

"You took the antidote," I said. "Where is it?"

"Why would I take the antidote?"

"Why, indeed?" Slash said.

Zizi shook her head in disbelief. "After all I've done for you—you're accusing me of being a thief? How could you?"

Sighing, I retrieved my phone from my purse and pulled up the video. I pushed play and the video of her swiping the antidote flashed across the screen. When it was finished, I returned my phone to my purse. "So, hand it over."

"You recorded me?" Her voice was surprised, outraged.

"Technically, I wasn't filming you. I was filming the antidote."

"How?"

"The laptop camera. So, seeing as how you stole the antidote, here we are."

She cast a furtive glance over her shoulder and then slid her feet into a pair of sandals by the door. Yelling something to someone in another room, she grabbed her purse and stepped outside. Without another word, she swept past us and down the stairs to the sidewalk. Gwen, Arthur and Elvis were waiting at the bottom where the stairs' opening met the sidewalk.

"Zizi?" Arthur said, walking toward her. "Please tell me I'm wrong, dear. You didn't take the antidote, did you?"

Zizi dug a scarf out of her purse and slipped it over her head. People passing by glanced at her, which wasn't surprising since she commanded that kind of attention, but today she didn't seem to appreciate their stares. "I suggest you lower your voice," she said to Arthur.

We moved to the side of the café where a low, black iron fence marked the boundary of the outside area. There were a couple of people at the tables, but all were deep in conversation and no one was near where we were standing.

"It appears we're at a stalemate." Zizi pulled out a pair of sunglasses and slid them onto her nose. "We both know too much and can't turn each other in without fear of incrimination."

The look of hurt on Arthur's face was painful to witness. "You *did* take it. Why? What would you want with an ancient antidote?"

"Must you really ask why, Arthur?" Zizi's voice was cool, unfamiliar. "Do you have any idea how hard it is for a woman scientist to make a name for herself in this country?"

I felt a small twinge of understanding, but it disappeared fast. There were women all over the world—including in Egypt—making a difference in science and math. They didn't go around lying, cheating and stealing to make their contribution.

"When I first started helping you, I thought you were like all the rest of the researchers, self-absorbed, single-minded and chasing after a ridiculous dream of a big find. But the moment you showed me those spores, I knew you were onto something extraordinary. For once in my life, an opportunity to move ahead presented itself without me having to fight for it."

"You never said anything," Arthur protested.

"Of course not. I had to move carefully." Zizi crossed her arms against her chest. "I was certain you'd found the spores in some artifact, and I wanted to know which one. When you refused to divulge the information, I tried to figure it out myself. I went through all the items you'd been researching at the museum. But without any clear idea what I was looking for, I couldn't find it. I'd hoped to access the notes on your laptop and I even considered stealing it, but I knew it was password protected and you like to encode your notes. I needed your cooperation, not suspicion."

Arthur's hurt look was turning to anger. "I had no idea."

"That was the idea. I'd hoped you'd let me study the spores further, but instead you mailed them to your son in America. When I came across the mailing slip, I was stunned. I had no idea you even *had* a son. Now, it became imperative for me to make you spill your secrets and tell me from where you'd retrieved the spores and where the rest of them were."

"So *you* were the one who hired someone to follow me."

"Yes. But unfortunately, you disappeared before we could get you to tell us what you knew."

I couldn't believe the cavalier tone of her voice. Like it was no big deal to talk about a plan to kidnap and potentially torture the man who stood right in front of her—a man she'd worked with for months.

Elvis stepped forward, jabbed a finger at her. "Then you were the one who was paying Merhu Khalfani. You sent him to my house to get the spores and the notes my father sent me. He almost shot Lexi's kneecaps off."

She shrugged. "Merhu is a friend of a friend, willing to assist me for the right price. Since Merhu is a British citizen, he was handily able to get into the US—not an easy feat these days. Unfortunately, that attempt failed as well. But it did have an unexpected and welcome consequence. It brought Arthur's son and his capable friends to Egypt to help me find him."

"You betrayed me from the beginning." Arthur's hands were trembling. It occurred to me he might have been fonder of Zizi than I had known. Maybe he'd thought of her like a daughter or a favorite student. "You were going to steal my discovery and use it to make a name for yourself."

"I didn't steal it…exactly. It fell into my lap. You didn't even know what you'd found, Arthur, or how significant it was. What a stupid thing to do, mail those spores across the world. You had no idea what you were dealing with."

"But you did," I said.

"Of course I did. I wasn't sure, but I suspected there was something unique about the spores. I wanted desperately to examine them. I knew if I could be the scientist to unveil an ancient biological material, it would be an enormous lift for my career. When I learned of the true lethality of the spores, I knew I *had* to get my hands on them so I could be the one to unveil the discovery of a new plague—an ancient one capable of horrific consequences. When Arthur revealed the possibility of an antidote or a defense against the plague as well, it was beyond my wildest dreams. Now, not only could I reveal the disease, but I could be acclaimed for coming up with the cure."

Arthur looked at her, aghast. "So, all of this was for…fame and recognition?"

Zizi laughed. "And you are surprised, Arthur, when you seek the same?"

He closed his eyes, a sick look on his face.

"So, why did you pretend to help us?" Gwen said. "You could have turned me in back at the museum."

"My dear, we were after the same thing. It was in my best interest to assist you."

"That was a big risk," Elvis observed.

"I assure you, the payoff will be worth it."

I angled my back so it was out of the sun. My skin seemed to be burning beneath my clothes. "But things didn't go quite as you planned, did they, Zizi?"

"No, they didn't." Zizi shifted on her feet, uncomfortable for the first time since the conversation started. "Arthur was the problem. After you found him, he refused to reveal much about his find—even to his own son. Seeing how important the laptop was to Arthur,

I figured there had to be some mention of the artifact in his notes. Even if there wasn't, between the spores, his notes and Gwen's analysis, I thought I could figure out where the antidote was located."

"*You* kidnapped Arthur and Elvis." Anger tinged Gwen's voice and her face was so furious, her cheeks had turned bright red. "You *hurt* them. They could have been killed."

"That wasn't the plan, I assure you. When Lexi, Slash and I went to the museum to find the chariot in question, I had my acquaintances capture Elvis, Arthur, the laptop and the spores. However, due to the delicate, not to mention dangerous, nature of the spores, I informed them that the vial Arthur had in his pocket had to be handled very carefully."

"I bet that raised their interest," Slash commented.

"It did."

"So, naturally, they wanted to know what they were dealing with," he said.

"Naturally." She lifted an eyebrow. "One of them, Khalil, insisted on knowing more before he'd grab Arthur. So, I told him the basics, about the possibility it was an ancient plague that could be deadly in today's world. That's why he had to take special care not to crush or break the vial when they took Arthur."

Slash shook his head. "That was a fatal mistake, Zizi. They no longer cared about your money after that. You hand-delivered them the perfect opportunity to strike against the West. A plague with no known antidote. An ironclad jihad."

Zizi pushed her hair off her shoulders. She didn't look so cool at the moment. In fact, a sheen of sweat had appeared above her upper lip. "They are stupid idiots with their senseless jihads and killings. This is science. They had no idea what they were dealing with and thought they could control it. They didn't listen to me."

"So, that's why you helped Slash and Lexi save us," Elvis said.

"Yes. I wanted you to get the endospores back at that point. But they got away with both Arthur's laptop and the spores."

"Wow." Gwen shook her head in disbelief. "You are, by far, the most awful person I've ever met."

"I never intended to release the plague on the world," Zizi said. "You must believe me."

Gwen glared at her. "None of us believe or care what you did or didn't intend to do at this point."

"That's certainly your right." Zizi lifted her shoulders. "Anyway, since Arthur confirmed the antidote was still in the artifact, its discovery was paramount. I was still trying to retrieve the laptop and the spores from the men, begging them not to upload Gwen's notes to the website, but they refused to cooperate. They offered to give me the laptop with Arthur's notes after they had uploaded the material, but they intended to keep the spores for reasons I don't want to imagine. While all this was happening, I discovered my museum card was missing. I wondered if you were all planning to steal the artifact, so I headed to the museum. When I ran into Slash and Lexi, I realized I had to help you succeed in order to keep everything quiet long enough for me to get the antidote and make first claim to the discovery. I knew it was only a matter of time before the authorities were involved and, if you were caught, that might make me a suspect as well. So, when Slash told me Gwen was still inside, I had no choice but to rescue her."

"That's quite an ambitious plan, Zizi."

"I'm an ambitious woman, Lexi. Why did you suspect me?"

"Your cell phone case."

She blinked. "My...what?"

"Phone case. See, Slash was careful to vet you. He checked your finances, your criminal record and even your phone records well before I'd even thought to do it."

"How *dare* you." She narrowed her eyes at Slash.

He shrugged, a slight smile touching his lips.

"Yeah, well, we kind of like dares," I said. "Interestingly, you were clean. But I have a photographic memory. The first time I met you, you were holding a cell phone in your hand. The next time I noticed your phone was when you handed Arthur it in order to display the online catalog of the chariots at the museum. It was a different phone case. Sure, some people change their phone cases now and then, but it still raised a flag with me."

"Why would my phone case matter?"

"Because most people don't have two cell phones, Zizi. So, I checked *all* the phones of the people in your family. Your younger sister, Lila, had a lot of phone calls to one particular number. A quick check and, bingo, we got a match and a photo of the guy you poked in the back at the apartment where Elvis and Arthur were kidnapped. After that it was just piecing together your motives."

"It was unfortunate my plan didn't work out as I planned, but none of us will walk away from this empty-handed," Zizi said. "Arthur will have his moment in the spotlight when he unveils Moses's staff. I presume you'll keep the actual plague secure. But I have enough information to publish on the unique characteristics of the spores. And, if someday the plague gets out, I will become famous for curing Moses's plague. My name will be right up there with Jonas Salk, who invented the vaccine for polio."

"You're delusional," Gwen said. "You can't even be sure the antidote is viable. It might not work. Even if it did, it would need to be evaluated by true disease professionals, not some two-bit microbiologist."

Zizi narrowed her eyes. "Oh, I assure you, I will be two-bit no longer. I'll have plenty of time to do my own analysis and have it checked. I can be patient. So, that leads me back to our stalemate. The antidote is in a safe place for the time being. If you think you can turn me in, blackmail me or otherwise threaten me or my family in any way, I'll tell the authorities everything about your break-in at the museum, including the theft of the staff. Add to that, I know you're not just friends of Elvis's, but some kind of American military or government agents. I'm not sure what a revelation like that would do for Egyptian-American relations, but I'm certain it wouldn't be good. So, with that in mind, I bid you farewell."

"Not yet, you don't." Gwen stepped forward and slapped Zizi so hard across the cheek it left a hand imprint. We all stared at Gwen in total shock, including Zizi and a couple of pedestrians who happened to be walking by.

"*That's* for hurting Elvis when he tried to protect me," she spit out. "You'd better believe you are *not* getting your own fan forum. You give women microbiologists a bad name. I hope you rot in hell."

She turned away and stomped down the sidewalk.

Zizi watched her go and then straightened her sunglasses. "I'm done here."

Arthur took a step forward. "Zizi, you must give us the antidote. You can't just leave."

"I can and I will. Goodbye, Arthur."

Elvis lunged forward as if to stop her. "You—"

Slash grabbed Elvis around the waist, restraining him. "Let her go."

Zizi turned and headed back up the stairs to her apartment without a backward glance.

Elvis whirled on me and Slash, furious. "How could you just let her leave like that? After what she did to Arthur? To me?"

I put a hand on Elvis's arm in an attempt to calm him. "Because we can. She'll get her punishment, Elvis. She just left thinking she has the antidote. Instead, she stole some dirt from the hotel garden wrapped in a piece of paper and hidden in a wooden box. Slash and I took the real plague endospores and the antidote to the American Embassy yesterday. They should already be in the hands of the CDC."

Elvis's mouth dropped open. "You…set her up?"

I glanced at Slash. "We did. Sorry we didn't tell you, Elvis. We just thought it would make the confrontation more authentic."

When it finally sunk in, he grabbed me around the waist, squeezing me so hard I could hardly breathe. When he pulled back, his smile was wide. "Really?"

"Really."

He looked down the sidewalk where Gwen was pacing, a furious look still on her face. He dipped his head in her direction. "You want to tell her?"

"Nah, I'll let you have the honor."

As Elvis walked over to Gwen, Arthur stuck out a hand. I took it, but instead of shaking it, he pulled me into a hug, too. "You, sneaky, wonderful little devil, Lexi Carmichael. From now on, I'm taking brains over beauty anytime."

FORTY-FOUR

"How did he get over there again?" I asked.

"Camel," Slash answered.

He passed the binoculars to me. I pressed them to my eyes and adjusted the view. Arthur came into focus across a wide swath of desert, sitting on a bench beneath a tent that had been erected to create shade for tourists who stopped during their camel rides to get pictures with the pyramids in the background. Tourists were coming and going, but Arthur just sat there forlorn and alone.

"How long has he been there?"

"Hard to say. Over an hour at least." Elvis's voice was glum. "Probably longer. Possibly the entire time we were in the pyramids. It's hard to say."

Slash, Elvis, Gwen and I sat at a café near the pyramids, sipping Coke from glass bottles and snacking on *feteer meshaltet*, which was a delicious layered pastry. We had the day to play tourists in Cairo before our plane was ready for departure, so we'd decided to visit the pyramids.

We could have taken a cab the thirteen miles to Giza, but given our experience driving in Cairo, we opted to take the train. Once we arrived at the pyramids, we purchased our tickets and fought our way through the surprisingly aggressive vendors to the pyramid entrances. The four of us had spent the past three hours tromping around inside the dark pyramids, navigating narrow ramps with only minimal light from manmade bulbs. It was remarkable examining the interior structure and marveling at the engineering ingenuity of the architects of the time. Slash, Elvis and I paused several times to debate on how or why something was constructed in a particular way as we walked through the astonishing structures.

Gwen held her own. She didn't seem to mind our engineering talk and offered interesting tidbits about the thermal imaging currently going on at the pyramids to determine if cold spots or significant changes in temperature might indicate hidden chambers or alcoves.

Basically we were four geeks in engineering and science heaven.

Arthur, on the other hand, had already seen the pyramids, but he wanted some alone time to think about what to do with the staff. He told Elvis he was going on a camel ride and would meet us at this café. The café provided the binoculars to tourists to admire the pyramids, which is how Elvis had spotted him at the picture area just sitting on the bench alone.

"We have to go get him," Gwen said, stuffing a piece of pastry in her mouth. Crumbs fell on the front of her T-shirt. "Our plane leaves in five hours."

Slash set down his coffee. He was the only one of us not drinking something cold. "She's right. We have to talk to him."

Elvis sighed. "I need backup. He's not going to listen to me. But he might listen to someone else." He looked at me pointedly.

I shook my head in alarm. "Oh, no. No way in hell am I getting on a camel."

"Come on, Lexi. I need you. Arthur needs you."

I set down my Coke bottle with a thud. "He can need me from here. Why don't you go get him and bring him back? Why do I have to go?"

"Because I'm afraid he'll bolt. Again." Elvis shoved his fingers through his hair. "We need him to listen to reason. He likes you, Lexi. He'll listen to you."

Wow. No pressure.

"If I'm the voice of reason in this situation, we're in trouble." I frowned. "How do you know he'll listen to me anyway?"

"I just know. Please, Lexi."

He was playing the pleading friend card. It totally wasn't fair. "This is a very bad idea, Elvis. Me on a camel? It's just alerting the trouble gods."

"Why? These camels are perfectly tame." Elvis swept his hand out toward the pyramid. "Look at them. They're plodding along as they do daily, carrying hundreds of visitors a month back and forth without incident."

"They are animals. They spit and have big teeth." I sighed. "You really want to do this?"

"*Want* might be too strong a word, but I'm willing to do it. I need to. I need you to do it, too."

"I'm in." Gwen finished off the last of the pastry and wiped her mouth with a napkin. "I've always wanted to ride a camel." She glanced at me. "Oh, come on, Lexi. Be brave. It will be a short ride. What could go wrong? You're coming, too, right, Slash?"

Slash glanced at me. "If Lexi gets on a camel, I wouldn't miss it for the world."

"I bet," I muttered crankily.

Gwen bounced out of her chair, her excitement showing. "Well, it's decided, then. Let's go."

I wasn't sure how it had happened, but somehow I had committed to go on a camel ride without actually agreeing to it. I'd been trapped.

Gwen and Elvis dashed off to secure our camel ride while Slash finished his coffee and I dropped some bills on the table. By the time we caught up with them, Elvis was animatedly talking to a guy whom, I presumed, was one of the camel owners. Gwen had linked her arm with his. They looked pretty comfortable together, talking and laughing. By the sounds of it, Elvis was bargaining and doing a pretty good job of it. The way he often glanced at Gwen, as if to gauge her mood and happiness, made me realize he was trying to impress her.

Bonnie might be in real trouble.

I leaned over to Slash and lowered my voice. "Do you see the way Elvis looks at Gwen?"

"Plausible deniability, remember?" He kissed my nose. "We know nothing."

"That continues to be the problem."

"If they want us to know anything, they'll tell us."

I sighed. "Fine. In my opinion, it would be a lot better if people just announced where they stood in relation to liking each other, then all would be clear."

"Sometimes, *cara*, people are still working it out."

After a few minutes of intense negotiations, Elvis and Gwen came over to us. Elvis looked determined. "It will cost twenty-two bucks per person for a thirty-minute ride that includes a stop at Arthur's location."

Thirty minutes.

I wanted to protest it was twenty-nine minutes too

long, but Elvis was nervous enough as it was, while Gwen was chatting happily in her enthusiasm over riding a camel. I sucked it up and tried to paste a happy smile on my face.

I felt sick.

As we approached the camels, my stomach squeezed. Regardless of everyone's assurance this would be a walk in the park, this wasn't a good idea. I *knew* it wasn't a good idea. Animals and I were not a safe mix.

But before I knew it, I stood with Elvis, Slash, Gwen and four tourists from Germany in front of the camels. They smelled—the camels, not the people. In fact, the smell was the first thing I noticed when we got close. The scent was overpowering and I hadn't even smelled a whiff of the animal's breath yet. Not that I was getting anywhere near a camel's mouth anytime soon. I wanted to pinch my nose shut, but no one else seemed to mind, so I just breathed through my mouth and hoped no one noticed.

The camel owner wanted us to pay before the ride, but Slash stepped up beside Elvis and insisted we would pay *after* the ride. He and the camel owner only argued for a minute or so, because the owner apparently knew a losing battle when he saw one. Finally, he nodded and motioned for us each to choose a camel.

"Why did you argue with him like that?" I asked Slash when he came back to stand beside me.

"What happens if we pay now and they demand more money later? I've heard of cases where they leave you on the camel unless you pay more."

That thought was so terrifying, I shuddered. "Oh my God. Good thinking."

He put a hand on my arm. "You sure about this, *cara*? You're shaking."

"Of course I'm not sure. This involves animals. But Elvis needs me, right? Besides, it will make a pretty cool story, provided I survive the ride."

He patted me on the back. "That's my girl. Okay, let's get you up. This one has seemed to take a liking to you."

The camel stuck his head between Slash and me and was trying to chew my hair. Its breath smelled so awful I gagged. "Gross."

Slash chuckled. "You've got thirty minutes to get used to it."

"It would take thirty years. Not like that's ever going to happen."

The camel owner went around getting all the camels to kneel so we could get on. I gingerly put my foot in a stirrup and Slash held me steady, pushing me a bit from the rear. My mounting strategy wasn't pretty.

I'd like to say I mounted with all the grace of an Egyptian princess, but by the time I finally managed to heft my leg over the camel, any shred of dignity was long gone. Half lying on the camel, my bottom was stuck up in the air and my nose was pressed against a colorful but pungent blanket. I was so nervous I was shaking. Sweat trickled down my neck and back. The sun was baking my head and shoulders.

Somehow, I managed to straighten myself into a sitting position and held the handle in a death grip. I watched as Slash climbed effortlessly onto his camel. Everyone else was already seated. The camel owner had the camels stand one by one and then came around making sure our feet were secure in the stirrups. When my camel stood, I almost fell off. I slid forward and then backward as the camel awkwardly unfolded his back legs and then front legs before coming to a stand. My knuckles were white on the small handle attached to a makeshift saddle, secured by ropes and held in place by the heavy blanket.

I looked down at the ground. It seemed far away. Reciting Fermat's Theorem, I tried to slow my breaths before I hyperventilated and fell off.

The camel owner and three young boys who were helping him ran around tying our camels together in a long train. Somehow I ended up at the end of the line. My reins were tied to Slash's camel, which was directly in front of me. Gwen was in front of Slash and Elvis in front of her. The German tourists were up at the front. I held on for dear life as the camel swayed back and forth. We weren't even moving yet and I was in serious danger of falling. I wiggled my butt in the saddle, trying to adjust.

As if sensing my palpable fear, the camel turned his head toward me, his tongue lolling out.

"Hey," I said weakly. "You're going to go gentle on me, right?"

Its answer was to snap at me. I yelped in surprise.

"Hey," I yelled at the camel owner. "This camel just tried to bite me."

The owner strode over in his red and white *keffiyeh*, the traditional Arabian headdress made of cotton. His white robe kicked up dust as he walked. He clucked his tongue as the camel jerked his head back toward me again, his tongue lolling out.

"No, no, you wrong. He like you."

"That's why he tried to bite me?"

"Exactly. Do you not know what male camels do when they like a girl? They stick out their tongue and do love bite." He stuck out his tongue and let it fall to the side of his mouth before he started laughing.

Ewwwwwwww.

Sensing my discomfort, the owner jerked the camel's head forward with the reins. "Eyes ahead, Arnold."

"Wait," I said. "I'm riding a camel named Arnold?"

"Yes. Good name. Big hump." He flexed his biceps and laughed again.

Slash turned around to see what was going on. "I'm riding a camel named Arnold," I told him. "He's got it in for me."

"Just stay in line," Slash said. A smile tugged at his lips. "Thirty minutes. You've got this."

"Easy for you to say," I grumped. "You aren't riding a camel named Arnold."

As if on cue, Arnold turned toward me and lolled his tongue.

"Did you see that?" I yelled, but Slash had already turned around.

I narrowed my eyes at the camel. "Keep it in your mouth, dude. No funny stuff."

Before I could add anything else, Arnold lurched forward, following the others. My stomach bottomed out and then lurched as I swayed from left to right, holding on to the handle in a death grip. My back was as stiff as a board and my jaw was clenched so hard I could feel the ache in my ears.

Yeah, I was having a great time.

Our camels were led by the three young boys. The owner was nowhere to be seen. It seemed completely unsafe to be led into the desert by three boys who may, or may not, still have baby teeth, but there you have it.

My life was in their hands.

After a few minutes of studying and determining the mathematical cadence of the camel's steady steps, I relaxed a fraction and felt brave enough to actually look around. In spite of my fear, my breath caught in my throat. It was a beautiful sight with the golden shimmer of the desert sand and the majestic rise of the pyramids. It was a completely different aspect in the daylight. I was awestruck.

A totally amazing vista. What a privilege to visit the oldest of the Seven Wonders of the Ancient World. Despite my precarious position, I considered myself truly fortunate at that moment.

Unfortunately, Arnold kept acting up. He bumped into the back and side of Slash's camel a couple of times before twisting his head around and doing that thing with his tongue, like he was laughing at me.

When Slash turned around once, I lifted one hand. "It's not my driving, I swear. He has a mind of his own."

Slash grinned as Arnold made some weird snorting noise.

I lowered my voice and leaned over the camel a bit. "If you are trying to knock me off, Arnold, it's not funny. I'm not amused."

We ambled along for a while without incident, so my mind drifted. I started to imagine how I would build the pyramids using ancient tools and mathematical calculations when I suddenly noticed two things.

One, my camel's reins had come untied. Two,

there was a large and growing gap between me and the group.

"Help," I yelled frantically, waving a hand. "I'm not connected anymore."

Looking back, I probably shouldn't have yelled with such terror in my voice. It immediately alerted Arnold, who until this moment had kind of been plodding along after the other camels without really noticing anything was amiss.

Now, Arnold lifted his head and checked out his current position in relation to the others. Then he turned his head to look at me, his damn tongue lolling out again.

"Be cool, Arnold," I said, a warning in my voice. "Seriously. Just stay where you are and someone will come get us."

But Arnold, apparently sensing freedom was within his grasp, had a plan of his own. He turned away from the group and started sauntering toward one of the pyramids.

"Oh, no," I breathed in terror. "No, no, no! Wrong direction."

The sauntering quickly turned into a full-fledged gallop.

Holy runaway camel.

"No, no, *NO*!" I screamed.

FORTY-FIVE

I'D NEVER SEEN a camel gallop before, but witnessing it firsthand, it was supreme awkwardness times a thousand. Now imagine me, the Queen of All That is Awkward, poised on its back, bouncing up and down like a freaking bobblehead.

"Whoa, whoa, *whoa*!" My teeth snapped together with every step. My eyesight blurred and my body flopped up and down on Arnold's back with all the grace of a beached whale as I held on for dear life.

He headed straight for some Japanese tourists. Somehow I managed to shout at them. "Get out of the way!"

I'm not sure they spoke English, but they clearly understood the visual of a crazy camel with a terrified tourist bearing down on them. They scattered, screaming.

Arnold swerved at the last moment narrowly avoiding hitting a guy with a large camera around his neck. I almost slid off.

"Help!" I screamed at no one in particular.

Although I was terrified beyond measure, Arnold seemed to be enjoying himself. Once he straightened his course, he picked up speed again.

Figuring I'd better secure my seat, I leaned down, like a jockey at the Kentucky Derby and pressed myself against him in an attempt to lower my center of gravity. My thighs gripped his side as tightly as I could clench them. My hands ached from squeezing the handle so hard, I wasn't sure blood could circulate there anymore. My head felt like a basketball being slammed up and down, and my brains were getting scrambled worse with every stride. The only good thing was, as far as I could tell, we were at least headed in Arthur's general direction.

I heard people shouting and suddenly Arnold came to a screeching halt. I lost my hold. I slid forward onto his neck, grabbing for fur, skin, whatever I could to keep from falling off.

Suddenly strong hands reached up to pull me down off of the camel's neck. I released my hold and fell into them.

Slash.

"Are you okay, *cara*?" he asked, setting me on the ground.

I nearly collapsed, my legs not willing to hold me up. Slash steadied me in his arms. A quick glance over my shoulder indicated someone had grabbed Arnold's reins and was leading him around and around in a circle, presumably to calm him down. I didn't think I could be calmed so easily.

"No, Slash. I'm not okay," I shouted. "I'm pretty sure I might be suffering from post-traumatic camel syndrome."

Slash patted me down, presumably checking for broken bones. "Does anything hurt?"

"Yes. My pride. I can't even imagine how it looked, the two of us married in supreme awkwardness, galloping across a desert landscape."

I saw his lips twitch, but he knew better than to

smile. Instead he cradled my cheeks between his hands and looked deep into my eyes. "Your pupils aren't dilated. I don't think you have a concussion from all the bouncing."

"Forget the concussion. I've got stress. That lunatic camel just led me across the desert at sixty miles an hour."

"It was probably more like thirty," Slash corrected. When he saw my expression he added, "Regardless, it was fast. You did a great job of holding on."

Elvis, Gwen and the German tourists all rode up, the young boys leading their reins looking wide-eyed and scared.

"Oh my God, Lexi. Are you alright?" Elvis asked.

"I'm alive. That's better than I expected."

"What the devil happened? You shot off like a bolt of lightning."

"The reins came unhitched and Arnold decided to make a bid for freedom."

"Arnold?"

"The camel," I said pointing at it.

"You named your camel?" He was clearly confused.

"No, I didn't name it. It was already his name." I glanced at Slash. "How did you get to me so fast?"

He reached into his pocket and pulled out a pocketknife. One push of his thumb and a small knife popped out. "I cut my reins from the train and came after you."

"You rode across the desert on a camel to save me?"

"It happened to be the only transportation available at the time."

"You've ridden a camel like that before?"

"No. Not like that. But I've been on a few horses in my life and figured the mechanics would be similar. Luckily, there was a guy near you who knew how to stop a camel. He managed to redirect and then stop your camel. I did the rest."

I threw my arms around his neck. "Oh, thank you."

He patted my back as one of the German tourists held up his phone. "It was all very exciting, yah? I caught it on camera and posted it to YouTube. It has sixty-two views already."

I closed my eyes. Great, now the entire world could have a visual of me racing across the desert on the back of a runaway camel.

Gwen misunderstood my concern. "Don't worry, Lexi. I got one good picture of you on the camel at the beginning of the ride. I'll post that one to the fan forum site. Then you'll have something to remember the ride."

Like I *wanted* to remember this?

"Lexi?"

I untangled myself from Slash's embrace and turned around. Arthur stood there.

"That was *you* on the runaway camel?" he asked.

I lifted my hands. "Yeah, I'm one for a grand entrance."

"Good Lord, woman. You're lucky you weren't killed."

"I told them mixing me and a camel was a bad idea, but no one listened."

"So, why on Earth did you do it?"

I pulled my hair out of a ponytail, shaking out the tangles. "Because I need to talk to you, Arthur. All of us do."

He glanced at Elvis and Gwen who were climbing off their camels and sighed. "You're right. It's time to talk."

Slash and I waited until Gwen and Elvis joined us. Together we moved to an area beneath the tent that was not too crowded by other tourists.

"We must know what to do with the staff, Arthur," Slash said, keeping his voice low. "It was your find, your years of work that led to its discovery. Therefore, the decision is in your hands."

"My hands?" Arthur studied Slash. "Why does it even matter what I want? You could do what you want with it. It's in your possession."

"True. I'm keeping it safe for the time being. But it's your find. Thousands have sought it over millennia, but you, Arthur Zimmerman, were the one to discover it. In my opinion, nothing connected to the staff is random. You were chosen for a reason, therefore, your actions matter."

"Chosen? Why me?" Arthur's cheeks colored as he looked at Elvis. "I am not the worthiest of men."

Slash's fingers strayed to his neck where I knew a gold cross hung beneath his shirt. He rubbed it between his fingers. "That's not for me to say. Perhaps it's because God has always used flawed men and women to share hope in a hopeless world."

Arthur closed his eyes, but I was pretty sure I saw a sheen of tears. He cleared his throat. "So, you believe the staff wanted to be found after all these years…or at least, God wanted it to be found?"

It seemed odd to be talking in otherworldly terms about a piece of wood. Like it had a mind of its own or something. But I'd seen enough unusual things connected to the staff, I wasn't going to be the one to point that out.

"But why now?" Elvis interjected. "Why would God want the staff to be discovered now?"

We all looked to Slash, but he just shook his head. "I can't answer that, Elvis. I'd never presume to know God's plan."

Arthur looked between Elvis and Slash. His expression indicated he was clearly uncomfortable with the religious turn in the conversation. "This is not at all what I expected upon unearthing one of the world's most elusive treasures."

"That's because you expected fame and fortune," Slash said. "That's not what the staff is about. It's about riches far greater than that."

Arthur sighed and mopped his damp forehead with his sleeve. "So, I discover the relic I've been searching for all my life—the extraordinary sum of my academic and professional career. But if I reveal it, it's only a matter of time before other researchers discover what was hidden inside. Once that knowledge is out in the world, it can't be put back."

"That knowledge, the plague endospores and its antidote, is already in the hands of the CDC," I pointed out.

"Yes, Lexi, but that knowledge can be contained in the hands of people who are experienced and who understand the consequences of that information getting out." Arthur's voice grew agitated. "That wouldn't be true if the staff went on display to everyone."

"Good point," I said.

After a moment, Arthur strode to the edge of the tent and looked out over the desert landscape, shielding his eyes from the sun with his hand. We watched him silently.

After a few minutes, Arthur turned to Slash. "Do you really think God chose me to find the staff?"

"*Si*, I do."

"Could you keep it safe? Keep its whereabouts a secret?"

Elvis's mouth dropped open in astonishment. "Wait. *What?* Arthur...you're actually considering giving it up?"

Arthur closed his eyes. The expression on his face was painful to see. Regret, disappointment, resignation. "It's not mine, Elvis. It never was. Zizi was right. I was chasing a dream that wasn't real. Now it's up to me to protect the staff and its secrets. It needs to go somewhere where it can remain hidden until it needs to be discovered again for what purpose, I do not know."

"Where could we hide it that no one would find?" I asked.

"What about that secret government warehouse, like in the Indiana Jones movie, where all those special otherworldly things, like the Ark of the Covenant, are stored," Gwen said excitedly.

I rolled my eyes. "That's Hollywood, Gwen. There's no such warehouse." I looked over at Slash. "Right?"

Slash stood silent. Now it was his turn to look out over the desert, thinking. After a moment, he spoke. "I know where the staff can go—where it will be safe and protected. I'm not at liberty to divulge where, for the protection of those who will keep it and for you who have found it. Will you trust me on this? All of you?"

We looked at each other, then back at Slash. It seemed an unspoken agreement that Arthur had to be the one to speak.

"Yes. We trust you," Arthur said. "Thank you."

"How will you get the staff wherever it needs to go?" Gwen asked. "I mean it's not like you can stick it in your suitcase, Slash."

"I have my ways…which is perhaps my role here. Thank you for your trust." Slash motioned toward the camels. "Now we need to get back to Cairo as soon as possible. I'll go see what I can work out for us to get back."

"Make sure my way doesn't involve a camel," I suggested. "I'm all for walking."

He flashed me a smile as he strode away.

Elvis turned to face his father. Blue eyes met blue eyes. "Are you serious, Arthur? You're going to give up your life's dream and the recognition that goes with it just like that?"

Arthur nodded. "Yes."

"How? Why?"

"Because it's the right thing to do. I know that now. I'm going back to England to reevaluate many things in my life. But first, I owe you an apology. A heartfelt one. No more excuses. Not that my apology could ever make up for what I've done to you, your brother, sister and mother. I'm sorry, son. Really, truly sorry for the poor excuse of a man and father I've been. I have a lot of amends to make. I just hope this is a beginning and not the end."

Elvis stared steadily at his father, as if he didn't believe it. *Couldn't* believe it. A storm of emotion crossed his face. He blinked a few times and then said, "I guess we'll see, won't we?"

"Yes. You'll see."

Elvis turned to face Gwen. Somehow, it seemed

significant he hadn't turned to me. He held out a hand to Gwen and she took it without hesitation.

"Come on," he said. "Let's go help Slash figure a way out of here."

Arthur watched them walk away before looking at me. "So, Lexi, was that better?"

"Yeah, Arthur, that was better."

"I know I have a long way to go with him...with my family."

"Yes, you do." I put a hand on his shoulder. "But at least you took the first step."

FORTY-SIX

SLASH TOOK ARTHUR to see the staff one last time and then he disappeared to take make sure the staff got to wherever he was sending it. When they returned, we said our goodbyes to Mr. Zimmerman and then headed for the airport.

The plane ride home was uneventful, maybe even pleasant. It was hard to say because we were all so exhausted, we slept nearly the entire time, waking up only to eat and then go back to sleep. Still, it didn't escape my notice that Elvis and Gwen were holding hands under the blanket. Whatever that meant.

It wasn't like I could ask.

Plausible deniability.

Slash had two drivers waiting for us when we got to the airport. After clearing customs, Elvis and Gwen were instructed to go in one car and Slash and I in another. Before we left I gave Gwen a hug. I had no idea how it had happened, but she had somehow wormed her way into my heart. Perhaps it was her genuine friendliness and fearlessness when it came to the people she had claimed as her friends. Or maybe I liked the way Elvis seemed to stand a little taller and be more confident when she was around. Or perhaps because I was impressed by the way she'd put her life on the line for people who weren't even technically her friends yet and whether that was determined by emojis or fandom.

Gwen was a redhead with a lot of smarts and even more heart. Whether I liked it or not, somehow we were friends. I watched the taillights of their car disappear.

The driver put our suitcases into the trunk. We climbed in the back and Slash gave the driver the address to our new house. As the car pulled away from the terminal, Slash put his arm around me. I rested my head against his shoulder.

"Well, we made it in one piece and in time for the wedding on Saturday," I said. "In the spirit of full disclosure, however, I'm pretty sure I feared Basia's wrath a lot more than an ancient plague if we'd failed."

"I won't argue with you on that one."

My eyes fell on a package on the seat beside him. I hadn't seen it before.

"Hey, what's that?" I pointed at the package.

"A present."

"You had time to go shopping? Really?"

"In a manner of speaking. I knew what I wanted, so I asked the hotel concierge to find one for me and have it delivered to the hotel."

I hesitated, hovering between being nosy and deciding I had to know. "Who's it for?"

"You, of course." He chuckled. "Want to open it?"

"Is that a trick question?"

He slid his arm out from behind me. Using both hands, he reached down to pick up the box. He slid it over to my lap. It was about the size of a large shoebox, wrapped in rough brown paper with a twine bow. It was unexpectedly heavy. I put my hands on top of the box, then paused. Guilt swept through me.

"Is it from Egypt?"

"It is."

"But I didn't get you a present."

He looked at me with affection. "We've had this discussion before. Giving a present doesn't require reciprocity. I bought it because it makes me happy to give you things. In this particular case, I wanted to give you something to remember our first trip to Egypt."

"First trip? Please tell me that means we're going to go again."

"We're going to go again. And next time, there will be no heists, plagues or runaway camels. Instead there will be a cruise down the Nile, three or four days devoted to nothing but museums, and a couple of romantic candlelight dinners with just the two of us."

"Oh, that sounds fantastic, especially the part about extra time in the museums."

"I knew you'd say that." He bumped my shoulder with his, grinning. "Just open the package, okay?"

"Okay." I pulled the twine loose and pulled open the brown paper. Carefully I lifted off the top of the box. My breath caught in my throat. "Slash…it's beautiful."

Laying nestled in the box was a replica of an ancient Egyptian merkhet. It was either partially made of gold or gold-plated. I lifted it out of the box by its top. The string with the heavy golden weight dropped down and swung slightly before I cupped it in my hand.

"It's a perfect souvenir. Thank you so much. You always think of everything."

"Not everything, but most of the time you make me feel like I can get close." He leaned over and kissed me. "We'll have to find a good place to put it in the house."

The house. *Our* house. My stomach did a little flip. I couldn't decide if it was nerves or anticipation. Tonight would be the first night we spent together in the new place. I wasn't sure how, if at all, it would change things for me emotionally.

Slash slid his arm around me again, so I settled back against him once more.

"You know we've been so busy I haven't even asked you how the move went." I adjusted my head slightly against his shoulder. "Hopefully without a hitch."

"As far as I know, that's correct. I got a text confirming that everything was successfully delivered from both your place and mine and the furniture moved to the most appropriate locations they could determine. It may mean we'll be moving many items around to suit us, but we'll manage."

"We always do. I just hope there is a bed somewhere."

"I'm sure we'll be okay on that front. By the way, I've set up another date to furniture shop at Marco and Marcella's place. Hopefully this time we'll come out unscathed and with some nice pieces."

"As long as Guido isn't part of the deal, I'm good."

He chuckled and then fell silent. He was probably reliving his favorite moment of me in the bathroom, dripping wet, my jeans hanging from my hips.

I looked at the window, watching the scenery flash past. Something still weighed on my mind.

"Slash, do you think Elvis and his father will be okay after what happened?"

He was silent for a bit, but I waited, letting him gather his thoughts.

"I don't know," he finally said. "Father and son relationships can be complicated. Just like any relationship."

"I think Arthur wants to make amends."

"Wanting something and actually doing something about it are two different things. Elvis may no longer desire that relationship, but at least he has a choice in the matter."

I reached out and took his hand. "Not that you had a choice, but do you regret not knowing your biological father?"

"Sometimes. I wonder if I'll ever know, and if I'll ever regain the memories from my childhood. But thank God, I have you. My life is full enough right now."

Still, there was something in his voice—a small catch—that made me wonder. I couldn't imagine how it felt to never know who your biological parents were, why they weren't able to keep you, and where you came from, even if where you ended up was just perfect.

For the rest of the ride we enjoyed each other's company in silence. When the driver pulled up in the driveway, we retrieved our suitcases and paid him. After he drove away, it was just the two of us.

Slash took my hand and pulling our suitcases behind us, we walked up the sidewalk to the front door. He punched in the security code and slid his key in the lock. The door clicked open.

Slash looked at me and squeezed my hand. "You ready for this, *cara*?"

I nodded, a smile crossing my face. Yes. Yes, I was. I was ready for this next step as long as I was taking it with him.

I squeezed his hand back. "I've never been more ready, Slash. Come on, let's do this."

Grinning, Slash pushed the door open with his foot. Hand-in-hand we crossed the threshold together into our brand new house...and life.

FORTY-SEVEN

LATER THAT EVENING, after the house had been thoroughly explored and a couple of boxes and our suitcases unpacked, Slash and I lay in bed. Suffering from jet lag, we'd fallen asleep about seven o'clock at night, snuggling in each other's arms. For some unknown reason, I'd just awoken. A glance at my cell indicated it was only nine thirty. I quietly slid out of the bed so as not to wake him, grabbing my robe and my phone.

I belted the robe as I walked barefoot down the stairs and into the kitchen. I drank a glass of water and then sat at the kitchen bar, winding my hair back into a ponytail and securing it with a scrunchie I'd pulled out of my robe pocket. I stared at my cell for a long moment before pressing my finger to the button and swiping to my contacts page. After pushing the call button on my cell, I waited as it rang a couple of times.

"Hello?"

The familiar voice made me feel warm and happy.

"Hey, Dad. It's me, Lexi."

"Hey, stranger. Your mom and I haven't heard from you for several days. Is everything okay?"

"Everything's fine. Actually, it's great. I've just been…busy. Sorry I haven't touched base lately."

"No problem. I know how you kids get all busy with your computers and technology."

I smiled. Perhaps I was just nostalgic, but speaking

to him brought back a flood of memories. The smell of his aftershave, the tickle of his unshaved stubble on my face, the goofy plaid golf pants and matching beret he used to wear, and the way he taught me to drive using two fingers. I remembered the Father's Day card I'd made him when I was six—a mathematical calculation that spelled out a numerical code that, once solved, read *Best Dad in the World*—and the sound of his off-tune whistle as he followed along to his favorite songs on the radio. He'd been a father who never pressured me to play with dolls, but he'd bought me my first laptop and given me a challenging wooden pyramid puzzle at age nine that signaled his early acceptance of who I was…and who I'd be. He'd vigorously defended me after I got caught at my first hack, then scared the pants off me so I understood what I risked by such behavior. Now I was moving on to another man in my life, I recognized that my dad, in his unique and sometimes exasperating way, had prepared me for that.

My father. The first man I'd ever loved.

"I, ah, just wanted to say hi." I cleared my throat. "And to let you know you've…well, you've done a really good job as a dad. I know it was hard work to raise someone offbeat like me, so I just wanted you to know I appreciate it. I'm really, *really* lucky to have you as a father. Thank you."

He was silent for a long moment. Finally, he said, "Are you sure everything is okay?"

"Yeah, it really is. I'm just feeling lucky tonight. You're the best. I love you, Dad."

"Back at you, pumpkin."

We chatted for a while longer and made plans to hang out at Basia and Xavier's wedding on Saturday.

It was then I wanted to tell my parents I'd moved in with Slash. It wasn't fair to keep my new home from them any longer and I was no longer scared of their reaction. No matter their initial thoughts, I was confident we'd work through it.

Because as painful as things might become, that's what families did.

When I hung up, I pressed the cell against my cheek. Life had certainly led me in unexpected directions and to unexpected places. But now I understood love would bring me home. It didn't matter where that home was, as long as the ones I loved were there.

I stood and turned off the light in the kitchen. Returning to the bedroom, I stood in the doorway for a moment and listened to Slash's even breathing. Finally, I slipped out of my robe and climbed back into bed next to him.

He stirred and rolled over, pulling me into his arms. His bare chest radiated heat. His eyes were still closed. "So, how do you like our new house?" he mumbled sleepily.

I snuggled in closer, resting my hands on his torso. "I like it. A lot. But I've had an epiphany."

"Really?" He cracked open an eye. "What would that be?"

"Home isn't a house."

"It's not?"

"No. It's you, Slash. Home is just another word for you."

Both of his eyes were open. For a moment he just stared at me before he murmured something against my cheek in Italian.

"What did you say?"

His hand stroked my hair. "I said welcome home, *cara*."

I sighed, my mind and body at peace. "Thanks, Slash. It's really good to be home."

* * * * *

Get 2 Free Books,
Plus <u>2</u> Free Gifts—
just for trying the
Reader Service!

HARLEQUIN
INTRIGUE

YES! Please send me 2 FREE Harlequin® Intrigue novels and my 2 FREE gifts (gifts are worth about $10 retail). After receiving them, if I don't wish to receive any more books, I can return the shipping statement marked "cancel." If I don't cancel, I will receive 6 brand-new novels every month and be billed just $4.99 each for the regular-print edition or $5.74 each for the larger-print edition in the U.S., or $5.74 each for the regular-print edition or $6.49 each for the larger-print edition in Canada. That's a savings of at least 12% off the cover price! It's quite a bargain! Shipping and handling is just 50¢ per book in the U.S. and 75¢ per book in Canada.* I understand that accepting the 2 free books and gifts places me under no obligation to buy anything. I can always return a shipment and cancel at any time. The free books and gifts are mine to keep no matter what I decide.

Please check one: ☐ Harlequin® Intrigue Regular-Print   ☐ Harlequin® Intrigue Larger-Print
                    (182/382 HDN GLWJ)   (199/399 HDN GLWJ)

Name _____ (PLEASE PRINT) _____

Address _____ Apt. # _____

City _____ State/Prov. _____ Zip/Postal Code _____

Signature (if under 18, a parent or guardian must sign)

Mail to the **Reader Service:**
IN U.S.A.: P.O. Box 1341, Buffalo, NY 14240-8531
IN CANADA: P.O. Box 603, Fort Erie, Ontario L2A 5X3

Want to try two free books from another line?
Call 1-800-873-8635 or visit www.ReaderService.com.

*Terms and prices subject to change without notice. Prices do not include applicable taxes. Sales tax applicable in N.Y. Canadian residents will be charged applicable taxes. Offer not valid in Quebec. This offer is limited to one order per household. Books received may not be as shown. Not valid for current subscribers to Harlequin Intrigue books. All orders subject to approval. Credit or debit balances in a customer's account(s) may be offset by any other outstanding balance owed by or to the customer. Please allow 4 to 6 weeks for delivery. Offer available while quantities last.

Your Privacy—The Reader Service is committed to protecting your privacy. Our Privacy Policy is available online at www.ReaderService.com or upon request from the Reader Service.

We make a portion of our mailing list available to reputable third parties that offer products we believe may interest you. If you prefer that we not exchange your name with third parties, or if you wish to clarify or modify your communication preferences, please visit us at www.ReaderService.com/consumerchoice or write to us at Reader Service Preference Service, P.O. Box 9062, Buffalo, NY 14240-9062. Include your complete name and address.

HI17R

Get 2 Free Books,
Plus 2 Free Gifts—
just for trying the Reader Service!

Get 2 Free Books,
Plus 2 Free Gifts -
just for trying the Reader Service!

Get 2 Free Books,

HARLEQUIN®
Paranormal Romance

Plus 2 Free Gifts—
just for trying the
Reader Service!

Get 2 Free Books,

Plus 2 Free Gifts—

just for trying the Reader Service!

LIS17R2

Get 2 Free Books,
Plus 2 Free Gifts—
just for trying the
Reader Service!